Cassie Miles, a *U[...]* n Colorado for many [...]. Her home is an hou[...]d an hour from the Cascade Mountains—the best of both worlds—not to mention the incredible restaurants in Portland and award-winning wineries in the Willamette Valley. She's looking forward to exploring the Pacific Northwest and finding mysterious new settings for Mills & Boon Heroes romances.

A *USA Today* bestselling author of over one hundred novels in twenty languages, **Tara Taylor Quinn** has sold more than seven million copies. Known for her intense emotional fiction, Tara's novels have received critical acclaim in the UK and most recently from Harvard. She is the recipient of the Readers' Choice Award and has appeared often on TV, including *CBS Sunday Morning*. For TTQ offers, news and contests, visit tarataylorquinn.com

Discover more at millsandboon.co.uk

SIGNAL IN THE STORM

CASSIE MILES

COLD CASE OBSESSION

TARA TAYLOR QUINN

MILLS & BOON

First Published in Great Britain 2025
by Mills & Boon, an imprint of HarperCollins*Publishers* Ltd
1 London Bridge Street, London, SE1 9GF

www.harpercollins.co.uk

HarperCollins*Publishers*
Macken House, 39/40 Mayor Street Upper,
Dublin 1, D01 C9W8, Ireland

Signal in the Storm © 2025 Kay Bergstrom
Cold Case Obsession © 2025 TTQ Books LLC

ISBN: 978-0-263-39733-8

1025

MIX
Paper | Supporting
responsible forestry
FSC™ C007454

This book contains FSC™ certified paper and other controlled sources to ensure responsible forest management.

For more information visit: www.harpercollins.co.uk/green

Printed and Bound in the UK using 100% Renewable Electricity at CPI Group (UK) Ltd, Croydon, CR0 4YY

SIGNAL IN
THE STORM

CASSIE MILES

To the memory of Chris Jorgensen,
a world traveller, artist, author and friend.
She will be missed. And, as always, to Rick.

To Summon a Loved One

Cherished, fond spirit
From the other side
   Come close to me
   And here abide.
Gentle, I summon thee.

Bring forth the solace
Only you can give.
I miss you, my dear one.
You are my will to live.
In whispers, I hear thee.

Walk through the mists.
Enter my embrace.
Memories fulfill me.
Never leave this place.
Forever, stay with me.

Chapter One

At the edge of sundown before daylight faded to dark embers, Gigi sat alone at a small table in the Lighthouse Tavern at Cape Seraphim on the Oregon coast. She sipped hard cider from a snifter and gazed through the western windows at the lighthouse on a cliff jutting into the Pacific. A few hundred yards away, the tall, white tower rose through the mist and stood out against the streaks of a vivid bloodred, tangerine and neon yellow sunset.

She hadn't come here for the view. From what she'd heard, this annual Valentine's Day event drew a good-sized crowd of about one hundred and fifty, most of whom dressed for the occasion in clothes suitable for the late 1800s, which meant ankle-length skirts, fitted jackets buttoned to the chin and hats for the women. Gigi's wide-brimmed hat included a veil to disguise her appearance even more than her fake tan, dark brown contact lenses and glossy, black wig. Nobody would recognize her. Her real home was nearly a thousand miles due south, and she didn't really know many people in this area.

The men in the crowd wore the garb of sailors or fishermen or gentlemen of the late 1800s, in waistcoats with gold pocket watches. Blake Schmidt—the bastard who drew Gigi to this tavern—had the nerve to dress like a pirate, which was exactly what he was: a liar, a scam artist and a cheat. He'd been dodging her phone calls, ignoring her emails and refusing to see her. That ended tonight. Her tense fingers tightened on the snifter. She knew he always attended this Valentine's Day event, and she intended to confront him directly and blast him with both barrels. Right here. Right now.

Tamping down her anger, she waited for the right moment. In contrast to her red-hot rage, the atmosphere in the tavern felt subdued. Whispers and sighs accompanied low-key conversations. An acoustic guitar and wooden flute played background music.

The program for tonight was a séance-like ritual to celebrate the return of Penelope Townsend, the Ghost Widow, who would open communication with loved ones who had passed away. Schmidt was here to connect with his late wife, who had died four years ago. His sensitivity surprised Gigi. She found it hard to believe that Blake Schmidt had a heart.

For the past two years, she'd been working with him and three others. They called themselves The Four and had rigged a real estate Ponzi scheme. By purchasing a membership in Fourscore and More, and encouraging others to do so, first-time buyers were promised low mortgages with a minimum down payment. Gigi had already built a significant fortune in real estate and didn't need more investments, but she thought Fourscore sounded like a good deal. At first, she made a good return. Then Schmidt showed his true colors. Too many of the mortgages turned into foreclosures, which allowed him to buy the foreclosed houses at bargain-basement prices. Good for The Four, and bad for everybody else. She'd felt sorry for the people she signed up, but they should have known they couldn't afford the loss. Investments were always risky. Buyer beware, as they say. And then Schmidt pulled a few strings and cheated her. *Big mistake.*

Nobody messed with Gigi Graham and got away with it. She spent the past few months compiling enough evidence against The Four to destroy their company and personally bankrupt each and every one of them. She couldn't wait to see the look on Schmidt's ugly face when she showed him the flash drive revealing corrupt banking practices and documented false promises—one of three copies. The paper evidence was hidden where no one would think to look.

She didn't intend to blackmail him. A tacky endeavor, not her style. Instead, she wanted legally documented payback on every cent of her own investment with 5 percent interest. If he tried to ignore her or threatened her…well, she wasn't helpless. She'd brought a weapon. A .38 handgun tucked under her voluminous skirt.

The dim lighting in the tavern, augmented by candle jars on every table, faded to a darker shade. Finally, the sun had set. Bridget Reid, president of the Cape Seraphim Historical Society, stepped up to a podium on the dance floor in front of the guitar and flute. She spoke into a microphone and gave a brief history of the *Lady Eve*, a 215-foot-long windjammer sailing from Australia to Portland with a load of coal. In February of 1897, the three-masted tall ship was assaulted by fierce winds and strong currents. She wrecked on the offshore shoals. There were no survivors.

Through the window, Gigi saw the beacon from the lighthouse automatically come to life as it did every night. The beam didn't rotate, but was set to a sequence of five seconds on, two off, two on, fifteen off. The pattern was unique and distinguished this lighthouse from all others on the coast.

The president continued her saga. "The honorable Christopher Townsend, captain of the *Lady Eve*, went down with his ship, leaving his young wife, Penelope, a widow. Overwhelmed by grief, she flung herself into the surf and nearly drowned. She developed pneumonia. In the months before her death, she often left her bed at night and went to the lighthouse, where she climbed the winding staircase to the circular walkway below the beacon. For hours, she stood, watching and waiting for a sign from her husband."

Bridget's melodious voice, underscored by the flute and guitar, compelled the attention of every person in the room. For a moment, Gigi forgot her revenge against The Four and imagined the young widow facing the raging sea. A lonely, tragic image.

"Even after death," Bridget said, "her vigil continued. Many have sighted the Ghost Widow on the lighthouse tower. Though her husband never returned, she vowed, as a spirit from the other side, to help others connect with their loved ones who have died."

With both hands, Bridget lifted a stout green candle toward the ceiling. "Penelope Townsend, we summon thee."

The crowd read from parchment copies. The conjuring poem was penned in elegant calligraphy. With one voice, they recited the words. "Cherished, fond spirits from the other side. Come close to us and here abide."

After the third repetition, individuals added their personal pleas, asking their dearly departed for a blessing, a sign or an answer. Gigi listened to their memories, questions and complaints, and she wondered if these gullible people received some kind of peace or pleasure from what seemed to her a fruitless exercise. She kept her eyes on Schmidt, watched as he bent his head and mumbled to himself.

In the midst of all this talking, she heard a gentle hum. A comforting sound, like a lullaby. A clear voice murmured in her ear. "It only hurts for a moment."

Gigi glanced over her shoulder. No one there. In a low voice, she asked, "What hurts?"

"She will find you."

Fear shot through her. She didn't want to hear voices from the beyond. Didn't believe this was happening. Not to her. "Who the hell are you?"

The answer came in the high-pitched wail of an infant. Alarmed, Gigi looked around. Where was the baby? Was anyone else hearing this?

She looked toward the spot where Schmidt had been standing. He was gone. *Can't let him escape.* She rose from her chair and went to the nearest exit. All the sound in the room—the flute and guitar, the people calling to their loved ones—blended into an ominous static.

Outside the Lighthouse Tavern, she saw him crossing the parking lot. During the ritual, night had fallen. Fog had rolled in. The temperature had dropped, and she shivered inside her costume jacket. The salty wind tugged at her veil, and she tore the hat from her head. No need for a disguise with Schmidt. She wanted him to see her, to know her, to understand her revenge.

A five-second flash from the lighthouse beacon illuminated him as he set out on the asphalt path toward the lighthouse. She stumbled along in his wake. From inside the tavern, she heard a low murmur and guessed they were chanting again, conjuring more ghosts. The flute and the guitar played along.

Schmidt skirted nearby businesses and a stand of leafless cottonwoods. He followed the path toward the lighthouse. Below the cliff, waves crashed against the jagged rocks that extended a few hundred yards into the Pacific. Southwesterly gusts blew the fog around her, shrouding her vision. But still she saw two other men join Blake Schmidt. *Part of The Four?* She stepped up her pace. They would not escape her.

The lighthouse beam flashed again. She was closer to them. Their baritone voices cut through the voices from the tavern and the sounds of the sea as they neared the white tower. A fourth man stepped away from the lighthouse. *The Four*. These men were criminals. Dangerous. Should she look for the sheriff? Call for help?

The beacon slashed through the darkness.

They stood outside the lighthouse, staring at her. With a nod to the others, one of them started walking in her direction. His posture tensed. Anger twisted his features. He wasn't looking for a pleasant conversation.

Frantically, she struggled to reach the gun hidden under her costume. If she screamed, no one would hear her above the chanting in the Tavern and the waves beating against the shore. She had the gun. Her trembling fingers tightened on the grip.

"Don't come any closer," she said.

He paused. A tall man, he loomed over her. There was no mistaking the fury in his eyes. "What do you want, Gigi?"

"You betrayed me," she said. "Betrayed the people I introduced to Fourscore. You stole from them."

"No one forced them to hand over their money."

"You and your three pals are going to make this right." She dug into the pocket of her jacket, pulled out a flash drive and held it up. "I have proof. Copies of bank records—all your bank records, even those in the Cayman Islands. Minutes from meetings of The Four. Recorded statements."

He held out his hand. "Give it to me."

"Take it." She threw the piece of plastic in his direction. It landed in the sand and dirt at his feet. "I have another, hidden where you'll never find it. And copies of the signed paper documents and evidence."

"We need to talk, Gigi." He took a step toward her. Close enough to make contact.

She shouted, "Back off."

He slapped the weapon from her hand. His fingers curled

into a fist. His elbow bent. With one fierce blow, he took her down.

Gigi sensed she was being lifted and carried. *It only hurts for a moment.* Away from the wind, there was silence and warmth. And then…nothing.

Chapter Two

Cape Seraphim, Oregon
Present day...

Outside, the wind picked up. Fresh spring leaves rustled. The purple, white and red rhododendron bushes shimmied and twirled like Cinco de Mayo dancers at last weekend's fiesta. Windows rattled in their casements while Ella Scarletti pulled down the shades on the side of the house facing the cul-de-sac and checked the front door lock. The evenings were still cool in May, but the rain everybody warned about when she moved to Oregon only occasionally darkened the skies. It was foggier than she was accustomed to, but no big deal.

She looked forward to an evening at home. In the casual living room at the back of the house, glimpses of the Pacific shoreline were visible through the beachfront shrubs and high grasses beyond the deck. She nodded to her boss. "Ready?"

"You betcha."

Hoping that streaming the old episodes would cheer him up, she pointed the remote at the 55-inch flat-screen television, adjusted the volume and leaned back to watch another episode of *The Taste of Murder* all the way through to the dramatic finale...

Justin Thyme stood at the chopping block in his custom-

ized kitchen. His Damascus steel chef's knife flashed as he diced Walla Walla sweet onions for soup. His skill was undeniable. His speed, impressive. He glanced up into the polished stainless steel bottom of a hanging skillet and saw the reflection of an armed assassin moving silently toward him. Detective Thyme rolled his eyes and gave an impatient snort, as if to say that he shouldn't be interrupted until the onions were in the pan and fully caramelized.

He whipped around and flung his sharpened blade into the chest of the assassin with an audible thump. The erstwhile killer backed into the fridge and slid to the terrazzo-tiled floor like a wilted celery stalk. A second attacker aimed his handgun. Justin Thyme beaned him with a rolling pin, which knocked him unconscious. Thug number three leaped forward to attack. Thyme responded with a high karate kick he'd learned from the Iron Chef.

He stood over the third man. "Are there more of you?"

"No, chef."

"Good," Justin said with a wink for the camera. "Too many crooks spoil the broth."

WHILE THE LAUGH track roared, the jazzy theme song for the popular detective show played over the credits. Ella cheered and gave a standing ovation. The series had ended production almost fifteen years ago, but was still entertaining, especially since she was watching with the actor who had played Justin Thyme—the brilliant chef detective—for all fourteen seasons.

Beaming a smile of approval, she looked over at the seventy-six-year-old man, Harrison "Harry" McKinsey, who was still nice-looking with thick white hair and rugged but symmetrical features. If she'd been sixty-seven instead of twenty-seven, she might have been attracted to him. His lean, sinewy body suited him better than his formerly muscular physique. Still seated in his armchair, he gave her a bow.

His smile waned. *Still depressed?* Harry turned his head aside and wiped away his tears with a linen handkerchief. "Forgive me, Ella. This was the first episode we filmed after Rosalie disappeared. It brings back memories."

"Good memories? Like nostalgia?"

"Mostly."

During the three weeks Ella had been working here, he'd repeatedly told her the story of his ex-wife, Rosalie, the true love of his life. She'd vanished twenty-five years ago while they were staying here in the mansion-sized house near the beach at Cape Seraphim. Her body was never found, and Harry refused to accept her death. He clung to the wildly improbable belief that she was still alive and would someday come back to him. "What's really bothering you, Harry?"

"I've got nothing to complain about," he said. "The critics praised my performance in this episode and others that followed. They said I imbued a slapstick role with gravitas. In spite of the tabloid headlines about Rosalie's disappearance, the fools never realized I was in mourning."

"She was a celebrity in her own right."

"A TV news reporter," he said. "She was tall. Like you."

Ella was five feet ten inches. "Only a bit above average."

"And slender," he added.

"I have seven pounds I need to lose." She gave a self-deprecating grin and asked, "Shall I make some chamomile for you?"

"You look so much like Rosalie," he said. "Have I ever told you that?"

Only about ten thousand times. Even if Harry hadn't mentioned the resemblance, Ella would have figured it out from the dozen or so framed photographs, and the life-size oil painting of a woman with streaked blond hair and blue eyes who could have been her sister. She believed the main reason Harry had hired her to act as his live-in housekeeper-companion—he called her a factotum—was because she reminded him of his lost love. "About that tea?"

"I'll have vermouth," he growled. "Three ice cubes and a splash of cranberry."

"Coming right up."

She went into the kitchen to put together his drink. Booze might help him sleep. Neither his nurse nor his physical therapist, both of whom visited twice a week, had mentioned restrictions when it came to alcohol. Depression was an understandable reaction for a man who had been active and was temporarily disabled.

Several months ago, the aftermath of a serious car accident put him in a full-time rehab facility. In addition to a broken ankle, he had muscle and nerve damage in his lower body. These medical issues—accompanied by arthritis and sciatica—made walking difficult and kept him in a wheelchair most of the time. His legs were a problem, but the rest of his body was in decent condition.

From a glass-front cabinet where liquor was stored, she took down a bottle of vermouth and started mixing. Though there was nothing organically wrong with Harry's brain, she worried about his emotional state. Crying over the disappearance of his ex-wife so many years ago? Refusing to accept her death? Depression? Obsession? *Stop!*

She warned herself to quit analyzing. Her education, training and certification qualified her to be a psychotherapist, and she'd worked at a clinic in Pasadena for four years. *But not anymore.* She couldn't handle the emotional burden after one of her clients died from suicide. Not her fault, but Ella had blamed herself. *Total burnout.* She needed a break.

Her good friend, Maggie Wright—a former sister at St. Joe's—told her about this temporary "factotum" job in a small town on the Oregon coast. Maggie knew Harry and could promise Ella that she wouldn't be taking on housekeeping tasks because he employed a cleaning crew, landscaper, driver-bodyguard and occasional chef. The position sounded like a good way for Ella to get centered, and it didn't hurt that Harry paid a salary that was twice what she earned at the clinic. Ella returned to their television-watching armchairs and placed his drink on the table beside him.

He took a sip. "Sorry for being morose."

"It's okay." But she didn't like the way he avoided her gaze. "If you want to talk, I'm happy to listen."

"I wasn't always a TV star, you know. When I started out, I performed the classics onstage. *Hamlet.* Now there's a challenge for an actor. And for a psychic."

"A psychic?"

"Because of the ghost of Hamlet's father. Shakespeare used the supernatural in several of his plays. There's Banquo's haunting in *Macbeth*, not to mention the witches. And the specter of Caesar appearing to Brutus. Do you believe in ghosts?"

This topic didn't connect to Rosalie's disappearance in any obvious way. Ella had the distinct impression that Harry was creating a smoke screen to keep something from her. "Do you? Believe in ghosts?"

"Many in Cape Seraphim do. The lighthouse is supposed to be haunted by the widow of a sea captain. The local historical society has monthly lectures at the library."

"Maybe we should go to one." Both the nurse and the PT urged her to get him involved in activities outside the home. "I'll look into it."

"And now, it's *Bedtime for Bonzo*," he said as he finished off his drink. "My favorite Ronald Reagan movie."

After he made the transfer from his armchair to his motorized wheelchair, which was lightweight and easily maneuverable, he zipped across the hardwood floor to the elevator that went from the wine cellar in the basement to the third-floor bedrooms. Harry and Ella had separate suites—bedroom, sitting room and bathroom—on the second floor.

After she changed into her peach-colored charmeuse nightgown, she threw on her robe and padded barefoot down the hall to his suite. Clearly, he hadn't gone to bed because light spilled out from under the door. He insisted on handling his nighttime routine by himself, but she always checked in with him in case he needed her assistance. She tapped on the door. "Harry?"

"Come in." Still in his wheelchair, he sat beside a reading lamp, flipping through a scrapbook. "Our conversation made me think of the old days."

"What did you find?"

He closed the book, as though he wanted to hide what he was looking at. "Don't worry. I won't stay up much longer."

"Good memories or bad? Nostalgia or nightmare?"

He shrugged.

She held up her bright blue two-way radio. "If you need anything, call me."

"I'm fine." When he met her gaze, his dark eyes appeared untroubled and his features relaxed. However, she reminded herself, he was an actor. He might be masking a darker reality.

A CRASH JOLTED her awake. Ella threw off her covers and sat up. According to the glowing numbers on digital bedside clock, it was 12:18 a.m. The door to her bedroom was closed, though she distinctly remembered leaving it open. *Something wasn't right.* She jammed her feet into the moccasins under her bed, grabbed her chenille robe and dashed into the hallway.

The door to Harry's room was open. She peered inside,

turned on the overhead light. His bed hadn't been slept in. His wheelchair wasn't in the usual spot. She checked the bathroom and the sitting room before running back into the hall. Amid the stacks of scrapbooks, she noticed an opened envelope from a medical lab. Was that the root of his problem tonight? Had Harry gotten negative news from a test?

Back in the hallway, she glanced toward the closed door to Palmer's suite of rooms. He'd been with Harry for fifteen years and acted as a sort of handyman-chauffeur-bodyguard—equally capable of repairing a broken cabinet door or whipping out his SIG Sauer P226 and blasting a garter snake. Palmer had the week off, which meant finding Harry was her problem.

She stood outside the accordion-style elevator doors that collapsed into a side pocket when open. They were closed, indicating the elevator had left the second floor. There might be a simple explanation for that. Harry might be on the first floor making himself a sandwich. He wouldn't leave the house in the middle of the night. Would he? Why would he?

Her heart skipped a beat. Tension squeezed the muscles in her back and shoulders. She heard another loud clatter. If he'd gone off somewhere, she feared the consequences. It was part of her job to keep him safe.

In her bedroom, she grabbed the two-way radio and called for him. "Harry? Pick up. Where are you?"

She was answered by empty static. "Harry, pick up. Now."

Grabbing her cell phone, she hurtled down the sweeping staircase to the first floor. The lights were on in the kitchen, and she dashed that way to check. *No sign of Harry.*

In the entryway, the heavy front door stood wide-open, and the screen door, which hadn't been properly closed and latched, blew in the wind and smacked against the wall on the covered porch. This was the source of the clatter she'd heard. The coded alarm box was unlocked and turned off, which made her think Harry had done it on purpose. What was he doing? Where was he going?

Call 911. With the door standing open, an intruder might have crept into the house. More likely, Harry had gone out, driving his wheelchair down from the veranda where a ramp had been installed. Her fingers itched to call for help in searching, but she hesitated, fearful of causing a scene. Harry had made it clear that he didn't appreciate the police or anybody else getting involved in his private business.

She ditched the two-way radio, pocketed her phone, locked the door and went to look for him. Her first guess was the beach. They often went there for walks, renting a wheelchair with oversize tires from a vendor who closed his business at sunset. Harry said the endless rhythm of the breaking waves called to him. The low tide came just after midnight, which meant the surf would now be rising.

In his regular wheelchair, he couldn't navigate over the berms and dunes leading to the sandy beach. She followed the same path he would have taken in his wheelchair—emerging from the cul-de-sac onto a narrow road that dead-ended at the edge of the rugged beach grass with a traffic barrier and a couple of no-parking signs.

Running at a steady clip with her nightgown and robe flapping around her, she circled around the signs and followed an asphalt path down to the sand. The shoreline stretched from chiseled, rock-and-basalt cliffs at the northern end, which were mostly invisible in the fog, to the towering Cape Seraphim Lighthouse at the south. The beam from an automatic solar-powered lens sliced through the night in a timed pattern. Otherwise, she was surrounded by darkness and the indistinguishable shapes of the offshore sea-stack rocks and driftwood on the sand. The glow from streetlights behind her didn't reach all the way to the water. And the waning moon cast dim light. Luckily, she and Harry had taken this route many times before. She could find her way in the dark.

The lighthouse beacon splashed the shore again as Ella approached the newly installed, 145-foot-long, wheelchair-accessible, nonslip, moveable mat that pointed in a straight line toward the waves. The rumble of the surf surrounded her, and the squawk of gulls warned her of trouble.

In a five-second flash of light, she saw through the lowering fog. Harry's wheelchair sat at the end of the mat. *His empty chair.* He was nowhere in sight.

"Harry," she yelled. "Where are you?"

Gathering her nightgown and robe around her thighs, she sprinted on the nonslip surface. The beacon from the lighthouse flared. The fog thickened and swirled above the white foam of breaking waves. He wouldn't go into the water, would he? If he fell into that freezing water, he might be overcome, go into shock and drown.

Bending over and peering at the sand, she saw what seemed to be footprints leading away from the chair. Stumbling, she followed them toward the south, toward the lighthouse. After a few yards the tracks disappeared. The sand showed signs of someone falling and then drag marks. Harry must have been crawling. "Where the hell are you?"

"I'm right here, Ella." He was sprawled on the beach about twenty yards away from his chair. "You can stop screeching."

Relieved and furious at the same time, she sank down beside him. "Are you all right?"

He rolled onto his side and forced himself into a sitting posture. In a voice that sounded like Justin Thyme, he said, "You know what they say. If life gives you lemons, make zest. A little excitement. That's all I want."

"Oh, Harry." Though she admired his devil-may-care courage, she abhorred his recklessness "I want you to stay safe. Your fans want you."

"And my agent," he said. "She'll want me as long as those residual payments for *The Taste of Murder* keep coming in."

She stared into his face, searching for signs of pain or dementia. "This isn't a joke, Harry. Coming out here alone was risky."

"I needed to get out. Rosalie and I used to run on this beach. Almost every day. From the cliffs to the lighthouse. Tonight, I needed to be close to her."

"Why now?"

"That's personal."

She took a guess. "I saw an envelope from a medical testing firm with your scrapbooks. Did you get bad results from some kind of test?"

"The opposite." He reached over and patted her cheek. "I received the perfect answer to my dreams."

She stared expectantly. "Are you going to tell me?"

"All in good time." He pointed toward the mat. "Can you bring my chair over here?"

"You know better than that. Those wheels won't go through sand. I hope the motor wasn't damaged by your adventure." He might have felt strong before, but she'd bet that surge of energy had already petered out. "We have to go to the chair. Can you stand?"

"If I could, I wouldn't be lying here, getting sand on my tweed jacket."

She whipped her phone from the pocket of her robe. "I'm calling 911."

"Absolutely not." He was vehement. "They'll report to the media, and I'll be a footnote in a tabloid with the headline Time's Up for Justin Thyme."

She couldn't believe he continued to toss out punch lines. "Once you're standing, you'll have to lean on me to walk. I can't carry you. You're too big."

"Used to be." Trying to move his legs into position, he

winced in pain. "All those years ago, jogging every day, I was in shape. Now, look at me. I'm as skinny as a julienned carrot."

After she dumped the sand from her moccasins, she crouched beside him, wrapped her arm around his shoulder and tried to stand him up beside her. He fell against her. His arm flailed, and they both went down in a slow-motion tangle of arms and legs.

She saw a form coming toward them through the fog. A baritone voice asked, "Could you use some help?"

She lurched to her feet, stood in front of Harry to protect him and aimed her phone at the intruder like a lethal weapon. "Back off. The police will be here any minute."

"The cops are already here, miss. I'm a sergeant in Robbery-Homicide."

"Where?"

"LAPD."

The lighthouse beacon flared for five seconds, and she stared at the stranger. Dressed in black cargo pants and a dark gray sweatshirt, he didn't look like any cop she'd ever known. His shaggy black hair almost reached his shoulders, and his stubble was too long and unkempt to be stylish. Slim and mysterious, he seemed to be a man with dark secrets. A bad boy. Damn it, her favorite type.

"My name is Colin Reid," he said.

Still, she hesitated. She'd be a fool to trust a guy who appeared from the mist, no matter how cute he was. But she needed help.

Harry made the decision for her. "Come on, Ella. Shake the man's hand. He's okay. Colin Reid is the hero cop from LA."

Chapter Three

The introduction embarrassed Colin. "You're mistaken, sir. I'm no hero."

"Which is exactly what a hero would say." The old man chuckled. "Come on, man. Take credit. You saved the day in that kidnapping case."

"How do you know that?"

"Let's just say that a little birdie told me."

With a shrug, Colin dismissed the topic. The fog, the wind and the constant rumble from the surf told him it was time to go home to bed. "How can I help you?"

The older gentleman gestured to the tall, slender woman wearing a midcalf lavender robe. "This is Ella Scarletti, my housekeeper and factotum. I'm Harry. Now then, let's get this show on the road. I need assistance getting back to my wheels."

The beacon from the lighthouse shone on Ella's face. Her eyes were suspicious, which Colin figured was a natural reaction to meeting somebody walking on the cold, foggy beach after midnight. Still, she didn't object when he took the initiative. He circled Harry, squatted on the older man's right side and slung his arm across Harry's back.

"Ella," Harry snapped, "get on my other side."

She followed his instruction. Together, they lifted Harry to his feet and scuffled through the sand toward the wheelchair.

The unaccustomed movement caused a stabbing pain in Colin's right leg, but he didn't moan, groan or whine. He accepted the pain. Dealt with it. No bones had been broken in the incident that changed his life forever, and the physical therapist promised he'd recover 95 percent if he followed her regimen of exercises.

Ella glanced toward him. "Are you all right?"

"Yeah, I'm fine."

"You're breathing heavily."

"No worries."

He angled his face away from the lighthouse beacon so she couldn't see him wince. Her sympathy annoyed him. Ella was the first attractive woman he'd met in this godforsaken town, and she saw him as a pathetic guy who couldn't even help an elderly man without huffing and puffing. When they reached the chair, Colin planted his feet and used his upper-body strength to lift Harry into the seat. A strain on his back. Three weeks in the hospital had done a number on his stamina.

As soon as he settled himself in the wheelchair, Harry activated the motor, did a three-point turn on the nonslip path to get himself facing uphill and whizzed ahead ten feet. Just as quickly, he reversed and came back to face Colin and Ella. In the spotlight of the beacon, he bowed his head. "Thank you both. I appreciate your assistance."

"Don't mention it," Colin said. Helping people used to be his job.

"This may seem odd," Harry said, "but I believe we were meant to run into each other. It was fate. Or karma. I heard you were in town, staying with Nathan Reid in the castle on the hill."

"Nathan's my uncle." His visit wasn't supposed to be general knowledge. "Can I ask how you heard about me?"

"Me and Nathan, we have history." Harry's voice took on

an edge. "But his wife and I go to the same acupuncturist. We're friendly, not that it matters. My point is that I wanted to speak with you. To make a proposition, as it were."

The more Harry talked, the more familiar he sounded. "Have we met before?"

Harry cleared his throat. "You're thinking of Justin Thyme."

Colin's memories clicked into place. "You're Harrison McKinsey, the guy who played the detective who was a chef."

"Guilty as charged, but I prefer just Harry."

Colin used to love that show. "I remember watching *The Taste of Murder* when I was a kid, staying at Uncle Nathan's house. I couldn't have been more than five or six."

"We're practically neighbors. Didn't your uncle tell you that I used to stay at Cape Seraphim in the summers?"

Colin didn't recall any mention of the famous actor, but he was only a kid and didn't remember much of his childhood, especially during the time he spent at Cape Seraphim while his mom and dad tried unsuccessfully to heal their marriage. "I don't think he said anything about you, but I tend to tune him out. He talks a lot. That's why he went into politics."

"But you watched the show," Harry said, playing to the beacon's spotlight. "Let me guess. Justin Thyme inspired your choice of career."

"Not exactly. Catching the bad guys didn't impress me. Lots of TV cops did that. But Thyme could whip up a veal parm while he solved the crime. And I love to eat."

Harry grinned. "Wish I'd paid more attention when those expert chefs were showing me how to do it. I wasn't a good cook back then, and I haven't improved. Isn't that right, Ella?"

"You make a nice caprese salad," she said. "And you're great at muddling mint for a julep."

"What can I say?" He gave a shrug. "I'm a better bartender than a chef."

When Ella turned toward Colin, her straight, shoulder-length hair blew across her face. She reached up to tuck the streaky-blond strands behind her ear, an absent-minded gesture that he found strangely appealing. When she tightened the sash on her robe, he realized she was wearing only that and a nightgown. Why was she out here on the beach in her nightclothes? Maybe he should be suspicious of her, rather than the other way around.

Colin's cop instincts were rusty. He needed to get back to active duty. When he'd been released from the hospital, the FBI tried to get him sequestered in a safe house until the kidnappers were apprehended, but his boss at LAPD Robbery-Homicide got him this deal with his uncle Nathan. Still on leave, Colin had promised to be careful.

"I really want to thank you," Ella said. The timbre of her voice lifted over the crashing surf. "Would it be too much to ask for another favor?"

After being defenseless in the hospital, it felt good to be needed, helping someone else for a change. He reached under his sweatshirt and touched the edge of the holster in the small of his back, reassuring himself that his Glock was still there. "What do you need?"

"When Harry came out here, he left the front door wide-open. I'm worried that someone might have slipped inside before I got it locked. Could you come home with us and check the house for intruders?"

Though the unaccustomed activity had activated his pain, and he wanted nothing more than aspirin and bed, he wouldn't refuse her. "No problem."

"Excellent." Harry engaged his wheelchair's motor and drove up the path toward the beach grass bordering the sand. "That gives me time to outline my proposition."

Following him, Colin made his way across the berm, shrubs and sea grass to a narrow street with a few houses on either side. The ocean noise faded, and the fog thinned. He couldn't see the lighthouse beacon from here.

A regular streetlight provided illumination and burnished the blond streaks in Ella's hair as she strolled beside him. He liked that she was tall, close to six feet, and easily matched his stride. Underneath that bathrobe, he imagined she had long, slender legs.

At the edge of summer, the night was pleasantly cool. For a moment, he let down his guard and allowed himself the simple pleasure of being with a pretty woman, hearing her breathe, feeling her warmth, catching a whiff of her citrus-scented shampoo. *Slow down, Don Juan.* Before dropping his guard, he ought to find out more about her. "Are you from Cape Seraphim?"

"Pasadena," she said. "A friend of mine heard about Harry's factotum job, and it sounded like what I was looking for—something temporary and low stress."

"What exactly is a *factotum*?"

"It's from the Latin and means *do all*. Whatever Harry requests, I'll do it. As long as it's sensible, ethical and moral." She shrugged. "My duties range from picking up his dry cleaning to organizing his medications to writing letters and answering fan mail."

"How do you train for that job?"

"You need an MFA," she said. "Master of Factotum Arts."

He recognized deflection when he heard it. She wasn't going to tell him much. But he tried again to break through. "Do you have family in this area?"

"My mom is in LA. No brothers or sisters. I'm adopted."

He filed that tidbit away. He'd known other people who were adopted. Half of them wanted nothing to do with the parents who had abandoned them. The others embarked on a lifelong quest to find their birth mom and dad, to get answers. "What did you do before you moved here?"

"I'd rather not say."

One of the worst things about being a cop was treating everybody like a suspect. Her prior occupation was none of his business, but he continued to press. "When you tell me you don't want to talk about your job, I wonder if you were a criminal."

"You wonder wrong," she said. "But when I tell people what I used to do, they get antsy and try to avoid me."

"You're a lawyer," he guessed.

"Ick. No."

"A dentist."

"No."

"Zombie princess?"

"Only on Thursdays."

In front of them, Harry reached the asphalt path that led to the street. He must have been listening to their conversation because he added his own comment. Looking over his shoulder, he said, "She used to be a shrink."

Colin gave her a look of mock horror. "That's scary."

"Not a psychiatrist, but a psychotherapist. And it is scary. You have no idea." She confronted him. "What about you? Why did Harry call you a hero?"

Harry whipped around in his chair to face the two of them. "Enough of the foreplay. Let me save you kids some time. Sergeant Colin Reid of the LAPD rescued two children— ages seven and ten—who were kidnapped for three days. The victims were unharmed, but Colin got shot in the leg and the head."

He saw compassion and a bit of curiosity in her gaze. And he reacted. "You're analyzing me. Please don't ask the typical therapist question 'How did that make you feel?'"

"Why not?"

"Too obvious." He'd seen a psychologist in the hospital and now had scheduled regular three-times-a-week sessions with a shrink in Coos Bay. Both of them asked him again and again about his feelings. He didn't want to hear the same from her.

"Okay, Colin. Give me the short version of what happened."

"Harry was accurate. Rescued the kids. Got shot twice in the right leg and once in the skull, which caused blunt force trauma and concussion."

"Ouch," she said. "I noticed your limp."

"No broken bones in my leg, but I have nerve and muscle damage. It's going to take physical therapy to recover. The concussion was worse. I was in a coma for five days. Stayed in the hospital for almost a month."

He left out the most devastating aspect to his injury. When he woke from the coma, his mind was a blank slate. Couldn't remember his own name. Or where he was. Or being a cop. Faces that should have been familiar were strangers.

He rapidly recovered most of his memory loss, but still had blank spots. Traumatic amnesia was a diagnosis that didn't need to be shared with her. He figured she'd be fascinated. All the psychology and neurology people were. And he'd rather not turn into a case study for her.

After his time spent in the hospital and rehab plus these five days at Uncle Nathan's house, he'd recovered a lot. But the night of the rescue never came clear. Colin remembered getting the kids to safety, but not who shot him. Couldn't identify the person in a lineup. Though his amnesia was kept under wraps, there were verifiable threats from people who didn't want to be identified when his memory cleared.

He glanced at Ella. "Any other questions?"

"You're holding something back," she said, "but you'll tell me when you're ready. Or maybe you won't."

Harry interrupted. "Step up beside me, Colin. I have something to discuss with you."

Signal in the Storm

On the street, he had plenty of room to walk beside the wheelchair. Thinking of Ella and how damned insightful she was, he kept pace with her boss. "What's up, Harry?"

"I want you to find my ex-wife."

Automatically, Colin switched to his cop brain. "That's a job for Missing Persons, sir. They have the resources and the cyber connections. How long has she been missing?"

"About twenty-five years."

His curiosity was engaged. "A cold case."

"Frozen solid. Her body was never found."

Because that would be too easy. In spite of his common-sense inclination to refuse to get involved, Colin was intrigued. Searching for an ex-wife was unusual, especially one who disappeared a lifetime ago. "Why now?"

"Ella," he said. "She looks so much like my darling Rosalie, I can't help thinking about my beloved, wondering if she's out there somewhere and thinking about me."

They rounded the corner and entered Chinook Circle, a cul-de-sac with five large homes, each with a distinctive style. The middle house was the largest by far, with three stories, peaked roofs and a tall gray brick fireplace. A detached four-car garage angled to the left and was overshadowed by lofty Sitka spruce and Douglas fir. The simple, modern design kept the house from seeming ridiculously pretentious. The color of the siding was slate blue with dark trim. Colin figured that was Harry's place because lights shone through several of the windows. The other houses were dark, except for the neighbor on the left where the porch light and another on the first floor were lit.

Ella stepped up beside him. "Doesn't look empty, does it?"

"Do you usually leave so many lights on?"

"I was looking for Harry," she said. "I don't remember lighting up the living room and kitchen, but I must have. The lights on the second floor are from my bedroom and his. It's weird that there's a light on the third floor."

"Does anyone live up there?"

"When Harry entertains, the chef, a bartender and a serving person or two might stay in the top-floor bedrooms. The only full-time residents are Harry and me and a bodyguard who is off this week and in Portland, I think."

"A bodyguard?"

"Palmer has been with Harry since his days as Justin Thyme. Attention from fans used to be a problem, I guess. Nowadays, Palmer is more of a handyman who happens to carry a SIG Sauer P226."

"How many people have keys?"

"Zero," she said. "All the locks have been redone to a digital system, and I change the number code often."

"Sounds like a good security system."

She gasped and pointed to the third-floor window. "Did you see that?"

Someone had been standing at the window. Quickly, the person disappeared. Colin reached behind his back, glad that he'd had the foresight to bring his weapon.

Chapter Four

Colin held his Glock G17 at his side while Harry burst into action like the TV series detective he had been fifteen years ago. He drove his motorized chair onto the sidewalk outside his house and raced toward the ramp.

Colin glanced toward Ella. "How fast does that thing go?"

"Top speed is usually four to five miles an hour," she said. "Harry had his chair customized to go twice that speed. He's the Mario Andretti of the wheelchair crowd."

Colin understood the need for speed and probably would have done the same thing for himself. "He's halfway to the front door."

"I'm calling the police." She punched 911 into her phone.

Even in the best-case scenario, the local cops would take a while to respond. They'd be too late if there was, in fact, an intruder in the house. Harry needed immediate backup.

Colin ran down the sidewalk. His bum leg slowed him down, and he didn't catch up to Harry until after he'd plugged in the code to unlock the door, yanked open the screen door and bumped over the threshold.

"Try to keep up," Harry hollered as the souped-up chair zipped across the hardwood floor to the elevator. "I saw somebody on the third floor. We've got to hurry."

"Stop." Colin automatically used the loud, aggressive voice he'd learned in the LAPD. "Don't get on that elevator."

Ignoring Colin's authority, Harry spun around and backed his chair into the open elevator door. "You can use the stairs."

Colin's leg wasn't well enough to dash up two sweeping flights and still have enough steam to confront an intruder. He reached into the elevator before the doors locked in place. His sneaker jammed the track to keep the door from closing and he was rewarded with a bleeping alarm.

Instead of wrangling the wheelchair out of the elevator and arguing with Harry, pointing out the dangers, Colin entered and pressed the button for the third floor. Before the rectangular pod started its ascent, Ella slipped inside.

"How did you get here so fast?" he asked her.

"Ran like hell." Breathing hard, she announced, "This time, the police really are coming."

The unlikely situation—the three of them and a wheelchair crammed into the creaky, slow-moving elevator—made him think of a TV drama…more likely, a sitcom. He missed his badge, missed having the proper backup and following standard procedures. "When we get to the third floor, Ella, I want you and Harry to return to the first. Then, go outside to wait for the police."

She bobbed her head and fanned herself to cool down after her sprint to the house. The overhead elevator light gave him his first clear view of her tousled, sun-streaked hair, her easy smile and the sprinkle of freckles across her nose. He liked what he saw, especially when she inhaled deeply, and her chest heaved. The front of her robe gaped, showing the lacy white embroidery on the bodice of her nightgown.

"You think we should retreat," she said. "Probably a wise move."

"I don't run away." Harry bumped Colin's injured leg with

his chair, causing a fresh stab of pain. "Is that a gun? I didn't know you were carrying. Ella, did you know?"

"I don't like guns. Even if you are a cop."

"She makes me keep my four handguns in a safe," Harry said. "Not much use to me now, are they?"

"Really, Harry?" She scowled. "And how do you think you're going to operate the wheelchair and shoot at the same time?"

"I was able to jump over a parked bus on a motorcycle," Harry claimed, "and disarm six criminals with nothing but a spatula for a weapon."

"I saw that episode, and I'm pretty sure your stuntman made the motorcycle jump. Retreat is a rational idea," she argued. "Maybe we should take the elevator all the way down to the wine cellar and hide."

"At least we could drink. I have a case of—"

"Enough." Colin forced his voice to a rational level. *What's wrong with you people?* "You're in danger. You need to get the hell away from here before the situation goes sideways and somebody gets hurt."

"What about you?" Harry asked.

"This is my job." Truer words were never spoken. In that moment, Colin realized how much he needed to get back to work as a cop. Hiding out with his uncle wasn't cutting it. He'd never fully recover if he sat on the sidelines.

The elevator came to a stop, and Harry pressed a button to open the doors. Pushing in front of Harry and Ella, Colin lunged out. The lights in the hallway had been turned on so he wasn't stumbling into darkness. Holding his weapon in a two-handed grip, he scanned the hallway, which was wide enough for Harry's chair. The decor showed a playful sense of style with fake portholes affixed to the wall above knotty pine wainscoting and undersea photos of fish and vegetation. The doors along the hallway stood open, except for the one at the far end that belonged to the room overlooking the street. That was where he'd seen a possible intruder.

He approached the closed door. Though he'd been out of action for over a month, all the right moves felt perfectly natural. His subconscious remembered how to hold his gun, how to keep an eye on the two civilians and how to take a position to the side of the door in case the person inside was armed and would shoot through the wood. "Police. Open up."

A distinctly feminine voice responded. "Don't shoot me. I didn't mean any harm."

Ella stepped up behind him and called out. "Lydia? Is that you?"

"Ella, honey, I'm so glad you're here. You've got to help me."

Just like that, another layer of weird had been added. Colin wanted to be out of this chaos before the local cops arrived and ran his identity through the system. After the kidnapping, the FBI wanted him to stay out of the way and keep quiet unless he had new evidence or overcame his amnesia.

Also, the Oregon cops would demand an explanation about why he'd been walking the beach in the middle of the night. Not that it was illegal. All the beaches and shoreline in Oregon were designated as public land and open to everyone. But he really didn't want to explain himself.

Still aiming his Glock at the closed door, he asked Ella, "What's the woman's name?"

"Lydia Rigby. She's a neighbor."

"Not dangerous, right?"

"Not unless you consider a retired makeup artist to be a threat. She's also president of the Harrison McKinsey Fan Club. Their motto is: Hungry? Well, Come and Get Him."

Harry whispered, "I'll go downstairs and wait for the cops."

As he wheeled back toward the elevator, it seemed like

he wanted to avoid his number one fan. At his age, he was probably tired of groupies.

"Hallooo," Lydia called in a shaky voice. "Can I come out?"

Colin lowered his Glock, but proceeded as if she had broken into the house with criminal intent. In his cop voice, he asked, "Are you armed?"

"I have a diamond nail file with a pointed tip."

"Open the door, place the nail file on the floor and raise your hands above your head."

Ella stifled a chuckle. "Is this really necessary?"

"You never know."

The door slowly opened, framing a short, skinny woman with a sprawling hairdo in turquoise that matched her claw-like fingernails and half of the swirls in her flowing tunic. Her eye shadow fanned out in green-and-blue feathery strokes. Sequins flashed on her eyebrows, and her nose resembled a beak. She looked like a wild peacock.

Colin holstered his weapon. "How did you get into Harry's house?"

"I come over here all the time. I'm the neighbor on the left. Isn't that right, Ella Bella?"

She nodded. "You can put your hands down, Lydia."

"Thank you, honey." When she pursed her lips, Colin thought she looked more like a parrot than a peacock. Definitely some kind of flashy bird. "Anyway, I heard a noise from over here, and I saw Harry in his wheelchair careening out toward the street. I didn't think he should be out so late, so I came over to tell Ella. You know, just being friendly."

And nosy. During his years as cop, Colin had encountered many people like Lydia. Those who couldn't sleep. People with binoculars and telescopes. Window watchers who observed and recorded everything that happened on their street. Sometimes, they helped solve a mystery. More likely, they complicated the situation.

Lydia straightened her shoulders and stuck out her skinny chest, preening. "Harry isn't as young as he used to be. He might wander off and get lost, you know."

"After you entered the house, what did you do?"

"Went to look for Ella in the kitchen. Couldn't find her. Then I heard her charging out the front door."

"And you were locked inside," Colin concluded.

"Which I really didn't think was a problem. Like I said, I visit often. And I know the code to unlock the doors. But it was different." Her sequined eyebrows lifted as she confronted Ella. "Did you change it?"

"Yes, and I'll continue to do so. At least once a week."

"What a terrible idea!" Lydia flapped her arms like wings. "I was stuck in here. Couldn't get out."

Changing the code was, of course, meant to limit the number of people with easy access to the house. He wondered if Lydia had taken this unsupervised opportunity to poke around in Harry's private things. How had she ended up on the third floor? And why? What was she looking for? Neighborly Lydia might be a good source of information about Harry's missing ex-wife, if Colin decided to take on that project. He asked, "How long have you lived at Cape Seraphim?"

"From now until the twelfth of never." She giggled. "Like the Johnny Mathis song."

"Could you be more specific?"

"More than twenty-seven years ago, I was a young thing, working as a makeup artist on *The Taste of Murder*. A maiden aunt died, and I inherited quite a chunk of change. Not enough to buy property in Hollywood or on the southern California beach, you know. But I wanted to own something. Harry told me about this place, and I invested. It was a fixer-upper, and I hired Doug Rigby, a local handyman, to do repairs."

"Were you and Harry close?" Doing the math in his head,

Colin figured that Lydia had known Rosalie before she disappeared.

"He wasn't my boyfriend. Dougie was plenty man enough for me. Know what I'm saying? Wink, wink."

Wink, wink? "So you and Harry never…"

"Heavens, no. Harry was in his fifties, too old for me. Besides, he wanted to get back together with his ex-wife. The love of his life, that's what he called her."

"Let's go downstairs," Ella said. "The police should be here any minute."

When they reached the elevator, Colin asked Ella to have the police search the house in case anyone else had snuck inside while the door stood open.

"Aren't you coming downstairs with us?" she asked.

"Don't want to get caught up in all the questioning."

He preferred to be anonymous, but realized that Ella would mention his name. And the word would spread, if it hadn't already. Tomorrow, Colin needed to inform his lieutenant at the LAPD. His hideaway with Uncle Nathan had been compromised. He should probably tell his therapist, as well. And notify the FBI…all the people who were waiting around for him to remember what had happened and make an identification.

After the elevator door closed, he returned to the room where Lydia had been hiding. Like the hallway, the bedroom had a bright, cheerful decor with mint-green walls, clean white trim and a striped duvet on a polished brass bed. A dresser, bookshelf and desk in blond wood were arranged against the walls. The artwork featured nature photos and more ocean pictures. Two casement windows with open curtains faced the street. If there had been a window on the southern wall, he might have been able to see the beacon from the lighthouse.

Though Lydia seemed like an innocent bystander, she must

have come to this room for a reason. Nobody had slept in that brass bed. Though the desktop held a laptop and charger, this wasn't an office. What did Lydia expect to find in this room?

Again, his years of police work—searching houses and serving warrants—kicked in and guided him through a quick, effective search. In moments, he hit the typical hiding places: under the bed, on the high shelves in the closet, behind the desk. He felt behind cushions on the chair and went through every drawer in the desk and dresser. Reaching between the mattress and box spring, he felt the square edges of a book and pulled out a five-by-seven-inch notebook with butterflies on the cover. The pages inside looked worn and yellowed. The handwriting was delicate. On the inner front cover, Rosalie McKinsey had written her name.

Not a diary with the days of the month on each page. Not a to-do list. The notes reminded him of the way he used to record data from suspects during interviews. Something to jog his memory or lead him toward another avenue for investigation. He suspected that a TV journalist like Rosalie might have had a similar notepad.

He thumbed through the pages, reading bits and pieces. A reference to an election. Winners of a beauty contest. An interview with a starlet. Apparently, the TV station where she worked was located in southern California, Burbank.

On the next to last page, the heading proclaimed: The Four.

Colin read a list of four names with a notation that called them scammers and pirate scum. He recognized one of The Four. Someone closely associated with the kidnapping that got him shot and caused him to lose his memory.

The last name on Rosalie's list was Nathan Reid. An Oregon state senator. Colin's uncle.

This clue deserved more study. Colin stuck the book into the pocket of his hoodie, hustled to the elevator, descended and raced through the house. In the front yard at the head of the sidewalk, he saw Harry in his wheelchair, waiting for the cops. Colin's decision was made. He wanted to undertake the search for Rosalie, to use his skills as a detective. This exercise might be enough to jog his awareness and get past the amnesia. Might literally wake him up.

Harry's mood was glum. "Lydia drives me up a wall. She's always getting in the way. Keeps offering to do my makeup."

Hearing the wail of an approaching siren, Colin didn't waste time with chitchat. "I want to talk about the project you mentioned earlier."

Harry looked up. His eyes brightened. "The search for Rosalie?"

"I'm in."

Chapter Five

At half past seven the next morning, Ella stood in the kitchen surveying the clutter left behind after last night's invasion by local law enforcement—a group ranging from the chief of the Cape Seraphim police to deputies from the county sheriff's office and other cops in uniforms she couldn't identify. Back in the day, when she was a money-strapped grad student, she'd reported a possible break-in at her apartment, and it took one LAPD cop three hours to show up. This response was incredibly different.

As soon as they had made sure there was no threat, these officers wanted to hang out with Harry, aka Justin Thyme, the gourmet chef detective. Because of his reputation, they expected exotic treats and designer espresso. The job of feeding them fell to her, the factotum.

Needless to say, the cop horde had left behind an epic mess. In addition to smudges from black fingerprint powder, sandy footprints and cookie crumbs, they'd spilled coffee, dirtied cups and crumpled napkins. She was fairly sure that one of them had swiped a cheap, customized mug with the logo from *The Taste of Murder*.

After they'd left the house, waving goodbye and calling out good wishes, Harry had nudged his wheelchair up beside her. Smugly, he'd said, "I warned you about the cops."

"Yes, you did."

"That kind of chaos is only one of the reasons I don't like to get the police involved. They might have scoffed at the inaccurate plots and procedures in *Taste*, but they followed every move Justin Thyme made."

Obviously, Lydia Rigby wasn't the only fan. People who had watched *The Taste of Murder* considered Harry to be their friend—somebody they could visit and expect to be greeted with warm croissants and truffle butter. Though he'd never admit it, Harry enjoyed the recognition, which meant Ella had to learn how to put up with the fanfare.

This morning, she ground the artisanal beans for the Williams Sonoma coffee machine and brewed a rich, gourmet blend. A delicious way to deliver caffeine. Definitely a perk of the job. As a therapist, she had never expected a ready supply of epicurean goodies. This was how the other half—or the top 2 percent—lived.

She perched on a stool beside the polished marble island in the kitchen and took out her phone. She had a text message from Maggie Wright: You have a strange inheritance. Call me.

An inheritance? Ella took another sip of coffee, hoping the caffeine would punch her awake. She couldn't think of anyone who would leave her money. She had no idea who her birth parents were, not from lack of trying to find them, but her adoption had been off the books, and the paperwork was sketchy. The sweet, kind mother who raised her, Franny Scarletti, was the only person still alive in her adoptive family, and Franny had been in Madison Rose, a memory care facility in Pasadena, for the past eighteen months.

Ella heard the back door open and saw the lean, rangy form of Jake Palmer, the bodyguard, step silently across the threshold. Dressed in his typical dark colors—a black windbreaker over a gray turtleneck and black jeans—he seemed to be trying to fade into the shadows. No way would that ever happen. Not with his chiseled features and hawklike gaze. His crest of neatly groomed brown hair swept back from his widow's peak. And he was tall, well over six feet. He had the presence and bearing of a natural predator and carried a SIG Sauer P226. Men automatically showed him respect. And women flirted. Palmer was hot.

Not that she cared. He was old enough to be her father. Over the years, she'd developed the habit of checking out men of a certain age and wondering if they could be her birth father. Not Palmer. He wasn't the sort of man who would abandon an infant.

"I thought you were in Portland," she said.

"There was trouble last night. I was needed here."

She didn't ask how he had heard. Palmer's ability to appear whenever and wherever needed came from surveillance he had planted around the house and grounds. He'd shown her where the cameras were focused, and promised he would never invade the privacy of her bedroom suite. "I'm glad to see you," she said, "even though last night was a false alarm."

Instead of pouring himself a cup of coffee, he took a bodyguard stance with both hands free and eyes on a swivel, looking for possible threats. "Tell me about Colin Reid."

"He's from LA, and he's a police officer."

"I know." Palmer gave a nod. "A boyfriend?"

"Met him for the first time last night. So, no. We're not dating." And there was no guarantee she'd ever see him again.

When Harry's wheelchair motored into the kitchen, Ella checked the time on a deco-style analog wall clock over the door. Not even eight o'clock, which was early for her boss to be up and about. He was fully dressed in a yacht club blazer and a captain's hat, even though he didn't own a boat. He made a beeline for the coffee, rose from his chair to pour himself a cup and carefully navigated the few steps across the kitchen to the island. "Morning, Palmer. Ella."

"Aye, aye, skipper." She gave him a sarcastic salute. "And where are you headed so bright and early?"

"Dinah's Diner. Palmer is going to give me a lift, but I smelled the coffee and wanted a cup before facing the tasteless brew at Dinah's."

Half a dozen retirees, including a lighting technician from *The Taste of Murder*, met every morning at the diner before 8:30 a.m. to get the bargain breakfast. Harry didn't need to worry about saving money, but he considered these guys to be friends. She was glad he had buddies his own age. "I'll bet you want to tell them what happened last night before rumors get started."

"You'd win that bet." He took a deep drink of his excellent coffee. "Also, I want to talk about Rosalie. A couple of these guys knew her. They could have helpful information."

His comment made her think he was still planning to look into his ex-wife's disappearance. "Anything else you want to tell me?"

"Colin Reid is on the case."

His voice resonated, and he made the announcement with dramatic flair. *Colin Reid. On the case.* Her heart beat a little faster. A smile bloomed on her lips, and she held her coffee mug to cover her expression. Not that she expected anything more than a nodding acquaintance with Colin. If something more developed, she wouldn't complain.

Palmer offered no opinion. "I'll bring the van around to the front."

"Thanks for interrupting your time off," Harry said. "I appreciate having you here."

The bodyguard's lips twitched, the closest he ever came to a smile. He went out the back door to the garage.

Ella took a gulp of coffee and asked, "When will you start the investigation?"

"Today, of course. The first forty-eight hours is crucial."

She didn't point out that Rosalie had disappeared over twenty-five years ago. Any timely clues were long gone. "What can I do to help?"

"Number one, arrange the food for the day. Colin will be here at one o'clock, and I'd like to serve lunch. My standard order from the Beach Deli. Or call Chef Sandra and have her come in early. She's scheduled to make dinner tonight, anyway."

"Got it," she said. Harry hadn't learned how to cook on the show, but he had developed a demanding palate. "What else?"

"Number two." He sipped more coffee. "I want you to join my sessions with Colin. With your background in psychology, you'd make a good profiler."

Though he'd made an inaccurate comparison between criminal profiling and therapy, she didn't correct him. She liked the idea of being included. "I'll get this place tidied up. And organize an office to conduct the investigation. What should we call it? Headquarters? We'll need whiteboards for notes and a corkboard to tack up photos. And computers."

"Well, look at you. I daresay you've learned a few things by watching my show." He finished his coffee, returned to the wheelchair and headed toward the front door. "Use the big office on the second floor."

The investigation, especially with Colin involved, sounded exciting. A change of pace. Not that her life with Harry so far had been boring. Far from it. These three weeks had given her a peek behind the curtain at the lifestyle of someone rich and famous. Harry wasn't ostentatious about flashing his money around, but he operated on a different level than most of the people she knew.

Colin added a whole new dimension. He'd popped up in her sleep last night. According to good old Sigmund Freud, her dreams might indicate some kind of wish fulfillment. She had a clear mental picture of the inscrutable stranger with bedroom eyes, a scruffy beard and tangled black hair in need of a trim. He'd made an impression. Being around him pumped up her heart rate and aroused her in ways she hadn't experienced in years.

Her body reacted to him. His casual touch sent shivers across her skin. His voice struck a deep, sensual chord. And his eyes? Hypnotic. Still, she wondered why he'd been wandering on the foggy, windswept beach at midnight like a twenty-first-century Heathcliff. Something about him just wasn't right.

She poured herself another cup of coffee and speed-dialed Maggie. The former nun turned real estate agent answered right away.

"Good morning, Ella, my child. God bless." Her energetic greeting made Ella smile. Maggie ranked high on the optimistic, upbeat scale.

"Good to hear from you." And that was the truth.

"And also from you," Maggie said. "First of all, how are you and Harry getting along?"

"You were right about him. He's eccentric and impulsive. But also kindhearted and generous. Not to mention he has a private chef. Working for him is a treat."

"You needed to get away."

Yeah, yeah, burnout is a bitch. When Harry didn't need her anymore, she might go back to being a therapist, but she wasn't sure she could handle the stress. Something to think about later. "Harry has a new project. He wants to investigate the disappearance of his ex-wife, Rosalie. Did you ever know her?"

"I've met her. She used to come to St. Joe's with him for

Mass. My sweet Lord, that was a long time ago. I was a postulant, training for service in the sisterhood."

"What was the deal with them? Divorced and then getting back together."

"It's a long story, my child. Something for another time."

"Okay." No point in rushing Maggie. She always set the agenda. Though she looked like a sweet, smiley lady, she was a major control freak. "Tell me about this inheritance. It's got to be a mistake. I'm not aware of any rich relations."

"The Lord works in mysterious ways." Ella imagined the pleasantly plump woman with salt-and-pepper hair settling her wide bottom in an overstuffed chair at her cozy Pasadena bungalow. Though Maggie had a successful career in real estate, she led a simple life, living with her longtime friend, Amelia. She donated most of her income to the church. Her main extravagance was a collection of brightly patterned scarves.

"Yesterday," she said, "I received a call from an Oregon-based lawyer who had attempted to contact your mom when he couldn't reach you. The nurses at Madison Rose Memory Care referred him to me. He said an elderly woman had passed away, and the proceeds from the sale of her house were supposed to go to you."

"Who was this woman?"

Maggie rattled off a name Ella had never heard. The address in nearby Florence was also unfamiliar. "Her home was purchased twenty-seven years ago for cash. Free and clear. No mortgage. A dedicated fund, administered by this lawyer, paid for homeowner expenses, like taxes and insurance, with the understanding that—upon her death—you would inherit."

Stunned, Ella said, "Doesn't make any sense."

"Actually, it does, my child. I've simplified the information sent to me by the lawyer, but this appears to be on the up-and-up."

Why? What? Who? "This fund, who owns it?"

"A holding company. It's not a single person, but a consortium."

"You're good at breaking through bureaucratic barriers and tracking down information," Ella said. "Can you find out who is behind this inheritance? Do you have any idea?"

"Actually, I do." Maggie paused and cleared her throat. Ella imagined her making the sign of the cross on her chest, silently seeking a blessing before she said, "Gigi Graham."

Mumbling an incoherent string of denials, Ella slipped off the stool in the kitchen and paced across the travertine tile on the kitchen floor. She went all the way to the back porch windows with a view of the Pacific and stared out at the dark, distant waves. *This can't be happening!* She'd come to Cape Seraphim to escape the stress of her failing career, but she couldn't hide from the core issues that had tormented her for as long as she could recall. Instability, insecurity and an inability to trust. That was her fate, her heritage. Literally, she had been abandoned at birth.

She plodded back into the kitchen. Her body was capable of movement. She could breathe. Her heart thumped in her chest, but she was far from well. She felt disconnected.

"Ella? Are you all right?"

"I'll never forget that name." The last time she had searched for her birth mother, she and Maggie had uncovered information about Gigi Graham, who had supposedly played a part in Ella's adoption and her placement with Oscar and Franny Scarletti. An elderly priest at St. Joe's had helped Gigi find care for an infant. He'd passed away twelve years ago. They couldn't find any other confirmation, couldn't locate current information or an address for Gigi. They'd hit a dead end. "I thought that trail went cold."

"Not yet, my child." Maggie exhaled a sigh, probably crossed herself again. "As you know, the lawyer didn't actually tell me her name, but I put two and two together. I figured out that the lawyer had been working with the elderly priest—God rest his soul—and Gigi."

"What does that have to do with the house in Florence?"

"The owner who died was a midwife who practiced in southern California. She knew Gigi. Twenty-seven years ago, she had moved to the house in Oregon after she had facilitated a home birth."

The timing was right. Ella was twenty-seven. "If she didn't report to a hospital, that would explain my obviously faked birth certificate."

"Exactly," Maggie said. "And I'm glad you mentioned the birth certificate. The midwife said the newborn girl's name was Gabriella Love."

"Shortened to Ella, thank goodness." She would have hated being known as Gabby. "Why is that important?"

"Gigi's full name was Gabriella. The nickname came from her initials."

"Coincidence." Ella tried to dismiss the unusual match. "What else?"

"In her will, she left you a necklace. A platinum chain with a pendant of pink crystal in the shape of a heart. The lawyer handling the house, Rob Patterson, has that piece of jewelry with the instruction to give it to you."

Only a desperate person would consider this proof, but Ella could easily imagine Gigi Graham using a midwife to avoid leaving a record of her child's birth. And then she paid the woman off with a free house and a crystal necklace.

Ella wanted to know the truth. No matter how much it hurt.

Chapter Six

Ella carried her coffee mug to the sink, rinsed it and stood staring through the window at the wind ruffling the wild beach grass at the edge of the manicured yard with blooming flowers and the sprouts of an herb garden. Her mind raced while her body retreated into a lethargic state of depression. Though she longed to hop into bed and bury her head under the comforter, she wouldn't quit her search or shirk her factotum duties. Harry needed her. And she realized that living up to her responsibilities felt good. Inhaling a breath, she fired a mental starter pistol and prepared to multitask. Maggie would have advised her to pray, but Ella preferred to juggle several balls in the air and keep them all from crashing to the ground. Housekeeping duties for Harry. Checking out her strange inheritance and the connection to Gigi Graham. And getting ready to meet Colin. *Bing. Bang. Boom.* No problem.

She charged up the staircase. On the way, she made phone calls to handle the immediate issues, namely, contacting Chef Sandra about lunch and rescheduling the three-person cleaning service to come earlier. After they straightened up the clutter, they could help her organize the upstairs office into headquarters for their investigation into Rosalie's disappearance.

Her focus shifted to Colin. His image flashed in her brain.

Was he really as sexy as she thought? How would he look in broad daylight? In her private bathroom, she brushed her teeth, washed her face and put on makeup to cover the shadows under her eyes from lack of sleep. Without enough time to spackle over the budding crop of freckles, she left her cheeks and nose *au naturel.* She dressed in white sneakers, straight-leg Levi's and a silky white tank top under a lightweight denim jacket. A wholesome look that was a tiny bit sexy. She didn't want Colin to think she was trying too hard. After all, he might not be interested in her. But she was pretty sure that he was. Last night, she'd caught him looking her over. The magnetic attraction seemed to go both ways.

By the time she was finished getting dressed, the crew from Clean as a Whistle had arrived and were making quick work of tidying up after last night's cop invasion. Ella pulled aside the supervisor and explained what she needed in the upstairs office. Furniture had to be moved. Whiteboards set up. A computer hooked into the Wi-Fi. *Multitasking.*

Ella took a seat at the dining room table, where she'd be available to answer questions from the cleaners and Chef Sandra when she arrived. Prepared for note-taking with her electronic tablet and stylus in hand, she placed a call to the Oregon-based attorney, Rob Patterson, who had contacted Maggie. He was absent from his Coos Bay office, of course, but his very helpful assistant named Hilary verified the basic information and made an appointment for early tomorrow. The location of the house Ella had supposedly inherited was close enough to drive there and back in an hour.

She noted the address on her tablet. Anxious to jump into action, she wanted to leave right now. If she talked to the neighbors, she might uncover more information about Gabriella and Gigi Graham. "Is the property listed with an agent?"

"I'd advise against going there," Hilary said. "You should wait until after you've talked to Mr. Patterson."

Her years as a therapist alerted Ella to a certain wariness in the assistant's voice. Was something wrong with the house? Had someone been murdered there? Was it haunted?

Hoping to create a rapport, she spoke in a friendly tone. "Thank you, Hilary, for your help. I don't know how this is supposed to work. I've never had an inheritance before."

"Me neither."

"Anything you can tell me would be greatly appreciated. What does the house look like?"

"A nice three bedroom. Well maintained, but I'd suggest putting in air-conditioning before you try to sell."

"Great idea. I'm excited to see it." Ella eased into the important question. "Do you really think I need to wait?"

"That's what my boss would say."

"I want to hear what *you* say, Hilary."

She continued in a whisper, "There was trouble. Last night, the place was broken into and ransacked."

Aha! "Any idea why? Or who?"

"Oh, shoot. I shouldn't have said anything."

"Not a problem," Ella assured her. She wanted to keep Hilary on her side. "I won't tell Mr. Patterson, and I'll keep my appointment tomorrow morning."

She ended the call and leaned back in the dining room chair, watching the quick, efficient movements of the tall guy in a light green T-shirt with a Clean as a Whistle logo while he mopped the hardwood floors. He didn't require her supervision, and she didn't want to be here. Instead, she could zip over to the house she'd inherited—*her house.* Why was it vandalized? Ella had heard of thieves who watched the obits in the local news to find people who had recently died, leaving their property unattended. But why would Hilary's boss avoid mentioning that? Maybe the break-in was more of a search than a burglary. Had the intruder or intruders been looking for something specific?

A ribbon of vaguely connected thoughts unfurled in her mind. She needed to research the midwife—her finances, her friends and her family. Her connection to Gigi Graham had been important enough to merit the gift of a house. Was she paid off to keep a secret? Why? Ella needed to know how she fit into that picture.

Ella reviewed the few verifiable facts she'd learned while searching for her biological parents. The elderly priest at St. Joseph's in Pasadena had told Maggie about an infant abandoned at the church. Around the same time, an anonymous donor contributed a significant amount to the St. Joseph Orphanage. After a lot of digging, the name of Gigi Graham replaced *anonymous*.

Ella's off-the-books adoption by Franny and Oscar Scarletti, an older couple who had never been able to have children of their own, had turned out to be a fortunate pairing. In spite of being old enough to be her grandparents, they gave her a kind, gentle upbringing and encouraged her to follow her dreams.

When Ella had decided to look for her birth parents, her quest wasn't a reflection on them. She just wanted to know where she came from. The only significant secret she had pried from them involved money set aside to pay for her college. Again, the mysterious source of these funds turned out to be associated with Gigi Graham. Who was this woman?

Like many people who were adopted, Ella fantasized about biological parents who were wealthy or royal or had some kind of exotic heritage. She dared to hope that Gigi—her elusive benefactor—was her birth mother. But why had she abandoned Ella? Why hadn't she made herself known after all these years? Gigi was as invisible as a ghost. No photos. No social media presence. Nothing but a lawyer—not the same one who had an office in Coos Bay—who administered her bequests.

While Ella juggled her car keys, wondering if she had time to make the drive to the house, Harry returned from his breakfast with the guys at Dinah's Diner. After hearing the gossip in Cape Seraphim, he was energized, ready to set up their headquarters and get started.

Riding up with him in the elevator, she said, "Maggie Burke says hi."

"How is the old nun of a gun? I owe her a debt of gratitude," he said. "She's responsible for referring you to me."

"She likes making people happy."

"How about if you do your factotum thing and send her some flowers or jam or something? As a thank-you."

"I'm on it, boss." Maggie loved the chocolate truffles from the Brigittine Monastery. "Have you ever heard of a woman named Gigi Graham?"

"Sounds like an actress name." His forehead wrinkled as he considered. "Or a model."

"I'm guessing she's in her midfifties. I thought she was from southern California, but I have reason to believe she has ties to this area."

"Why are you asking?"

"She left me an inheritance. A house in Florence."

"Talk to Colin," Harry suggested with a shrug. "He has access to LAPD resources for finding people."

On the second floor, they went down the hall to the office—a long room with desks, bookshelves and a wall of windows facing the Pacific. Best view in the house. Ella had the idea that Harry wanted to recreate the investigation room from *The Taste of Murder* so she told the supervisor from the cleaning crew what they needed and where to find it.

His favorite piece of furniture was a wooden swivel chair—an actual prop that he'd taken from the set of *The Taste of Murder*. He wheeled into the room and transferred himself into the chair. As he gave orders and shuffled through file folders, his voice dropped into the cultured, resonant Justin Thyme tones. After playing the role for fourteen years and winning a Golden Globe, he easily slipped back into character.

At half past twelve, she left Harry with the crew from Clean as a Whistle and went downstairs. In the kitchen, she watched while Chef Sandra whisked a combination of finely chopped anchovies, minced garlic and lemon juice for the Caesar salad dressing. The energetic woman wore workout clothes under her pin-striped apron and was almost as tall as Ella at five feet, eight inches. Her skillful fingers performed delicious magic as she put together a lunch of sourdough bread, fresh butter, clam chowder and the aforementioned salad.

Ella inhaled the fresh, creamy, fishy aromas and sighed. "You're so fast. How did you put all this together and still have time to do a flower arrangement for the table?"

"The daffodils come from your own garden. A quick pick." She peeked over the rim of her round gold glasses. "Who's the important guest? A celebrity?"

"Not this time." Ella wasn't sure how much she should say about the investigation. "His name is Colin Reid. He was a cop in Los Angeles, and he's helping Harry with a project."

"Mmm-hmm. It's something to do with Rosalie."

"How'd you guess?"

"Did you know Harry made an album many years ago? I think it was called *The Taste of Christmas with Justin Thyme*."

Ella groaned. "He's played it for me."

"Most of the songs were standard carols. But 'Beyond the Sea' doesn't fit that mold. He insisted on including it because Rosalie loved the song. He's been humming it all week."

"I didn't know," Ella said. She exchanged a look with the chef that said it all: Harry's unrequited love for his ex-wife was sweet, touching and deeply weird. Didn't take a degree in psychology to figure that one out.

Chef Sandra tsk-tsked. "Well, if I'm not going to meet Hugh Jackman, I have a few errands to run before dinner. Can you manage serving?"

"I've got it." Ella shooed her out the back door. "See you tonight."

Though Chef Sandra had cleaned up after herself, Ella wiped down the counters. She set the table in the dining room with three woven place mats, beige stoneware and plain glasses. The long-stemmed wineglasses were crystal because Harry wouldn't use anything else. Ella continued to putter around, trying not to watch the minutes slowly tick by on the wall clock.

When the doorbell chimed, she ran to answer. Colin stood waiting. And she was happy to see him…happy and surprised. Last night in his sweatshirt with his baggy cargo pants, he looked sloppy and disreputable. Today, he was transformed. He wore gray trousers, a blue button-down shirt and a lightweight, navy-blue sports jacket. No necktie, but it was a perfectly acceptable off-duty cop look. His black hair still hung down to his shoulders, but was clean and combed. A pair of dark sunglasses perched on the bridge of his nose. And he had shaved. The scruff was gone.

She showed him the way to the dining room. "Hope you like chowder."

"Love it," he said. "Living on the coast, I'm getting into seafood."

"Duly noted." She paused at the table. "Wine? Harry prefers pinot grigio with chowder, but we've got a selection."

"I'd rather have beer. Seven Devils, if you've got it."

"From the local brewery. I hope Lighthouse Session is okay."

He followed her into the kitchen, where she grabbed a

bottle from the fridge. At the counter, she poured the pale ale into a beer glass. Colin spoke in a low tone. "I want to pick your brain, Ella."

"Okay." Beer in hand, she turned to face him.

He was close, very close. When he stripped off his sunglasses, his dark brown eyes mesmerized her. The man was breathtaking. She struggled to speak. "Is there something you want? Other than beer?"

He took the glass from her. "Information. Harry said the police categorized Rosalie as a missing person. The cold case is still open."

Still off-kilter, she nodded like a bobblehead doll. "Still missing. No body."

"I saw the police report." His natural intensity gave weight to his words. "Her phone was never used. No bank withdrawals. No credit card purchases. Her car wasn't on the road. She didn't take a plane. It's highly unlikely that she ran away or changed her identity. She just disappeared. No indications of foul play or violence."

Ella had heard all this before. "I don't have any other information."

"Harry insists that she's still alive. Why?"

Because he wants her to be alive. By searching for Rosalie, Harry could project his own idea of the future, whether or not it was accurate. His obsession was similar to the way she felt about the mysterious Gigi Graham. If she existed and was Ella's biological mother, her life would take on new meaning, even though Ella doubted she'd like the woman. What kind of monster abandons her newborn baby? "I can't give you a logical reason for Harry's quest. It's emotional."

"Psychological?"

"Yes."

"Suppose we determine Rosalie was killed. I'm sure you've watched enough movies and read enough books to know that in the murder of a wife, especially an ex-wife, the first suspect is always the spouse." He pinned her with that deep, dark gaze. "In your opinion, is Harry capable of murder?"

His question struck a chord within her. As a trained psychologist, she knew the shocking variability of human behavior. Nobody could be categorized as the *type* to be a murderer. Nor could they be ruled out. Atypical behavior was just that… not typical. She hadn't been able to predict the death by suicide of her client. A bright young woman, she seemed to have everything to live for and had no history of violence toward herself or others. The fact that she was adopted meant nothing. Probably.

Ella shook her head, hoping to dispel the idea of Harry as a cold-blooded murderer. "If he killed her, why would he want to reopen the investigation?"

"Guilt."

A valid motivation. Ella tried to be a rational, fact-seeking detective, but felt a knot in her belly. Tension. Their investigation involved real people. It wasn't like Harry's TV series, where the crime would be solved with a witty comment, like "That's the way the cookie crumbles."

Colin's demeanor reminded her that a real woman had disappeared and possibly had been murdered. His world was much darker and scarier than hers. "Are you saying that Harry is a suspect?"

"A person of interest."

And she was living in his house, sleeping down the hall. She spent a great deal of time with him. Ate dinner with him. Watched TV. Until now, her life hadn't seemed risky.

Chapter Seven

At the mechanical rumble of the elevator door opening, Colin looked up. He saw Harry zoom into the dining room in his motorized wheelchair, park against the wall and rise to his feet. Using the cane hooked over the back of the chair, he walked to the head of the table. His gait was so sure and steady that Colin experienced a flash of envy. Maybe he'd be better off using the cane the way his physical therapist suggested.

Harry gestured expansively. "Welcome, Colin. Let's eat and then get rolling. This investigation won't run itself."

The old gentleman looked excited and alert—ten years younger than last night. And he sounded like Justin Thyme, with a dramatic cadence and a slight British accent that was probably meant to make him seem smarter. Colin took a seat to Harry's left. "Good afternoon, sir. Did you get caught up on your sleep?"

"No time for napping. We need to dig in."

Ella lifted the lid on a ceramic tureen and ladled out steaming bowls of clam chowder with chunks of seafood and fragrant bacon. Then she darted into the kitchen and returned with the Caesar salad in a wooden bowl so they could serve themselves. Colin thought she was avoiding his gaze and had noticed that she'd never answered his question about Harry being capable of murder. Did she have doubts about her employer? Colin hadn't meant to scare her. Or maybe he had. Maybe she needed to suspect everybody and trust no one, which had always been his mantra.

She poured from a chilled bottle of pinot grigio, half filling her wineglass and Harry's. Looking toward Harry, she asked, "Do you like the way your headquarters is getting organized?"

"Reminds me of the set for *Taste*. Sitting up there, looking at the whiteboard, I wish I was as clever and intuitive as Detective Thyme."

"Not a fair comparison," she said. "Thyme had a roomful of scriptwriters to make him a super sleuth. I doubt that happens with real cops. Does it, Colin?"

"A script would be handy." If he'd known all the details in the kidnapping case, he might have avoided getting shot. "What's the headquarters you're talking about?"

Harry answered. "I want a place where we can devote all our attention to the investigation without interruptions from nosy neighbors or the cleaning crew or my physical therapist or anybody else. I've got whiteboards to write down comments and clues. And a bulletin board with photos of suspects. And a map. You'll be surprised by how many boxes of evidence I've accumulated over twenty-five years."

"Have you been searching all this time?"

"I haven't," Harry admitted. "At first, I accepted the police opinion that Rosalie had run off on her own. She was an adult and that was her right. Besides, I was in the middle of shooting for *Taste* and busy as hell. I had to accept her disappearance, even though it hurt."

Many alternatives occurred to Colin. "Some people offer rewards. Or hire a private detective. You had contacts with the LAPD. Did you consult with them?"

"I tried all of the above." He dipped his spoon into the

chowder. "Nothing worked. I got zero results. Nada. Bubkes. Rosalie vanished like a vampire at sunrise."

Colin recalled that vampires planned their disappearance to avoid the sun, which made him wonder if Harry's ex-wife had some dark secret to hide. "At the time of her disappearance, you and Rosalie were living together?"

"Only when we were in Oregon. Los Angeles is too frantic. You know she was a TV news reporter, right? Always chasing after a story. Our separate careers kept us running. There was barely time to spend an afternoon together."

Though his questions sounded more like an interrogation than polite lunchtime conversation, Colin continued along the same vein, trying to understand Harry's relationship with his ex. "Did she date other men?"

"Occasionally," Harry reluctantly admitted. "After the divorce, our relationship was open-ended. No commitment. No jealousy."

A great idea, even though Colin doubted that kind of arrangement could ever work in real life. Jealousy might have been a motive for Rosalie's disappearing act. "And you? Were there other women?"

"I never lacked for female companionship, if you catch my drift."

"Caught it."

Colin loaded his salad bowl with greens and sprinkled shaved Parm on top. Harry was correct. Southern California was a good place to find female companions. He'd spent most of his youth in the LA area after his parents had split up. High school turned into a shallow blur of surfing, skateboarding and hooking up with beach babes, starlets and sweet girl-next-door types.

He glanced across the table at Ella. She didn't fit any of those categories. Nor was she typical of the women he'd dated in college, or when he started out in the LAPD. Not a professional like a lawyer or a doc. And she definitely wasn't a woman of action—a cop or a federal agent. She occupied a unique space of her own. A psychotherapist who chose not to practice. A smart lady who seemed to be dialing back her intellect to work as a caretaker. He suspected that, similar to Rosalie, Ella had secrets.

His curiosity about her had very little to do with their investigation. Something about her beckoned to him, made him want to know more. He wondered if the sprinkle of freckles across her chest extended all the way to her belly button. And if her lips were naturally that dusky rose color. The streaks in her hair probably weren't natural, but he didn't care. She looked great.

She made eye contact, then slowly blinked. The electric blue of her iris burned like a butane flame and spread throughout his body.

The doorbell rang. Though Harry shook his head and told them to ignore it, the door handle jiggled and somebody shouted an unintelligible comment. Ella pushed back her chair and went to answer.

Colin couldn't see the entryway from the dining room, but he heard the door being opened. Ella said something about this not being a convenient time. Then Lydia charged into the dining room with her tunic-of-the-day flapping around her. The tiger-striped pattern matched the orange of her eyeshadow.

She planted her fists on her skinny hips and stared daggers at Harry. "You need to fix the code on the door lock, you know. I couldn't get in. What if there was an emergency?"

"I changed it," Ella said calmly. "As I told you before, I change the code every week. Doesn't do much good to lock up if everybody has the combination."

"You!" Lydia stabbed the air with a clawlike fingernail. "I came here with the best intentions. I have information for you, Ella Bella. Doug Rigby called this morning."

"Your husband?" Ella asked.

"For lack of a better word. Anyhoo, he said you inherited some property up in Florence, and you should contact him if you need help with repairs."

"What property?" Harry shot her a confused glance.

"I only heard about it this morning," Ella said.

"Doug told me it had something to do with Gigi Graham." Lydia rolled her eyes. "She was nothing but trouble, that one."

"Do you know her?" Ella asked.

"She's been dead for years, you know. Cremated and interred in a columbarium at Forest Lawn in Glendale, with the likes of Mr. Walt Disney and Miss Bette Davis."

"Why did Gigi buy a house in Florence?" Ella asked. "What was her connection?"

"My Dougie never had a single good word to say about her. And he's a very forgiving guy. Forgiving and sweet, a perfect combo."

"Thanks for stopping by," Ella said. "Now I have to ask you to leave. We're in the middle of something."

"Are you sure I can't—"

Ella herded the tiger lady toward the door. "Bye now, Lydia."

She returned to the table, took her seat and looked at Colin. "What were you saying?"

His train of thought had completely derailed, but he managed to get back on topic. "Harry, when Rosalie disappeared, were you here or in LA?"

"Both places." He paused and took a sip from his stemmed wineglass. "I have a sweet little town house in Burbank. It's not an area considered to be elite, like Brentwood or Beverly Hills, but there are some outstanding properties. This place is stucco with a red-tile roof. Two-story, three bedrooms. No swimming pool, just a hot tub. It perches on a hillside with a terrace that overlooks the city. I still own it. Comes in handy when I do business in LA."

"Like a pied-à-terre," Ella said.

An extra house for business meetings. Colin never ceased to be amazed by the extravagant habits of the wealthy. The interruption from Lydia had caused him to veer off track, and he got back on topic. "You said living in LA was frantic. And so, you and Rosalie took a break and came back to Oregon."

"It was a matter of timing. *Taste* was in the middle of the shooting schedule, but the producers wanted a two-week break—a miniature hiatus. Since February is the beginning of award season, our tapings were frequently interrupted. Rosalie and I moved to Cape Seraphim so we could enjoy the downtime. We flew back and forth for red-carpet events."

"You must have been busy," Ella said. "You were nominated for awards."

"I won a Golden Globe." He beamed proudly. "But that was in January."

"Your career was going well." She looked directly at Colin as if making the point that Harry hadn't been depressed and certainly not homicidal. "It was a good time in your life."

"The best." His expression relaxed as he stared up at the modern glass chandelier with sprawling octopus tendrils that reached across the ceiling. It looked like an original Chihuly. "Rosalie and I seemed to have found a perfect balance."

His gaze softened. For the first time, Colin understood why Harry had been a heartthrob. Even at age seventy-six, he had charisma. "Tell me about the day she disappeared."

"I got called back to the studio to reshoot a couple of scenes. I grabbed a private flight and zipped down the coast to the soundstage in Burbank, fully expecting to be back before dark. But the shoot took longer than we had thought. I called Rosalie to tell her I'd be late, and she snapped at me.

Told me I didn't have to check in with her every minute, and I should stay at the town house."

"That must have ticked you off."

"As arguments went, this was a squall. Not a hurricane. I didn't think it was any big deal until I came home the next day and found her gone."

"Had she packed?"

"The details are in the police report. She took her purse and keys, of course. I remember her carry-on suitcase was gone and a few other things. But she didn't take her makeup or her lotions. The car she used when she was in Oregon was still in the garage."

"She didn't leave a note?"

"Not a note or an email or a text."

His description matched the police information. Colin had already gotten a copy of the missing person report and investigative files of the lead detective in LA, which were sent to his phone by his partner, Dwayne Perez. His boss in Robbery-Homicide, Lieutenant Rankin, hadn't been pleased when Colin told him about his intention to investigate Rosalie's disappearance. His recuperation time was supposed to be used for regaining his memory. Rankin wanted an arrest, and Colin agreed. He'd been dutifully attending sessions with a new shrink based in Coos Bay. Dr. Lowell Tindahl was a specialist in amnesia—a big reason Colin had come here, rather than hiding out in an FBI safe house.

"Okay, Colin," Harry said. "I have a couple of questions for you. Starting with the obvious. Do you think you can find Rosalie?"

"I make no guarantees."

"Have you ever investigated a case like this before?"

"No case is exactly like another," he said. "Rosalie's disappearance is especially unique. The original investigators didn't find a body or a note. There's no trail to follow. Common sense tells me there are two possibilities. Either she disappeared of her own free will, possibly catching a ride with someone else, or she is deceased."

"She was the love of my life. Sometimes, I think I see her walking on the beach. Or I turn on the television and—swear to God—I hear her voice." Harry drained his wineglass. "I just want to know what happened to her."

Colin tipped back in his chair and raised his Seven Devils to his lips. The beer went down smoothly, and his mood lightened with the anticipation of starting a brand-new investigation. This felt right. He was a detective, and this was what he did. His brain cranked into gear. A little bit rusty, but the wheels were turning.

He reached into the inner pocket of his jacket and took out the butterfly notebook. "I found this in the third-floor bedroom. Rosalie's name is written on the first page."

Harry nodded. "She always carried one of those with her to jot down details and thoughts, usually about a story she was developing for the news. She had dreams of becoming the west coast Barbara Walters." He held out his hand. "I don't think I've seen that one before. Can I take a look?"

"In a minute." He flipped to a page toward the back. "At the top of the page, there's a title—The Four. Then, there's a list of four names. At the bottom is a note that says 'Scammers. Pirate scum.' What does this mean?"

"It's probably a story she was working on. Scamming sounds like a computer thing, which is more focused on southern California than Oregon."

In spite of Harry's Golden Globe–winning acting talent, Colin could tell the old man wasn't being truthful, not telling the whole story. He blinked. His gaze flickered. His hand reached up to rub his chin, almost as though he was erasing the words before they came out of his mouth.

Much as he hated to hear negative stories about his uncle,

Colin asked, "Nathan Reid is one of the names. What was the nature of Rosalie's relationship with him?"

Harry's hand clenched into a fist. "Among other things, he was her lover."

Chapter Eight

Though bursting with curiosity, Ella managed to contain her questions while they crammed themselves into the elevator. While Harry and Colin made small talk about the weather and the warm June temperatures, she wrapped herself in a cloak of silence and tried to put the pieces together.

The house in Florence had been ransacked. *Her house.* Lydia said that Gigi was nothing but trouble. More importantly, Gigi was dead. Added to that was Rosalie's list of The Four.

At the dining room table, when Harry made his announcement about Colin's uncle Nathan, she'd almost choked on her chowder. Her concept of Rosalie, the supposed love of Harry's life, was sweet, gentle and romantic, like the Edgar Allan Poe poem about Annabel Lee in her kingdom by the sea. Ella hadn't expected an accusation of infidelity. Not that Rosalie's affair with Colin's uncle fell into that category. She'd been divorced with no strings attached and no expectation of monogamy. She wasn't cheating. Nathan was.

Their affair wasn't a total surprise. Harry had previously mentioned that he and Nathan had "history," which usually indicated some kind of dispute. At the same time, she knew Harry was friendly with Nathan's wife, Bridget. She'd been the "little birdie" who told him about Colin staying at their house. Harry had even suggested that Ella take a tour of their home—known as the Castle—accompanied by Bridget.

After exiting the elevator, they trooped down the hallway to the long, large office with a wall of windows facing west and looking down on the beach grass, the sand and the rolling sea. Harry had already claimed the central desk in front of a floor-to-ceiling wall of leather-bound books. To his right was a bulletin board with several photos of Rosalie in different outfits with different hair styles. On his left, a whiteboard stocked with markers in different colors. With an imperious gesture, he directed Colin toward a long table with a computer, printer and television monitor. She was assigned the less impressive desk near the door.

Before they went to their separate stations, she leaned close to Colin and whispered, "Are you okay with having your uncle dragged into this?"

"If there's one thing I've learned as a cop, it's this—everybody is a suspect. Nobody gets a free pass. And I don't really know Nathan and Bridget well. I mean, I lived with them for almost a year when I was a kid, but that was a hella long time ago."

"How long ago was that?" Colin might have been staying at Uncle Nathan's castle during the time when he had his affair with Harry's ex-wife. "Did you meet Rosalie?"

"Don't remember. I was only five." He shrugged. "I didn't notice much about the adults. Aunt Bridget baked butterscotch cookies. Uncle Nathan was kind of cold. We never had much in common, but they're okay. Family, you know. Blood relatives. Know what I mean?"

"Actually, I don't. Remember? I was adopted."

Harry made a harrumphing noise from the swivel chair behind his desk. "Are you two going to stand there whispering? Or can we get this show on the road?"

"I'm ready," Colin said.

"Good." Harry cleared his throat. "Write those four names on the whiteboard in a horizontal line. We'll fill in the space under each name with information."

"I'll start with my uncle." He wrote the name. Underneath, he added details. "Married to Bridget for thirty-five years. Two kids, neither live at home. Nathan is a state senator who is campaigning to be the US senator from Oregon. He used to practice law. Manages investments. Dabbles in real estate. Unlike the rest of my family, he's filthy rich."

"And you're currently living in his house," Ella pointed out.

"Temporarily. When I'm recuperated, I'm back to LA." He wrote another name. "Douglas Rigby, the guy Lydia mentioned. I did a quick online search for Dougie."

Ella asked, "Are he and Lydia married?"

"Not officially," Harry said. "She uses his name because they've lived together off and on for years. When she bought her property, he was Mr. Fix It. Eventually, he moved in. He expanded his business and runs several crews, specializing in flipping run-down properties."

"Another connection to real estate," she said, thinking of how much she'd appreciate Maggie's advice on this topic. Before the house in Florence, she'd never owned property.

Colin moved down the whiteboard. "Number three is Dean Santiago, a developer based in Los Angeles. Do you know him, Harry?"

"Nope. Houses were Rosalie's thing. She did a lot of buying and selling of property, always made a tidy profit."

Ella noticed Colin's hesitation. Did he have more information about Santiago than his stated occupation? She probed. "What else can you tell us? Is Santiago wealthy?"

"Very much so."

"Married?"

"Yes. With two kids. Ages seven and ten."

"Seems young," she said.

"Second marriage."

She asked, "Is there anything else about him that we should know?"

"A lot." Colin slipped off his jacket, revealing a shoulder holster that reminded her, once again, that they weren't playing a parlor game. Right now, he looked like a cop, a person in authority, somebody who solved crimes.

She tried to read behind his expression. "Do you know this Santiago?"

"Yes."

"I'd like to hear about your connection to him," she said. A lifetime ago, Rosalie had branded Santiago as one of The Four. "Can you tell us your impressions of him?"

"Finish the list," Harry said in an impatient tone. "Who's number four?"

"Blake Schmidt." Under his name, Colin drew a giant question mark. "I couldn't find much on him. He was an accountant. His wife died a long time ago. No kids. Never remarried. Worked for Uncle Nathan in Cape Seraphim and Santiago in LA. He has a finance business of his own. Specializes in malls and apartments."

Ella stared at the whiteboard. Four names. Not much to go on. She wondered if most investigations began with a kernel of suspicion that ultimately blossomed into a full-fledged case.

Harry rose from the wooden swivel chair and walked a few paces to the whiteboard. With his cane, he pointed to the names. "They sound like a law firm. Reid, Rigby, Santiago and Schmidt. Four suspects. Ella, you should get started on profiles for each of them. What do you need?"

"A crystal ball."

"Not funny."

"Let me explain. Again." Sitting at her table near the

door, she laced her fingers together, holding her frustration in check. How many times would she need to go over this simple point? "I'm not a forensic psychologist. Never had training as a profiler. Though I have no problem with online research or digging through documents, my skills require face-to-face, personal interaction, and I rely on a number of psychological tests. Only then can I come up with my diagnosis of a disorder."

His forehead scrunched into a scowl. "Are you saying that you can't give me a reading on these men without meeting them?"

"I'm not a psychic, Harry."

"Do you have any observations at all?"

She'd never been a fan of stereotyping, but she had noticed obvious similarities among the four men. "They're all about the same age, which is somewhere around sixty. Reid, Santiago and Schmidt are successful. Probably wealthy. I doubt Rigby started out that way, but he seems to be doing very well—at least Lydia thinks so."

"You're right about that," Colin said. "According to the Internet, the carpenter is a self-made multimillionaire. Twenty-five years ago, he was just starting out."

She continued, "All four are connected to the housing market. Like Rosalie. That's the place I'd start an investigation. Determining if they were, in fact, scammers or real estate pirates."

"I'll follow up on that angle." Colin sat behind the computer, booted it up and scowled at the screen. "I'm not great at researching, but if I figure out the right questions, I know people who can get me answers. I'll look for housing scams, starting twenty-five years ago."

Ella had an idea about a useful contribution she could make. "I'll take the personal angle. Looking into the backgrounds for each of these guys and how they knew Rosalie."

"Like a profiler?" Harry said triumphantly. "I knew it! I knew you'd be good at that."

Without acknowledging his crowing or explaining how researching the personal history of a subject—including ethnicity, family, friends, work, hobbies and so on—was different from forensic psychology, she continued, "I can start by talking to Nathan Reid."

Colin's eyebrows raised. "You want to interview my uncle?"

"Is that a problem?"

"No reason we can't pay him a visit." He stood and stepped away from his computer before making a single keystroke, seeming happy to leave it behind. He looked toward Harry. "How about you? Want to come along?"

"Given my past disputes with Nathan, it's better if I stay here."

Colin led the way through the hall and down the sweeping staircase. Outside on the veranda, she stood beside him at the banister and inhaled the salty coastal air while listening to the echo of the surf and the squawking gulls. In spite of the hazy clouds, sunshine warmed her cheeks and her nose, probably creating another unfortunate spray of freckles.

With his sunglasses in place, he smiled down at her. "Let's walk. It's uphill, but not far, and the approach to the Castle is kind of spectacular. When the afternoon sun hits just right, the rocks in the circular towers seem to glow. Much of the base is stone. The upper level and gables are weathered wood. Sequoia, I think. Built in the late 1800s by a shipping baron."

"One of your ancestors?"

"Nope. Uncle Nathan didn't inherit a fortune, but his wife's family had a lot of property. They deeded the Castle, which required major renovation and repair, to the young couple for a fraction of its true value."

He directed her across the street toward the northeast side

of the cul-de-sac, away from Lydia Rigby's house. Leaving the sidewalk, they followed a worn path through the trees and foliage that ran parallel to the street where a couple of cars paused at a four-way stop.

Walking felt good. In her jeans, sneakers and denim jacket, she was prepared to be on a hike. Glad to be outdoors. Especially glad to be with the tall, lean cop who accompanied her.

COLIN STAYED SLIGHTLY behind Ella on the path so he could keep an eye on her. Without a doubt, she was the most attractive partner he'd ever had. Not that looks counted for much in an investigation. His last three partners in the LAPD hadn't been fashion models, but they were all smart, quick thinking and loyal. One of them—Sergeant Dwayne Perez—had saved his life.

At the corner, they left the forest path, crossed the street and turned uphill. Concentrating on his stride, he moved comfortably, but the quad in his right leg began to ache. Occasionally, the muscles hitched, and he limped. *Not fair.* Hadn't his sweet-faced PT promised 95 percent recovery? Side by side, he and Ella went up the wide sidewalk. Several of the houses had green yard signs saying Nathan Reid for Senate. Clearly, they were on his uncle's home turf.

"When I was a kid," he said, "I used this route to get to the beach. I wasn't supposed to go into the water past my knees, but rules and restrictions were lax at the Castle."

"I've been wondering about you and the shore," she said. "May I ask a blunt question?"

"Isn't that what therapists do?"

She flashed a grin but didn't deny his accusation. "Why were you out there last night after midnight?"

A fair question, but he didn't want to delve into the complicated explanation. Still, he owed it to his new partner to tell the truth. He crossed another street. Their route continued northeast on more sidewalks. "It's the lighthouse," he said.

"I'm going to need a little bit more."

That's what worried me. He didn't want their investigation to be about him, didn't want to reveal too much about himself. "Part of my recuperation process is to relax and meditate, but I'm not what you'd call a mindful person. Don't know why, but watching the lighthouse helps. My therapist told me to go with it."

"A physical therapist?" She tilted her head to look up at him. "How does a midnight walk on the beach help heal your bum leg?"

"My injuries included a serious concussion, and I was in a coma for five days. When I woke up…" He hated admitting to his weakness. But here it was, staring him in the face. "I couldn't remember anything, not one damn thing. Stuff came back, little by little. But not all of it. I still can't recall the final rescue. The investigation is stalled until I identify the shooter."

She came to a halt in the middle of the sidewalk. "You have amnesia. That's the thing you haven't told me. Amnesia. I should have known."

"Yeah? Are there obvious signals? Are my eyes supposed to get crossed? Do I start barking like a dog or drooling?"

"Not funny, Colin." She shook her head. "It's a serious disorder, a frequent cause of which is concussion. I once treated a concussed high school football player who developed selective amnesia where he couldn't remember the hours before and after his injury. He recovered in a few weeks."

"How did you pull that off?"

She shrugged. "I had the distinct advantage of being able to show him the video recording of the game where he was injured. And I used a combination of treatments developed for PTSD. One of them must have gotten through. Or maybe… his brain healed itself."

"Sheer dumb luck?" He couldn't hide his bitterness. She, of all people, should understand how hard this was.

"I'd like to think his recovery took some skill on my part."

He directed her off the sidewalk onto a roadside path at the edge of a forested area. Untended thickets of shrubs and ferns bordered the gravel shoulder. Beyond, the forest thickened with moss-covered fir, cedar and ash. The two-lane road with a worn double-solid yellow line down the middle seemed to be an S-shaped curve. "Near the top of this hill, you can see the Castle through a clearing in the forest."

She stepped up beside him. "Who's your therapist?"

"Dr. Lowell Tindahl in Coos Bay. A psychiatrist. He's a specialist in amnesia recovery, and I see him three times a week. He's one of the reasons I'm staying here with my uncle, rather than in an FBI safe house. I had an appointment with Tindahl this morning."

"Did you tell him about our investigation?"

Colin nodded. "He wasn't thrilled."

The doc advised against getting too involved, even though the disappearance of Rosalie was ancient history and shouldn't be dangerous. Tindahl didn't like to see Colin wearing his shoulder holster—an indication that he was expecting trouble, either on a conscious or subconscious level.

Ella asked, "Did the doctor think our investigation would slow your recovery?"

"He didn't offer an opinion, but admitted that my return to crime-solving might shake something loose in my head. Like you said, my brain might heal itself." He came to a stop three-quarters of the way to the hilltop and pointed through a clearing. "There it is."

A few hundred yards away and surrounded by forest, the Castle occupied the high ground above the small town of Cape Seraphim. Though Colin didn't particularly like his uncle and his political rhetoric, he appreciated the beauty and the history associated with the Castle. Sunlight shone against the curved surface of the three-story towers, similar to short lighthouses but without beacons. The wood on the siding and gables had faded to a rich, variegated gray. Beveled glass panes in some of the windows gleamed. Thick bushes of red-and-coral roses lined the sidewalk.

"Wow." Ella stood and stared. "I can't believe I haven't noticed this gigantic house before. It's really tucked away among the trees."

"It's purposely remote. My uncle likes it that way. There are only twenty or so other houses in the area."

"Your Castle looks like a fairy tale."

"Yeah? Sometimes, I think it looks like a place where vampires live in the basement."

"Possibly true. Fairy tales don't always come with happy endings."

Directly across the road, a white gull stood on a fence post at the edge of the forest. Colin could have sworn the bird turned its head and stared at him, squawked a warning and took off. What the hell was that all about?

He gestured for Ella to cross the narrow, curving road. The moment she stepped onto the asphalt, a black Escalade with dark-tinted windows rounded the curve at the top of the hill. Appearing out of nowhere, the SUV almost seemed like it had been waiting for them. Instead of slowing down, the rhino-sized vehicle sped up. Coming right at them.

Acting on instinct, Colin grabbed Ella by the arm and threw her into the foliage between the road and the forest, out of harm's way. He dropped to his knee. Pulled his weapon and aimed. He fired a warning shot, high and wide, and shouted, "Halt. LAPD."

Not true, but that had always been an effective way to stop in assault. The Escalade swerved and kept coming. The car was going after Ella.

Chapter Nine

Ella sprawled backward into a clump of maidenhair fern, vines and prickly brush at the side of the road. Twigs and gravel scraped her palms. She heard Colin yell. Saw the SUV veer off the road onto the narrow shoulder. The wide grill and headlights aimed toward her.

She scrambled to her feet and charged up the slight incline, hurtling toward the moss-covered trees. Behind her, she heard the engine rev. Gunfire exploded. Shooting at her?

Her muscles quivered as adrenaline surged. She forced herself to keep going through the foliage and into the forest. She tripped over a root. Fell to her knees. *Get up. Get moving.* She lurched forward. Ducked behind the thick trunk of a Douglas fir.

Peeking out, she saw the SUV return to the paved road. Colin stood in a classic shooting stance, with both hands holding his gun. He fired at the rear bumper. The back window shattered.

And then, the Escalade was gone.

Her vision dimmed. For an instant, she felt as weightless as a helium balloon. She'd been attacked. How could something like this happen to someone like her? Who would try to kill her? She wasn't a cop or a secret agent. Had never even held a gun. Didn't know kung fu.

Confused and terrified, she forced herself to breathe. The rules of engagement had changed. Her skills as a factotum and psychotherapist counted for nothing. She needed to learn how to be a warrior if she wanted to survive.

Colin crashed through the forest and came toward her. Still holding his weapon in one hand, he grasped her arm above the elbow with the other and pulled her to her feet. "Ella, are you okay?"

She nodded and tried to speak, but no sound passed through her lips.

"Take a breath." He ripped off his sunglasses and stared into her eyes. His fierce intensity wakened her. "Talk to me, Ella. Are you injured?"

"Teach me how to shoot a gun." She heard the anger in her voice. Her instinctual rage came from being attacked for no damn reason. "I need to know how to defend myself."

His eyebrows raised. "I get it."

His arms wrapped protectively around her, and she welcomed his embrace. He still held the gun, and she felt the heat of the weapon. Breathing hard, she inhaled the acrid, sulfurous scent of gunpowder. Not that she knew what a recently fired gun should smell like.

Though tempted to relax against his chest and let him take care of her, Ella feared the approach of more danger. The hairs on the back of her neck prickled. Beneath her fear was a wellspring of anger. Like it or not, this was her battle. "Will they come back to finish off what they started?"

"Don't know." He stepped back, holstered his weapon and pulled out his phone. "I'll call for backup, but we both know how long it takes for the local cops to respond."

In the meantime, they couldn't just stand here like a couple of immobile targets on a shooting range. She gazed past his shoulder toward the gleaming Castle on the hill. "We should go to your uncle's house."

"Follow me." He stepped in front of her. "I know my way around these hills and a safe approach to the house. If any other car comes along this road, don't signal them. They could be working with the driver of the Escalade."

Crouching, she moved as quickly as she could through the trees. The forest stretched wide but not deep, similar to the road through the Van Duzer Corridor that gave the impression of being a massive, old growth forest. Those trees and shrubs extended less than a mile outward from the pavement in some areas. The rest had been clear-cut.

She heard Colin's end of the conversation as he gave phone directions to his uncle's house and warned that the driver of the SUV was dangerous. He hadn't managed to get a license plate, but had shattered the back window and embedded a bullet in the rear bumper.

He finished his conversation, put the phone back in his pocket and lowered himself onto a flat rock, hidden in the green spring foliage. He pulled her down beside him. "Still okay?"

"I'm so sorry, Colin. I didn't mean to put you or your family in danger. Believe me when I tell you this. I don't know why that driver came after me."

He smoothed her hair and tucked a strand behind her ear. "What are you talking about?"

"This morning…" She could hardly believe Maggie's phone call had taken place only a few hours ago and turned her life upside down. "I was informed that I'd inherited a property in Florence. The house had been ransacked, probably searched. There are secrets about that place, starting with the former owner, Gigi Graham. You heard what Lydia said about her, right?"

"I'm not sure I'd trust anything Lydia says."

"Gigi is dangerous," Ella said. "Somehow, I'm connected

to her. And now, an Escalade tries to run me down. The two things are related to each other. They have to be."

"Why do you say that?"

She didn't want to go into details based on speculation and wishful thinking. She had no verifiable proof that Gigi was her biological mother. Since she was dead, there was no chance of a DNA test. "It's the only explanation I can come up with."

He reached into his jacket pocket, pulled out his sunglasses and flipped them open. "You're not the only one with enemies."

"The shooter from the kidnapping." But the Escalade had been aiming for her.

He gestured toward a break in the trees. "When we get to that spot, we'll hit an open field. About twenty yards across. You'll need to bend over, make yourself as small a target as possible. And run like hell."

"I don't like this plan," she said. "You make it sound like somebody is hiding in the forest with a rifle, like a hunter. Maybe we should wait for the police."

"Ella, I *am* the police. In my judgment, we should get to shelter. Immediately."

"Who did you talk to on the phone?"

"Deputy Sheriff Grant Angstrom."

She'd met him last night at Harry's house. "Did he give you an ETA?"

"ASAP."

But she didn't hear the reassuring screech of sirens coming closer. There had only been one other vehicle—a yellow VW Bug that looked more like a bumblebee than an assassin. She knew better than to expect the police to drop everything and come to their aid. "Let's go."

When he maneuvered toward the break in the tree line, she fell into step beside him. His right hand held his Glock.

His left arm curled around her. When she glanced up at him, he dropped a light kiss on her forehead. "I'll do everything I can to keep you safe."

"Harry was right," she said. "You really are the hero cop from LA."

Another kiss. This time on the tip of her nose. "I'm no hero."

"We'll see."

His little kisses encouraged her with exactly the right degree of intimacy. When they paused at the edge of the open field, her blood pumped…in a good way. She was ready to run.

"I'm going to move fast," he said. "Try to keep up."

Though she'd barely noticed his limp while they made their way through the trees, she had to wonder about his ability to sprint. "Should I go first?"

"What kind of hero would I be if I shoved you into danger?"

"A smart one."

"See you on the other side."

He darted through the trees into the field. The grass was knee-high in places. At the edge of the road were lupines, daisies and milkweed. Colin tore across the landscape. She saw little sign of his disability, perhaps because she was so utterly focused on her own gait. She managed to stay close behind him. Breathing hard, she heard her pulse pounding in her ears.

Ella wasn't a runner. Her physical conditioning tended toward yogic exercise—stretching and flexing—that Colin would dismiss as philosophical. Not cardio. Not frantic exertion based on fear and rage. *Run, Ella, run.* She leaped into the shadow of the trees on the far side of the field. *Made it!*

Colin took her arm and dragged her forward, guiding her toward a wide tree trunk. She leaned her back against the rough bark, glad that she'd worn her denim jacket. Gasping, she peeked up at him.

With his forearms braced against the tree, he surrounded her with his body. "It's not far from here. We go up this hill and come down at the rear entrance."

She was energized and excited. Running for her life made a good motivation for more vigorous exercise. Her lips parted. Seeing herself reflected in his sunglasses was a bit of a turn-off, but she still wanted him to kiss her. For real. No pecks on the forehead. She wanted to feel his mouth on hers.

Instead, he stepped back and peeled her away from the tree. Cautiously, they continued the rest of the way to his uncle's house. Without knocking, Colin entered through a back door into a mudroom filled with rain gear, and proceeded into a huge, high-ceilinged kitchen. A tanned, out-doorsy-looking woman with a long, ash-blond ponytail stood at the kitchen counter chopping veggies. Her firm grip on the handle of her chef's knife told Ella this woman knew what she was doing.

Colin introduced her as Aunt Bridget. She wiped her hands on her patterned apron and beamed. Hers was a happy face with round, rosy cheeks. "You're the young woman who works for Harry. What does he call you? A factoria?"

"Factotum," Ella said and returned the smile. She took an immediate liking to Bridget and was irritated on her behalf that Uncle Nathan had been messing around with Rosalie.

"Would you two like coffee? Or tea? Or anything else?"

The screech of a police siren echoed from the front of the house, and Colin went toward it. "That's Deputy Angstrom. I called him."

"Whatever for?" Bridget asked as she took off her apron and smoothed her soft blue sweater over her casual, midi-length linen skirt.

"Nothing to worry about," Colin said as he patted her shoulder. "Somebody is trying to kill us, Aunt Bridget. That's all."

UNACCUSTOMED TO BEING a witness, Colin followed the others into the small, informal dining room off the kitchen and waited while they seated themselves around the eight-person oval table covered by a light gold damask tablecloth set off by a low centerpiece of coral roses from the front yard. Bridget served coffee and tea. Cookies appeared. With his aunt handling hostess duty, the atmosphere was more like a birthday party than a police interrogation.

Ella was the only person who looked worried. Deputy Angstrom sat at the head of the table with a small spiral notebook for jotting down notes. Nathan and Bridget shook their heads, tacitly dismissing the idea that an assassin driving an Escalade had purposely attacked Colin and Ella. After all, this was a good area, a nice neighborhood. Not a place for criminals and killers. Besides, Nathan and Bridget were the lord and lady of the Castle. What sort of person would dare assault their guests? Colin must be mistaken.

But he knew the danger was real. A month ago in LA, he'd almost been killed, which made him doubt that today's attack was related to Ella's strange inheritance. Yes, the SUV seemed to be aiming at her. Still, Colin believed he was the target. The kidnappers must have figured out his location and come after him, fearful that he'd be able to identify them.

Retreating to the FBI safe house offered the safest option. If he went there, he could concentrate full-time on curing his memory. Much as Colin hated the idea of hiding, he couldn't stay at the Castle if it meant putting his aunt and uncle in danger. He glanced across the table at Nathan Reid. Tall, dark and rangy, like all the men in his family. Nathan's shining black mane didn't show a single hair of gray. No doubt, a dye job—another example of his phony facade. Over the years, he'd cultivated a broad, ultrawhite politician's smile designed to make people think he was open and honest. Nothing could be further from the truth.

Colin knew better. He hadn't been surprised when he found Rosalie's notebook with The Four scammers, including his uncle. Nathan leaned back in his chair, folded his arms across his chest and scowled. "All right, Colin, tell us exactly what happened."

In concise, factual language, he described the black Escalade with tinted windows that had tried to run them down. "No guardrails along that stretch of road," Colin said. "Deputy, you'll be able to see tire tracks across the gravel and shrubs at the shoulder."

The deputy nodded. "I already put in a call to the sheriff. He'll contact the state forensic team to take evidence. Also, we have a BOLO on the Escalade."

"I wouldn't make too big a deal of this," Nathan said. "Sounds like an accident. Somebody driving too fast. At the worst, it's a DUI."

Ella piped up. "He came right at me. On purpose."

Nathan flashed his toothy smile. "I'm sorry. I've forgotten your name."

His wife nudged him. "This is Ella Scarletti. I told you about her. She's working for Harry until he gets back on his feet."

"Right, right, right." Nathan continued to grin. "You must have been very frightened."

Ella straightened her shoulders. "I'm angry."

"Of course you are."

His uncle's voice dripped with so much slimy condescension that Colin wanted to hose him down. Crisply, he said, "Ella is correct. The Escalade was aiming for her."

"I'm sure it felt that way," Nathan said. "Sometimes, people are so careless."

Ella rose from her chair. Her cheeks flushed. "Thanks for the cookies and coffee, Bridget. I'll wait on the porch to give my statement to Deputy Angstrom."

"Now, now, now," Nathan said. "Don't go storming off in a huff."

"A huff? This was attempted murder." Her voice rang with authority, and Colin stifled an urge to applaud. Ella could take care of herself. She continued, "I demand to be taken seriously."

After she pivoted on her heel and left the room, Nathan gave a dismissive snort. "She's making a big fuss about nothing. If this incident was anything more than an accident—which I seriously doubt—it's obvious that the driver was coming after you, Colin. The FBI took the threat so seriously that they wanted you in a safe house."

"What's this about the FBI?" The deputy jolted forward in his chair.

"Not your problem," Nathan said. "My point is this. Little Miss Ella is a nobody. Why would she be attacked?"

"That's why the deputy is here," Colin said. "To investigate."

"What's the big mystery?"

"Ella learned that she inherited a house from a person she had never met. Last night, the house was ransacked. Today, a car tries to run her down. The coincidence bears looking into."

"Fine, fine, fine." Nathan liked to repeat things for emphasis. "I'll back off, son."

Even when he was a kid, Colin hated when his uncle called him *son* or *sonny*. As an adult, the nickname was pure insult. *You're not my father.* He glared across the table. His dad wasn't a perfect parent or an exemplary human being, but he had the guts to follow his dreams. His dad might have been the only person Colin had ever truly trusted to tell him the truth.

"Just out of curiosity," Nathan said, "who is this mysterious person who left your little girlfriend a house?"

Colin could have gone off on a tangent about how he and

Ella had just met, and she wasn't his little anything, but he wanted to check his uncle's reaction to this name. "You might have known her."

"Spill it, son."

"Gigi Graham."

Nathan's gaze darted. Looking for a place to hide? His mouth snapped shut. With very little of his former bravado, he said, "I knew her."

Chapter Ten

On the long veranda stretching across the front of the Castle, Ella stood beneath the center arch, fuming about the way Nathan Reid had insulted her. In her work as a therapist, her clients experienced rape, abuse, addiction and many psychological issues that had—in the unenlightened past—been swept under the rug while the victim was blamed or discounted as being unreliable. With a figurative pat on the head, Colin's uncle had dismissed her. She'd be damned if she sat silently and allowed him to pull that kind of patronizing attitude.

She paced to the northern end of the veranda and gazed past the thick, leafy vegetation and tall trees. Far below, the Pacific horizon stretched below a hazy sky. From this angle, she couldn't see the beach that ran past Harry's house. Nor was the lighthouse visible, though she imagined that after dark she'd see the beacon sweeping across the waves.

She pivoted and marched to the other end of the veranda where the clumps of trees were sparse, allowing a view of the housing development on the hills. Large homes with landscaped yards connected to a curving side road that led to the Castle's long, twisting driveway. The Escalade might have come from that direction, which was something she'd point out to the deputy. The development could be a starting point for his investigation. Gazing out to sea, she watched the progress of a massive container ship headed toward Portland or Seattle. Still no lighthouse view, which was why Colin had to go down to the beach to see the tower. Definitely an odd obsession, but he was supernormal compared to his chauvinist political uncle.

Who did Nathan think he was? King of the hill? The facade of the Castle gave the impression of being more majestic than it was. Five Gothic-style arches stretched between the stately towers. When she stood by the iron railing at the outer edge of the veranda, Ella felt like she should be peering down into a moat filled with snapping alligators instead of a pleasant flagstone sidewalk lined with rose bushes.

The front door opened, and Bridget stepped out. Gently, she asked, "May I join you?"

"Of course." Ella had no problem with the lady of the house. A lot of decent, friendly, intelligent women chose to stay married to jerks. In her therapy practice, Ella had learned to curb her natural impulse to advise them to dump the bum. Life didn't work that way. Neither did the cognitive behavioral therapy that had been the cornerstone of her practice.

Treating Ella like an unpredictable feral creature, Bridget cautiously approached. She took a seat in a wicker chair with a rose-patterned cushion that seemed more laid-back than the castle theme. "I apologize for Nathan's behavior. He had no right to be disrespectful."

"Thank you." Ella sank into the matching chair beside her. "Your home is incredible."

"We've owned the Castle for almost thirty years. The purchase was one of the few things Nathan and I agreed upon one hundred percent. He liked the idea of being the lord of the manor. And I saw a chance to preserve a significant historical structure. The shipping magnate who built this place in the late 1800s was the owner of the *Lady Eve*, a three-masted vessel that sank off the coast and left no survivors."

The Castle was well over a hundred years old. "Did you need to do a lot of repairs?"

"When we moved in, the place was falling down around our ears. Buying it in a run-down condition was the only way we could afford the mortgage." She waved toward the houses on the nearby hills. "Nathan figured we'd make our money back with a development on our property, which is called Castle Bluff. I've got to admit, he was correct."

Ella recalled Colin's summary of The Four. One of them was a developer. "Did you work with Dean Santiago on Castle Bluff?"

"As a matter of fact, we did. Nathan had many business dealings with Dean. He was a bit of a playboy, but he's settled down and become a real family man."

Or had he? Once a pirate, always a pirate. "For the repair work, did you use Doug Rigby?"

"We did." Bridget looked surprised. "How do you know Rigby?"

"Harry's neighbor is Lydia, his wife."

"Only in her head," Bridget said. "Rigby has half a dozen women who think they're married to him. As far as I know, he's never actually tied the knot."

"Sounds like he offers more than carpentry in his home improvement services."

"Indeed, he does." She gave a good-natured chuckle. "He's wiry and cute, a little short for my taste. And I'm not a fan of men who wear gold chain necklaces. Rigby is okay. He offers discounts on repair work for older homes. I've recommended him to several folks."

"Harry mentioned that you were president of the local historical society."

"More than president," she said. "I'm the head of the nonprofit that oversees the lighthouse and several other local properties. Once a year, we open all the historic houses and businesses to sightseers. The Lighthouse Tavern where we hold an annual Valentine's Day séance—complete with ghosts—is a favorite."

Bridget would be a helpful resource for local information. She'd lived in the area forever and had deep roots in the community. "Maybe you can help me understand something."

"I know what you're going to say." Bridget reached over and placed her warm hand on Ella's forearm. "Colin told us about Gigi Graham."

Exhaling a quiet groan, Ella said, "Swell."

"How are you connected to her?"

"I heard about her a few years ago when she lived in the LA area. And I was surprised when I learned she'd purchased a house in Florence. Even more shocked that she left it to me when the person who lived there passed away. Did you know Gigi?"

"Can't say I ever met the lady, but Nathan did business with her. From what he said, she was hostile and incompetent." Bridget scowled. "Not sure I believe him. He's never been supportive of women in business."

"What else can you tell me about her?"

"It was a long time ago. Over twenty years." Bridget cocked an eyebrow. "If you don't mind me asking, what is your connection with Gigi?"

Ella hesitated. She seldom talked about her past. Not because she had anything to be ashamed about. Her childhood with Franny and Oscar Scarletti had been warm and loving. Their little family wasn't wealthy, but they wanted for nothing. Nobody cared to hear about such a normal upbringing, but when she revealed the sad tale of a newborn baby abandoned in a church, people looked at her differently. They assumed she must have been traumatized, even though she couldn't remember her infancy.

"I was adopted," Ella said. "I have reason to believe Gigi Graham might be my birth mother. I don't have tangible proof, but the inheritance is making me rethink things."

"How old are you, dear?"

"I just turned twenty-seven. Why?"

"Just trying to get a perspective," Bridget said. "I've lost track of Gigi. Do you have any idea where she lives or what she does for a living?"

"Lydia said her ashes were in a columbarium at Forest Lawn Cemetery in Glendale."

"I'm so sorry."

"Thank you." How strange to accept condolences for a woman she'd never met. Later today, Ella would call and get a date for the interment. Though it wouldn't be a precise time of death, she'd have a better idea of continuity. "I wasn't shocked to hear she was deceased. On some level, I already knew."

"But you never had a chance to mourn."

Ella nodded. Bridget's comment was similar to something she'd say to a new client, encouraging them to share more information about their past and their feelings. "It would have been nice to meet my bio mom…if Gigi was that person, I have questions I'd like to ask about her skill and talents. And other people in the family. Like my bio father. And medical issues, of course."

Bridget frowned for a moment, then she sat up straight in the wicker chair and raised her index finger. "I have a brilliant idea."

"Okay."

"Do you believe in ghosts?"

Ella paused for a moment, letting the question sink in. Though she wasn't a superstitious person, she was open to the opinions of others. People not only believed in ghosts, but some actively searched for spirits from the other side. "Tell me your brilliant idea."

COLIN KNEW HE couldn't stay at the Castle any longer. Not when his presence might put his aunt and uncle in danger. Though Nathan had left the offer open, Colin didn't want to be in the same house with him. Mostly because of the details Nathan had revealed about his past. His uncle had skated at the edge of criminal behavior for too many years.

While Ella was downstairs on the veranda giving her statement to Deputy Angstrom, Colin retreated to the upstairs bedroom to pack his clothes, computer, medical supplies and shaving equipment. Trying to maintain a semblance of organization, he filed his stuff in a multipocket backpack that doubled as a suitcase. Though not sure where he'd spend the night, he decided to skip the protection of the FBI safe house. His talk with Nathan had opened several avenues toward evidence he wanted to explore, including a disturbing link to the kidnapping that robbed him of his memory. Colin wanted to be the cop to follow these leads.

Also, he didn't feel right about revealing Ella's strange inheritance and her possible connection to Gigi Graham to the FBI. Though he doubted the SUV attack was meant to hurt her, he didn't like the idea of the FBI poking around in her past.

After they left the Castle, he figured their first stop would be Harry's house, where he'd parked his rental car. He needed a chance to talk to Ella alone before they confronted Harry and told him that the Rosalie investigation needed to go on the back burner. Shouldn't be a problem. A former TV detective like Harry ought to understand that handling current death threats came before solving cold cases.

He slung the heavy backpack onto his shoulder and slowly

descended the staircase to the first floor. His bum leg had stiffened after the exertion of their escape through the forest. He paused in the gracious foyer of the Castle with the inlaid pattern of slate-gray-and-white marble and lowered his backpack to a carved oak bench. In the front pocket was a container of pain relievers. He swallowed three without water.

"Is it your leg?" Aunt Bridget asked. She had a habit of popping up when least expected. "Is there anything I can get for you?"

He grabbed his ebony cane from a hook by the door. "I think I've got everything I need."

"If I can help, call me." She came closer and took his hands in hers. "I like Ella. Take good care of her."

He leaned down and kissed Bridget's forehead. "Thanks for your hospitality."

"I'll see you again. Maybe even sooner than you expect."

He stepped out onto the veranda in time to see the deputy close his spiral notebook and hand his business card to Ella. Angstrom promised to be in touch, and she did the same.

Speaking to both of them, the deputy consulted his phone and offered an update. "No hits on our BOLO for the Escalade. Our forensic team has taped off the area where the SUV went off the road. We'll wait for the staties to take castings of the tire tracks. Ella suggested that I canvass the residents of the Castle Bluff development to see if anyone noticed a car that didn't belong, which is a good idea. I'll get right on it."

The deputy seemed calm and competent. Maybe a bit behind the times, but Colin wasn't surprised. Cape Seraphim wasn't exactly a hotbed of criminal activity, which was one of the reasons Colin had reestablished contact with his former LAPD partner. Sergeant Perez was fluent in computer investigation, a handy talent for fact-finding in cold cases. That wasn't the only reason he needed to return to LA. He needed to get some answers from Dean Santiago.

Deputy Angstrom glanced from Ella to Colin. His gaze rested on the backpack. "Are you going somewhere?"

"Can you give us a lift back to Harry's? My rental car is parked there."

Angstrom gestured to his gray SUV with the sheriff's logo emblazoned on the side. Not the most subtle form of transportation. "Hop in."

"I'd appreciate it if you don't use the siren," Colin said.

"Trying to sneak past Harry?" The deputy chuckled. "Good luck with that. The old man is pretty sharp."

"That he is," Ella agreed. "Justin Thyme would say he was sharper than a Damascus steel chef's knife."

She climbed into the passenger seat beside the deputy, leaving Colin and his backpack in the rear. Leaning back against the seat, he inhaled a deep breath. Since he didn't usually sit back here, he noticed the distinctive smell, common to most police vehicles. A combination of metal from all the equipment they carried mixed with the scent of fear from suspects under arrest and, of course, a whiff of doughnut.

From the back, he had a good angle to study Ella's profile without her noticing. Her small nose turned up at the end, making her pretty and perky. Her prominent cheekbones and high forehead balanced out the cuteness. In spite of her height, Ella didn't seem to be a woman who would stand out in a crowd. At the same time, she was special. Once a spotlight shone on her, it wouldn't move away. The variegated strands of blond in her hair shimmered. When she ruffled her fingers through her bangs, she shook loose a twig from their run through the forest.

She glanced over her shoulder. Her gaze connected with his, and she said, "I think you should stay at Harry's tonight."

"The reason I left the Castle was to avoid attracting danger toward the people who live there. The same applies to you and Harry."

"What if the Escalade was coming after me?" she asked. "I might be the trouble magnet, and I wouldn't mind having you nearby to protect me."

"Good point."

"Also, Harry's alarm system is state-of-the-art. And he has Palmer."

"The bodyguard," Colin said. "Why does Harry need to be guarded?"

"At times, his fans get carried away. Palmer is good at removing them."

The deputy spoke up. "I can vouch for Palmer. He's a former navy SEAL."

Staying with Harry began to sound like a practical option. It wouldn't be for long. Colin planned to leave as soon as possible and get down to southern California.

When the deputy parked beside Colin's rental, Palmer was standing like a sentry at the top of the ramp on the front porch. Colin greeted the former navy SEAL with a wave and called out to him. "We'll be back in less than an hour."

As he herded Ella into the car, she asked, "Where are we going?"

"Once again, I need to talk to you alone. Nathan gave me some interesting details."

"About Gigi Graham?"

"Yes. And another person on Rosalie's list of The Four. Dean Santiago."

"Do you know him?"

"For a while, we were close."

They didn't have a long-term connection, but their bond was deep. He'd seen the rugged, stoic Santiago at his worst and his best. Comforted him when fear stabbed him in the heart. Celebrated with him when he achieved success. Both times, Santiago had wept.

The wealthy, successful developer based in southern California had built a multimillion-dollar empire. But he was more than a businessman. He had two children, ages seven and ten, and they had been abducted. Colin had tracked down the kidnappers and saved the children's lives.

Then, he lost his memory.

Chapter Eleven

Ella belted herself into the passenger seat of Colin's rental SUV—a Land Rover more suitable for off-roading than puttering around town. They were alone, shielded from the rest of the world. She wondered what he wanted to tell her and why he needed privacy.

He slid behind the wheel, lowered his sunglasses and peered over the rim with his gorgeous, chocolate-brown eyes. "There's a place up the coast I want you to see."

"Okay." Not that she minded being alone with him. The opposite, in fact. "But why?"

"From what Nathan told me, Gigi was involved with The Four who were listed by Rosalie. We need to put those details together before we talk to Harry." He pushed the sunglasses to the bridge of his nose and started the engine. "Also, I need space to think. To figure out what to do next."

She tried to read his expression and pay attention to vocal cues, hoping to understand how his mind worked. "What can I do to help?"

"I like to bounce ideas around, exchange opinions, make plans. That's what I used to do with my partners." A muscle in his jaw twitched. "But our relationship is different. I'm in charge, responsible for what happens."

"I can listen," she said. "I'm good at that."

He gave a nod. "Top priority, I've got to make sure we're safe."

"Harry's house is very secure."

"I know." In addition to a navy SEAL bodyguard, the doors and all the windows were hooked into a security system.

"He might be a bit paranoid," she said. "A good trait for someone in real danger.

"Also, we need some privacy, you and I." He drove out of the cul-de-sac and navigated the side streets until he was headed north on Highway 101, following the shoreline. "We're talking about sensitive stuff, and I don't know if you want Harry to know about your past and Gigi Graham. Didn't want to shoot off my mouth and make things uncomfortable for you."

"I've got nothing to hide." *Or did she?* There might be more to her situation than she realized. "To be perfectly honest, I'm not sure how much I've told Harry. I might have mentioned that I'm adopted, which is not a big secret. I don't think I ever spoke about Gigi until today."

"Just to be clear, you didn't tell Harry that Gigi Graham might be your birth mother. Right?"

"How could I? I don't know if it's true." Though she hadn't been aware of dark secrets in her past, she felt barriers crashing down and leaving her exposed. She didn't like being vulnerable. "You mentioned our relationship. What exactly is that?"

"I know what I want it to be." He reached across the center console, placed his hand on her shoulder and gently squeezed. "Tell me about you and Gigi. Start at the beginning."

Oddly enough, she didn't feel compelled to hold back. Instead, she felt like she could tell Colin anything. Was it possible she trusted this guy she barely knew? "I've been looking for my bio parents ever since I learned I was adopted."

"When did that happen?"

"During my junior year of high school in Pasadena." She recalled the day very well. The dining room table was cluttered with the paperwork she needed for college admission. With her good grades, solid participation in activities and decent entry-level testing, she had options for schools she could attend in California. Some scholarship money was available, but finding enough for tuition would be a struggle. "My parents and Sister Maggie told me I didn't need to worry about finances. A college fund was set aside for me when I was born."

"Who's Sister Maggie?"

"Maggie Wright, a real estate agent. I think I've mentioned her before. She's a good friend. Used to be a nun."

He exited the highway and took a series of twisting, two-lane roads that descended from the hills toward the coastline. "Who created this fund for you?"

"It was administered by the lawyer who handled business for St. Joseph's, and all he'd give me was the name of a closed corporation. The officers were unidentified…or so he said. The man took his attorney-client confidentiality more seriously than most priests honor the secrets of the confessional, but I discovered a name. Gigi Graham."

"How did you get him to tell you?"

"I didn't. That was all Maggie. She pried the information out of him. Too much of it was hearsay and gossip, not factual enough to be proof. More like a starting point."

"What else?"

"A lot. Maggie had been waiting until I was old enough to tell me everything she knew about my birth and adoption."

Gazing through the windshield, she related the story of the elderly priest at St. Joseph's, the midwife, the abandoned infant and Gigi Graham. Her attention shifted to his profile. Without the facial scruff, his features were sharp and strong. "Sounds like a fairy tale, doesn't it?"

He shrugged. "The truth isn't always simple."

"I didn't know until today that Gigi was dead and interred at Forest Lawn."

"Do you have the heart necklace that the midwife left for you?"

"I'll probably get it tomorrow when I see the lawyer and the house."

"Do you want me to come with you?"

She could use the emotional backup, but didn't want him to get sidetracked by her problems. "I feel guilty about taking up your time."

"All part of the investigation."

The Land Rover emerged from a narrow road onto a sand-and-gravel trail at the edge of a twenty-five-to thirty-foot-tall outcrop. Mostly volcanic rock, it stretched out into the surf. Late afternoon sunlight glistened on the white caps and shone against the jagged basalt wall of the cliff. Gulls, puffins and long-necked cormorants dove through the misty sky and swaggered along the sand.

Growing up in southern California, she expected beaches to be bright and sunshiny, populated with sunbathers, surfers and builders of sandcastles. Oregon was different. Rugged. Foggy. Mysterious. The temperature on the coast was usually lower than inland, and the water was too cold for extended swimming without a wet suit. These were perfect beaches for wading or jogging or sitting on a driftwood log and staring out to sea. Typically, not crowded.

When he parked about ten feet away from the breaking waves and opened his door, a rush of sound poured into the Land Rover. Rumbling surf, whooshing winds and the cries of birds. "Follow me," he said. "We don't have much time. The tide is already coming in."

Ella stepped onto sand at the base of the cliff. Theirs was the only vehicle this close to the water. A few people strolled, kids played on the sand and others flew kites that looked like giant blue-and-green butterflies.

The late afternoon sun beat down. She slipped off her jacket, tossed it inside and closed the car door. The cool spring breeze brushed across her bared shoulders under the sleeveless top. The rhythm of the waves mesmerized her. For a moment, she forgot about the danger. *Inhale. Exhale.* After the attack from the Escalade and her conflict with Uncle Nathan, she needed a break. *Exhale, again.* Colin hadn't taken his sports coat off—he probably didn't want to reveal his shoulder holster.

When she took a step, her white sneaker sank into the sand. "I'm not really dressed for beach walking."

"We're going to be climbing around on the rocks and wading through a tide pool. Nothing strenuous. If you want to keep your shoes from getting wet, take them off. I'm leaving mine on. The rocks can be painful on bare feet."

She bent over and rolled up her jeans to her knees. His suggestion to keep her shoes on was smart. During the three weeks she'd been at Cape Seraphim, she'd done enough hiking to know that scratchy plants and pebbles could hurt. "Why here? I appreciate the need for privacy, but this seems a little much."

"It's my happy place."

She recognized the phrase. The idea was a bit dated, but still valid. When a therapist advised a client to find their happy place, the idea was to calm and comfort them. "I get it."

"When I lived at the Castle as a kid, I explored all over the coast. I had instructions not to go in the water so I wouldn't get washed away by the undertow, but nobody told me I couldn't climb on the rocks." He moved to the edge of the outcrop that extended beyond the waterline and sliced twenty yards farther into the Pacific. Waves crashed against the pockmarked basalt, sending up plumes of white spray. "I used to imagine hiking at the water's edge like Lewis and Clark, going the whole length of Oregon from the mouth of the Columbia to the California border."

"Exploring." His imagery gave her a clearer picture of who he was. A searcher. Someone with goals and dreams. "You might be better at meditation than you realize."

"Yeah?"

"You don't necessarily need to close down your mind. Sometimes, it's better to open yourself to new experiences."

He pinned her with a gaze. "You're better at figuring me out than my high-priced shrink."

But she wasn't treating him, which was a very good thing because she felt herself responding to Colin in a way that would be totally inappropriate in a therapy context. For the first time since the attack of the Escalade, his jaw had relaxed, and the tension had left his body. He still favored his left leg, but he moved with more agility. "We're going to climb along this ledge," he said. "Not too narrow, is it?"

"Looks okay." *If you're a gymnast on a balance beam...*

"Even if you fall, it's not a steep drop, only a couple of feet. We're going almost to the end of these rocks."

"Into the water?"

"Over the water. To a couple of tide pools and a sea cave."

She concentrated on following him without tripping and falling. Mist from the churning surf moistened her arms and shoulders. Her hand rested against the basalt wall, and she balanced easily. Much of the Oregon coast—including the dramatic offshore rocks—had been formed by lava flow and erosion.

At a turning point at the far end of the cliff, Colin took her hand. His hand was surprisingly warm and sent a searing blaze from her fingertips to her shoulders. He helped her maneuver between a grouping of waist-high rocks that encircled a kidney-shaped tide pool with sand on the bottom. A high wave shot water over the edge, but the puddle quickly drained, displaying tangled seaweed, sea urchins, purple anemone flowers and two orange starfish. A magical glimpse, surprisingly colorful. She could have hunkered down on the rock and observed this small, strange environment for a while, but Colin pulled her deeper through a wide arch into the cave.

The interior was over ten feet at the highest point. The damp, irregular walls sloped downward until they disappeared into the shadows. The front faced the ocean and was open to the rising tide and misted sunlight. Colin guided her past the splotches of water on the sand floor to a tumbled-down pile of rocks worn smooth by the waves.

"You can find a place to sit, if you want," he said as he perched on a high rock and removed his sunglasses. "Watch out or you'll get your bottom wet."

"I'll stand." In the dim glow of otherworldly light, shadows outlined his features. His obsidian eyes glistened. This was his happy place. A little weird, yet somehow perfect. "When you're here in the cave, how do you feel?"

"At peace. I feel protected. It's like being in a fortress or a lair." He stood and brushed the sand off his trousers and sports coat. "It also feels like I'm wearing too many clothes."

She wrapped her arms around her middle. "And I was just thinking that I should have left my jean jacket on."

"Are you cold?"

"A little," she admitted.

Stepping carefully on rocks, he moved toward her. "I'll warm you up."

I'll bet you will. Now would be the time for her to back up and put distance between them. Instead, she found herself leaning toward him, wanting his warmth. "Okay, partner. Why did you bring me here?"

"Planning. Tonight, we'll stay at Harry's. Tomorrow, we go to LA."

A number of things had to happen before they left Oregon. "We can't just leave. What about the investigation with Harry? And I need to see the house in Florence tomorrow morning. I have an appointment with the attorney."

"You can reschedule. The house will still be there a few days from now."

Almost everything could be reshuffled to accommodate a trip, but there was something more bothering her. She took a step toward him. "Is it safe for you to return to LA?"

"It's a chance I need to take." He shrugged. "I'm not going to hide away in an FBI safe house. I need to figure out what's going on. I've got to remember what happened."

"At what cost?" She shivered. "Sounds risky to me."

"With great risk comes great reward."

"Who said that?"

"Not sure. Either Thomas Jefferson or Spider-Man." He was close enough to rest his hand on her shoulder. "Should I warm you up?"

"Yes." She gazed into his midnight eyes and exhaled a sigh. When he stroked the length of her arm all the way down to her wrist and back up, she trembled. His touch sparked a chain reaction, sending ripples of warmth from her arm to her chest. The heat penetrated to her core and moved down her body to her stomach, then lower. "Again."

He stroked the other arm, arousing the same response. "I didn't say I felt peace and quiet in this cave because sound is caught and magnified in here."

"Is it?" His words resonated, buzzing in her ears.

"Listen." He spread his arms and yelled her name. "Ella Scarletti!"

The echoes were nearly as loud as his original shout. The sound ricocheted off the cavern walls. Not quiet, not at all.

She copied his action, throwing her head back and yelling. "Colin Reid!"

They faced each other and repeated their names. The echoes overlapped. Each time they spoke, their voices were softer until finally they were whispering.

"Ella."

"Colin."

He embraced her, pulled her against his chest and kissed her. The contact was hard, sudden and swift, almost over before she realized what had happened. But her lips tingled. And her heart fluttered frantically inside her rib cage. She couldn't claim that it hadn't happened. No doubt about it, she had been thoroughly kissed.

And then, he did it again. This time, he slowly pressed his mouth against hers. His teeth caught her lower lip and gently pulled. He hummed in the back of his throat, and she heard herself moan in response. The sound that came from her was not unlike a kitten's purr. Without planning what came next, her tongue darted into his mouth and engaged with his.

He gently separated from her and took a step back. They stood, staring at each other and breathing heavily. She knew that neither of them had planned for that kiss to happen. He cleared his throat. For a moment, she feared he'd spoil this moment with an apology. Instead, he spoke in a husky voice and said, "We need to talk about Uncle Nathan."

Talk about making a turn on a dime! He'd gone from a sexy, hot, amazing kiss to a cool, analytic detective in the blink of an eye. She couldn't turn off her emotions or her passions so quickly. *Inhale. Exhale.* She used every relaxation technique in the book to bring herself back into sharp focus.

In a ridiculously formal tone, she said, "You're referring to your conversation with your uncle back at the Castle."

"Right."

In spite of the chill in the cave, she radiated heat from

her core. She was sweating, struggling for control. "Nathan claimed to know Gigi."

"He remembered a conversation they had on Valentine's Day, a couple of decades ago. At the lighthouse."

"Why did he recall that specific day?"

"There's a Cape Seraphim tradition for Valentine's Day. Local folks, especially those in the historical society, gather at the Lighthouse Tavern and call forth the spirit of the Ghost Widow in the hope that she will put them in touch with someone beloved who has passed away."

"A séance," she said. "Your aunt told me about it. She suggested we have a ritual of our own to call forth the spirit of Gigi Graham."

"Of course she did," he muttered. "And I suppose Harry will want to be a part of this. Reaching out to Rosalie."

"I'm not so sure," she said. "He still thinks his ex-wife is alive."

"You're shivering," he said. "Take my jacket."

"I'm fine." And she wanted to keep him as far away from her as possible.

Pivoting, he turned away from her and picked his way through the rocks toward the front of the cave. "Earlier today I talked with my partner in the LAPD."

"Dwayne Perez." She remembered the partner who saved Colin's life.

"I asked him to search databases for information on Rosalie. He couldn't find recorded evidence of her death. Likewise, no documentation proves she's alive."

"She vanished. Just like Gigi." What were the odds of two young women disappearing from the same place at nearly the same time? "It's a huge coincidence. Is it possible that Rosalie and Gigi are one and the same?"

"I wondered the same thing, but Gigi didn't disappear twenty-five years ago. Nathan was in contact with her in LA years later, and he knew both women." Colin took her hand and pulled her toward the late-afternoon sunshine that sparkled on the waves. "The tide is coming in. We should leave before the cave gets swamped."

"It doesn't seem right to run off to southern California. We promised Harry we'd investigate Rosalie's disappearance."

"Which is related to Gigi. The whole reason I started looking into The Four was the list in Rosalie's notebook. She was a reporter, digging for a scandal."

"Rosalie might have uncovered the same information that Gigi had." She finally felt the mental click of a meaningful connection. Different women who had discovered the same threat. "Maybe the two of them were working together."

She watched as he slipped on his sunglasses and said, "You've probably heard people talk about their instincts."

"Yep." Some of her clients blamed instinct for impulsive actions. Others used instinct as justification. Sometimes instinct was a primal force, like's Freud's definition of the id. "I've worked with cops frequently. They talk about instinct all the time."

"My gut is telling me something."

"Okay." She waited for him to confide.

"One of The Four didn't want his dealings made public. He couldn't risk having Rosalie or Gigi talk, and he caused one or both women to disappear."

She hated to agree, but his instinct made sense. An unspoken word whispered through the cave and echoed. *Murder.*

Chapter Twelve

Cruising along Highway 101 on the way back to Harry's house, Colin reviewed the moments he'd spent in the otherworldly sea cave with Ella. *My happy place.* Visiting the cavern had refreshed him, and Ella had been on target when she said this was his version of meditation. No matter where he was or what he was doing, he could always escape into the cave.

Ella was the only person he'd ever taken there. In his mind, he would forever hear her name echoing off the walls. Likewise, he'd never forget their kiss. What the hell had he been thinking, with all that yelling and jumping around? Not exactly the way the strong, silent type should act. Somehow, she threw him off his game. Or maybe the opposite was true. Maybe she was good for him.

Distracted by a spectacular view of the coast on the right side of the Land Rover, he glimpsed her profile. With her streaked hair tucked behind her ear, her high cheekbones and sharp little chin were visible. She was on the phone with Harry, planning for tonight. Abruptly, she turned toward him, and her vivid blue eyes flashed an unspoken invitation that had nothing to do with her employer. Colin could tell that she wanted another kiss, maybe more than that. *Talk about a happy place!*

His body responded in a predictable way, and he grounded himself by gripping the steering wheel and focusing on the road. Her kiss had startled him awake. And the reminder got his motor running. Their brief physical contact counted as a workout with more cardio exertion than fifty push-ups. He remembered her little moan and the way she'd kissed him back…with tongue.

He might want something deeper with Ella. But he knew that, even in the best of times, he wasn't good at relationships. His ex-wife—the marriage lasted less than three years—had told him he just wasn't a trusting sort of person. And she was right. As far back as he could remember, he had preferred to keep to himself. His shrink called it compartmentalizing his emotions. A natural tendency for a cop. Maybe a necessary one.

Colin needed to construct walls to protect himself from the natural rage, frustration and sorrow that came with his job. If he tore down the soundproof barriers, he couldn't block out the screams from victims and the heart-wrenching pleas from those who were near death. He'd never forget the horrors he'd seen. The stench of a rotting corpse or the metallic smell of fresh blood was permanently imprinted in his mind. Better to keep those doors closed. Those barriers had been constructed for a reason. To protect his sanity.

He suspected that Ella had similar compartments where she filed the sessions with her clients. She couldn't allow herself to take on their trauma. Hadn't she mentioned that she was taking a break from her work as a therapist because she felt burned-out?

She ended her phone call. "Harry insists that you sleep at his house tonight. He'll inform Palmer."

Colin had considered the alternatives and decided that staying in a house equipped with heavy-duty security and a former navy SEAL bodyguard was as safe as he could get.

The only way Harry's invitation would be better was if he insisted that Colin sleep in Ella's bed. "I'll be sure to tell him thanks."

"I'm sure Nathan told you more about Gigi and The Four."

"Yep."

"Well, tell me."

"Don't you want to wait until we're with Harry, so I don't have to repeat myself?"

"I'd rather have you talk to me now. When we're back at the house, Harry always has little tasks—factotum jobs—that he needs done right away." She crooked her index finger, calling him toward her. "Give it to me now. You have my full attention."

"All right, here we go. If Nathan saw me as a cop instead of his nephew, he wouldn't have been so forthcoming. Which also makes me think there might be something illegal in his actions."

"Makes sense that he'd know. He used to be a full-time lawyer."

"According to Nathan, Gigi Graham was in real estate and worked with The Four. These guys created a financial pyramid scheme that allowed people to invest in a club called Fourscore and More, or FAM. Members could purchase a home for a minimum down payment on a special mortgage with a FAM loan. They could reduce their membership dues by bringing in new members."

She nodded. "Kind of a Ponzi scheme, like Bernie Madoff. I get it."

"Once the buyers were locked in, the money pool dried up, mortgage costs accelerated and interest compounded. Bottom line, within two years, over half the houses were repossessed. The buyers lost everything. The four pirates and people like Gigi made a fortune."

"Isn't that against the law?"

"Not ethical, but it's borderline legal. Nathan drafted the contracts and set the terms. Blake Schmidt, an accountant, made the money work for them. Rigby—the charmer in the group—and Gigi were salespeople who recruited new members. And Dean Santiago provided cash incentives and properties to purchase, both in the LA area and here. By the way, he's the developer who built those high-end houses near Nathan's place. Castle Bluff." He gave an ironic laugh. "They were bluffing, all right."

"I've lived in southern California all my life and have never been able to afford real estate. But I understand the need for people to own a home of their own. A powerful urge, nearly primal. Shame on The Four and on Gigi, too. It's wrong to exploit people like that."

"Apparently, Gigi thought so."

"Good for her," Ella said. "Did she turn them over to the authorities?"

"Like I said before, their scheme didn't break any laws. It took advantage of gullible, trusting people. Besides, FAM is ancient history. The Four had a falling-out. They disbanded and covered their tracks."

"What about Gigi?"

"Nathan put the blame on her for the breakup and claimed she was a terrible businesswoman who didn't understand the realities of the marketplace."

"I'm not surprised." Her gaze sharpened. "Uncle Nathan doesn't have much respect for women in business. What do you think really happened?"

"She wanted out. Her conscience was bothering her."

"Conscience," she said thoughtfully. "Now, that's something I understand better than a Ponzi investment scheme. Gigi thought they were hurting people. It was wrong."

"And she had the insider information to prove they were cheating and lying. Nathan said he dismissed her, refused to listen to her. I think he called her accusations poppycock." At this point in his conversation with his uncle, Colin had made assumptions to fill in the blanks. "I think Gigi might have threatened him. Told him that she'd give the story to Rosalie."

"Aha!" Ella gasped aloud. "And Rosalie would expose them on the news. She was a journalist. She had the power to ruin their reputations on the evening news."

"I think that's how the two women connected."

"What happened next?"

"Here's where Nathan's story comes to an end." He claimed that The Four decided the time was right for them to go their separate ways and dismantle FAM. Each of them had developed a significant bankroll for future endeavors. "My uncle was on the verge of going into local politics and didn't want to be involved in anything shady. He walked away."

"But he saw Gigi again."

"That's right." He drove the Land Rover toward the exit from the highway, which led toward Harry's house. "On a trip to LA, he met with Santiago, and they talked to Gigi, who seemed to be doing well as a real estate investor."

For a long moment, they both were silent, allowing the story to sink in. Colin dreaded her next logical question.

"What about Rosalie?" Ella's voice was quiet. "She disappeared before she made a report on the news that implicated The Four and FAM. I'm guessing that wasn't a convenient lapse."

He applied logic to the little they knew about Rosalie's disappearance. "Maybe she quit her job and moved on to other things. Happens all the time in broadcast news. Something bigger and better comes along."

"But why wouldn't she tell Harry? Why wouldn't her publicist talk about it?"

Colin considered the natural avenue of investigation. Rosalie's businesspeople—agents, lawyers, publicists and such—went on the list of people they needed to talk to when they got to LA. He tossed out another possibility. "Rosalie might have dropped the story. Might have been convinced it wasn't true."

"Who would have done this convincing?" Ella shook her head, unwilling to accept an easy solution. "The Four could have paid her off. They were powerful, wealthy guys with a lot of influence. Or…" She paused. Her eyes widened. "I hate to say this, but The Four might have made an offer she couldn't refuse. Maybe she was whacked."

"Let's not go there."

Over the years while working close to Hollywood, he'd become accustomed to movie references, like *The Godfather*, and he tried not to get carried away. Life wasn't cinematic. And real estate investors based in Cape Seraphim weren't the Mafia.

"You know I'm right," she said. "We've both been thinking she was dead."

"Sure, Rosalie might have been whacked…" He glanced toward her. "Is that the right term? Whacked?"

"Not funny. Murder is no joke."

If he turned this cold case over to the LAPD, they'd file it away and nothing would happen. Like it or not, this was his investigation. Moving forward meant finding new evidence, tangible facts. Uncle Nathan had said that Gigi had threatened them with proof of fraud. A long shot, for sure.

Gigi wasn't exactly a reliable source. His aunt didn't like her. Nor did Lydia Rigby. Nathan thought she was a double-crosser. Not even Ella liked the woman who might be her birth mother. Gigi had abandoned her infant daughter, left her at St. Joseph's. What kind of person did that?

Even though her vague threats were a long way from murder, that had to be their starting point. They needed to find Gigi's data and confront The Four.

AT HARRY'S HOUSE in the center of the cul-de-sac, Palmer stood waiting for them on the covered porch. He'd been with Harry for nearly fifteen years and was probably close to sixty. Palmer still looked dangerous as he stood there, absolutely motionless. In his black-and-gray clothes, he melted into the shadows. From the first time they met, Colin pegged the bodyguard as former military and was glad to know he'd been a navy SEAL, which meant he was not only a skilled marksman, but had all sorts of tactical know-how. Palmer's brain was as much a lethal weapon as his physical abilities—probably including martial arts—and surveillance techniques.

When Ella went inside to change clothes, Colin stayed behind to brief the bodyguard, starting with the story of the Escalade trying to run them down. "I'm not sure whether he was after Ella or me. Recently, Ella uncovered a connection to Gigi Graham. Do you know her?"

Palmer frowned. "No."

"Years ago, Gigi offended some local scammers, and they might be looking for revenge. It's more likely that the driver of the Escalade was coming after me."

"Why?"

Apparently, Palmer hadn't heard Harry's references to the hero cop from LA. "Before I came here, I worked a case in LA where I was shot in the head. Lost part of my memory. The guy who pulled the trigger knows I can identify him if my memory comes back. He wants me gone."

"A loose end."

Palmer wasn't much of a talker—a trait that Colin appreciated. "These guys are violent. I don't want to do anything to put Ella or Harry or anybody else in danger. Is it a problem for me to stay here?"

"Not at all. I've got it covered."

"There's backup. Lots of people know I'm here. The local

sheriff's office and police. My uncle Nathan Reid. My shrink. Probably even the FBI."

Palmer cleared his throat. "I have one request."

"Name it."

"Don't let Harry carry a loaded weapon."

"Fair enough." Colin didn't bother mentioning his own Glock. The bodyguard had probably taken note of the gun when they had met. "How should we handle surveillance?"

"We're on lockdown all night. All alarm systems are activated. Everybody sleeps on the second floor. You and I trade off, keeping watch."

"Okay. Anything else you need?"

"Get your ass upstairs to the room Harry is calling his headquarters. He's keeping Chef Sandra from making dinner."

Palmer had his priorities set. Food came first.

Inside, Colin climbed the staircase to the second floor, ignoring the twinges from his injured leg. The upstairs hallway echoed with the sounds of Harry making grand pronouncements. When Colin entered the big office that had been transformed into headquarters for the investigation, the sunset view through the west-facing windows momentarily robbed him of forward momentum. Spectacular. Beautiful. He stood and stared at hazy skies that had turned crimson, orange and gold with streaks of dark purple and mauve clouds hanging above the ocean horizon. On the rocky coast to the south, he could see the lighthouse.

"It's about time you showed up," Harry said in his cultured Justin Thyme voice. He thumped his cane on the floor, even though he was sitting in his motorized wheelchair. "Chef Sandra has been filling in for you and Ella. Doing a bang-up job, if I do say so myself. But her talents are needed in the kitchen."

The tall, athletic-looking chef—still wearing her pin-striped apron—stepped away from a corkboard filled with photos and drawings of Rosalie. She gave a jaunty wave of her hand and fled. "I'm going downstairs to finish dinner. Ta-ta."

When she left, Colin scanned the large room. Their notes on the whiteboard outlining info on The Four were untouched, but Harry had added the corkboard on wheels filled with various pictures of Rosalie. Several boxes of evidence had been opened and the contents scattered. Office supplies littered the desktops and tables. The large-screen computer showed clips from Rosalie's news show. The array of clutter reminded Colin of a bullpen at the LAPD. There was even a rotary-dial phone, a Rolodex and an empty doughnut box.

"Well, Harry, I like what you've done with the place."

"After fourteen years on *The Taste of Murder*, I learned quite a lot about set dressing."

"Right down to the doughnuts." He picked up the box and opened it, delighted to find a sugary apple fritter, which he immediately munched.

"I never ate them," Harry said. "My job as Justin Thyme meant I had to stay in shape. Couldn't allow myself to turn into a pudgy chef."

"What about now?" Colin took another bite. It seemed criminal to avoid crullers, muffins and Jelly Belly candies for the rest of his life.

"I've lost my taste for sugar. And my career isn't quite over, not yet." He navigated his way across the headquarters and came closer to Colin. "There's something we should discuss before Ella joins us."

He licked his lips. "I'm listening."

"Before you two left, she mentioned Gigi Graham. I did some investigating on my own and talked to someone Ella has known for years. Sister Maggie."

Ella entered the room. Her hair was damp from the shower,

and she'd changed into brown leggings and a long, yellow Oregon Ducks T-shirt. "What's this about Maggie?"

"I figured she could help. And I just happen to have a private plane standing by."

"Wait." Ella raised both palms and gestured for him to slow down. "You sent a plane?"

"Maggie couldn't get away until tomorrow," Harry said. "She'll be ready to go tomorrow morning at seven thirty. I told her it would be okay to wait until later in the day, but she said she's an early riser."

"That's true," Ella said. Her scowling expression made Colin smile. He knew it was a cliché, but she looked cute when she was angry. Especially when she wore an oversize T-shirt with the Ducks logo and no makeup.

"I've always found Maggie to be down-to-earth and helpful," Harry said.

"I know."

She stamped her bare foot on the floor, drawing Colin's attention to her long, slender legs. The Ducks T-shirt was barely long enough to cover her bottom. Her intention probably hadn't been to look sexy, but he appreciated her curves. Tonight, they'd be sleeping down the hall from each other.

Harry gave her a helpless look. "You're not angry, are you?"

"I'm always happy to see Maggie. She's one of my nearest and dearest friends." Again, she stamped her foot. "But I wish you'd consulted with me before making arrangements."

"Would you have said no?"

"Yes. I mean, no. I mean, let's move on. Colin?"

Distracted by her legs and the rest of her body, he hadn't really been listening to her words. He needed to focus on the investigation. They were blundering into uncharted territory. He was the only one with real-life experience, and he needed to get a grip.

Chapter Thirteen

Ella wasn't the least bit surprised that Harry didn't apologize for dragging Maggie into their investigation without telling her or Colin about his plan to send a private jet. Harry did what he wanted, when he wanted it. After a lifetime of having people cater to his whims, he wasn't inclined to ask permission. Instead, he spun his wheelchair around and moved closer to the second whiteboard, which was, so far, blank.

Harry tapped the surface with his cane. "We can use this for a murder board."

"Do you know something we don't?" Ella asked. "Who was murdered?"

"I misspoke," Harry said. "We'll call this Rosalie's Disappearance Board. We'll start with the last time I saw her. Twenty-five years ago, on the day before Valentine's Day. Colin, write that in the center of the board."

"Before we do anything else, I need to make something clear. I'm still employed by LAPD. I'm on sick leave while I recuperate, but I'm still a cop."

"Understood," Harry said.

"If we uncover something illegal or actionable about Rosalie's disappearance, you agree to turn over the information to the authorities."

"Fair enough." Harry glanced over at her. "Do you think I should involve my attorney?"

"Up to you." She went to the chair behind the long table that held photo albums, folders and interesting little notebooks similar to the one with butterflies that Colin had found in the third-floor room. "My job as a factotum doesn't include legal advice."

Colin continued, "From years of working with celebrities, I know they need an NDA. I promise I won't reveal any of our findings without your permission."

"A gentleman's agreement," Harry announced in his Justin Thyme voice. "Sounds reasonable to me. Let's get started. What's our next step?" She was impressed with how quickly Colin had taken control. Harry tended to be uncooperative and liked to be in charge, but he'd agreed without a fight.

"First, an interview," Colin said. "Harry, I want to know how you and Rosalie met. Your wedding. Your divorce. When you got back together. Give me specific names and locations."

"That's a tall order."

"You can handle it. You've had more practice talking about yourself than most people."

"Too true," Harry said. "Hundreds of celebrity interviews."

"That's not what this is." Colin peeled off his sports coat, hung it over the back of a chair and rolled up the sleeves of his blue Oxford shirt. "You don't need to be clever or funny. Don't try to impress me."

"Just the facts." He shrugged. "We should record this for future reference. Ella can set up one of these camcorders, so we'll have a permanent record."

She looked toward Colin for confirmation, and he nodded. "Let's do it."

Not the first time she'd recorded her boss. He'd lived half his life in front of the camera and preferred live action to writing things down. He figured it never hurt to have video footage of important moments in case Steven Spielberg decided to do a biopic of him. Home movies of Harry and his friends occupied a massive amount of cloud storage—cumulonimbus or bigger.

While he moved into the swivel chair he'd swiped from the set of *The Taste of Murder*, she arranged the camera on a tripod to frame him and checked the overhead lighting to make sure there were no shadows across his face. "Ready?" she asked.

"Clapboard." He pointed to the table with computers and recording equipment.

She spotted it immediately—a notebook-sized blackboard with an arm that snapped down. Using the attached piece of chalk, she wrote the title. She turned on the camera, placed the board in front of the lens and announced, "Harry and Rosalie. Take one."

Harry straightened his shoulders. Somehow, he had arranged his features in a way that made him look younger and camera-ready. His voice was modulated but didn't mimic Justin Thyme. Once an actor, always an actor. He knew how to present.

"I'm here with Colin Reid, an LAPD cop. He's interviewing me in connection with the disappearance of my ex-wife, Rosalie. Colin, did you have a question?"

"Give me a few sentences about Rosalie's background."

"She grew up in California. Glendale, I think. Typical suburban family. She had a sister, and a cat named Boots. Her dad was in sales and her mom…"

Harry kept talking. The few sentences Colin had asked for became paragraphs filled with extraneous details, which was no big surprise to her. Unchecked, Harry could rattle on for hours. Outside the several windows facing west, the magenta and mauve of sunset deepened. Half-listening, she meandered through the so-called headquarters and ended up standing before the whiteboard filled with photos of Rosalie, often with Harry standing beside her.

In the early years of their relationship, they made a handsome couple. Harry's thick, chestnut-brown hair was combed back from his forehead. His casual style included jeans, leather jackets and loafers without socks. Ella would have guessed his age was in his late thirties, but knew he was older than that.

Rosalie wore short skirts or jeans combined with simple sweaters and pastel blouses. No busy patterns. Her outfits would look good on television news shows. Her hairstyles shifted from a crimped perm to a platinum blond pixie that was probably a wig. Expert makeup highlighted her blue eyes. She looked like she was in her late twenties, but was probably younger. In several of these long-ago photos, she wore a simple necklace with a pink crystal pendant, like the one Sister Maggie had mentioned belonging to Gigi. *But this was Rosalie. Not Gigi.*

Ella concentrated on Harry, waiting for a break in his monologue so she could ask a question. She was on the verge of interrupting when Colin took control.

"About these early years," he said. "Give me a list of people among her friends and family who she might have turned to when she disappeared."

"Ella," Harry said, "make a note on the Disappearance Board. Under friends and family."

"May I ask a question first?"

"Absolutely," Colin said.

She pointed to a photo of Rosalie with layered 1990s hair. "This necklace with the pink crystal, did she take it with her?"

"We're jumping to the end of the story," Harry said with a frown. "All her expensive jewelry—the diamond tennis bracelet, a Rolex, her five-carat engagement ring and a pair of sapphire earrings—were gone. Both from here and from my place in Burbank."

"Evidence that she was planning ahead," Colin said. "Her disappearance wasn't a spur-of-the-moment thing."

"I don't like that," Harry muttered.

"Look at it this way." Colin paced closer to the whiteboard. "If she was making plans and then disappeared, she wasn't murdered."

Loudly, Ella interrupted, "The pink crystal?"

Harry shook his head. "Don't know where it is."

An odd coincidence. The pendant didn't look particularly expensive. If she searched online, she could probably find dozens, ranging from Swarovski to plastic.

Her focus returned to the list of names. She wrote them on the board with a marker, then erased half of them when Harry decided they weren't useful. As it turned out, there were only a few. Rosalie had been estranged from her sister, and both parents were dead. There were a couple of girlfriends and former roommates, and one ex-boyfriend.

"Next topic," Colin said. "Her lawyers, accountants, agents and publicists. Did she have an assistant? I need to know about her coworkers who might have helped her disappear."

"You're making this sound like a conspiracy," Harry complained. "And the police already investigated all these people."

"I know." Colin held up his phone. "I have the missing person report and the follow-up investigation. I asked my LAPD partner to send the files when I considered taking on the investigation of Rosalie's disappearance."

When Harry swiveled in his chair and turned his profile, Ella stopped and stared, surprised by his unprofessional behavior in front of a camera. His eyebrows drew into an unflattering grimace. He grumbled, "If you already knew all this, why question me?"

"Memory is a complicated thing," Colin said. "When you

look back, you might see something that didn't register the first time around. An unusual purchase. A change in habits. Rosalie might have paid too much attention to something you barely noticed before. You said she had an affair with Nathan Reid, my uncle."

"He never admitted it," Harry said. "But I knew."

"She might have turned to him to help her disappear."

"Damn it." Harry spoke in a harsh whisper, as though suppressing his outrage. "She didn't need anyone else. I was here for her. I would have done anything for her."

Ella believed his performance, but wasn't sure that Harry was telling the truth. Was he hurt or angry? She'd never actually seen him lose his temper.

"Your divorce cited irreconcilable differences," Colin said. "I need specifics."

"Like what?"

"Every couple has sore spots. Certain issues that infuriate or irritate. She spends too much on clothes or flirts with everybody or never shows up on time. Tell me about you and Rosalie."

"Most of our disagreements came because we were competitive." He averted his gaze from the camera, as if embarrassed to admit the problem. "She resented my series and photo shoots. Didn't like playing second fiddle. She was secretive about her successes and her failures. Always kept a separate bank account. She didn't trust me."

In her role as a therapist, Ella had heard many variations on this tune. Both Harry and his wife were in extremely competitive occupations. The stress had to be intense. She probably shouldn't interrupt Colin's questions, but couldn't help asking, "Did some event trigger her competitive instinct? A better job in the news department or a new title? Or the opposite. Maybe she was demoted."

"Come to think of it," he said, "before she divorced me,

she decided to take her career in a different direction, putting together an investigative story."

"A story about the real estate scam," Colin said. "And The Four."

"That came later," Harry said with a glance at the other whiteboard where the four names were written. "She wouldn't tell me about her investigative reporting, but I have video of her final reports, something about a bank failure and another talking about drug cartels in LA. Complicated stuff. She might have made dangerous enemies."

"When did these reports air?"

"After the divorce," he said. "She never asked me for alimony, but I gave her a big lump sum to show her I was willing to take her back."

"Money didn't drive your relationship," she said.

"Hell, no. I loved Rosalie. I wanted to support her, but she cared more about her damned career than about me."

And he was so jealous that he couldn't let her go. Twenty-five years later, he wanted to find her and tell her that she should have chosen him over success. He wanted to win.

Colin said they needed a frame of reference for what had happened. So they developed a timeline for Harry and Rosalie's relationship. Ella sketched in the high points.

Thirty-two years ago, Harry (age forty-four) met Rosalie (age twenty-three).

Thirty years ago, Harry and Rosalie got married. *The Taste of Murder* aired the first episode.

Twenty-seven years ago, divorce.

Twenty-six years ago, reconciled.

Twenty-five years ago, Rosalie disappeared.

Fifteen years ago, The *Taste of Murder* ended a fourteen-year run.

Ten years ago, Harry (age sixty-six) moved to Cape Seraphim.

IF THIS HAD been psychotherapy instead of an investigation, Ella would have tried to process Harry's feelings about Rosalie's disappearance using techniques for handling PTSD. Having her duck out of his life represented a serious trauma for him. Ella suspected the same was true for Rosalie. But this wasn't therapy.

While they studied the timing, she walked away from the board and went to the windows where the glow of sunset had faded to night. If she opened the window, a salty breeze would sweep through the house, and she'd hear the rhythm of the waves breaking on the shore. After these hours of concentration, she longed for something to revive her. Apparently, she wasn't the only one. The stubble on Colin's chin had reappeared, and his black hair was disheveled. Harry, who was always well-groomed, looked more exhausted than she'd ever seen him.

He moved carefully to his wheelchair and collapsed into it. "Chef Sandra should have dinner ready. Halibut, I think. I'm going to my room to freshen up, and I'll see you downstairs."

Colin stepped up beside her and slung his arm around her shoulders. "Harry has the right idea. I wouldn't mind taking a shower before dinner."

"That's the first thing I did when I came in." She smoothed her yellow Oregon Ducks T-shirt. "You can use my private bathroom."

"Private, huh. Just you and me."

As they strolled down the hall, she snuggled against him, adjusting her position so the Glock in his shoulder holster wouldn't poke her in the rib cage. "My bathroom and bedroom have one special feature you'll appreciate. Palmer has surveillance all over the house, but he promised me there were no cameras in my rooms."

"I'm glad the bodyguard is thorough. Even more glad that your rooms are truly private."

They reached her door, and she pushed it open. She had personalized the pastel blue room with photos of Oscar and Franny Scarletti, her adoptive parents, as well as a photo of Ella and her softball team with their coach, Sister Maggie. A stack of books yet to be read were on the small cherrywood desk, and others on the bedside table. A raku pottery vase filled with flowers perched on the matching dresser. She thought it was a welcoming room, and he must have agreed, because Colin didn't hesitate to make himself at home, slipping off his shoulder holster, stretching out on her queen-size bed and pulling her down beside him onto the puffy white comforter.

"It's a good thing you took off your gun." She propped herself up on her elbows and looked down at him. "If things get hot between us, I don't want to trigger a misfire."

"Are you hotter than a pistol?"

"Oh, yeah."

He pulled her down on top of him. "Prove it."

She didn't plan on having sex with him. Not with Harry down the hall and Palmer patrolling the floor. But one kiss wouldn't matter.

She molded her body to his. A perfect fit. Their long legs entwined. Her breasts flattened against his muscular chest. Her mouth pressed against his, arousing a burst of passion that banished her encroaching exhaustion. Wide-awake, she succumbed to the waves of sensation that crashed through her, shaking her to her very core.

In her rational mind, she doubted the wisdom of hooking up with Colin. He was an LAPD cop who wanted to return to his job, and she was a burned-out therapist who didn't know what she wanted. They both had personal issues to overcome. Now wasn't the time for either of them to jump into a relationship. *Tell that to the endorphins and oxytocin hormones flooding my system.* Kissing him was a matter of biological need, not psychology.

He rolled on top of her. The weight of his body pinned her to the mattress, struggling and aroused. She wriggled beneath him, not objecting to the pressure. She wanted more, everything he could give her. And more.

Then, she heard the screams. It sounded like someone was hammering against the front door.

Colin reacted to the sounds. He bolted from the bed, grabbed his gun and ran for the door.

In the hallway, the unintelligible screams increased in volume. Ella heard the echoes of raw terror. This person wasn't playing a trick. Not making a joke.

At the top of the staircase, she stood behind Colin and looked down as Palmer approached the front door. He gestured for them to stay back.

When he pulled the door open, he aimed his weapon at Lydia. Her hands, turquoise hair and silky, hot-pink negligee trimmed with black feathers were streaked with blood. "You've got to help me," she pleaded. "It's Dougie, my Dougie."

"Who?" Colin asked as he descended the staircase.

"Douglas Rigby. My husband. My lover," she shrieked. "He's bleeding. You've got to help me."

Chapter Fourteen

After Palmer took Lydia home and the police arrived at her house, the bodyguard returned to Harry's house with the news that Rigby had been stabbed to death. Colin stood at the front window and stared at the array of flashing red-and-blue emergency lights. Local law enforcement, including Deputy Angstrom, had arrived quickly and deployed. Colin wanted to charge next door and view the crime scene, but that wasn't his job. On recuperative leave without a badge, he had to respect the jurisdiction of other cops. This wasn't his crime scene, and he had no right to barge in.

Another reason for him to stay away from the murder was his conflict of interest. Though he'd never met Rigby, the guy had been listed as one of The Four. He was a suspect in the disappearance of Rosalie.

Ella appeared at his elbow. "Go on over there," she said. "I know you want to draw your own conclusions."

Less than an hour ago, he'd been in her bed. Kissing, caressing, on the verge of making love to her. Protecting her gave him another reason to stand down and not get involved with Rigby's murder. "Doesn't seem right to leave you and Harry unguarded."

"What are you saying? Palmer is right here. He's got the

house locked up tight and surveillance activated. Not to mention, he's armed and kind of dangerous himself."

Palmer stood behind her. "Go."

"What about you?" Colin asked.

"I'm a bodyguard." He tapped his chest. "You're an investigator. Go. Investigate."

Without further encouragement, Colin went to the door and waited for Palmer to deactivate the alarm system. As soon as he got the nod from the bodyguard, he stepped onto the covered porch into a breezy, moonlit night. A welcome surge of adrenaline whooshed through his veins. Reluctance left him. He felt alive, ready to do the job he'd trained for all his life.

In a stroke of good luck, Deputy Angstrom was one of the first people he encountered at Lydia's house. The wiry, blond officer had changed from his khaki uniform into a black thermal vest over brown Carhartt pants with his badge fastened to the belt. After he introduced Colin as a cop from LA, he led the way into Lydia's house, past the living room, down the hallway and through the kitchen.

The calm, almost conservative furnishings and wallpaper surprised Colin, who had expected something more flamboyant from Lydia. Outside the laundry room, a lieutenant from the Oregon State Police supervised a forensic tech who had just finished recording the scene with a portable camera.

"The body hasn't been moved," Angstrom said. "We're waiting for the coroner."

The metallic stink of blood mingled with the stench of death. Rigby was curled on the floor in front of the top-loading washer. Bloody handprints and smears marred the enamel surface. His arms wrapped around his gut, as if trying to hold back the blood that drenched the white T-shirt under his plaid flannel. A quick glance told Colin that the stab wounds in his abdomen weren't what killed him. Those came first. Then Rigby's throat had been slashed.

After Colin was introduced to the OSP lieutenant, he asked, "Is it okay for me to take a closer look?"

"Booties and gloves are over there. This scene is a mess. You might want to put on a Tyvek suit."

"Thanks, I'm okay." He slipped disposable shoe covers over his sneakers and entered the laundry room, which was large enough to have two storage cabinets, pegs for hanging up jackets and a boot shelf, in addition to the washer, dryer and folding table. Some of Lydia's wildly colorful caftans hung from a rack. The door had a nine-pane window and opened directly into the backyard.

The lieutenant pointed to the broken windowpane nearest the door handle. "That's the way the killer got inside."

"Which must have made noise," Colin said. "Did Lydia say she'd heard anything?"

"She's been talking nonstop, but not saying much. She was upstairs, changing into something she says is more comfortable."

"The pink thing with feathers."

"Yeah. Real comfy." The lieutenant rolled his eyes. "Anyway, she was in her closet for about half an hour. When she came downstairs, she couldn't find Rigby until she went into the laundry room. As you can tell from the prints on the floor, she tried to revive him."

Colin noted the telltale footprint of a stiletto heel, something Lydia would wear, and a small handprint. "Then what?"

"After she figured out he was dead, she freaked out and ran to the neighbors."

"Lydia is kind of a busybody. You might want to question her about suspicious people or vehicles in the neighborhood."

He nodded. "Her and everybody else in the cul-de-sac."

Colin looked down at the linoleum floor. "Did you find other useful footprints?"

"Sneaker prints in size ten, probably Nike. Got plenty of pictures of them."

Ten was a common shoe size, and everybody had Nikes. The company headquarters and many outlet stores were only a few miles away in Beaverton. Still, the prints were better than nothing. "Murder weapon?"

"Nothing on site." The lieutenant narrowed his gaze. "You're LAPD, right?"

Ignoring the edge of hostility in the statie's tone, he said, "Robbery-Homicide Division." Hoping to avoid a spitting match, Colin purposely didn't mention that he was a sergeant, a rank lower than lieutenant.

"What can you tell me from your observations?"

"Broken window seems to indicate that Rigby and Lydia didn't know the attacker." He studied the spatter and splotches. "Minimal arterial spray means the killer came in fast and hard. The victim went down, bleeding heavily from the gut. I doubt he could have taken a single step. After the slicing wound to the throat, he hit the floor and bled out."

"We didn't get many clear fingerprints. It's safe to say the killer wore gloves."

Colin crouched beside the body, ignoring a painful twinge in his bum leg, and leaned closer to inspect the damage. "Looks like three deep stab wounds in the lower abdomen. Underhand strikes using a hunting knife or something like a Ka-Bar."

Like a lot of former military, Palmer had a Ka-Bar combat weapon strapped to his leg. Hunting knives—both straight edge and serrated—weren't unusual in this area. No evidence had been left behind to identify the attacker. "This was fast and simple. The killer broke in, making noise. He waited for someone to come looking for him. When Rigby entered the laundry room, he struck. Three quick jabs to the gut. Then a firm swipe across the throat to sever the carotid."

"The killer had a plan," the lieutenant said.

"He knew what he was doing. I don't see hesitation marks in the wounds. This guy is a professional, and this wasn't his first assassination."

Deputy Angstrom still hovered in the kitchen, keeping an eye on things. "I knew Rigby. He did carpentry work for us when my wife renovated the kitchen. Nice guy. Good sense of humor."

"How tall was he?" Colin asked.

"A little shorter than average. Maybe five feet seven. Kind of square-built, but not in bad shape. Over the years, he'd gotten a little paunchy." Angstrom cocked his head to one side. "Why are you asking about height?"

"Your forensic techs might be able to determine the relative height of the killer based on the angle of the wounds."

"I'll remind them to check."

Colin stood and faced the other two officers. "Any idea who did this?"

Both Angstrom and the OSP lieutenant shook their heads. The statie said, "We haven't had a chance to search the house. Or question anybody except Lydia."

"Do you mind if I tag along?" Colin looked toward the deputy. "This murder might be connected to the SUV who tried to run me and Ella down this morning."

Angstrom spoke up. "Let me check with the sheriff first, but I'd be happy to have your input. We don't get a lot of murders up here. I'll bet LAPD gets one a week."

"More like one a day. In 2023, there were over 327 homicides reported in Los Angeles."

The screech of a siren announced the arrival of the ambulance and two paramedics who came through the house to the laundry room. They took charge of the scene while waiting for the coroner. The other police conferred, and Angstrom returned to Colin's side.

"We'd appreciate your help. As a consultant."

"Believe me, I won't challenge your jurisdiction. I've got enough on my plate."

Angstrom gave a quick nod. "Here's what we discovered so far."

Colin listened while the deputy told him about finding Rigby's overstuffed wallet with several credit cards and $113 in cash. His driver's license used Lydia's address as his own. He had business cards with a Coos Bay address and a different phone number than the cell phone he carried with him.

Apparently, Rigby used his fat wallet as a portable filing system. There were three cards with the names of local women, including a travel agent, and their phone numbers. Also, he had a card with an address in the Castle Bluffs development near Uncle Nathan's house. The name on that card was Dean Santiago.

Colin frowned. It was late to make a phone call, but inconvenience wasn't an issue when it came to Santiago. Colin had been on duty 24/7 when he worked on the kidnapping, and when he finally rescued the kids. The billionaire developer would answer. "What else have you got?"

"At your suggestion," Angstrom said, "we canvassed Castle Bluff, looking for the SUV. The address listed for Santiago appears to be a show home for the development. But there was mail for Rigby in the box. When we looked through windows, we saw evidence that someone was living there."

"Do you have enough for a warrant?" Colin asked.

"With Rigby's murder, we do."

The OSP lieutenant and two other officers joined them for a search of the house where Rigby was an occasional resident. Lydia had recovered enough to lead the guided tour. Though she'd washed her face and hands, she still wore her hot-pink negligee spattered with the blood of her supposed husband. It crossed Colin's mind that she might have killed him. According to his aunt Bridget, Rigby had a harem of Cape Seraphim ladies. But Lydia didn't seem like the jealous type and had recovered quickly from her grief. Already she was flirting with the OSP lieutenant.

The connection with Santiago seemed more relevant. A big shot like him wouldn't dirty his own hands with a murder, but he wasn't above hiring a professional hit man. Their scam from twenty-five years ago might have criminal echoes that influenced the present.

WHEN ELLA STOPPED pacing through the first floor of the house and went to her bedroom at eleven o'clock, she doubted she'd be able to sleep. Not only had there been a murder next door, but their investigation into Rosalie seemed to be creating more questions instead of finding answers. To call her life *unsettling* would be an understatement. Ironic that she'd come to Cape Seraphim to escape the stress of her job and find a measure of mindful peace.

Her bedroom window faced southwest. In the distance, she could see the beacon from the lighthouse. She didn't have a view of Lydia's house, but saw the reflection of emergency lights from the police cars and ambulance next door. She heard conversations and the static noise from police radios. Snapping the blinds closed, she turned away.

Harry had gone to sleep shortly after an incredible dinner of halibut and risotto with Alfredo sauce. Palmer silently patrolled. And Colin still hadn't returned from Lydia's house. Memories of their kiss in the sea cave and the passion they shared less than an hour ago flooded her mind. He was a whole different brand of trouble. Someone she would do well to resist.

Still wearing her Ducks T-shirt and leggings, she flopped

onto the bed. Since her favorite white sneakers were still wet, she lined up her moccasins at the side of the bed. By the light of her bedside lamp, she started reading a mystery she'd started the day before. Her bed felt really comfy. She slipped under the comforter and closed her eyes…just for a minute.

Before she knew it, she had tumbled into a chaotic dream about a pink crystal necklace, a lighthouse beacon and a long, slow kiss. Sleeping, she must be sleeping. She opened her eyes and realized that her bedroom was dark. But she hadn't turned off the light. There was a rustling noise and the sound of breathing. An indefinable change in the atmosphere alerted her to the presence of someone else in her bedroom. A muscular arm wrapped around her and pulled her close. Her back pressed against his chest, torso and groin. He was aroused. His hot breath tickled the hairs on the back of her neck. She should have been alarmed. Instead, she recognized him and reveled in the tactile sensation of being in bed with a virile man…her virile man. "Colin."

"Don't wake up. Stay like this."

Perversely, she wriggled in his firm embrace. "You want me to lie still. Why?"

"Feels good." He squeezed her. "I want to tell you what we found at Lydia's."

But she couldn't listen while he was so close. After a struggle, she'd turned around to face him on the bed. A sliver of light from the edge of the window blinds gave enough illumination for her to see that he was on top of the comforter wearing a gray T-shirt and pajama bottoms. If he'd been naked, she wasn't sure what she would have done. If her dreams were any indication, it would have been something sexy. She groaned and banished that temptation. Then she reached out and turned on the bedside lamp.

He blinked in the sudden light. Then he stared with his inky black, liquid gaze. Though she'd seen him only a few hours ago, it seemed like his stubble had thickened. She'd heard that the rapid growth of facial hair could be related to high testosterone levels. *Don't go there.*

She cleared her throat. "What did you find next door?"

"The furniture and stuff on the walls were tasteful on the first floor. Not what I expected from Lydia. The place looks like a show home at housing development, which reminded me of Castle Bluff."

"Near your uncle Nathan's house."

"High-end houses on big lots. Rigby lived there part-time in one of the demo houses. It belonged to Santiago."

Another link between the two men. "Maybe you should talk to Santiago."

"Already tried. I left a message on his answering machine and with his answering service. He's avoiding me. The only way he'll talk is if I go to LA and track him down."

"That doesn't seem right." She was angry on his behalf. "You saved his children from their kidnappers. The least he can do is answer your phone calls."

He smoothed her long bangs off her face and tucked them behind her ear. "Moving on to the second floor of Lydia's house. The primary bedroom has a circular canopy bed draped in silky pink curtains. The furniture is white and gold. Four naked, faux marble statues lurk around the walls. And it smells like a tsunami of roses. The closet is bigger than this room."

Ella could picture it in her mind. "That's more like Lydia."

"The guest bedroom—probably where Rigby stayed when he visited—has a jungle theme with tiger stripes and a zillion plastic plants."

"Also predictable."

"In the jungle room, Rigby left a stack of paperwork, including bids, billings and contracts. And his passport. The passport and a phone number for a travel agent in his wallet made me wonder if he planned to leave town."

"To get away from whoever was after him."

He brushed a light kiss across her forehead. Though she doubted his intention was to have wild, erotic sex with the ubiquitous presence of Harry and Palmer just outside her bedroom door, Ella's engine revved. She was like a Ferrari at the starting line, ready to zoom into action.

Colin kissed the tip of her nose. "I think Rigby's murder was a professional hit."

"I can't believe his murder had anything to do with the Fourscore scam. That was over twenty years ago. Isn't there some kind of statute of limitations on fraud?"

"Typically, it's five to ten years. Only capital crimes, like murder, have no limitation." He planted another quick kiss on her lips, then pulled away from her and swung his legs down so he was sitting on the edge of the bed. "If I stay here, I'm going to make love to you. It's not the right time or place."

Though she agreed, Ella didn't want to stop now. She felt primed and ready, barely able to look at him without ripping off his clothes. With a loud sigh, she fell back against her pillow. "Was there anything else you found at Lydia's place?"

"In her garage," he said. "Locked up nice and tight, we found a black Escalade SUV with tinted windows and bullet holes in the back."

The car that tried to run them down. As they guessed, it had come from the Castle Bluff development. Rigby had been behind the wheel.

Chapter Fifteen

The next morning, Ella brushed her streaked-blond hair, smoothed on tinted moisturizer to cover her freckles and dabbed on a smudge of peach lipstick. Dressed in her version of business casual with olive green slacks, a striped shirt and a taupe blazer with deep pockets, she tried to look like a mature, responsible professional for her meeting with the local lawyer at the house in Florence. She was ready.

But he wasn't. When she checked her phone, she saw a text from Hilary, the lawyer's assistant, postponing her appointment until after lunch at two. Not a great start to the day, but not necessarily a bad thing. Maggie was arriving this morning, and Ella needed to talk to her about Gigi and her ties to The Four. Though the woman—who was likely her birth mother—had threatened to blow the whistle on their scam all those years ago, Ella couldn't imagine why they'd look for her now. Though she'd claimed to have evidence, why would it matter? Who holds a grudge that long? The psychotherapist voice in her head answered: lots of people. Though The Four had shut down their operation, and the statute of limitations had expired, they still wanted revenge. Confusing, unsettling and weirdly dangerous when she considered Rigby's murder.

The good news: Chef Sandra had dropped by earlier and whipped up breakfast for them. Definitely a treat. The dining room table looked like a banquet with an array of bagels and lox, spinach-and-mushroom frittata, bacon, tomatoes, avocado and assorted fruits. Harry had already dived in, filling his plate with a bit of each.

He looked up when she took a seat beside him. "I was right," he said, "when I told you we needed a murder board. Rigby's name will go front and center."

Overwhelmed by the many flavors and foods, she started with black coffee and retreated to her comfort zone: personal relationships. "How well did you know the victim?"

"Victim." He shuddered. "I don't mean to make light of his murder. From what Palmer told me, the scene was horrific and bloody. It's got to be tied to our investigation. I think he was killed for revenge."

Which was what she'd thought about Gigi. She wondered if Harry knew more than he was saying about The Four. "What makes you think so?"

"It's one of the major motives for murder. I learned that on the show." He assumed the chef-detective pose. "You know what they say about revenge. It's a dish best served cold."

"Thank you, Justin Thyme."

"My reasoning is obvious." He gave a huge, dramatic gesture encompassing the whole room and erasing any objections she might have. "Rosalie discovered The Four and their scam. They threatened her. And she disappeared to protect me from them. Obviously."

"Hate to burst your bubble," Colin said as he strolled into the dining room. "There's no evidence to back up your nifty theory."

"What about the notebook with butterflies?" Harry demanded. "We need to go through all Rosalie's other papers and see what else we can find."

Ella fully expected to be tasked with that tedious bit of research, but she wasn't sure how much time she'd have for digging through files and watching videos of Rosalie. Maggie would be here soon, then Ella wanted her to see the house in Florence.

Colin brandished a bread knife, halved a plain bagel and popped it into a toaster oven on the table. "I need to make a trip to LA. To look into Dean Santiago's connection to Rigby and the other two of The Four."

"You know I have a private jet service on call," Harry said. "I don't use them as much as when I was working full-time in Burbank, but I can still make it happen. Matter of fact, I'd like to come along. I talked to my agent. Might have suggested looking into a real-life reality TV series about Rosalie's disappearance."

The line between reality and Harry's televised detective was beginning to blur. She had to wonder if this whole investigation was part of a grand scheme for Harry to make a comeback. *At age seventy-six?* As Harry had pointed out many times, William Shatner was in his nineties, Betty White worked until she was practically one hundred and Tom Selleck was in his late seventies. *Why not Harrison McKinsey?* "Tell me about this series."

"We need to investigate more and come to some conclusions," he said. "I'm thinking of a happy ending where Rosalie and I are reunited and live happily ever after."

"When can we make the trip?" Colin asked.

"Tomorrow. First thing in the morning."

"The timing works for me." Colin prepped his bagel with a schmear of cream cheese and sprinkles of onion, capers and dill on thin-sliced lox. "I can go to my shrink appointment this morning. My last appointment."

She didn't like the way that sounded. Surely he wasn't giving up on the amnesia specialist. After she indulged in a savory serving of frittata with a splash of Tabasco, refilled her coffee mug and went upstairs to their headquarters, she returned to the subject of therapy. "Are you dropping out of treatment?"

"Why keep banging my head against the wall? We're not getting anywhere."

Standing at the windows, she glanced toward the door to the hallway. Since Harry was busy making phone calls to his agent and other LA people, she figured this was a good time to talk privately. "Do you mind telling me about the treatments Dr. Tindahl has already tried?"

"Will you give me your expert opinion?"

"Sure." As long as he wasn't her client, she could speak freely.

"At our last session, the doc suggested a barbiturate similar to sodium pentothal for a guided tour inside my head. I said no. I've seen too many well-meaning people become addicted. I don't play around with drug therapy."

"There are natural medications to encourage remembering."

"Yeah, yeah, I've already vetoed marijuana, ginkgo biloba, something with turmeric and Omega 3. Tindahl also mentioned magic mushrooms. Psilocybin is supposed to help with memory loss and PTSD."

"It's proven effective when used in microdoses." She'd never tried it herself, but knew many who spoke highly of shrooms. "But you need guidance by a trained therapist."

"Nothing seems to work for me. A shrink at the LA hospital tried hypnosis. Totally ineffective. According to that doc, I'm not a good candidate for any therapy that requires trust and an open state of mind."

He went to the table with electronics spread across it and turned on the computer. Picking at the keys, he avoided her gaze. This wasn't the first time he'd mentioned trust. He'd talked about building walls to protect his inner self. She asked, "Do you trust me?"

He fired a hard-edged look in her direction. "I've got the same question for you."

She exhaled a big sigh and murmured, "I'm so glad you're not my client."

His intense manner and fierce defenses made it nearly impossible to get close to him. The only time those barriers came down was when they kissed. A form of therapy she could never ethically suggest to a client.

He turned back toward the computer screen. "I'm going to email questions to my partner. I want him to check registration for the Escalade and the ownership of the house in Castle Bluff. Plus, the criminal record for Doug Rigby. And Santiago. And Lydia."

"Why her?"

"She seems harmless, but I want to know if she played a bigger role. Did I mention that she has a full makeup room and hair salon on the second floor of her house?"

"I would expect no less."

"She could easily slap on a wig and change her identity. People do that."

"I know." She knew plenty about disguises from philandering spouses and thieves and cheats. "People who have something to hide."

He looked up from the computer screen. "You're coming with me to LA, right?"

"I'm not sure why I would."

"You've got your own search going on. Looking for Gigi. She's buried at Forest Lawn, but you don't know how or when she died. My partner can look up the records and maybe put you in touch with whoever worked on her case."

Taken aback, she said, "You make it sound like she was murdered."

"Any unusual death gets investigated. Could have been

a fatal accident. Or an illness. Don't you want to know the details, Ella?"

"I do." She'd come too far to bury her head in the sand. "I guess I'm going to LA with you."

Palmer tapped on the door frame and entered. He placed an eight-by-twelve-inch black-and-white photo on the table beside them. "Caught these shots last night. On the backyard surveillance cam."

She knew about the layer of protection he surrounded them with, but it hadn't occurred to her that Palmer's cameras also caught scenes from the neighbors' homes. In this picture, she recognized the foliage in the backyard and the beach grass bordering the sand. Squinting, she could make out the shape of a person in a baseball cap who seemed to be approaching Lydia's back door.

Palmer set down another picture that zoomed in on the intruder. His features were mostly in shadow.

The third shot was clearer. The intruder had lifted his chin. Though his face didn't strike her as being remarkable in any way, Colin lifted the photo in both hands and stared into the eyes of the killer. He cocked his head to one side and nodded, almost as if he knew the guy. "You gave copies to the police?"

"Yes," Palmer said.

"And Deputy Angstrom will contact us after they run facial recognition software."

"Good guess."

Colin went to the murder board and attached the photo. Still focused on the picture, he said, "His approach to Lydia's house was crude but effective. Breaking a window could have set off an alarm. He didn't know who, if anybody, would come into the laundry room. Not a brilliant assassination, but he got the job done. I still think he's a pro."

"I concur," Palmer said. Without another word, he left their headquarters.

She stepped up beside Colin. Tension radiated from him. "All these weeks with all these therapists," he said, "I've been looking for a face. This might be the man who kidnapped Santiago's kids."

"A huge breakthrough." But she saw uncertainty in his gaze. "What is it?"

"I'm not sure."

"You might want to mention this to Dr. Tindahl," she suggested.

He shook his head. "When my memory comes back, what happens? A pop. Or an explosion. Or a warm sensation of peace. A feeling that all's right with the world."

"Different strokes," she said.

"I'm so damn ready."

When Harry buzzed into the room on his wheelchair and took his position at the center of their so-called headquarters, he was charged up. He'd gathered a ton of information about how a reality series would work and how they should start filming everything. "My agent says we don't have to use a special camera because this will be integrated with the later, more professional video. Ella, you can use your phone and don't bother with the clapboard. Send it all to the cloud. Oh, and would you please frame the shots so my wheelchair isn't in the picture? I'll be able to walk by the time we settle down to filming."

She kind of hated this idea, but she'd signed on as a factotum dedicated to fulfilling Harry's needs. "What time does Maggie's flight get in?"

"In about an hour," he said. "You don't need to worry about picking her up. Palmer has all our transportation needs covered, including Colin's trip to the doctor in a little while."

Certainly was handy to have a former navy SEAL as a

bodyguard. Not only had he turned Harry's house into a fortress, but he knew enough reliable security guys to run a protective fleet of cars. A bodyguard's version of Uber.

With her phone at the ready to record any exciting moments that might occur, she settled down to read through notes Rosalie had used on potential stories for her TV news segment. Almost all of them took place in the Los Angeles area.

Ella's attention wandered. Not surprisingly, she focused on Colin. She noticed that when he concentrated, he had parallel furrows between his eyebrows, and he ran his fingers through his straight, black hair. He bit his lower lip and frowned. Like a voyeur, she kept watching his every move, imagining how sweet it would be to trot across the room, sit beside him and glide her hand along his jaw. He hadn't shaved this morning, and the stubble had thickened.

When he left with Palmer for his session with Tindahl, she felt like she'd miss him, even though he'd only be gone for an hour and a half. Ella dove back into the files. Rosalie's scratchy writing became more legible but still not interesting. She hadn't expanded on The Four or written about anything else dangerous.

Time crept slowly as she read about engagement parties and black-market wedding dresses and a feline jazz band. Ella was delighted when she heard the front door open and Maggie's voice calling out, "I'm here, Ella."

She scrambled from behind the piles of notebooks, fled from headquarters and raced down the staircase. Maggie's navy-blue dress and sensible shoes were nearly as plain as a nun's habit, but her paisley-patterned silk scarf swirled with all the colors of the rainbow. Her salt-and-pepper hair was neatly arranged in braids that encircled her head. The only makeup on her plump-cheeked face was bright scarlet lipstick.

As soon as Ella fell into her warm embrace, she could tell something was off. Sister Maggie felt tense, almost anxious. Nervous? Maggie Wright? Sister Maggie? No way!

"What's wrong?" Ella asked.

"It's not for me to say." Her red lips twisted into a scowl. "There are some secrets that aren't mine to tell. Be careful, Ella."

Chapter Sixteen

"You're warning me?" Ella shook her head. "Well, that's kind of ominous."

"I don't like keeping things from you," Maggie said.

"Then tell me your secret. I'm not a kid anymore. You don't have to protect me."

"Let it go, dear." With the strap for her oversize purse slung over her left shoulder, Maggie strolled deeper into the house, brushing off her earlier comment. She'd never been a woman who changed her mind easily. She had decided not to speak of secrets, and that was final. "These furnishings are beautiful. That painting looks like a Degas."

"It's a copy. From a movie that Harry was in."

"I should have guessed." With her free hand, she adjusted her paisley scarf. "So much about Harry is…"

"Fake." Ella supplied the missing word. "Don't get me wrong. He's also kind and generous and as witty as the detective he played on TV. But Harry sometimes lives in an imaginary world."

"It's a better place, my child. The place where his beloved Rosalie lives."

"I understand." She was well aware of the similarities between Harry's quest and her own search for her birth mother. "I hope we all find what we're looking for."

"Perhaps we should start with a cup of tea."

Ella escorted her friend into the kitchen, where Maggie gushed over the top-of-the-line appliances. "I've never been much of a cook, but I do love to eat. Amelia would kill for a kitchen like this. Oh dear, that's not a good choice of words, given the murder next door."

"And how is Amelia?"

"As always, she's excellent."

Amelia had been Maggie's roommate for seven years, ever since she had left the convent. Amelia had short, spiky hair and tattoo sleeves. She worked as an executive chef at a three-star Michelin restaurant in Highland Park near Pasadena. Though nearly the same age, the two women didn't seem to have much in common, but Ella had once bumped into them at a Renaissance festival when Maggie's long hair was unbraided and fell nearly to her waist. They both wore bohemian-style clothes and matching grins. They were a complicated twosome, and Ella trusted both of them, which made Maggie's comment about secrets even more worrisome.

While Ella heated the kettle on the stove, she asked, "Have you seen my mom lately?"

"Franny is doing well."

Ella had visited Madison Rose on the day before she left, three weeks ago. Her mom couldn't remember her name, then she thought Ella was still in high school and finally decided she was a well-meaning stranger. They had a nice chat with undertones of painful sorrow. Though their visits were fraught, Ella missed her mom. "I hope to see her tomorrow when we go to LA."

Maggie perched on a stool beside the kitchen island and started digging through her oversize purse. "During our last visit, your mom was going through old photo albums, showing me pictures of you and Oscar. She was truly happy, enjoying the good memories. Arranging for you to be adopted by Oscar and Franny was the best thing Father Lawrence ever did."

If only the priest had still been alive when Ella had started her search, she might have had more luck finding her birth family. But she couldn't complain. "They were great parents."

Maggie pulled a brown five-by-seven-inch envelope from the purse and held it out. "Franny found this among the Halloween photos. She didn't know when it had been taken, but Gigi was definitely in costume."

An actual photograph of Gigi Graham? Ella carefully withdrew the photo from the envelope. Her only other pictures of Gigi were distant group shots where she was a blur among other blurs. In this picture, she wore a fitted jacket buttoned up to her chin and fastened with a large cameo brooch. Her wide-brimmed hat had a veil, but her glossy, dark hair and big, brown eyes were clearly visible. She gazed fondly at the man standing beside her wearing a bow tie and bowler hat. Nathan Reid!

Ella recognized him immediately. In his youth, he resembled Colin. Tall, dark and handsome. Living in the Castle, he considered himself to be the lord of the manor, and he looked the part. Gigi suited him as a partner with her aloof attitude and fancy brooch. Her dark hair and eyes didn't match Ella, but there was a similarity around the jawline and pointed chin. An attractive woman but still a stranger. Probably, this woman had given birth to her. Shouldn't she have felt some kind of connection?

Ella dunked an organic orange spice tea bag into hot water and placed the delicate cup and saucer on the island at Maggie's elbow. "Cream and sugar?"

"My dear, sweet child. You know what I want."

Ella went to the liquor cabinet and found an opened bottle of spiced rum. She placed it on the island and watched as Maggie added a generous dollop to her dainty teacup. "I wonder why Mom never showed this picture to me. It's not like she hid the fact that I was adopted. And she was straight-forward about the trust fund that paid for my college. She must have known Gigi's identity."

"Your mom did what she thought was best for you."

"Like you." Ella climbed onto a stool beside Maggie. "What should you be telling me?"

"They miss you at the clinic," she said in a lightning change of topic. "Wouldn't hurt for you to drop them a line or send a text."

Ella knew she ought to stay in touch with her friends and family, but she had needed a break from everything that re-minded her of the client who died by suicide. On her drive from her apartment to the clinic, she passed the deli near Caltech where her client Cassandra had worked. Sometimes, she thought she saw the seventeen-year-old woman on the street. Ella couldn't stop remembering…a song Cassandra had liked. Her hairstyle. Her way of walking, swinging her arms. Cape Seraphim held none of those memory triggers for her.

In some ways, Ella was the opposite of Colin. While she was trying to forget, he struggled to remember. His fascina-tion with the lighthouse and the sea cave must be relevant memory triggers. She wondered if Dr. Tindahl had gone there with him.

Maggie reached across the island and patted her hand. "Penny for your thoughts."

"It's nothing important."

"I know that dreamy look in your eye and the flush on your cheeks." Maggie pursed her scarlet lips. "You're think-ing about a new boyfriend."

Ella gave an exasperated sigh. She hated the way Maggie

could read her mind. Especially since that talent wasn't recip-rocal. "I'm twenty-seven. Too old to be yakking about boys."

"I'm told you're never too old." The former nun leaned back and sipped her rum-and-tea. "It's not that bodyguard, is it?"

"Palmer? No way. He's not my kind of guy."

"Are you saying you don't like the strong, silent type?"

"I'm not saying anything." She mimed zipping her lip. The rumble from the elevator alerted her to Harry's arrival on the first floor. "Here's somebody who is definitely not silent."

Maggie rose to greet him. Though she wasn't statuesque—not even as tall as Ella—she seemed to tower over Harry in his wheelchair. She bent slightly to accept his embrace. Ella saw him whisper in her ear.

Maggie stood up straight. "Speak out loud, Harry. Ella needs to know."

When Harry looked toward her, Ella pulled her phone from her pocket and held it up. "Do you want me to video this moment?"

His gaze ran up and down Maggie, and he scowled. "I wish you'd worn your habit."

"I don't do that. Not anymore." She scowled right back. Fiercely. "I want to thank you for the private plane ride and the chauffeur service from the airport. But first, I want you to tell Ella what you just told me."

"Fine." He confronted Ella directly. "Your dear friend Maggie is the reason I hired you. She sent me your photo, and I couldn't get over the resemblance to Rosalie."

"I know." Ella had already heard variations on this story.

"That photo is why, after all these years, I'm digging into the past. It's her fault, Maggie's fault. She couldn't stop her-self from meddling."

"There's more," Maggie said. "Go on. Tell her."

A heavy silence descended upon the kitchen. Morning

sunlight spilled across the marble countertops and the island. The faint scent of orange spice and rum teased Ella's nostrils. She heard the front door opening. Colin was back. Finally.

WHEN HE STRODE into the kitchen, Colin couldn't help noticing the intense quiet wrapped around these three people, holding them together and keeping them apart at the same time. He wasn't a part of this moment. Calmly, he said, "I'm interrupting something."

"Harry is being a stubborn donkey." Maggie came toward him and introduced herself with a polite handshake.

"I've heard a lot about you," he said.

"Indeed." Maggie looked from Ella to Colin and back again. "Ella says I shouldn't refer to you as her boyfriend. What shall I call you?"

"He has a name," Ella said.

"I also answer to Mr. Reid. Or sergeant."

"Or the hero cop from LA," Ella said. "That's how Harry introduced him to me, which is neither here nor there. This conversation is over. Harry, you can keep your damn secrets."

Her tone sounded more furious than anything Colin had heard from her. Even more outraged than when Uncle Nathan had been hurling his misogynist insults. He said, "You don't have to stop talking because I'm here."

"It's not about you." Ella hopped down from her stool and stalked toward the elevator. "We should go upstairs. Maggie can get settled in her room. And we can run through the clues before we leave for the house in Florence at one o'clock."

While Maggie and Harry rode in the elevator, Colin followed Ella up the staircase. By the time they reached the landing, she'd recovered her equilibrium. Though her cheeks flushed an angry red beneath the freckles, her jaw had unclenched and the parallel lines between her brows had eased.

She didn't look like a woman who wanted to bash something. Or someone.

He asked, "What was that all about?"

"Harry and Maggie have known each other for decades, and they have issues. Both of them think they know what's best for me."

The doors to the elevator rattled open, and the twosome emerged. Harry in his wheelchair shot toward his bedroom while Maggie stiffly marched by his side. Without saying a word, Maggie closed the door behind them.

Ella winced. "Hard to believe they're good friends."

His phone gave a no-nonsense ring. Caller ID showed his aunt's name. "It's Bridget," he said to Ella. "Mind if I take it?"

"Actually, no. I have a question for her."

After he greeted Bridget and told her that Ella was with him, he said, "I'm going to put you on speaker."

They entered the headquarters room, and Ella closed the door so they wouldn't bother Harry and Maggie down the hall. Bridget's calm, sensible voice came through the phone. "I heard about Doug Rigby," she said. "A murder right next door to Harry's house? Unbelievable. Are you kids all right?"

Even though she couldn't see him, Colin gave a quick nod. His career as a homicide cop never seemed to alert the women in his family to the fact that he faced violence nearly every day. He'd just been released from the hospital after being shot in the leg and in the head. His work was unavoidably dangerous, but he had the training and the skill to deal with threat. "We're fine. Lydia is pretty broken up."

"What can I do to help?" Bridget asked. "I just baked brownies. Or I could throw together a hot dish for your dinner."

"You know Harry has a professional chef on call, right?"

"Of course. I've swapped recipes with Chef Sandra." She

made a harrumphing noise. "I just can't stand being so help-less."

As if cookies would fix everything. Justin Thyme would probably agree. "Not to worry."

"Actually," Ella said, "I could use your help. I unearthed a photograph of someone wearing old-fashioned clothing, and it made me think of the Valentine's Day séance you have every year."

"Not really a séance," Bridget corrected. "It's more of a remembrance. Go on."

"Nathan told us that he met with Rosalie at the, um, re-membrance twenty-five years ago. It might be helpful if you could set up a similar event to remember those who have died."

"Absolutely," she said cheerfully. "I'd be delighted to help. Let's do it tonight at the lighthouse. Nine o'clock."

Colin didn't know what Ella was plotting, but he had no objection to digging deeper into the past events. "You could bring Uncle Nathan. He must be shook up about Rigby's mur-der. After all, they were close."

"That was a long time ago," Bridget said. "Nathan and Rigby don't run in the same circles anymore. A shame, re-ally. I've always appreciated Rigby's carpentry skill."

More than her husband's political aspirations? "He'll be missed."

When they finished the call, he turned to Ella. "You're full of surprises today. What made you think you wanted one of Bridget's séances?"

She reached into the pocket of her taupe jacket and pulled out an envelope. Inside was a photograph of a dark-haired woman in an old-fashioned jacket and a hat with a veil. Be-side her was his uncle. "According to Maggie, this is Gigi Graham. The woman who might be my birth mother. Looks like she's all dressed up for Bridget's séance."

He had to agree. "That means they were both there. Nathan said that was one of the last times he saw Rosalie McKinsey."

"And Gigi," she said.

Must have been one hell of a dramatic night.

Chapter Seventeen

While Ella and Maggie looked at photos and went over Rosalie's notebooks in Harry's headquarters, Colin compared notes with Deputy Angstrom on the murder investigation. The deputy joined him in the front room by the windows that looked out at the other houses in the cul-de-sac. Crime scene tape was draped around various areas outside Lydia's house, and a Coos County Sheriff's Office vehicle sat in the driveway.

Angstrom reported that facial recognition software hadn't produced a definitive match for the intruder caught on video as he crept through the backyards. Studying the photos showed a couple of details: he wore gloves. He was average height and build. And his baseball cap had a logo for another college team from Oregon. The Beavers were represented by a ferocious orange-and-black rodent with buck teeth. Angstrom referred to the intruder as the Beav and told Colin that they were investigating possible connections in Corvallis, where the school was located.

Since the autopsy hadn't yet been done, the deputy had little other evidence. Lack of identification for the murderer meant they couldn't look for motel registrations or credit card use or cars being rented. The cops had been canvassing diners and pubs, looking for information about the mysterious

Beav and coming up empty-handed. It was as if the Beav appeared out of nowhere, killed Rigby and disappeared, which was the typical MO of a professional assassin. A good one.

Though this murder wasn't Colin's case, he enjoyed the systematic police work, tracking down the evidence and discovering answers. He was eager to get back to his job in LA, but he'd be damned if he left Cape Seraphim before he figured out who was menacing Ella. With a professional murderer on the loose, her safety was his numero uno consideration.

After they grabbed a quick but delicious lunch prepared by Chef Sandra, including arugula with mustard dressing accompanied by tuna wraps, they separated into two carloads. Maggie and Harry would be chauffeured by Palmer, who would act as bodyguard for the entire group. Colin drove Ella in his Land Rover.

Being alone with her felt good and right. Almost everything about her pleased him. She stretched her long legs in the passenger seat and leaned back against the seat, getting comfortable. When she lowered her window and glided her hand through the salty breeze, he couldn't help smiling. Ella liked being close to the shore, hearing the surf and watching the swoop of gulls…and he liked being with her.

As he followed the GPS directions to the house in Florence, he let his guard down. "I told Dr. Tindahl that I wouldn't be seeing him on a regular basis. This was my last regular session."

"I'm sorry you didn't have better results."

"Not as sorry as my boss in Robbery-Homicide. The lieutenant expected me to recover from amnesia and remember the guy who shot me. That might never happen."

"Does this mean you're done with Cape Seraphim? Will you be headed back to LA?"

"Depends on what we learn when we go there tomorrow."

He glanced at her and did a quick read of her expression. He didn't see tears in her beautiful blue eyes, but her jaw tensed, and her eyebrows twitched. "Don't worry, Ella. I won't leave until I know for sure that you're not in danger."

"You won't abandon me." She gave a self-deprecating shrug. "I appreciate the thought, but I don't expect you to rearrange your life for me. I've spent twenty-seven years not knowing my mother's identity. If I find out it's Gigi, I won't change. Not much, anyway."

He wished he could give her a reassurance that the connection with her birth mother would make a difference. "What do you expect to learn from the séance?"

"If your uncle is there, we can use his memories to learn something new. Maybe the spirit of Gigi will drop in and we can interview her."

"A ghostly interrogation." He grinned. "I like it."

"Bridget might have information. She might have noticed something that she didn't realize was important." Ella reached across the console and rested her hand on his sleeve. "I've been thinking about memory triggers. Someone like you—suffering from post-traumatic stress disorder—might need to focus intently on the triggers to reveal a deeper truth."

He and Tindahl had discussed the same thing. "What exactly are you thinking about?"

"The lighthouse," she said. "You're drawn toward it."

"Yeah, I am."

"Maybe that's the key to opening up your memories. I'm glad we'll be doing the séance there tonight."

He doubted Uncle Nathan would agree to participate. He'd made it clear that he considered Bridget's fascination with remembrance to be a waste of time and energy, except as a fundraiser for the historical society. Still, he'd been caught in the photo with Gigi, and he'd been dressed like a gentleman from the 1890s. Maybe he was more into it than Colin suspected.

At ten minutes before two o'clock, he parked the Land Rover at the curb in front of the ranch-style house in Florence. Similar to other homes in the neighborhood with attached garages, the slate blue, one-story building had clean white trim around the door and windows. The hedges were neat and three tall rhododendron bushes—red, orange and yellow—were in full bloom. Two Adirondack chairs stood together on the porch. A cute little place. Nothing spectacular.

A thin man wearing a casual, lightweight jacket in a neutral beige stepped away from the chair where he'd been sitting. Something about the way he charged toward them told Colin this wasn't the Coos Bay attorney. Instead of approaching with a handshake, he halted six feet away and stared at them with cold, gray, granite eyes that matched the color of his hair. If he stood up straight, he'd be a bit taller than Colin, probably six feet, five inches, but his posture was stooped, robbing him of height.

"Excuse me," Ella said. "Are you Mr. Patterson?"

"The name is Schmidt. Blake Schmidt."

He was the most secretive member of The Four. An accountant, he'd done work for Santiago in LA and Uncle Nathan in Cape Seraphim. Colin's LAPD partner had been able to uncover a bare outline of Schmidt's businesses. Very successful, he had clientele in the top 1 percent. He owned several properties, including a small hotel in Cuba. Not married. No kids. Schmidt was notoriously reclusive, spending most of his time alone on a fifty-foot cabin cruiser.

Colin stepped forward, introduced himself and shook Schmidt's hand.

"You're a cop," Schmidt said. "You work for Santiago."

"I'm LAPD," Colin said, glad that he wasn't on the Santiago payroll. "I'd like to ask you a few questions."

"I don't talk to cops. Nothing personal. It's just good business." He shifted his focus to Ella. "You must be the woman who inherited this place."

She cocked her head to one side. "What makes you think so?"

"You remind me of Gigi. You're tall like her. And you've got that…attitude."

"Did Gigi ever talk about me?"

"I wasn't friends with her. We were more like business partners." His expression turned sour. "So don't expect you and me to be buddies. I only want one thing from you, and that's to buy this house."

"Why?" she asked.

Schmidt scoffed.

"You heard her," Colin said. "She wants to know. Why do you want this house?"

"I don't have to give her an answer. Not her. And definitely not you." His lower lip stuck out, and he frowned. "You don't have the right to question me."

Colin longed for his badge and the inherent authority to insist that Schmidt answer his questions. The accountant-recluse was rude and uncooperative. Still, Colin pressed for answers. "You knew Doug Rigby. You were both part of a group known as The Four."

"So what?"

"He's dead. Murdered last night just after dark." He watched Schmidt for a reaction. The tall man slouched lower and stared down at his Top-Siders. He looked evasive, but not guilty. Colin asked, "Where were you last night?"

"Back off, cop."

Though Colin hadn't discussed interrogation techniques with Ella, she spoke in the calming voice of a therapist. Her gentle approach provided a contrast to his no-nonsense aggression.

"I'm sorry for your loss," she said. "At one time, you and Rigby were close. It's hard to lose a friend."

"Damn right," he muttered.

"You don't have to talk to us, but the police might want an alibi. They might want to know what brings you to Oregon?"

Defiantly, he said, "Business. I'm here on business."

"You know Nathan Reid. And his wife, Bridget." Ella was positively chatty. "You remember Bridget. She was the person who did the Valentine's Day séances. Maybe you attended one or two of those."

"I remember." Schmidt's expression softened. "It's been a long time."

She asked, "Do you believe in ghosts?"

He almost smiled back at her. "Anything is possible."

"Would you like to talk about it?"

"Maybe." He paused, then nodded. "Maybe I would."

Harry's van pulled up, and Palmer jumped out. Though he wasn't holding his SIG Sauer, he moved with purpose and had probably already deduced there might be trouble. His hawklike gaze fixed on Schmidt.

Colin inserted himself between the two men, offered a quick introduction and said, "You're in luck, Mr. Schmidt. The woman in that van is Ms. Scarletti's real estate agent. You can talk to her about purchasing the house."

Rob Patterson parked his shiny Lincoln Navigator behind the van, introduced himself and joined them. He carried a large briefcase and the key to the front door. Taking charge of the group, he directed Ella and Colin toward the entrance. Palmer followed, guiding Harry's wheelchair up the step to the porch. Schmidt and Maggie stayed on the sidewalk, apparently discussing the asking and selling prices of real estate in Florence.

The Coos Bay attorney explained what they were about to find inside. "My apologies for the break-in two nights ago.

The police were notified, took fingerprints and warned me about robbers who read the obituaries and target abandoned properties."

"A damn shame," Harry said emphatically.

"Yes, it is." Patterson pushed open the front door and gestured for them to enter. "I haven't hired a cleaning service because I wasn't sure what you wanted to do with the place."

As soon as Colin entered the front room, he knew this ransacked mess wasn't the result of a robbery. The TV and stereo system hadn't been taken. And the chaos didn't show signs of random violence. Walls hadn't been marked. Plates hadn't been broken. Pillows hadn't been slashed. Colin recognized a search. Drawers were opened, and the contents strewn. Furniture had been flipped upside down. The kitchen had been dismantled with cabinets emptied. Even the food in the fridge and freezer had been systematically removed.

"This was a search," Colin said.

"What do you suppose they were looking for?" Ella asked.

"Something small enough to fit inside that cookie jar." The ceramic honey bear had been turned over and Oreo cookies spilled across the counter. "Doesn't look like they found it."

"How can you tell?"

"If they'd located the object they were looking for, they would have stopped. This hunt shows no sign of concluding." It occurred to him that Schmidt might want to buy the house so he could dismantle it for a more thorough inspection. Overkill, for sure.

Harry launched into a diatribe about burglary. He forced himself to stand and took a position in a particularly messy corner. "Ella, get a video of this."

Silently, she obeyed while Harry straightened a row of books on a shelf and lectured about the harsh realities of crime.

Patterson brought the focus back to more practical matters. He cleared a space on the dining room table, pulled up a chair and opened his briefcase. "I hate to rush you, Ms. Scarletti, but I have another meeting at four, and I'd like to make a start on the necessary paperwork."

Ella sat beside him and watched as he stacked several file folders on top of each other. "That's a lot."

"Twenty-seven years of records," he said. "The house was initially purchased with cash. Other stipulations paid taxes, insurance and miscellaneous expenses. I'm sure you'll want your lawyer or Realtor to take a look at all this."

Maggie buzzed into the room. "She most certainly will. It's an unusual arrangement, especially since Gigi and the woman who recently passed away were not related."

"What was her name?" Ella asked. "The woman who died."

Patterson flipped through some of his paperwork and read. "Alice Quincy. She was fifty-five when she moved in."

Colin leaned over his shoulder to read the document. "Her occupation is listed as licensed midwife. Did you know her, Mr. Patterson?"

"The initial arrangements were made with my father. I only met with Ms. Quincy once, and that was ten years ago." He looked toward Ella. "If you're looking for information, you might want to talk to someone from Blessed Sacrament Church or any of the local hospitals that used midwives."

"That will be my job," Maggie said firmly. "You have enough to worry about, Ella."

"Then there's this." Patterson placed a small, blue velvet rectangular box on top of the file folders. "I'll need for you to sign this receipt before you take possession."

Ella snapped it open. Inside was a pink crystal heart on a silvery chain. It didn't appear to be a valuable piece of jewelry, but Colin wasn't an expert. Quietly, he asked, "Have you seen it before?"

She opened a note that had been folded inside the box and read it. "'I wish you all the best, Gabriella Love.'"

A tear slid down Ella's cheek as she lifted the necklace from the box and went toward Harry. The pink crystal dangled before his eyes, reflecting sunlight. "Do you recognize this?"

"It belonged to Rosalie."

Chapter Eighteen

The Cape Seraphim Lighthouse and souvenir shop were closed to the public at five in May, but Bridget had arranged for Ella and her five-person group to meet there after dark at nine o'clock. Though Ella didn't realistically expect to see or hear spirits from the other side, she kept an open mind about the conjuring. Her practical reason for being there, which she and Colin had discussed, was to trick Blake Schmidt into telling them about Gigi Graham and confess to his part in the scam that The Four had perpetrated twenty-five years ago.

At the far end of the parking lot outside the Lighthouse Tavern, Colin eased his Land Rover into a space beside Harry's van. Their small cluster of vehicles—the Land Rover, the van, Schmidt's rented sedan and Bridget's SUV—perched at the edge of a five-foot-tall cliff that overlooked the approach to the lighthouse. Other vehicles were parked closer to the Tavern. Ella peeked over her shoulder at Maggie in the back seat.

"Are you sure you're okay with this?" Ella asked the former sister. "I mean, a séance is kind of a witch thing, isn't it?"

The overhead light in the Land Rover gleamed on the stained-glass pattern of Maggie's silky neck scarf. She smiled. "I talk to dead people all the time."

"You do?"

"I call it prayer."

Well, that put me in my place. "Okay."

"I'll always remain true to certain rituals of the faith, but my beliefs have changed considerably since I left the sisterhood."

Knowing that it sounded odd, Ella asked, "Do you ever talk to Gigi?"

"I tell her about you, my child. She's never seen fit to respond."

Of course not. If Gigi actually turned out to be Ella's mother, she'd abandoned her infant daughter at birth and never looked back. Sure, she'd done her fiscal duty by setting up a college fund and bequeathing some property, but she'd never shown interest in being a parent. Why would she care about events in Ella's life?

They left the Land Rover and joined the others. The beacon from the lighthouse slashed an intermittent pattern across the bay, reminding Ella of the night she met Colin on the shore. So much had changed. Her first impression of a scruffy-but-sexy beach bum had morphed into respect for his intelligence and cop instincts, which had developed into a relationship, if that was what she would call this. He'd acknowledged her as his partner, but his incredible kisses didn't fit that definition. Last night, they nearly collapsed onto her bed and ravished each other. Did that make them lovers?

Standing beside her at the edge of the parking lot, he linked his hand with hers in a warm grasp. His dark-eyed gaze communicated gentleness and encouragement and was somehow…hot. Partner. Boyfriend. Lover. The therapist part of her personality demanded a clear psychological definition, and she exerted a conscious effort to stop dwelling on her abandonment issues. *Time to terminate analysis and just live my life.*

But the glow from the moon and stars highlighted his features, and she couldn't look away from this really, truly handsome man. Though she could probably spend hours staring and admiring, she tore her gaze away and concentrated on the flashlight in her hand. "Guess I don't need this."

"Better to be prepared," he said.

"Is that why you carry a Glock? Or is the gun a fashion accessory?"

He raised an eyebrow. "You think my weapon is sexy?"

No way was she going to wade into those waters. "I'm still not sure what we're expecting to accomplish here."

"That's the trouble with cold cases like this one. You can't tell what's hidden in the deep freeze until it thaws and starts to stink. You'll know it when you smell it."

Bridget interrupted their quiet conversation and motioned them forward. "This way."

She marched their five-person group through the light fog to an asphalt path that extended a few hundred yards into the Pacific. The headland—a long, rocky finger pointing to the lighthouse—was wide enough for two people to walk side by side comfortably. Maggie stayed beside Bridget. Next came Harry in his motorized wheelchair. He was followed by Blake Schmidt. Ella didn't know what to make of this guy. He might be a killer or a thief…or simply misunderstood. She and Colin, still holding hands, hiked behind Schmidt. Colin's gait using his cane was smooth and athletic with almost no sign of a limp. Last but not least was Palmer and his trusty SIG Sauer P226—also not an accessory.

In spite of the sound made by the biting wind and crashing surf, Ella didn't want to risk a conversation with Colin that might be overheard by Schmidt. Instead, she ran through questions in her mind. What made him come all the way from LA to see Ella? Did he believe Gigi had hidden evidence of the scam? When was the last time he saw Gigi? And what about Rosalie? Did he even know her?

She and Colin had already agreed that he would conduct the ghostly interview. Given that he was a cop and knew what to ask as follow-up questions, he could direct this odd interrogation. Though Ella's career as a therapist also involved Q and A, she leaned toward the emotional rather than fact-finding. Her goal was to help her clients. Not that she gave a damn if Blake Schmidt was troubled by his criminal past.

Bridget unlocked the door to a small, white house attached to the base of the sixty-two-foot-tall Cape Seraphim Lighthouse tower. Palmer herded them inside and fastened the lock, shutting out the noise of wind and surf. In spite of the trinket-filled shelves, circular racks of sweatshirts and book displays, the atmosphere of the gift shop felt welcoming, possibly because of the cheerful, gold-tinted overhead lights—a color Ella found too stimulating when she had experimented with mood lighting in her office. She'd opted for a cooler, blue-tinted shade.

Beyond the shop and attached offices for the Cape Seraphim Historical Society was a paneled room—also lit in a golden light. There was one window with the curtain closed. And an electric fireplace, which Bridget turned on to chase away the chill. An oak table with seating for twelve faced a podium. Folding chairs were arranged in rows behind it.

"This is where the Cape Seraphim Historical Society, also known as CSHS, meets," Bridget said. "Please take a seat at the table. Gather at this end and leave the other seats empty."

"Places for the ghosts to sit," Harry said. His boisterous voice hinted at nervousness. "How many will be visiting tonight, Bridget?"

"That depends on all of you. Who do you want to contact, Harry?"

"Me?" he blustered. "Nobody. I don't believe Rosalie is deceased."

Everyone except Palmer found a place. The bodyguard posted himself in front of the entrance.

Clumsily, Harry maneuvered from his wheelchair to a padded chair near the head of the table. "This is a nice setup you've got here. Good place for a book signing or a private screening. I've lived in Cape Seraphim for years and only visited the lighthouse two or three times with out-of-town visitors."

"After the conjuring, I'll give you a tour. Unfortunately, you won't be able to see the best feature." She sat at the head of the table. "It's a hundred and eighteen steps to the top of the spiral staircase, where you can exit onto the circular balcony."

"I won't be making that climb. At least, not until next month," he said with a self-deprecating chuckle. "Tell me what I'll be missing."

In the practiced tone of a guide who had escorted hundreds of tours, Bridget said, "The tower and attached lightkeeper house—which is now the gift shop, offices and meeting room where we're sitting—was completed in 1881. Construction was difficult because of the narrow access road. Much of the building material had to be delivered to the site by boat."

"What's behind those two doors?" Schmidt pointed to the wall beside the window.

"One is a private bathroom for the volunteer staff. The other is always locked."

"A secret passage?" Colin asked.

"Nothing so dramatic," Bridget said. "In 1954, CSHS tried to tunnel down and connect with a sea cave under the lighthouse. The staircase wasn't successfully completed, and we keep it locked because the descent is unsafe and the cave often floods."

"What can you tell us about the beacon?" Schmidt asked. He'd taken a seat beside Harry. His sallow cheeks flushed with color, and his flat gray eyes sparkled. His interest in construction and architecture seemed sincere, and Ella wondered why he'd chosen to be an accountant rather than a builder.

"In the early years," Bridget said, "the beacon used kerosene and required tending throughout the night. The Fresnel lens was imported from France, and the original lens is still in use today. In 1935, the beam was electrified and a thousand-watt lamp installed. It was automated in the late 1990s. The beacon can be seen from twenty-one miles out to sea."

"The property seems to be well maintained," Schmidt said. "Who's in charge?"

"The Oregon Parks and Forests Service and CSHS," Bridget said. "In 1977, our lighthouse was listed in the National Register of Historic Places."

"Congratulations," Maggie said. She sat beside Bridget and across from Harry. Then came Ella and Colin. "You must be very proud."

"We are," Bridget said. "Whenever the lighthouse needs repair or reconstruction, the community steps in with contributions and volunteers. Our annual Valentine's Day event is always a good fundraiser."

"What happens at the event?" Maggie asked.

"It's dedicated to the memory of Penelope Townsend, the Ghost Widow, who died on February 14, 1897. In her honor, participants dress in historical costumes from the 1890s and participate in a conjuring ritual based on a legend."

"About the Ghost Widow," Harry said, obviously enjoying the dramatic story. "More, more, more. I want to know more about Penelope."

"Why?" Ella asked. She hadn't expected him to be so enthusiastic.

"This would make a great TV movie. Perhaps featuring the return of Justin Thyme, the chef detective. Tomorrow when I contact my agent, I'll mention it."

"For right now," Colin said in his calm, rational voice, "we focus on the conjuring. Bridget, tell us a bit more about Penelope."

"For several months, she mourned her deceased husband, the captain of a three-masted windjammer that wrecked offshore. Every night, she climbed the one hundred eighteen stairs to the circular balcony below the beacon. For hours, she stood there keeping watch. After she died, people claimed to see her ghost on the balcony. In her will, she promised to come back every year on the anniversary of her death. She vowed to lift the veil between living and dead and make communication with loved ones possible."

"When I lived here," Schmidt said, "I never missed a single Valentine's Day."

Ella raised a skeptical eyebrow. Blake Schmidt was a puzzling individual. From what she'd learned about him, he was a loner, an introvert who didn't enjoy the company of others. A cutthroat businessman. He didn't seem like the sort of person who would enjoy dressing in a costume and participating in a group séance.

She made eye contact with him across the table. "Do you mind if I ask why you made a point of attending?"

His lips pressed together in a straight line. His pale cheeks flamed crimson. "My wife, Wendy, died twenty-nine years ago."

"I'm so sorry."

"She promised we would be together again. Someday. At the séance, I had a feeling she was near."

"Exactly how I feel," Harry said, not to be outdone. "Except my Rosalie isn't dead."

And she never said she'd return. From what Ella saw, the disappearances of these two women had very little in common. Schmidt had a far more romantic version of a lost love. She wondered if he'd remarried or found another to replace

Wendy. Hard to believe he'd spent his whole life pining away for his one true love.

After Bridget asked Palmer to dim the lights, she placed a huge needlepoint satchel on the table and started taking out her tools: votive candles in several colors, which she lit and passed down the table. A fat green candle in a silver holder. Two brass Tibetan singing bowls. And several sheets of parchment with a long verse written in calligraphy.

She gave one of the bowls to Harry and another to Ella. After brief instructions, they learned to make a resonant chime. Harry harmonized by humming Rosalie's favorite song, "Beyond the Sea," which seemed to be his own private way of communicating with her.

Bridget passed around the parchment verses. "After I light the green candle, we'll read this together to summon Penelope. I think of her as a friendly presence. Ask anything you want in a conversational manner. Maybe she'll answer. Maybe not."

"I have a question," Ella said as she studied the parchment entitled To Summon a Loved One. "Who wrote these verses?"

"After much research," Bridget said, "I believe it was Penelope herself, trying to reach out to her beloved captain. Ready?"

They started with the verse. "'Cherished, fond spirit from the other side, come close to me and here abide. Gentle, I summon thee.'"

Ella watched the wavering flames of the votive wicks and the larger green candle. The subtle music of the singing bowls opened her ears. When her gaze skipped around the table, she noticed Maggie was holding her rosary and murmuring. Harry stared off into the distance. A soothing heat emanated from Colin, and the scent of the ocean clung to him.

She looked across the table at Blake Schmidt. Earlier, she and Colin decided that she would make the first inquiry to Schmidt because he seemed to trust her more than him. Schmidt's head bowed. The parchment in his hand trembled. He murmured so softly that she couldn't make out the words.

Her concern for him was natural. "Are you all right, Blake?"

He glanced at her, then looked away. "'Walk through the mists,'" he read from the parchment. "'Enter my embrace.'"

"Do you hear her?" Ella asked. "Is Wendy calling to you?"

"Not her." He shook his head. "It's another."

Bridget cleared her throat. "Please don't interrupt, Ella. We'll read the verse again, starting at the beginning."

Harry responded in a booming, actorly voice. "'Cherished, fond spirit from the other side. I summon thee.'"

Colin directed a question to Schmidt. "The voice speaking to you, is it Gigi Graham?"

"I liked her," Schmidt said with a catch in his voice. "She reminded me of Wendy."

"You were friends," Colin said. "More than friends."

"I'll say. We made a lot of money until…" Schmidt's head jerked to the left. He looked distressed. "Do you hear that? It's a baby. A crying baby."

A shiver went through Ella. Though she didn't hear the cries, she felt Schmidt's gut-wrenching pain. He was caught up in the illusion.

Colin asked, "You and your wife, did you have children?"

"We tried and tried. Wendy wanted a baby girl. It never happened, not for us, not in this lifetime." He exhaled a heavy sigh. "Gigi understood."

Colin leaned across the table toward him. "You and Gigi argued. She had information she could use against you. She threatened you."

"Never. She would never hurt me."

Harry rose to his feet and braced his arms on the tabletop. "Rosalie is not a spirit. She's a living, breathing woman, and she'll come back to me."

"Blake Schmidt." Colin commanded his attention. "When was the last time you saw Gigi?"

"Valentine's Day." His mouth relaxed into a smile, and he looked across the table at Ella. "It's you, my baby Gabriella."

The name the midwife had given her. Her secret identity. How could he know? He called her *his baby*.

"No," she said.

This couldn't be happening. She refused to believe that Blake Schmidt was her birth father.

Chapter Nineteen

The next morning, Colin stood outside Ella's bedroom door and twirled a lock pick between his fingers. With a few practiced twists, he could open the door, but wasn't sure what he'd do when he got inside. Last night, after the conjuring-séance-event, she'd made it clear that she needed time alone. Didn't give him a reason. Didn't explain. Instead, she squeezed her eyes closed and looked away when he asked what was wrong. Even during the ride back to Harry's house, she was quiet. All she'd say was that she didn't want to talk.

Rather than pick the lock, he tapped on her door and spoke quietly. "Ella, it's Colin. We need to talk before we get on the plane."

She whipped the door open, almost as though she'd been poised on the other side waiting for a cue. She gestured toward her queen-size brass bed, which had already been made. Maybe she hadn't slept at all. The thought bothered him. "Sit," she said.

When he sauntered into her room, he felt the leftover steam from her shower still hanging in the air, and he noticed that she'd changed into cropped jeans and a striped T-shirt. Her hair was damp. Her eyes were bright. She looked better this morning. He gave her what he hoped was an encouraging grin. "As soon as you're ready, we need to leave for the airport."

"I'm not sure I should go to LA."

He sure as hell wasn't going to leave her here alone. Two days ago, they'd been attacked by an Escalade. Rigby, the driver of the SUV, had been stabbed to death yesterday. And Blake Schmidt presented an unexplained, but present, threat. "It's too dangerous for you to stay here."

"Palmer can arrange something to protect me."

"You've come a long way toward solving the puzzle. If we clean up the loose ends in LA, we might be able to find out whether Gigi is your birth mom."

"It's not Gigi I'm worried about." She stalked loudly across the room, her ankle boots clunking with every step. "I'm thinking about my birth father."

He refrained from making jokes about her baby daddy. "Why?"

"Something Schmidt said. He referred to a baby and used the name Gabriella, which is what the midwife wrote on my birth certificate." She pivoted and faced him. "What if Schmidt is my father? He's a crook and obviously wants to buy the house in Florence to gut it in a search for… I don't know what."

"You can ask him for a paternity test."

"As if he'd agree." She shuddered. "What if it's another member of The Four? It could be Uncle Nathan. You and I could be related."

The worst-case scenario. He shook his head. His lips pursed as if he'd sucked on a lemon. He wanted to believe it was impossible, but Nathan had a reputation for playing around. "We need DNA."

"I should pack up my suitcase and head for home."

"Quitting is never the right answer. If you don't follow

through, this big unanswered question will haunt you for the rest of your life."

She muttered, "Exactly what I'd tell one of my clients. Be brave. Don't give up. Blah, blah, blah. Easy to give advice."

"Good advice," he said. "Let me tell you the plan."

"Fine."

"Tonight, we're staying at Harry's town house in Burbank. He notified the property manager, who fluffed the place. That's what Harry called it."

"I know," she said. "Fluffing means fresh sheets and towels and a well-stocked pantry. Harry didn't make the call. I did. I'm the factotum, remember?"

"Sounds like a great place with a hot tub and a view of the city lights. Harry said he'd join us there with Palmer after he talks to his agent."

Though she hadn't said yes, she shrugged into the linen jacket draped across the foot of the bed. "Then what?"

"We meet with my LAPD partner for an update on his research, then we check with Santiago. I need your help to figure him out. He won't take my phone calls, but he owes me big-time for rescuing his kids. He could be a victim. Or a perpetrator. Or a suspect."

"Or all three," she said. "It's not uncommon for a victim of one crime to engage in other criminal activity. It's called victim-offender overlap."

Her matter-of-fact tone sent his thinking in a new, more useful direction. "I need you with me to figure things out."

"Flattery?" She arched an eyebrow. "Really?"

He saw her resistance fading. "And, of course, we'll visit your mother at Madison Rose."

"Was that your Hail Mary pass?"

"If I need more, I could talk about you and me, sharing the hot tub and the view from Harry's town house in Burbank."

"You win, Colin. Not because of the hot tub. I just can't say no to Mom." She tromped across her bedroom to the closet, opened the door and pulled out a small overnight bag. "Let's get this over with."

Before she could make her exit, he stepped in front of her and blocked the way. "I feel like there ought to be something I should say. Offer you a brilliant piece of advice. Or a promise to get this settled and make everything right. But I'm not a liar."

"You're being negative." She blinked. "You don't sound like a therapist at all."

"Because I'm not. I'm a guy who doesn't make promises he can't keep. A cop who has seen the worst, but still believes good things can happen." He slung an arm around her waist, pulled her close and kissed her soft, beautiful lips. "Trust me, Ella. I'll do my level best for you."

She kissed him back, and a tear spilled from the corner of her eye. "Oh, Colin."

"Yeah?"

"I really hope you're not my brother from another mother."

COLIN FIGURED THAT a two-hour flight on a private Citation jet from the airfield near Coos Bay to Burbank, California, would lighten Ella's mood. The sheer luxury of swooping through low-hanging clouds while drinking espresso and nibbling fresh fruit and croissants sure as hell lifted his spirits. Schmidt sprawled in one of the reclining seats, closed his eyes and looked more relaxed than Colin had ever seen him.

On the other hand, Harry had gone into high gear, leaning into his persona as a former Hollywood producer and star. He'd parked his wheelchair behind a desk at the rear of the jet in front of the galley kitchen and was carrying on two phone conversations simultaneously while surfing the depths of the internet. Given his ascot, his maroon blazer and his whitened teeth clenched on an old-fashioned cigarette holder without an actual lit cigarette, he should have looked ridiculous. But Harry pulled off the mogul image. He was a much better actor than anybody gave him credit for.

In the seat beside Colin, Ella napped. He tucked a cashmere blanket over her, and she wiggled like a cuddly kitten getting comfy. For a moment, he shoved reality aside and imagined what it would be like when he returned to full-time duty. They had started a relationship, and he wanted to continue. Living apart wouldn't be an obstacle. When she was done being a factotum, she'd come back to southern California. Her mother lived here, and her former job at the clinic awaited her return. They would have a chance to build on the shaky foundation they'd established in Cape Seraphim.

He tucked her streaked blond hair behind her ear and glided his hand along the smooth line of her jaw. They had only shared a few kisses. Too soon to expect more. Yet, he knew her at a deep, personal level. And vice versa. He'd told her things about himself that he'd never spoken about. Not to mention that he'd taken her to his happy place. Leaning back in the leather seat with the hum of the jet engine crooning in his ears, he quietly sneered at the psychobabble. A happy place? He didn't believe in stuff like that. He was a tough guy, a cop who'd survived a bullet in the head. Not some holistic, metaphysical yo-yo.

Still, he couldn't deny his amnesia. And he truly felt safe in the sea cave. He glanced over at Ella. He felt safe beside her.

COLIN HAD STRATEGICALLY picked a restaurant to meet his partner, Sergeant Dwayne Perez. They needed to be far enough away from the precinct to avoid accidentally bumping into coworkers who could report Colin for violating his recuperation time, putting himself and his work at risk. In a similar caution, they stayed away from Ella's clinic in Pasadena. Colin opted for Maxwell's, a bistro that was close to the Brentwood mansion belonging to Dean Santiago, the next suspect on their list. The menu offered a standard array of burgers, salads and burritos. Nothing as delicious as the gourmet meals prepared by Chef Sandra.

After placing her order, Ella went to the ladies' room. Perez rested his elbows on the tabletop, stared at Colin and confided, "I like her. She's tall. What's the deal with you two?"

"Does there have to be a deal?" Perez had gotten married last year and kept pushing for Colin to settle down. "She's okay."

"She's a lot more than that." He grinned like the cat that swallowed the canary. "Here's how I know. You shaved. You put on real trousers instead of sweatpants. And you're wearing cologne that smells like Christmas trees."

"I cleaned up. So what?"

"You didn't get all fancied up for me," Perez said. "Maria is going to want to have you and Ella over for dinner so she can talk about wedding dates and venues."

"Don't start." Colin expected the teasing. Perez was a big guy—as tall as Colin and twenty pounds heavier—but he had the sense of humor of a nerdy adolescent. Not in the mood for games, Colin said, "Ella and I have a lot in common since somebody is trying to kill one or both of us."

"I understand how you and your smart mouth might tick off somebody enough for them to want you dead. But Ella seems like a nice lady. You said she's a shrink."

"A psychotherapist. Right now, she's taking a break from work."

"In the boondocks. Why did she go there?"

Colin wasn't about to argue about the healing power of forests and ocean shores with a man who'd grown up in East LA surrounded by gangs. Perez considered peace and quiet to be the absence of explosions and gunfire. "Big paycheck."

"Got it." He reached into a battered briefcase and pulled out a thick folder. "I already sent you the rundown and case files on Rosalie McKinsey."

"Thanks for all that," Colin said.

"Where do you want to start with this new data I was so kind to get for you on my own time?"

"Thanks, partner." Colin was anxious to get back to his regular duties. "Any hits on facial recognition?"

"The geniuses in the cybercrimes division honed the image of the guy in the Beavers cap and were able to ID him. He's got seven active aliases, which means that tracking his activity through credit cards or rental receipts is a no go. He's been arrested twice on suspicion of murder, made bail and disappeared. Never been tried, convicted or spent time in jail."

"The Beav is a professional hit man," Colin said.

"Not the kind of guy who lets himself get caught on camera. Big mistake."

The hit man must have underestimated the cops in Cape Seraphim, much the same way Colin himself had turned to the LAPD for crime analysis. He hoped the Beav's next assignment wasn't him or Ella.

She returned to their table, and Perez stood and held her chair for her. Then he gave her a magnificent smile. His partner knew he was hot. His nickname around the precinct was Denzel the Second. He returned to his chair. In a deep, sexy voice, he said, "We're discussing the investigation, Ms. Ella, and I don't want to say anything that might offend."

"You won't upset me," Ella said, "as long as you tell the truth."

Colin put an end to their casual flirting with a direct question. "Were you able to trace any of Rosalie's missing jewelry?"

"Nada." Perez eyed the pink crystal pendant at Ella's throat. "There was mention of a necklace like the one you're wearing."

Supposedly, the pendant was a gift from Gigi and not con-nected to Rosalie, even though Harry claimed that it belonged to his ex-wife. "Nothing else? Not diamond tennis bracelets or sapphire earrings?"

"Nothing from the usual pawnshops or resale locations. It's hard to track jewelry unless it's one of a kind. Even then, jew-els could be repurposed or disappear into a foreign country."

Colin asked, "What about the Escalade?"

"The vehicle belongs to a corporation that ultimately traces back to Santiago."

At the mention of his former good buddy, Colin's jaw clenched, and a jolt of anger pumped through him. Dean Santiago had a lot to answer for.

Colin aimed his questions in a different direction. "What about Blake Schmidt? When did he arrive in Cape Sera-phim?"

Perez leaned back in his chair and watched as their wait-ress refreshed their drinks and served burgers all around. While he chowed down on the hamburger, he sketched in the info he had obtained from credit card activity and car rentals. Schmidt arrived in Florence about three days ago, shortly after the midwife's death.

"Three days," Colin repeated, fixing the time in his mind. "Schmidt had time to ransack the house in Florence. Were you able to get his phone records?"

"Not for his regular phone. He could have used a burner to contact Rigby or Santiago or the hit man. We'll never know." Perez drank from his iced tea. "Here's a nugget for you. He arrived by boat and is anchored at Coos Bay."

"What kind of boat?" Ella asked. "How long would it take for him to go from LA to Coos Bay?"

"Three days at least," Perez said. "But Schmidt left from San Francisco, which meant only a couple of days at sea."

Colin hadn't thought he was hungry, but he polished off

his mushroom burger in a wink. Aware of time slipping away, he got down to business. "Switching gears," he said. "Tell us about Gigi Graham. When did she die? Cause of death? Place of death?"

Perez chewed slowly, swallowed and looked over at Ella. "He demands a lot, doesn't he? Kind of a diva. High maintenance."

She grinned. "It's a good thing he's cute."

"Here's the scoop on Gigi. Eight years ago, her bones were discovered off a trail in the San Rafael Hills outside Pasadena. Determining time of death wasn't possible. The bones were picked clean, mangled, broken and scarred by tooth marks from scavenger critters."

"How was she identified?" Ella asked.

"Attempt to extract DNA proved inconclusive. But the forensic anthropologists got lucky with having a fairly intact skull. They found a match with dental X-rays. Apparently, Gigi had a great deal of work done on her smile. She also had cheek implants."

"Not surprised," Ella said. "We're within shouting distance of Hollywood, one of the top cities in the world for facelifts."

"Gigi wasn't old enough for cosmetic work," Perez said. "The forensic people guessed she was in her early thirties. Their conclusion was that she'd been in a profession that required perfect features."

Colin returned to the discernible facts. "Cause of death?"

"Undetermined." Perez finished his fries. "Though her bones were plenty beat up, there were no signs of gunshot wounds. The forensic people wouldn't take a guess."

"Could they tell if the San Rafael Hills were where she died?"

"Nope."

"Have you got anything else?"

"Sorry," Perez said. "Even when we had her identity

pegged, her background was shielded. No family. No close friends. She had an estate worth nearly a million. It was managed by the lawyer who supervised her cremation and internment at Forest Lawn."

"And the house in Florence?" Ella asked.

"Different attorney," Perez said. "The original guy referred us to the executors of Gigi's will—Oscar and Franny Scarletti."

She sprang to her feet. Her phone was in her hand. "Excuse me, gentlemen. I need to call my mother."

Chapter Twenty

On the sidewalk outside Maxwell's Bistro, Ella stared so intensely at her phone's screen that her vision blurred. Her hands trembled as she hit the speed dial for Madison Rose Memory Care. She'd learned long ago that phone calls confused her mom, so Ella asked to speak with Amy, her mom's favorite nurse. On hold, the phone played soothing classical music. Ella inhaled and exhaled slowly, trying to regulate her racing pulse.

Mom should have told her about the million-dollar estate. Withholding the name of her birth mother didn't make sense. Ella had been old enough to understand.

According to information from Sergeant Perez, who had no reason to lie, Franny and Oscar Scarletti had been named executors of Gigi's estate eight years ago when her father was still alive, and her mother was mentally sharp and healthy. Ella slipped back through time. Eight years ago, she would have been nineteen, living at home, dating a guy who majored in engineering, working at a day care center and going to college. Her tuition had been paid by Gigi's college fund.

The voice that answered her call to Madison Rose wasn't Amy. "Ella? It's me, Maggie. Why are you calling?"

"Why are you answering?" Maggie had flown back to LA

with them and had been dropped off only a few hours ago. "Why are you at Madison Rose? Is Mom all right?"

"I got a message that Franny was agitated and wanted to see me. I came right away, even before I unpacked."

Putting emphasis on each word, she repeated, "Is. Mom. All. Right?"

"The episode seems to have passed. Thanks be to God."

Ella watched the traffic streaming past, wishing for a futuristic transporter machine to zoom her to Franny's bedside. No matter how angry she was at her mother, she loved the woman who raised her. "Okay, fine. I can be there in an hour."

"There's nothing you can do, my child. The doctor prescribed a mild sedative, and Franny is sleeping."

"We can wake her up." Even as she spoke, Ella knew forcing her mother to suddenly awaken wasn't a good plan. Still, she persisted. "I need to talk to her."

"Wait until early tomorrow morning. You know as well as I that she's at her best right after breakfast."

"Good advice." But it didn't make Ella happy. She didn't like being put off again. "Did you know, Maggie? Eight years ago, my parents learned that they were the executors of Gigi Graham's will. They must have known her. Is this the big secret you're keeping from me?"

"Did I know? Yes, I did." And she didn't sound in the least bit guilty. "Was this the secret I couldn't tell you? Partly."

"Why?" Ella wanted an answer.

"It's Franny's secret. If your mother decided, for whatever reason, that she shouldn't share this information, it's not my right to disclose."

Ella imagined a door slamming shut. Maggie had decided she couldn't—or wouldn't—betray Franny's trust. She'd probably prayed about it, and Maggie never changed her mind once she'd reached a conclusion. Coldly, Ella said,

"Please tell Amy I'll be at Madison Rose tomorrow morning. Goodbye, Maggie."

"Wait."

"We have nothing more to say."

"I have a document for you. I'll leave it with Amy at the front desk."

Ella huffed a frustrated sigh. "I'm done playing games."

"I don't expect you to understand," Maggie said. "People tell me very private things, probably because I belonged to a religious order, and they feel they can trust me. I don't betray their secrets. Not ever."

Ella felt much the same about her therapy sessions. Her clients needed to know she wouldn't tell anyone else their secrets. Of course, there were exceptions. If a client threatened violence to others or to themselves...

Maggie continued, "I'm leaving this document for you. It's in an envelope and addressed to Harry. That's all I intend to say."

Apparently, Maggie had found a way around her conscience. Though she wasn't telling Harry's secret, she had provided Ella with a clue. "Goodbye, my friend. Thanks for taking care of Mom."

"Be careful, dear."

FOLLOWING THE GPS map on the dashboard, Colin drove the rental car he'd picked up at the Burbank airport to the gated entrance outside Dean Santiago's mansion. The five-bedroom, six-bathroom, English Tudor–style manor was modest by Brentwood standards, but extravagant to most everybody else. Before he pressed the button on an entry box, Colin looked toward Ella and asked, "Are you sure you don't want to go to your mom's place?"

"Tomorrow morning will be soon enough."

He could tell that she was holding back. "Anything you want to tell me?"

"So much, starting with your scruffy beard. I like facial hair." She reached across the console to stroke his cheek. "If you want to stop shaving, I'm fine with that."

Good distraction. But he wasn't easily diverted. "Tell me about Franny Scarletti."

"It's hard to know what to expect when I visit Mom. Sometimes, she's chipper and alert. On her bad days, she doesn't recognize me and isn't sure of the time, the season or even the year. Today, she's having a downer episode."

"Perez dropped a bombshell when he said your parents were executors of Gigi's estate. When you went running off, he felt bad."

"Not his fault," she said. "He can't be blamed for my family keeping secrets from me."

Colin turned his attention to the entry box. He knew Dean was working from home because he'd talked to his head of staff. If Colin had been wearing a badge, he would have taken the straightforward approach by punching the button and demanding to see Dean. But he didn't have that authority. "I'm not sure what to say. A friendly greeting. Or a concerned warning. Or an outright threat."

"A threat?"

"You know, let me in or else."

"Not a threat." She peered through the windshield and the iron gates to the grounds. "It looks like he has good protection. I see an armed bodyguard patrolling near the house."

"My fault," he mumbled. "After the kidnapping, I told him to beef up his security."

She turned to face him. "How about a bit of role-playing? Let's hear your friendly attitude."

"Hey there, it's your favorite cop, Colin Reid. I happened

to be in the neighborhood and thought I'd drop by to see you and the kiddos."

"So phony," she said. "You sound like a weirdo."

"What do you suggest, Ms. Smartie?"

"This might sound like a radical idea, but how about telling the truth?"

He had a nasty feeling that Santiago would send him away without a second thought. The Richy Rich contractor didn't have a problem with ignoring Colin's phone calls. "We could park around back and climb over the fence."

"And maybe get shot by one of the new bodyguards."

"You're right." He pressed a button on the entry box. When a gravelly voice answered and asked if he had an appointment, Colin stated his name and rank. "I'm the guy who took a couple bullets protecting Dean Junior and Brandi."

"Yes, sir." The voice sounded more alert. "Pull up to the front and somebody will park your car."

Under her breath, Ella said, "Told you so, told you so."

"You're a trained pro. You're supposed to understand social interactions."

"And a cop isn't?"

He drove around the curved flagstone driveway to the entry for the two-story brick house with four peaked gables and two soaring chimneys. A young man wearing a forest green windbreaker with the Santiago Construction logo on the left breast dashed up to take the car keys from Colin.

Dean's pixie-sized wife, Trudy, appeared in the doorway and scampered down the stairs to give Colin a great big warm hug. When she stepped back, her cheeks were wet with tears. "I can never thank you enough. You saved my babies and gave my life back."

He'd been told that she had inquired about his progress in the hospital daily and came to visit every few days with cookies and doughnuts for the staff. Trudy was as friendly as a puppy and twice as adorable.

Nobody would ever call her husband cute. Dean Santiago had a muscular, athletic build, unruly brown hair and a year-round tan from working outside. He reminded Colin of Paul Bunyan, striding through forests of redwoods with Babe the Blue Ox at his side.

He greeted Colin with a manly slap on the back and a nod, making no mention of dodging his phone calls. "Any new developments on the kidnapping case?"

"There's something else I'm working on. Let me introduce Ella Scarletti." Colin watched Santiago for a reaction and saw nothing. Not even a blink. "She's related to Gigi Graham, a woman you used to work with."

"I remember Gigi. A pretty gal from Cape Seraphim."

"She worked with The Four on a housing project called Fourscore."

He shrugged his massive shoulders. "I don't recall." Again, Santiago's expression was blank. The best damn poker face Colin had ever seen.

Trudy had looped her arm through Ella's and pulled her into a tour of their house. Her nonstop chatter filled the air as she talked about her plans for raising her children, renovations, diets and a possible spring vacation in Hawaii. As soon as Ella mentioned Harry, the conversation switched to movie stars. Colin listened while their voices faded to a murmur.

He followed Santiago into an office with floor-to-ceiling books and heavy furniture. Instead, sitting on the throne behind the huge desk, Santiago sank into a cordovan leather chair at the end of a coffee table. With virtually no change in his expression, he said, "I heard about Rigby. You were there in Oregon."

"Staying with my uncle Nathan," Colin said.

"The guy who lives near Castle Bluff. What's he been up to?"

"Running for the senate."

"Good for him."

Santiago gave the impression that Rigby and Nathan were vague acquaintances rather than partners in a Ponzi scheme that made them all a boatload of money. Plausible deniability, that was what politicians called it when a member of a group or the leader claimed to know nothing about what the others were doing. Their defense was forgetting or not being informed.

Colin called the ruse undeniably implausible. Santiago was lying, and Colin had evidence that proved the connection of The Four. He sat on the matching leather sofa and stretched out his long arms along the back. "Rigby drove an SUV owned by your parent company. That Escalade has bullet holes from where I shot it."

"I don't get it. Why were you taking target practice on a car?"

"Your lousy Escalade tried to run me and Ella down. Also, Rigby was living in one of the show homes at Castle Bluff."

"I know nothing about that. The problem with running a big company in several locations is that it's hard to oversee everything. I'll have somebody look into where Rigby was living."

"What about Rosalie McKinsey, Harry's ex-wife?" Colin asked. "Remember her?"

"Afraid not."

"Uncle Nathan said the two of you ran into her about twenty years ago in Burbank."

"I hate to be the one to break this to you," Santiago said, "but Nathan Reid is known for being a convincing liar. Politics is probably the best career for him."

"Blake Schmidt showed up in Cape Seraphim." Colin

pinned him with a sharp gaze. "I doubt you've forgotten him. He has invoices from the accounting work he's done for Santiago Construction."

Santiago leaned forward with his forearms resting on his thighs and glared. "I'm not a man who lives in the past. In my work, I come in contact with hundreds of people. I pass their names and addresses to my secretary, and she makes sure they get promo ads and Christmas cards. I don't bother remembering their names unless they owe me money or are bringing new business."

"Schmidt was looking for something. He wants to buy the house in Florence that Gigi left for Ella in her will." And had probably ransacked the place while illegally searching. "It's been suggested that Gigi Graham compiled information that implicated The Four in criminal activity."

"I don't know what the hell you're yammering on about." He surged to his feet and confronted Colin eye-to-eye. "I've cut you some slack because I felt guilty about your injuries."

And I saved your children. Colin stared back at Santiago, unblinking. They were equal in height, but the contractor had more bulk, more muscle. "What did Schmidt think Gigi hid from you?"

Their hostilities eased when they heard the voices of Ella and Trudy approaching the office. Trudy popped her head around the door frame and flashed a smile. "Colin, would you like coffee cake? Or something to drink? I have cider."

"I have something to show you." Ella stepped into the room and held up two framed photographs. "Trudy has a whole wall of pictures in the family room."

"That's only the tip of the iceberg," the perky little woman said. "Every year or so, I put them into scrapbooks. People say I should do this online, but there's something wonderful about being able to look at all these memories."

Ella handed him a five-by-seven-inch photo of three men:

Santiago, Rigby and a guy wearing a baseball cap with the logo for the Oregon State Beavers. Colin pointed to the Beav. "Who's this?"

Trudy peeked around his shoulder. "I think his name is Kevin, or Ken. Something like that. Dean, do you remember? He's the guy who did the cabinetry work when we renovated the kitchen."

Finally, Santiago's expression faltered. His ruddy complexion faded to pale. Worry lines scrawled across his forehead. "I don't remember."

Identifying the hit man, aka the Beav, was the key to figuring out everything else. The fact that Santiago had a professional hit man working for him as a carpenter was damning evidence. Colin couldn't believe how neatly all the twists and turns had led to this conclusion, until he took a look at the other photo Ella held.

In a posed picture with mugs held high, The Four offered a toast. They were dressed for a Valentine's Day séance in clothes from the 1890s. Rigby was the shortest in the group. Instead of his current clean-shaven look with a buzz cut, he had a thick mop of reddish-brown hair, muttonchops and a huge mustache that changed the shape of his face.

Colin's memory clicked into place. Although Lydia had probably used her makeup skills to further disguise him, Colin recognized Doug Rigby. The man who shot him and gave him amnesia.

Chapter Twenty-One

Colin insisted that Ella be part of the FBI debriefing at their field office on Wilshire Boulevard. She rode beside him in the back of a car driven by two agents—one male and one female—while they navigated the seemingly disorganized tangle of streets, shops, businesses and neighborhoods that made up Los Angeles and the surrounding cities. Though she'd asked if they could turn on a siren and flashing lights, the agents said they preferred not to cause traffic jams, and this debriefing wasn't an urgent mission.

She and Colin had left Santiago and his sweet wife, Trudy, at his Brentwood manor with other agents who might or might not arrest them. Santiago's defense of plausible deniability seemed to be holding firm, and Ella agreed with the idea. If he *really* couldn't remember and *really* didn't know what was going on, he couldn't be held responsible. After all, his children had been kidnapped, and he deserved their empathy.

But she doubted he was telling the truth about anything. Santiago claimed that Nathan lied, and they hadn't seen Rosalie five years after she had supposedly disappeared. A clear case of the pot calling the kettle black.

As they stalked through the offices of the FBI, she was glad she'd dressed for comfort in cropped jeans and a linen jacket. Her ankle boots made a satisfying clunk with each lengthy stride. On the seventeenth floor, they entered a small conference room with a rectangular table, several chairs and a large mirror that Ella assumed was a window to a viewing room. They were joined by two special agents carrying file folders. A psychiatrist accompanied them.

"Ms. Scarletti," he said, "I'm Dr. Bromwell. I worked with Colin shortly after his diagnosis of amnesia, and I'm interested to hear how xhe recovered his memory."

She shook his hand. "Wish I could offer a cogent explanation, but I don't know how or why he remembered. Other than to say, the photo triggered his suppressed memories. As soon as Colin recognized the man, his memory block cleared."

"Too bad we can't link his recovery to any particular therapy," Bromwell said. "Colin would make an interesting case study."

She recalled her other client who recovered from amnesia. "Sometimes, the mind just heals itself. Not everything has an explanation."

The psychiatrist gazed intently at her. "Wise statement, Ms. Scarletti."

"I try."

After making sure their unobtrusive equipment was set to record video and audio, the two agents—one older and one hyperenergetic—arranged them around the table. Ella, the only woman in the room, was seated at one end on the opposite side of the table from Colin. Each person introduced himself, and they got down to business. The hyper guy, who was wearing two American flag pins on his lapel, opened his file folder and began. "Colin Reid, you recognized the man who shot you twice in the leg and once in the head. Correct?"

"Doug Rigby," Colin said. "He lived part-time in the house next door to Harrison McKinsey."

"The chef detective," the silver-haired agent said with a

chuckle. "I loved that show. *Too many crooks spoil the broth.* Great line."

Two Flags refused to digress. "Did you meet your neighbor, shake hands with him?"

"Actually, I did not. I met Lydia, the woman who called herself his wife. And I saw Rigby after he was stabbed. At that time, he was clean-shaven and his hair cut short. That's how he looked in every other picture I saw of him."

"Except for one," Two Flags said. "Rigby looked different in the photograph taken twenty-five years ago. The picture showed to you by Mrs. Santiago."

"Thick, curly hair, muttonchops and a handlebar mustache. All his hair was reddish-brown."

"And at the kidnapping?"

"Mustache and curly hair." Colin shot her a glance. "Probably a wig and fake facial hair. He might also have been wearing prosthetics. His partner, Lydia, is a retired makeup artist."

"Tell us what happened at the kidnapping when you confronted him."

Colin straightened his posture, rested his hands on the tabletop and spoke in a calm voice. Not a monotone but a rational tone, as though reading a story aloud. First, he described the abandoned warehouse property where Colin and Sergeant Perez suspected the two children were being held.

"And how did you make that determination?" Two Flags asked.

"I refer you to the various details included in our report," Colin said. "Short answer—solid police work and good luck."

While Ella listened, she became more and more proud of him. Colin loved his job, and he was good at it. He described how he had led a task force of five officers. He and Perez had entered a large, three-story building filled with cardboard boxes, wooden pallets and other clutter. They searched and located the room where the kids were being held.

"Our priority," he said, "was to rescue the children with as little trauma as possible."

Bromwell spoke up. "Tell us about the room where the captives were held."

"It wasn't a dungeon. About twenty-five feet square, clean and well lit. There were discarded candy wrappers and evidence of other junk food. The kids were playing video games on a fifty-five-inch LED screen."

If Santiago had participated in the kidnapping scheme, he might have insisted that the children be treated well. Still, Ella had to wonder about motive. Why would a father agree to having his children kidnapped?

Colin continued, "We decided Perez would direct the kids out of the room and through the warehouse to a rear door we had left unlocked. We contacted the other members of our team and alerted them to our position and to summon backup. That was when we heard movement outside the room. The kidnappers were closing in."

"Why didn't you stay where you were?" Two Flags asked.

"There wasn't much cover in the room, and we wanted to avoid having the children in the middle of a fire fight. We decided to move. I left first, hoping to clear a safe pathway to facilitate the escape. And that's when I lost track of what was happening. My recall is spotty."

"The onset of amnesia," Bromwell said. "The memory loss didn't come when Colin sustained the head wound. It happened earlier. I find that fascinating. Do you, Ms. Scarletti?"

"Yes," she said curtly, wanting to hear the rest of Colin's story.

He continued, "I glimpsed the man I now know was Rigby. He stepped out from behind a stack of pallets. He aimed his weapon at me."

"Did you seek cover?" Two Flags asked.

"I probably should have done so," Colin said. "My job was

to create a diversion. I grabbed a three-foot length of rebar and flung it into a stack of broken-down packing crates. It made a racket. When I looked over my shoulder, I saw Perez taking the kids toward the exit. I switched my position several times. Discovered two other active shooters. I kept up a steady barrage of gunfire."

Ella's pulse kicked up a notch as she imagined the danger Colin had faced. Though he spoke calmly, she heard an undercurrent of tension.

"Rigby maneuvered his way around until he was behind me. I spun around and saw him. He fired before I could react. I felt the pain in my leg. Everything went dark." He paused. "I thought I was dead."

She exerted all her self-control to keep herself from diving across the table and wrapping her arms around him. He had come so close to death.

Tonight, she'd give him something to live for.

HOURS LATER, WHEN the debriefing ended, Ella and Colin were given a lift to Harry's Burbank town house, which had been properly fluffed with clean sheets and basic food supplies. The two special agents who drove the SUV stayed behind to observe and protect. They were still in danger. Though Colin's memory had returned, the threat from the professional hit man hovered over them like smog in the San Fernando Valley.

Ella used her key to open the door, and the agents entered first. Guns drawn, they swept through the house, declared it safe and bid them good-night. She locked the door behind them and engaged the motion-sensitive alarm system. Though they were close to her Pasadena apartment and his little house in the San Rafael Hills, they had opted to stay at Harry's place, which was especially attractive since Harry wouldn't be here. He'd decided to spend the night with his agent.

Ella and Colin would be alone. An expansive silence wrapped around them. She'd never visited Harry's Burbank pied-à-terre before, but she was familiar with her boss's tastes. The sheets would be five hundred thread count. The towels would be fluffy. Gourmet snacks and fine wine would be stocked in the cupboards and refrigerator.

When she took a tentative step forward on the terra-cotta floor, Colin caught her arm and turned her toward him. He pointed to a wall of windows. "I should close the curtains."

"For privacy?"

"I don't want the Beav watching."

She glided her hands inside his sports jacket and pulled him closer. "I'm not scared, Colin. I trust you to take care of me."

"Weren't you listening at the debriefing?" He kissed her forehead. "It should have been obvious to you that I'm not the world's best bodyguard."

"The story I heard told me that you're brave and gallant. You laid down your life for those children." She rested her head on his shoulder, enjoying the sensation of being with a tall man. "Do you think Santiago arranged the kidnapping? How could a father do something like that to his own kids?"

"Ruthless," Colin said. "How would Dr. Bromwell diagnose Santiago?"

"Psychopathic narcissist." She'd studied criminal psychology, but wasn't an expert. "His motivation is greed. He runs his life based on profit. Possibly, he justified the risk to his children by thinking of the money he'd make."

"I think you've got it. I wasn't surprised to learn that he has a hit man on the payroll. Or that he told Rigby to run us down with the Escalade."

"And then had Rigby killed."

"The FBI thinks the whole kidnapping scheme was about money laundering. Santiago would pay a ransom to himself and avoid taxes." With his arm around her waist, Colin went to the windows and drew the curtains. "Like I said, the place where the kids were hidden looked like a fun place to chow down on junk food and play computer games. The only person who got hurt was me."

"And you have your memory back."

"It's going to take my leg a lot longer to rehab."

With the barest hint of a limp, he hiked to the kitchen. The interior of the town house was furnished in the minimalist style of the 1990s. A long counter divided the galley kitchen from the front room where the sofa and chairs were arranged for the best view of the hillsides beyond. If the curtains had been open, they would have looked out on a private terrace with a hot tub. According to instructions she gave the crew who prepared the house for their arrival, the four-person tub was ready to go. All she needed to do was push a button and adjust the temperature.

She opened the refrigerator and saw a premade salad and meats for sandwiches. She opened the sliding door of a bread box on the counter. "Hungry?"

"I could eat." He joined her at the fridge and assembled the makings for a ham on rye while she plated the salad. "Strange thing about my memory."

"Can't wait to hear. You'll make a lovely case study."

"There's more going on in my head than the kidnapping. Odd little threads keep weaving into my thoughts."

"Give me an example."

"The bread box reminds me of my grandma, which made me think of her funeral. A really sad day for me. I cried and don't like to remember it." He took a jar of mustard from the fridge. "There's good stuff, too. Like the day I got my driver's license."

She filled two glasses with water from the tap. Harry

had special filtration systems installed in all his residences. "What about less important events?"

"I ran away from home when I was nine and took a bus into downtown. I was protesting my parents' miserable divorce, and I thought I'd show them. Those were the scariest six hours in my life. When I got home, nobody even noticed I was gone. I never talked about it."

They talked and ate and took off their shoes. She wasn't sure how or why they ended up in the guest room on the California king–size bed, but there they were. She stretched out full-length, enjoying the extra four inches head to toe. Gazing up at him, Ella was certain that this was exactly the place she needed to be. "Sometimes, things just fall into place."

"But sometimes, we need to take action." He slipped off his shoulder holster, removed the Glock and placed it on the bedside table before he flopped onto the snowy white duvet beside her. He tugged at her beige-and-blue-and-black-and-white-striped T-shirt and wriggled it up over her head.

"Action-packed," she said with a chuckle. "Not exactly a smooth move."

"But necessary."

He traced a line from her throat to her belly button, setting off a chain reaction of tremors. When she arched toward him, he reached behind her back, unhooked her lacy white bra one-handed and yanked it off. "Very nice," she said. "You've done this before."

"Once or twice." He ducked his head and kissed his way across her shoulders. "Have I told you how much I like your freckles?"

"I've never liked them. When I was thirteen, I used a formula of apple cider vinegar and honey to make them go away." Breathing in gasps, she couldn't believe she was talking about a freckle cream. "It didn't work."

"I'm glad."

He suckled at her breasts, licking and nipping until her nipples were almost painfully hard. He went lower, waking sensations she hadn't felt in a very long time.

He kissed her mouth, gently at first and then with a more demanding pressure. Her heart thumped in a fast, heavy cadence. So loud. All-consuming. He had to be able to hear the drumbeat. She needed him, trusted him, wanted him.

She tore at his shirt, not caring if the buttons popped off, but grateful when he took over with a steady hand. Colin wasn't a man who lost control. In seconds, he was naked from the waist up. She stroked his black chest hair and caressed his firm chest, enjoying the masculine feel of his body. She unzipped his trousers. Her hand slipped inside the waistband and went lower until she found his hot, hard arousal.

He reacted in a flash, turning the tables and removing her jeans. Except for her red lace panties, she was naked. Then he took those, too. He started a trail of kisses at her collarbone and went south. Sensations ran wild in her blood.

"You're perfect," she gasped.

"Not exactly," he said. "But I'm very, very good."

He showed her once, then twice. And then they moved to the hot tub.

Chapter Twenty-Two

The next morning, Colin insisted on a quick omelet breakfast before they visited Ella's mother at Madison Rose Memory Care. He knew this was going to be a hectic day and wanted to grab something to eat while they could. His night with Ella had taken a lot of energy, and he needed to refuel. Not much sleep. But he wasn't complaining.

She stood at the counter, sipping Harry's excellent coffee. In the guest room closet, she'd found a short, silky, black robe that gave him an excellent view of her long, long legs. "Now that you've recovered your memory," she said, "will you go back to work?"

He knew what she was really asking: Would he leave her? "I won't abandon you. Until we have the situation under control and I know you're safe. One hundred percent safe. You're stuck with me."

"No place else I'd rather be."

When she glided into his arms, he felt himself getting hard. If he didn't exert some self-control, he'd make a nest with her at Harry's place and stay forever. He forced himself to step back. "We should get going if we want to make it to your mom's place by nine."

She gave him a kiss, pivoted and went back into the guest room.

Not trusting himself to stay away when he heard her in the shower, he invited the FBI special agents inside for coffee and food. Though they were casually dressed, they maintained the air of formality that went with black suits and knotted ties. Colin stroked the stubble on his jaw, glad that Ella liked facial hair. He was changing in ways he didn't completely understand.

His earthshaking recovery from amnesia still had aftershocks—echoes of other memories he'd buried or hidden. Oddly, he kept seeing the distant lighthouse on Cape Seraphim, rising through the fog and beckoning to him.

They left Harry's town house with the bed stripped and the trash taken out. Ella had called the people who took care of the place to tell them the hot tub could be put to rest. After they stowed their overnight bags in the SUV, she climbed into the back seat beside him, rubbed shoulders and gave him a kiss on the chin.

"Here's what to expect from Mom," she said. "Wait! I don't know what her mood is going to be. Or if her memory will be engaged."

"What do you hope to learn from her?"

"Thanks to Perez, I learned that my parents knew about Gigi. They were told about her death eight years ago and never mentioned to me that my birth mother had died. I suppose they had their reasons."

"They were appointed as executors of a million-dollar estate."

"Unlike Santiago, Franny and Oscar were never motivated by greed."

"Money is always a motive." He wasn't cynical, just realistic. "I suspect some of Gigi's legacy is being used to pay for your mom's memory care center."

"I don't really care," she said. "All I want to know is why they kept Gigi's identity from me."

MADISON ROSE MEMORY CARE spread over several manicured acres where rose bushes mingled with palm trees and birds-of-paradise. The buildings were white stucco with red-tile roofs. Ella directed the special agent who was driving to a long one-story structure with a covered walkway leading to the doors.

Inside, she marched to the front desk and asked for Amy. The receptionist on duty recognized her immediately. "Good morning, Ella. Your mom ate a good breakfast."

Ella didn't read too much into her opinion. The staff generally tried to be upbeat. "Is she in her room?"

"I think so." She took an envelope from a desk drawer and passed it to Ella. "Amy left instructions that you were to be given this letter."

A sticker with Maggie's return address decorated one corner. *Another secret.* "Thank you."

The corridor smelled faintly of hospital antiseptic and air freshener, but the decor reminded her of an apartment building with framed photos on the walls and a tasteful carpet on the floor. Colin walked beside her to her mom's room. Her mother's dark brown eyes lit up when she saw him. "It's about time," she said. "You finally have a boyfriend."

"Mom, this is Colin Reid."

He took her veined hand, lifted it to his lips and lightly kissed it. "I've heard so much about you, Mrs. Scarletti."

"Aren't you a charmer." She chuckled, adjusted her tiny, thin body in her overstuffed chair and looked out the window at the sunlit landscape. "My daughter deserves a good man, a good husband. She's quite wealthy, you know."

If Ella hadn't recently been informed about the estate from Gigi, she might have thought her mom was hallucinating. Trying to pry more information from her mother, she tossed out another bit. "I inherited a house in Florence from that midwife. Do you remember her?"

"Of course." Franny bobbed her head. "A lovely person. But lonely. Did you say she was a midwife?"

"How did you meet her? Did Gigi introduce you?"

Franny bisected her lips with her index finger. "Shh. I'm never ever supposed to talk about Gabriella."

Gabriella was Gigi. "It's okay, Mom. She wants you to tell me everything."

Ella bent down next to the chair and looked into her mom's careworn face. Franny gasped. She reached out and touched the pink crystal necklace. "Oh, I'm so very glad you found this sweet little pendant. Some of my other jewels are missing."

Amy came into the room to check on her mom while she greeted Ella and Colin. Before Franny's room turned into a party scene, Amy pulled Ella into the hall so they could have a quiet talk. She was glad when Colin followed.

"Maggie was here yesterday." Amy pointed to the envelope in Ella's hand. "I see you got her message."

"Thanks," Ella said. "I really appreciate the way you watch over Mom."

"Just doing my job."

"She mentioned something about her jewels."

"A very nice collection. Some expensive stuff. We keep it in the safe at the front office." Amy frowned. "I'm sure you know about it. She's talked about it several times before."

Ella had always dismissed her mom's chatter about her precious fortune as delusion. "Tell me more, Amy. Specifics."

"There's a beautiful ruby and gold pin she likes to wear at Christmas."

Colin spoke up. "A Rolex, a diamond tennis bracelet, sapphire earrings, a string of pearls. Was there a cameo brooch made into a bracelet?"

"That's the stuff. Franny likes to take it out every once in a while and look at it."

Ella recognized the list of Rosalie's missing jewelry. Those items had belonged to Harry's ex-wife. Not Gigi. She sought Colin's gaze. "I don't understand."

"Either the two women knew each other well enough to share jewelry," he said, "or they were one and the same."

She knew what he was suggesting. The thought had been forming in the back of her mind. "We've been looking for only one missing woman. With two identities."

Gigi was Rosalie. And vice versa.

Chapter Twenty-Three

Harry wasn't flying back to Cape Seraphim with them. He'd left last night after an argument with his agent, who apparently told him that the search for Rosalie might make a decent story, but Harry was too old to play himself.

A tough break for Harry, but a stroke of luck for Colin. After they read the document Maggie had left at Madison Rose, Ella was furious with her boss, and Colin was legitimately worried about her reaction. She'd torn open the outer envelope while they were riding in the rear of the FBI's vehicle to the Burbank airport.

Inside the larger envelope with Maggie's address was a smaller one with a window. She turned it over in her hands. "I saw this in Harry's room on the night he took off in his wheelchair. The night I met you on the beach."

He read the return address for Sinclair Medical Laboratory. "Open it."

The seal had already been broken. All she had to do was reach inside. She pulled out two separate charts. "DNA fingerprinting," she said. "I don't know how it's interpreted, but the clinic where I used to work uses this technique to determine paternity. Oh my God, I don't think I want to see this."

He took the charts from her and passed them to the FBI

special agents in the front seat. "You guys have more experience with this than I do."

The agent in the passenger seat nodded. "DNA analysis creates unique patterns using polymerase chains and electrophoresis."

"In English," Colin said.

"The chart for this individual—H. McKinsey—is a match for Ella Scarletti. Congrats, Ella, he's your daddy."

She growled like a jungle cat, feral and vicious. "I spent so much time trying to figure out who was my mother that I ignored the other parent. That's why he hired me. He's my father. Why didn't he tell me?"

"You can ask him when we get back to Cape Seraphim."

She muttered curses about the unfairness of twenty-seven years not knowing. "I'm done waiting."

"To be fair," he said, "Harry got these lab results only a few days ago. Maybe he didn't know."

When they got to the airport, the two agents escorted them to the plane and refused to leave until Colin promised to call them with the final report on Ella's birth parents. The story was—in their opinion—better than a soap opera.

On the plane, Colin tried to construct a possible scenario. "Okay, if Harry didn't know Rosalie was pregnant, she wasn't far enough along to have a baby bump when she left him."

"We had the answer in front of us all along," she said. "On our timeline, we show Rosalie's disappearance twenty-seven years coinciding with my birthday. She left Harry while she was pregnant with me. After she delivered me and I was adopted, she took some time away from television appearances and made a small fortune in real estate with Fourscore and More."

"Using her alias. Gigi Graham."

"Why change her name?" Ella asked.

"Maybe she didn't look great," he suggested. "Remember the skeletal remains for Gigi Graham showed cosmetic surgery."

"But how did she get away with having two separate identities?"

"You remember the picture of Gigi? She had dark hair and eyes. Not like Rosalie, the sunshine blonde with electric-blue eyes. Also, they led separate lives. Not too many people knew both Gigi and Rosalie."

He could think of only two: Maggie and Uncle Nathan. Maggie said nothing because she had a moral dilemma, not wanting to betray confidences. For some reason, his uncle had purposely clouded the issue by pretending to see Rosalie a few years after she was already dead. Why was he lying? What was he hiding?

There was one thing for sure. Harry had to accept the inevitable conclusion that Gigi-slash-Rosalie was deceased, probably murdered.

When they left LA, the sunny California weather stayed behind. Springtime in Oregon often meant storms and fog. By the time they reached Cape Seraphim and drove to Harry's house, a light rain had begun to fall. Colin parked at the ramp to the front door and said, "I'll leave you here to have a private conversation with Harry."

"My father." She shuddered.

"You have a lot to talk about. A lifetime of experiences to reconstruct."

"Though I'm angry, I can't really blame him. He didn't know he was abandoning me." She unfastened her seat belt and leaned across the console to kiss him on the cheek. "Thanks for supporting me."

"Works both ways," he said. "You taught me how to trust, unlock my barriers and overcome my amnesia."

On the tip of his tongue were the three little words he hadn't spoken in years. *I love you.* As he watched Ella walk up the stairs to the porch, he tasted the sweetness of that simple statement. And he swallowed hard. Loving her could be complicated. In the short time they'd been together, she'd had her life threatened, had learned of the death of her birth mother and discovered the identity of her birth father. A lot to take in.

He needed space to consider all that had happened to her and how it affected their potential relationship. He wanted to help her carry the load. After he drove out of the cul-de-sac, he decided not to go all the way to his sea cave. If Ella needed him, he wanted to be nearby.

He parked at the beachfront and switched his jacket for a charcoal hoodie. Barefoot, he rolled up his khakis and went for a walk at the water's edge. Peering through the veil of rain and fog, he saw the lighthouse. The sun, hidden by purple clouds, slid lower toward the horizon, leaving only a glow struggling to break through and be seen.

At a little after five o'clock, the lighthouse souvenir shop would be preparing to close. He wondered if Aunt Bridget was there, if he could talk to her about her liar husband, who could have put Ella out of her misery when he met her. Uncle Nathan could have revealed the mystery: Rosalie and Gigi were one and the same.

Colin knew there was more to that story, and the mystery had something to do with the lighthouse. With his hood pulled up, he sat on a driftwood log and stared at the tall, white tower. If it took all night, he'd stay right here, waiting for his mind to clear. He needed to know the truth.

WHEN ELLA CONFRONTED HARRY, she couldn't attack him the way he deserved. He looked too miserable. Shoulders hunched, slouched over in his wheelchair at the dining room table, he swallowed a giant bite of tiramisu gelato. "I'm sorry I have to tell you this," she said. "It's time for all of us to face the truth."

"Rosalie is gone. Dead. Not really a surprise. On some level, I knew she was never coming back. Not after the first time she left me, divorced me."

"What happened, Harry?"

"I ask myself that same question," he said. "She wanted fame and fortune. I was in the way. She didn't need a husband."

"Or a daughter," Ella reminded him. He wasn't the only person Rosalie had left behind.

He spun around in his wheelchair. "Don't give up on me, Ella. Let me make it up to you."

"The man who raised me, Oscar Scarletti, was a good person. He taught me how to listen, how to be loyal and how to grow. He was my father, and you'll never replace him. But I think we can have a different relationship."

He held his arms wide, and she leaned down to embrace him. "By the way, your agent is wrong. You're not too old. You're the only person who can play the role of Harry McKinsey."

She left him to drown his sorrow in gelato. At the front door, she grabbed a rain jacket and stepped outside, thinking she could find Colin. He couldn't have gone far. She took out her phone to call him. Before she could plug in Colin's number, Nathan Reid drove up to the house and waved.

Her anger grew as she left the porch and approached his car. Though she didn't want to make enemies in Colin's family, she couldn't ignore Nathan's lies. She blurted, "I have a bone to pick with you."

"You're getting wet," he said. "Hop in."

Rain splattered around her. No matter how furious she was, standing outside would be foolish. She slid into the passenger seat. "I'm guessing you were the leader of the Four. You set up the Ponzi scheme."

"Ancient history." He turned toward her. His features showed the family resemblance with Colin, momentarily disarming her. "What are you doing in the rain?"

"Looking for Colin."

"You're in luck. He talked to Bridget and said he'd meet her at the lighthouse. I'll give you a ride."

She didn't like Nathan, didn't want to be stuck in his car. But it would only be a few minutes. While they drove to the Lighthouse Tavern, she told him that she and Colin had been in Los Angeles. Though she could have said more, she held back the information about Santiago hiring a hit man and possibly kidnapping his own children. "Your old friend, Dean Santiago, told us that he'd never seen Rosalie in LA, didn't even know who she was. That's not what you said."

Nathan shook his head. "He's a liar."

Takes one to know one.

Outside the tavern, the rain had stolen the last glimmers of sunlight. Wind off the deep, dark water churned across the beach. Nathan parked at almost the same place they left their cars on the night of the séance. Though she said goodbye, he stayed with her, walking beside her on the path to the lighthouse. The few people she saw were covering their heads and dodging away from the tower. Not toward it.

"Goodbye," she repeated. "You don't have to walk all the way out here with me."

"I insist."

She heard an edge to his voice, a warning, a reminder that he was a powerful man. She took a few steps away from him. "I want to be alone."

He held her arm in an iron grip. "You're coming with me."

She cried out. Her voice was carried away by the droning wind and crashing surf. No one would hear her.

Nathan used a key to unlock the lighthouse door and shoved Ella inside. When she tried to break away, he took a stun gun from his pocket. "We can do this the easy way or the hard way."

"What do you want?" She remembered Gigi's threats about damning information that could put The Four out of business. With Rigby murdered and Santiago implicated in the crime, there were only two left: Blake Schmidt and Nathan. "Is this about a flash drive and documents?"

"Why would you think that?"

"The house in Florence Schmidt was searching."

"Schmidt is an idiot. I've told him a thousand times that Gigi's secrets don't matter. The statute of limitations has run out."

There was another crime. One that didn't fall under the statute. *Murder.* Nathan had a reason to worry. Finally, Ella understood. "You killed her. You killed my mother."

"Gigi or Rosalie. Or both." He sneered. "Two bitches with one stone."

"How did you do it?"

"She died right here. Then I convinced Schmidt to load her body into his boat and sail down the coast so she wouldn't be associated with Cape Seraphim."

Rage built inside her, a force almost as violent as the storm.

Nathan continued, "We transported her to the dumping ground. The hills outside LA. Lucky for us, her bones weren't found for over a decade."

She lashed out at him. Using every bit of her strength, she flung him away from her and made a mad dash for the souvenir shop door. She tore it open, but before she could escape, he caught her with the stun gun. Thirty thousand volts shot through her. She collapsed on the floor.

ON THE BEACH, Colin stood staring, mesmerized by the beacon from the lighthouse as it struggled to slice through the storm. He thought of the first time he saw Ella. So much had changed since then. Then he saw the shadows. A tall, dark-haired man strode toward the tower, dragging a woman with him.

In his mind, Colin was transported back in time to when he was five years old. He spied his uncle Nathan—dressed up in old-time clothes—on his way to the lighthouse. A lady in a long dress was with him. He carried her in his arms. Colin took a step toward the lighthouse. Something bad was about to happen. He knew it, but couldn't stop it from happening.

Memory ambushed him again. Uncle Nathan was at the top of the lighthouse. At the edge of the wrought-iron balcony. He lifted the woman, and then he threw her limp body down, down to the jagged, rocky shore.

Not again. Not Ella.

He shoved his feet into his Top-Siders and took off at a sprint. Climbing with desperate speed, he reached the long path leading to the lighthouse. The wind exploded around him. Heavy rain pelted him. With his phone clutched in his hand, he called for backup. They wouldn't get here fast enough to save Ella.

The door to the souvenir shop was closed but unlocked. Colin flung it open. His first thought was to climb the stairs to the balcony above the sea. Halfway up, he could tell that Nathan hadn't taken that route.

Colin remembered the sea cave below the conference room. A door that was always locked stood wide-open. Inside, a curved staircase hugged the damp stone walls that descended at a treacherous angle. The stink of rotting seaweed and fish swept over him. He heard the lapping of water at the bottom of the cave. Halfway down the staircase, there was a light. Otherwise, the cave was completely dark.

He heard Ella talking in a soft tone, trying to convince his lying uncle that she'd never tell anyone his secret. "You're too important to go to jail, Nathan. You're almost a senator."

"True. Nobody is going to believe you."

Colin drew his gun. "But they'll listen to me."

"Colin? What the hell are you talking about?"

"My memories came back, Nathan. All of them. When I was five years old, I witnessed the murder of Gigi Graham."

"No. You're wrong."

Nathan turned toward Colin. His clumsy movement was just the distraction Ella needed. She shoved him away from the wall. His arms pinwheeled as he tried to get his balance. And then, he fell down the stone staircase. Far enough to knock him out.

Colin heard her shouting, the way they had called to each other in the other sea cave. "Colin Reid." She called his name. "Colin."

"Ella Scarletti." He descended the stairs. "Ella, I love you."

ONE YEAR LATER, Ella was back at work in the clinic, and Colin had returned to the LAPD. The newlyweds both had secondary careers as producers.

Their docudrama premiered on a cable station. *The Taste of Murder: The Real-Life Adventure of Harrison McKinsey.* Starring the one and only Harrison McKinsey.

In a Burbank studio, Ella and Colin joined Harry, Palmer, Maggie and the production crew to watch as the screen filled with Harry in the kitchen giving an introduction.

He spoke in his Justin Thyme voice. "I've said it before. Revenge is a dish best served cold. This adventure is about vengeance, heroism and love."

"You tell them, Harry." Maggie nudged her roommate and continued, "The bad guys all ended up in jail. Nathan, Santiago and Schmidt. I'll still pray for them, but not very hard."

"Concentrate on the happy ending," Harry said. In his Justin Thyme voice, he added, "And the bun in the oven."

Colin took Ella's hand and lifted it to his lips. His gaze met hers and their deep love grew even more permanent. Harry was correct. They already had another production underway. Ella was due to deliver in four months.

* * * * *

COLD CASE
OBSESSION

TARA TAYLOR QUINN

For Brit Kelly, may you always hold tight
to your soul's need to create words and pictures
that let little ones see a path to their happiness.

Chapter One

"I've already taken a leave from my forensics research position in Little Rock and signed a three-month lease on an apartment here in Phoenix, Dr. Thomas. This cold case—finding Simon Billingsley—I've been working on it since high school. I've made it my life's work. I have to figure out what happened to him." Dr. Lorna Schwann, already a renowned scientist at twenty-nine years old, groaned inwardly as the words she'd plotted over and over tumbled out with no order like some pubescent hormonal overload.

The frown on the powerful-looking, clean-shaven scientist's face told her she was blowing it. Less than two minutes into the Monday morning meeting.

Sitting behind his massive desk, pushing up his dark-framed lenses, he said, "Excuse me? *You* have to figure out what happened to him? Your note said you wanted to discuss the possibility of Sierra's Web *taking on* a cold case."

She nodded. Adjusted the edges of her lab coat, tucking the white fabric over the tan pants she was wearing. "That's right. I need Sierra's Web's resources," she said, also out of sequence with her rehearsed spiel. She tried to get herself back on track. "The local police and the FBI never had a suspect," she continued, dropping key points that should have been distributed first. "Simon was two years old and just disappeared from the neighborhood park while his mother was right there, tending to Simon's twin, who'd fallen, cut her knee and had blood dripping down her leg. Her four-year-old daughter was crying as well, because she had to go to the restroom. Simon was behind the park bench where his mother had taken a seat to look at his twin, Selena. When she'd assessed that the little girl didn't need stitches and stood up to gather all three little ones and get them to the bathroom, Simon was gone. Her husband had called in the midst of it all, and when he'd heard that Selena might need stitches had stayed on the line with her. Back then it was just those little cell phones that only allowed talk and minimal text, so no way he could see anything. But neither of them heard Simon cry out. Or heard any shuffling, either. He was just there and then gone."

Telling the story got her somewhat on the even keel that defined her life. She'd meant to start with it. Laying out the facts clearly. Concisely. Not blundering about with her current living conditions.

But meeting Glen Rivers Thomas in person—the expert forensic scientist she'd been following for the entire twelve years his firm had been in business—she was uncharacteristically gobsmacked. Lorna couldn't remember a time she'd ever felt so lacking in self-importance. Would have nervously tucked her hair behind her ear if she'd had any long enough to do so. She fiddled with the messy dark mass instead, working ends at her neck between thumb and forefinger.

"I was only six at the time. I didn't know Simon, but I lived in Morrilton, the small town where the Billingsleys lived and where this happened. Simon's disappearance changed everything." She was segueing off track again. Pulled herself back. But blew the effort with an inane comment. "Morrilton is only an hour and a half to two hours from Searcy."

Dr. Thomas's expression didn't noticeably change. But

his gaze seemed to pierce her for a second, rather than just observe. She'd hit a nerve. And if that was what it took to get her in, then she'd go with it. "I know you got your undergraduate degree there. And that your friend disappeared during your senior year."

The knowing wasn't the point. Anyone who looked up Sierra's Web, or had ever visited their website, could easily find out about the woman, Sierra Wendel. Her murder would likely have gone unsolved if not for the seven friends, all straight-A students in different fields, who'd banded together to petition the police department for a more thorough look. They had all assisted in the investigation. They'd been too late to save Sierra's life, but they'd led the police to her killer. And had managed to uncover a major illegal sports gambling ring in the process. They'd finished the job Sierra had set out to do. Had given Sierra justice.

And had gone on, after completing postgraduate studies in their fields, to form their now nationally renowned firm.

Dr. Thomas's past was part of what had led Lorna to him. She was counting on him to at least partially understand, and relate to, her need to solve Simon's case.

And she had to hit harder or she was going to be out. "I developed an age progression facial recognition algorithm when I was younger. I have perfected it over the years, and a month ago, finished a trial run with it with the slimmest margin of error anyone has ever achieved. With my system, and Sierra's Web access to a plethora of databases, we might be able to find Simon in short order."

"You just said you rented an apartment for three months."
Right. She had.

"He'd have to be in a database in order for quick closure." She pointed out what he already knew. Just to let him know that she wasn't a complete imbecile, the sheet of credentials she'd sent when she'd made the appointment notwithstanding. "Sierra's Web also has a department of tech experts with national access to public and some not-so-public cameras. Beyond that, finding Simon doesn't necessarily mean that the case is solved. He was two at the time of his disappearance. I'm guessing he's not going to remember much." And she had to know how it had happened.

How did a two-year-old with his siblings and parent just disappear without a sound? A trace? And unless they knew, they couldn't prevent it from happening again.

"I'm assuming, since you've already indicated as much, that you have an evidence file?" The scientist's gray-eyed gaze wasn't encouraging. But it wasn't exactly unfriendly, either.

She hoped that didn't change as she shook her head and said, "Not an official one, no." Filling with tension, mixed with the thread of hopeless desperation she'd been carrying around with her since Simon's disappearance, she said, "I have my own file. Everything I've compiled. Tests I've done all over the park. The dirt. Digging down deeply enough at sixteen that I could be relatively assured that the readings I was getting would be similar enough to the abduction ten years before…"

He hardly blinked. Didn't look away at all. And his brow rose. She figured she had his full attention. But wasn't sure it was in a good way as he reiterated, "You dug holes in the park to get dirt?"

"Yes."

"And the city allowed this?"

She shook her head again. Cursing herself for going off key. She'd known certain things would not show her in a good light. But he'd seemed to doubt her aptitude. The amount of work she'd put into the forensic study of Simon's disappearance. Her dedication.

No way he was going to give her access to his firm's superpowers if she was dishonest with him. For all she knew, he'd already done a thorough background check on her, not that the arrests would show on anything official. But if he'd made a call to Morrilton, introducing himself as a partner in Sierra's Web, someone on the police force might have spoken off record. "I was arrested for doing so," she told him. "Did community service for the misdemeanors. And my juvenile record was wiped clean when I turned eighteen."

His brow rose again. "Misdemeanors? In the plural?"

Without batting an eye, she stared him down. "I raided the Billingsleys' trash when I was a senior in high school and had access to the biology lab. I wanted to see if I could get any familial DNA."

For a second there, she thought he looked impressed. But his face was soberly expressionless as he asked, "Did you?"

She cocked her head then allowed a little smile as she said, "I did."

"What did you find out from the dirt?"

"Back then, not a lot. But I now know what kind of fertilizer was being used at the time of Simon's disappearance. Park records hadn't been computerized, and the landscaping department had a flood and a whole cabinet of records was lost. But the fertilizer could matter. If we ever found something else that had any remnants of the dirt on the ground in the park that day." During her years of forensic research and working on commission for various law enforcement agencies across the state of Arkansas, she'd seen a lot of things more far-fetched than that.

She didn't believe until she saw proof. But she didn't ever close the door on possibility, either. Simon's bizarre disappearance from their small town had brought both truths home to her. Hard.

"I also know various rock compounds that could be lodged in the sole of a shoe. I know all of the vegetation that was growing in the area that day, including the bed of tulips that the local legion had just planted, the type of grass in the park. Which trees were growing, the type of paint on the park bench, the wood it was made out of and the kind of screws holding it together, too. It's all in my evidence file." Along with a hundred other potentially innocuous pieces of information. All things that could also lead to a break in the case if put together with evidence yet to be discovered.

The renowned scientist's gaze narrowed as, in a white lab coat over a brown knit shirt, he studied her for long seconds.

She had more to say. Years' worth of pent-up thoughts on the case. But was loath to put any more nails in the coffin of her best hope of finding the answers that would bring a lifetime of anxiety to some kind of rest. She let him stare. Withstood the awkward rudeness with head held high. Shoulders straight. Hands folded in her lap.

When he opened his mouth, coupled with a newly formed frown on his face, her heart dropped. "I'm not sure what you're envisioning here," he said. "You aren't asking us to just take the case, you want to work it with us?"

She shook her head. "I don't want to take up anyone's valuable time," she told him. "I just need access to all of your forensic amenities. Camera feeds. Databases. State-of-the-art laboratory capabilities." Her lab at the university was the best in the state of Arkansas, but nowhere near as equipped as Sierra's Web's would be.

And as she heard her own words, she knew how ludicrous her quest really was. That she'd wasted a brilliant man's time, taken a leave from work, and wasted money on an apartment she wasn't going to need because she was too far in to see straight.

Her need to find Simon had superseded common sense.

She didn't need the shake of Dr. Thomas's head or the oddly kind look in his eyes to know that she'd failed. "Not for any reason, or any person on earth, could I ever see Sierra's

Web, my partners and I, agreeing to allow our resources to be used in such a fashion." His words weren't kind. The tone was.

Her hero worship for the man she'd thought would understand her quest almost rose a notch. If there was anyplace up for it to go. And she wasn't cascading downward in a pool of disappointment.

She was supposed to relay that she'd already made the temporary move to Phoenix after the rejection. Along with some conversation about Sierra. She'd already sent both ships out to sea.

Gathering the leather satchel she always carried with her most faithful companion—a powerful, state-of-the-art laptop/tablet combination that had its own dedicated phone line and internet connection—she stood. Nodded. "Thank you for your time…" she started to say, with an apology for wasting the scientist's time ready to launch, when he frowned again.

"You have somewhere to be?" the man asked, pushing his black frames up on his nose as though they'd actually slid down to begin with.

An old habit? She noted the observation. Glommed on to it, actually, as she stood there awkwardly, unsure what to do, and then dropped to the edge of the chair she'd vacated. Still holding the strap of the satchel draped over her shoulder.

"I can't grant your request," he started, and she wished she'd had the gumption to have remained on her feet. Standing up to him. Or, even better, had gotten herself out the door already. "But I'm open to some conversation about hiring you, on a temporary basis, to work under my command—so to speak—alongside other experts who have proven themselves invaluable and have chosen to join my team."

Heart pounding so hard she could count her pulse, she stared at him. "You want to hire me?" she asked, and continued without giving the slightest pause for an actual response. "You're offering me a job?"

On a temporary basis. A short-term position.

Excitement shot through her so sharply it hurt to move. To breathe.

"I'm open to conversation about doing so for the one case." Dr. Thomas pushed at his glasses again. And just sat there. Watching her.

Lorna took her bag off her shoulder, set it on the floor at her feet, folded her hands in her lap.

And waited.

WHAT WAS HE DOING? The case had validity. Along with over a thousand other missing person files Sierra's Web had been approached about over the course of the past year alone.

And because of their current urgent workload, cold cases were mostly off the table. Unless a partner felt a need to pursue it.

He was a partner. He felt a need.

He just wasn't sure the need was sufficient to drain any of the firm's much-needed resources.

The woman was getting to him.

Much like Sierra had.

It wasn't a mistake that Dr. Lorna Schwann had mentioned his old friend. The one tragedy that he'd never gotten over.

Scientist to scientist, she'd known how to get to him.

And that knowing sat with him still. It wasn't entirely unpleasant. To be enough like another to understand—and be understood.

More like a call to him to pay attention.

To the case. To the science.

Not to the woman.

Except by way of Dr. Schwann being at least a partial solution to the manpower equation, were Glen to agree to take a Sierra's Web kind of look at the Billingsley case.

"Why us? Why now?" He was a facts guy. They had to add up.

"Simon's twin sister, Selena. She's engaged to be married. Her wedding is coming up in a couple of months. She keeps asking me about the case. We have Simon's DNA, and the more recent DNA testing capabilities have given her new hope. If there's any way to give her the miracle she's craving—her twin at her wedding—I want to do so."

He believed her. No doubts. But he needed more. "I assume you've already run the DNA against family finder databases?" She didn't need Sierra's Web for that one.

She nodded. "And the FBI and state police have run it against their own sources."

He hadn't made up his mind what to do. And wasn't done, either. "What would be your first step here?"

"Run my age progression/facial recognition program against all databases you could hook me up with."

Her again.

"You just arrived today." He gave her the reality frankly. "With an impressive résumé, credentials I've already verified, and a spotless background check, granted, but no one walks in off the street here and has immediate access to anything." Not anymore. Win's wife was one of the team now, trusted, adored, and a great asset to the firm, too—but her less-than-stellar advent into their lives had shown them all that there had to be protocols followed before anyone had free rein among them.

Dr. Schwann's facial expression flattened. She didn't reach for her bag again. Which impressed him. She was dedicated to the case. He'd give her that.

"Say we get no hits with the new program," he started in, more eager than he was letting on to get a look at that particular piece of the conundrum. "What's next?"

"Not *next*," she said, sitting calm and still. As he might

have done. Keeping focus on the facts, the job, not on whatever might be trying to unhinge inside him. "At the very start I'd also ask for both the Arkansas and FBI case files. I'd expect them to have arrived by the time we do or do not get facial recognition."

His gaze narrowed. "You've never had access to anything official?"

Maybe not FBI, but, with her credentials, her forensic research position, he'd have thought at least her local police would have turned to her.

"My juvenile behavior precluded it," she told him. "And then lack of a position that gave official capacity to my work on the Billingsley missing person case also prevented means of entry." She stopped. Blinked. Her shoulders stiffened and then relaxed. "I've seen a list of evidence, though," she finally allowed.

And Glen relaxed a bit more. Intrigued beyond normal. By the case. And the woman. "I'm guessing there are things you're eager to get a look at?"

"A particular pen," she told him. "First. And then…everything."

Thinking about how she'd analyzed the hell out of the park years after the abduction, he could well imagine what could come of her attention on more pertinent items.

And wanted to see what came of it, too. What her mind and honed skills might lead her to that others hadn't found. Due to lack of time, funding, technology, or skill.

Glen blurted out the starting salary for his most junior technician position. He knew what she was earning. His offer was an insult, at best.

"Does this mean you're going to hire me?"

He hadn't made up his mind yet.

"You wouldn't have any access to any secure areas or databases without another Sierra's Web team member present."

She stared him down. "You think I'm going to argue about that?"

"Are you?"

"No."

He was beginning to enjoy himself. Something else he hadn't done in a while. "I'm the boss," he told her—just as he did every single technician he'd ever hired. "I keep my mind open to other thoughts, ideas, theories...welcome them, actually, expect them...but the lab is run to my specification. Anything done behind my back is cause for instant termination."

She shrugged. "I'd be worried if it wasn't."

"I'll need to set up a meeting with the rest of the partners," he said then, wishing he'd already done so. That he could jump on a video call and get their nods.

She lowered her head a bit, but was still looking at him as she said, "Does this mean I have the job?"

The woman was determined. And seemed to be in possession of a one-track mind. Similar to his.

"I'll let you know once I speak with my partners."

She nodded. Stood, pulling her bag up, strap over her shoulder, as she did so. "Is there someplace here I can wait?"

"Most of them are on cases. It could be a while."

"I'd like to be here, ready to start, in the event I get the job."

She was new to the city. In one of the nation's vacation meccas. Surrounded by natural wonders as well as more urban pursuits. And she wanted to sit around in an office and wait.

Glen held back his smile as he showed her to the break room.

"There's just one other thing," Dr. Schwann told him as he told her to help herself to coffee or other refreshment. She'd put her bag down on the conference table in the middle of the room. "It doesn't have anything to do with the case, but I need to give you full disclosure."

Expecting to hear that her local police department wasn't overly fond of her, Glen turned back toward her.

She'd opened her bag. Pulled out a half sheet of paper, bearing large, typed letters. "This was on the floor by the front door of my house in Morrilton when I woke up yesterday morning. It had clearly been slid through the mail slot."

Back off.

Glen read the words.

And all enjoyment in the moment fled.

Chapter Two

"Did you call the police?" Dr. Thomas's entire demeanor changed as his gaze landed, and stayed, on the note she held.

Lorna shook her head. She'd purposely waited until she'd succeeded in her mission before exposing the little problem she had on the side. "I know who sent it," she quickly assured him. Then, scientist to scientist, had to add, "I don't have proof, obviously, since I haven't had access to a lab in the past twenty-four hours and was on my way to catch my flight here when I saw it, but once I can pull prints from it, I will have the proof. I figured I'd call the Little Rock police at that time."

"You're being threatened by someone? You might have mentioned this earlier…" Dr. Thomas's gaze narrowed, and he took a step back. "Is this why you're really here? To find out who this person is?"

He shook his head, as though not sure he stood behind the question. But it was out there. And if she wasn't so certain that Sierra's Web was her only good shot at finding Simon Billingsley, she'd have walked past him and out the door without looking back.

Instead, she took a deep breath and said, "I discovered that a technician in our lab, Leonard, was fabricating some of the results he'd been working on to determine levels of drugs in someone's system without needing to wait for blood test results. He'd been successful enough in his preliminary findings that he'd been given a national grant to further his research. But he'd run into some roadblocks—not necessarily showstoppers, but they could be. His grant was due to run out and the only way he'd be able to renew would be to provide more evidence that his theories were proving successful. He knew I'd seen him. Begged me to look the other way. Success of his theory would help not only the medical field, but criminal investigations as well. And give him a household name in the field of forensic science, which, as you know, would basically let him write his own ticket to whatever research train he wanted to hop on next." Lorna was telling him far more than his question required, but the longer she talked the more she delayed the request to leave the premises that she feared could be coming.

And she continued. "I just nodded and moved on," she said, seeing Dr. Thomas's eyes narrow on her as she did so. Pausing just long enough for her words to fully sink in so the next ones would hit him equally hard.

"That was last week. I'd already put in for my leave. Knew I'd be gone for the months of the fallout. Knew also that nothing was going to happen with his research or grant in the week I had left. So waited to report him until my last day. Which was the day before yesterday."

When the impressive scientist in front of her nodded, Lorna took her first full deep breath since he'd shown her to the break room and she'd known she had to complete the end of her rehearsed spiel.

"I come with baggage," she said before he issued any opinion on the matter. "But it can be easily cleaned up as soon as I have access to a lab again. I can call the police from here."

And she'd felt safer getting out of town before she did any

more reporting, too. Because she'd been afraid of the bad guys since she was six years old.

"Who knows you're here? Family? People from work? Friends?" His questions came succinctly, rapid-fire. As though he was as much cop as scientist.

Frowning, she shook her head. "My parents think I was invited to guest lecture at a university for three months. They know I'm in Arizona, but when they asked, I blurted out the University of Arizona, not Arizona State University, thinking U of A was in Phoenix, and ASU was in Tucson, not the other way around. They'd never have believed I got the name of the school wrong, so...they think I'm in Tucson." She was back to babbling.

He hadn't kicked her out.

Didn't even seem about to do so.

"What about friends? Coworkers?"

She hesitated to shake her head, as telling as it would be that she had no life outside her lab. But she did so because a man like Dr. Thomas would surely detect subterfuge, and lies between them would make it impossible for them to have the kind of working relationship scientists had to maintain. But to bolster herself the bit that she could, she said, "Only Selena Billingsley knows I was coming to Phoenix to meet with you. She contacted me after her mother died several years ago. And then again after her father died. She'd heard talk about my teenaged antics and originally just wanted to know if I'd ever found anything pursuant to her twin brother. I eventually told her that I was still looking at things. We aren't friends. We don't hang out. But when she calls—generally every three to six months until she got engaged last year and the calls became more frequent—I answer. I am her hope."

That last word ended her babbling.

Hope.

It's all she had. All Selena had.

And maybe all Simon Billingsley had ever had, too.

Asking Lorna to stay put, Glen strode from the room. Realizing as he did so that he had no right or business suggesting that his recent appointment not leave. He wasn't even her boss. Not yet.

But he wanted to be. Or rather, wanted to take her on, to work the Billingsley case with her. Almost as though, if he could help set her free, he could somehow come to better terms with his culpability in Sierra's death.

As though, from above, Sierra was telling him that if he solved this case, helped this woman, she'd forgive him for not pushing her for information when he knew something was off, not trying harder. Not solving her own case in time.

Hudson Warner, partner and tech expert, was behind his desk with his office door open. A closed door wouldn't have stopped Glen. But he was pleased to see that he didn't have to barge in.

Barging had never been his style.

"If someone has already reported an infraction, the perpetrator isn't likely to immediately leave a threatening note at the home of the reporter, ordering her to back off, right?" he asked. Hud was their liaison with the police, and together with Savannah, their law expert, oversaw the team of private investigators and bodyguards that worked for Sierra's Web.

Hud's brow rose, then fell, as he said, "Depends on whether or not the reporter had more evidence to produce, or other people to report to."

Glen shook his head. "It's a workplace infraction, the only thing of any real value at stake is some research and a grant associated with it. Not grounds for criminal threats, I wouldn't think." It didn't seem logical to him.

Enough so that he wasn't going to let it go.

He'd failed to listen to his instincts where Sierra was concerned. He wouldn't with Lorna. Why then, why that woman, he didn't know.

Could just be that she'd played him with the Searcy card. And maybe not.

Either way, he wasn't going to take the chance. Because of her, but for the safety of the rest of them—and of his lab and full-time Sierra's Web forensic scientists, too.

He told Hud about his morning appointment. About Lorna's refusal to let go of the case bordering on obsessive behavior. "Until now, while she's analyzed a lot of evidence and has proof of many things, if they were to show up on anything that was at the crime that day, she's made no headway on finding out what happened to Simon. Or who else was involved. But the morning she wakes up to head here, to give three months to the case with our official weight behind her, she gets a note to back off."

His chin tightening, Hud rested his elbows on the arms of his chair, steepled his fingers, and nodded. "Is that the note?" he asked, nodding toward the paper still in Glen's unprotected fingers. When he had protective gloves in his pocket.

Always.

Glen nodded, realizing that his friend had just made a mental note regarding him. He didn't like it. But after so many years together, he wasn't going to bother trying to challenge it, either. The partners couldn't spend all that time with each other, celebrating holidays as family, and not profile their partners. Came with the territory of being observant and the best at what they did. "I'm taking this to the lab to dust for prints and run it through our systems," he said. "Can you please call the others, fill them in, and, assuming all agree, give me the heads-up to take the case, and get Dr. Schwann on it and into some kind of protective living situation?"

He was jumping ahead—solving a problem he didn't yet know they had, but Hud didn't call him on that, either.

Nodding, the tech expert picked up his phone. By the time Glen heard Hud's voice again, he was already at the elevator, heading downstairs to the state-of-the-art lab they'd moved into their office building the year before.

TIME PASSED. LORNA, sitting at a vacant conference table, going over case files, didn't care if one hour became two. She wasn't leaving unless she was kicked out.

Waiting had been her initial idea, even before he'd told her to stay put. She had no place else to be.

She'd made a plan of action, had a list of things she'd check in order of priority, as soon as she had access to Sierra's Web's lab and databases. And she was reevaluating every one of them. Again. Looking for any other ideas, potential tests to run, or rerun, to verify what she already knew. And find what she didn't know, too.

To think outside the box.

She'd had the room to herself for the entire length of her stay. Not even the sweet older woman who'd greeted her as she'd stepped off the elevator and then had shown her to Dr. Thomas's office had come in.

Because Glen Rivers Thomas had asked that she not be disturbed? Because he didn't want them exposed to her zealousness? Didn't trust her not to try to get information from them?

The science expert had made it definitively clear that Lorna would, at no time, be entrusted with access to their information and resources unaccompanied.

"The fingerprints on the note don't match anyone at Stellar Laboratories."

Lorna's breath caught, and she jumped as the voice came at her in the silence. She looked up to see Dr. Thomas just entering the open door of the room. He'd started talking before she'd had any idea he was approaching.

It took a second for the message his words had delivered to hit her. Confused, she frowned and said, "Excuse me?"

Instead of speaking, Glen put the note she'd given him on the table. Except that it was no longer just the piece of paper. It was encased in an evidence bag.

The science expert didn't sit, and Lorna didn't like looking up at him. She stood, looking at the paper, feeling as though she couldn't touch it in its new state.

It represented something that didn't belong to her.

A serious crime.

And then it hit her. "You've been in touch with Stellar? They weren't supposed to know I'm at Sierra's Web, or even in Phoenix. I just said I was taking personal leave."

Her mind was tumbling on a much more important aspect of the situation. Focusing on what her boss must be thinking was easier. The only logical reason someone who worked for a private lab would lie about visiting a different private lab would be for a job interview. Or potential permanent job change. She loved her job. Had every intention of returning to it.

"I had Savannah call," Dr. Thomas said then, still frowning. And seemingly unaware that she was bothered by what he'd done. "And told her specifically not to mention your name. Just that we were working on a case, that someone from the lab had been exposed to some evidence and we were trying to rule out known fingerprints so that we could narrow down our suspect pool."

The professionalism and logic behind his words knocked into her that time. She nodded. Impressed.

And no longer able to hold all fear at bay.

Though she tried. "You knew that Stellar requires all employees to be fingerprinted for just that purpose?" she asked.

An embarrassingly unintelligent question based on the information he'd already imparted.

Whether he didn't hear her, or was just choosing to ignore her ineptitude, Dr. Thomas didn't respond to her query. Instead, he said, "It didn't make sense, threatening you *after* you reported the incident. And right when you were departing on an extended leave. Too late to frighten you into silence. And you were already backing off—all the way out of the state for three months."

There'd been a niggle in the back of her mind as she'd headed to the airport. She'd chosen to believe the note had come from Leonard, the Stellar scientist who was possibly losing his grant. "I don't handle controversial research," she said softly, meeting the concerned look in the man's gray eyes.

He'd know that from the bio she'd sent him when she'd asked for the meeting.

"Which is why I asked who knows where you were going and why."

She shook her head. "There's no way Selena told anyone. Not even her fiancé. Everyone thinks that she needs counseling, professional help, because she can't let go of Simon's disappearance. So she quit mentioning anything about him to anyone. Instead, she talks to me."

"Where were you when you were talking to her? Did you meet her at a coffeehouse? A restaurant?"

Eyes wide, she shook her head again. Slowly. And admitted, "We've actually never met in person. We've done video calls—my insistence so I'd know for certain she was who I was talking to, and so she could see my face and look me up on the Stellar website. Because of everyone in her life having a negative reaction to her inability to let this go, she only calls me when she's alone. And I only talk to her in privacy." For the same reason, but she didn't bother telling Glen that part. He could deduce on his own that absolutely everyone in her life who knew of her quest thought she'd lost perspective where Simon Billingsley was concerned, but she wasn't outright handing him the information.

And didn't want to dwell on the warning note, either. Whoever wanted her to leave things alone would get their wish. She'd already left town.

"Did you talk to your partners?" she asked then. Getting access to Sierra's Web was what really mattered to her.

The damned note had been an afterthought in the event Leonard's case exploded into more than she expected it would. And during her time in Phoenix.

The scientist nodded, still clearly preoccupied with the note resting alone on its portion of the table. He continued to look toward it. As though the thing could shoot bullets or something.

"And?" she prompted, butterflies swarming through her stomach and up into her esophagus.

He nodded. "We'll take a look at the case with you. You're in as my assistant, answer to and work only with me. If we need help from other departments, or lab techs, those requests go only through me. Which is all protocol now when any one of us takes on a new hire. We've had too many close calls…"

His words dropped off as Dr. Thomas shook his head. Leaving Lorna with a strong desire to hear more. To know what kinds of challenges the firm had faced that made such stringent protocols commonplace. But she knew better than to ask.

And in the next second, the desire to do so waned.

She was in!

Glancing at her watch, seeing that it was still early enough in the day to get some answers, she asked, "Do you have time now to take me to the lab? To familiarize myself with equipment and set up so that when you're able to get started with the actual work, I'll be up to speed." She didn't want to be pushy, but…where Simon Billingsley was concerned, she had to…push.

Glen pulled out a chair across from where she'd been set up. "Have a seat," he said, nodding at the space she'd just vacated.

With her hand on the back of the chair, Lorna stood her ground. "Dr. Thomas…"

The wave of his hand stopped her words. "Glen, please. I'm not likely to respond to Dr. Thomas. And, officially it's Rivers Thomas," he said before continuing with, "We don't stand on formality here. When life and death are at stake, which, for us, is often the case, what matters is the facts, not the titles. Now, please sit."

She was wasting time.

He was the boss. Giving her a shot at fulfilling her life's quest.

Lorna sat.

Chapter Three

Her eyes were green. And focused sharply on him. Glen noticed, but the information didn't faze him. He noticed the fingers fiddling in the unruly dark hair, too. She could be impatient all she wanted—he, with input from his partners, had set a course.

And his sudden interest in a woman's hair wasn't going to detour him.

"The timing of this warning is too critical to ignore," he told her, pushing the clear evidence bag in her direction. He needed her to see it. Really see it. To feel the fear the note was meant to impart. Not to just let it lie there as an afterthought.

Before she could argue, he continued. "I don't know who knew what, but the fact that it was laying by your front door the morning you were flying here, while it could be coincidental, seems to clearly not be."

The shake of her head had him leaning in toward her as he held her gaze and said, "The sender of this missive needs you to know what he wants you to back off from, or his warning is moot." He told her what he and his partners had surmised. "The only thing going on in your life right now, by your own admission, is the Billingsley cold case."

He paused then, giving her a chance for feedback. She remained silent, her eyes watching him. He didn't detect fear, but he relaxed just a smidgen, knowing he had her attention.

"It's just smart to assume that someone besides Selena Billingsley knows you're here. And why you're here. Someone who was in Morrilton the night before last, or who had access to someone who was to get that note slid into your mail slot."

She shook her head. "I can't just give up, if that's what you're asking. I risked going to jail, I've lost credibility with my siblings and somewhat with my parents, too. I've spent all my free time on this. I'm not going to stop."

With a long stare, half hoping she'd look away and change her mind, Glen finally nodded. Sat back. "We aren't suggesting that you give up," he said then. "What we *are* going to require is that you agree to protective custody. Meaning you go nowhere without a bodyguard. And we want you to move to a location that is already secure and set for our people to best keep you safe."

Her brows rose. He saw her chest rise and fall with a long heavy breath. Did not allow an ounce of compassion or understanding to seep into his stern glance. He would not be responsible for another promising young woman's death.

Any death at all, actually, but...he'd failed Sierra.

If she was up there testing him, ready to forgive him if he'd learned his lesson, then fine. He'd pay acute attention to every nuance put in front of him. Seek out the ones that were hidden. Give every ounce of himself.

He'd help Lorna find her peace and make damn certain she was safe as she did so.

He'd show Sierra he was better than he'd been. That her death had not been in vain.

And, maybe, just maybe, somewhere in the process, he'd show himself, too.

"THIS POINT IS NONNEGOTIABLE." Glen Thomas didn't seem to have an emotion in his body as he delivered his final mandate.

She was between an immovable boulder and a mountainside. "I make good money," she said, "but I'm also still paying eight years' worth of school loans, and I've only been at my position for four years, so not long enough to amass a small fortune. The only way I was granted a three-month leave was by agreeing to do so without pay." She was giving him the facts. In the same manner he'd just dumped them on her. "I do keep my medical benefits, however," she assured him, as he seemed so bothered by her personal safety.

Afraid that Sierra's Web would have to bear the financial burden if something happened to her? Not that she blamed them. Business was business.

"I had to pay the three-month lease in advance—turns out Phoenix is not an easy place to find housing—and no matter how much you lay down the law, I simply don't have the money to pay a second rent, let alone hire a day's worth of twenty-four-hour protection, let alone ninety of them."

He hadn't budged. It was as though the man had noise cancelling headphones on. So, partially just to be contrary, but also willing, she said, "Unless you let me set up camp right here in this room." There was a small bathroom, she'd noticed it when she'd come in. And every laboratory that met even basic standards had some kind of shower. "I can afford a camping cot. And make do with the rest."

Of course, that would mean she'd have at least partial access to Sierra's Web's resources while everyone was gone at night.

Glen blinked, and seemed to change right before her eyes, returning to the man she'd seen in his office. One who was wholly human. Kind, even.

"I apologize," he said then. "I hadn't considered the financial ramifications."

She refrained from smarting off about him probably not needing to. Clearly, with his firm's success, money wasn't an issue in his world. But the words would only have been said in defense. Not because she meant them. Or even wanted them out there.

"I have a tendency to forget about the financial aspects of life as well," she said instead. Because those words were true. "Automatic bill pay is a godsend," she added with a chuckle. And then immediately sobered and said, "But I meant it when I said I was willing to stay here. All locked up and safe. I'd make sure that I had everything I needed for the night before the last person leaves…" Her mind raced forward, seeing possible need scenarios and ways to solve issues before they became problems. "I've spent many nights in my office in the lab at work," she added, another concrete fact that would strengthen her proposal.

When Glen shook his head, her heart sank. She was so close. Who could she ask to loan her the kind of money they'd be talking about for the three months? She'd have to explain why she needed it, which knocked her parents and siblings out all in one fell swoop.

Selena had access to it, but until she turned twenty-six, the money her father left her was in a trust, meaning she had to go through others—give just cause—to access it. Lorna would have to lie, and if anyone found out who Selena gave it to, or why…she could end up under family-induced psychological care.

The scientist sighed. Loudly. Sat forward. Didn't quite meet her eyes at first as he said, "There's no way you staying here would work. In the first place, the building is zoned for business and office space, not residential. But beyond that, there's no protection detail here at night, other than the security guard in the lobby of the building. And we can't leave you in our suite of offices alone, either. There's too much here that's confidential and as a temporary employee, you won't have access to any of it without a partner present."

Yes, she knew. He'd already explained…

Lorna's gaze dropped, as her mind dived deep, grasping for the solution she wasn't seeing. No way she could get this close and fail. Her and Selena aside, Simon Billingsley deserved better than that.

"I do have a solution that could work." Her gaze flew back up and over to her potential new boss. "It's highly outside the boundaries of conventional business…"

He paused, as though rethinking even admitting what he had come up with. Lorna didn't let herself blink. Wouldn't take the chance of losing his help.

"You could stay with me."

Not only did her gaze remain locked on him, it grew wide. Embarrassingly wide. She didn't speak. Was afraid she hadn't heard him right.

Had he just offered…if he thought…was he suggesting that she offer more than scientifically professional duties in exchange for gaining what she'd clearly shown meant the world to her?

Not that she hadn't found him attractive the second she'd first laid eyes on his photo years before…and there'd definitely been a spark when he'd first stood at his desk and welcomed her into his office earlier that day. Warmth when her hand had been engulfed by his.

But…surely…nothing about the man, his bio, the many articles on his work, his manner, or his closeness with his partners…nothing about Sierra's Web alluded to even the possibility of being asked for sex in exchange for work.

"After a case I had not long ago, I've hired a full-time protection detail for myself. Just until the case goes to trial. My home is in a gated community, and on gated property, too, with full, state-of-the-art security both inside and out.

There are two master suites, at opposite ends of the home, both with televisions and reclining chairs as well as beds, and other than any necessary moments in the kitchen, we wouldn't even see each other. The agreement with my partners was that I would have eyes on you all the time you're on the premises here, and since I spend most of my waking hours in the laboratory downstairs, you'd have ample time to work, and we'd have very little time at the house. You'd travel to and from work with me."

At some point, in the middle of his soliloquy, Lorna's mouth had fallen open. When she became aware of the fact, she still didn't close it.

"Really, other than the car rides back and forth, and a potential two or three minutes a day inside the house, it would be no different than if you were staying in a safe house and meeting me here each morning."

Relief flooded her so profusely, she almost teared up. She was shaking with excitement and had to clasp her hands together.

But she wouldn't let herself believe. She was on the cusp, but… "Your partners would need to know." She stated the obvious. "You think they're going to approve of such an arrangement?"

"As long as you sign whatever agreement Savannah draws up for me to offer you a room on my premises, providing you with grounds for compensation to the full extent of the law if I were to in any way misstep where you're concerned. She'd provide me with the same, along with whatever phrasing she finds necessary to protect mine and the firm's assets. I suspect they'll not only all agree, but will probably rib the hell out of me, too."

The last was offered with a bit of a grumble. Voicing some valid grouching, but a degree of affection, too.

Leaving Lorna wanting to know why they'd rib him. But no way was she asking.

"I'll sign away my home and all of my earthly possessions if that's what it takes," she said. And then added, "Is Savannah here? Is this something we can take care of right away?"

Glen stood without answering. Was at the door before he turned and said, "I'll be back shortly," and then disappeared.

Leaving Lorna with a curiously new sensation flowing through her. Hope, sure, but more than that. She felt lighter than she could ever remember feeling. Like if she stood up, her steps might float a bit.

Not wanting to test her theory, to find out that her steps were completely normal, she sat back. Looking outward.

Through the opened door and into the hallway.

And smiled.

If she sat there, and didn't move, she could almost convince herself that she'd just walked into a whole new world.

THE FINGERPRINTS ON the note were not in any database anywhere that Sierra's Web had ever accessed. Military, all branches of law enforcement, and justice systems. Even private companies like Stellar, whose employees had been required to provide fingerprints upon hiring and to sign an agreement that the organization had the right to turn the fingerprints over to authorities.

It was possible that the prints had been left on the note by someone who'd handled the paper, and that the perpetrator had worn gloves.

While Glen's bodyguard, Jamison, took Lorna Schwann to pack up the few things she'd unpacked the night before and turn over the key to the apartment she'd rented, Glen spent time in the lab, analyzing the ink in which the note had been written, the handwriting itself, the paper. Hud put someone on security cameras at the Little Rock airport, tracking Lorna's time there, looking to see if anyone appeared suspicious, was following her, maybe finding out where her flight was headed?

No one mentioned that they were expending a lot of valuable time and energy on a woman they'd just met, for a cold case that was not noticeably different from ones already waiting in the vault for them to have time to assimilate.

But from the inception of Sierra's Web, back when it was just a passionate goal shared by seven grieving college friends, they'd said that their mission was to listen to their instincts and give their all to wherever those instincts took them.

Because they'd all failed to do so, and to talk to each other about their concerns for Sierra.

Glen's instincts had been awoken by the initial email he'd received from Dr. Lorna Schwann of Stellar Laboratories. He'd been gripped by the amount of time and effort she'd put into finding even the most minute piece of a puzzle missing its box.

Meeting her, hearing firsthand about her experience with the case, had significantly strengthened the drive inside him to find out what happened to little Simon Billingsley. A two-year-old did not disappear without a trace.

And so, for the first time in Sierra's Web history, Glen had brought a case to the partners of his own accord. A loner who spent most of his waking hours in his lab, a man who didn't get out much except to purchase perishable items, and bring in the deliveries he ordered for everything else, he wasn't generally exposed to life in the world.

He was busy living life in his head, through critical thinking, aware that every second he spent doing anything else was another minute someone suffered from his lack of answers. He'd found purpose, peace, through his work with Sierra's Web. For the first time since he was born, he'd found home.

Not in the house the firm's earnings had allowed him to

buy with cash. But in the life they'd all built together. The day-to-day activity. The communication between them. The resources that allowed them to get results.

And in the smiles of those they'd helped.

He didn't say much as he drove—with Jamison in the passenger seat and Lorna in the back of Glen's full-size luxury sedan—to Glen's place. Mostly just responding to a direction or two from the tall, muscled dark-haired protector who was watching mirrors, traffic, and pedestrians outside the vehicle. Lorna didn't say anything at all.

Glen, for one, was glad the trip was short. Less than five miles, and yet his bodyguard insisted that he take a different route each time he drove it.

At home, Jamison retired for the night to the guest house on the other side of the pool in the half-acre walled-in backyard. Jethro, one of Sierra's Web's longest-standing employees, had insisted on taking night duty. He'd be watching the grounds, patrolling, until morning.

Glen explained the protocol to Lorna as he unlocked the door between house and garage, and stood back to let her precede him into the hallway that led to the kitchen. A chef's delight, he'd been told. He wasn't a chef.

Didn't stop him from trying out various concoctions his scientist mind came up with. Things that should coagulate, gel, or blend in interesting fashion. He ate them all.

Had yet to create something worth repeating.

With her satchel over her shoulder, Lorna stopped at the entrance to the large room. Turning her head as she seemed to take in every cranny and corner. "This is incredible," she said. "When you said we'd only be a minute or two in the kitchen, I was picturing some little galley thing with just a refrigerator, microwave, and sink." She glanced over her shoulder, looking at Glen. "Would it bother you if I took over the cooking? As my way of earning my keep, at least in small portion…"

He should have been surprised, but didn't feel particularly so as he asked, "You like to cook?"

"I actually have a cooking blog," she told him, moving around to peer more closely at the built-in double oven, running her palm lightly across the cooktop stove. "You have an Ankarsrum," she said, touching the dial on the base of his mixer.

"And Le Creuset pans," he said, feeling in unusually lightened spirits as he pointed to the hanging rack over the cooking island. He didn't bother to point out that he hadn't chosen any of his kitchen's furnishings. Mariah and Kelly—child life and psychology expert partners—had taken care of it for him while he'd been at work. "And you're more than welcome to prepare whatever you'd like," he told her. "Grocery delivery is once a week on Saturday night. The list is in this drawer." He pulled on the handle next to the double-doored refrigerator.

"You have groceries delivered on Saturday night?" The question, or rather the surprise filling it, brought him a notch or two back to reality.

"I wasn't exaggerating when I said I work all hours in a day. Pretty much every day," he admitted. If she was expecting weekend sightseeing, or availing herself of the hundreds of tourist attractions in Phoenix and her surrounding areas, she was going to be disappointed. But then, he'd already told her as much when he'd described her protective custody detail. "Saturday evening is when our building is cleaned." Under surveillance, of course.

Success most definitely had its shadowy side.

And if his revelation made him appear pathetic to the woman currently checking out the pull-down faucet on his kitchen sink, she didn't indicate as much.

Nor should it matter to him. The thought bringing him fully back to earth, Glen ended the kitchen admiration fest with an offer to show Lorna her living quarters, walking quickly through a tour of the house, pointing out the hallway that led to his suite, and then on to hers. He didn't wait to see her reaction to the guest suite that Kelly and Mariah had also furnished. He went and collected her baggage instead, so that he could grab something quick to eat—a frozen dinner for sure—and head to the office just outside his bedroom suite.

The place where he spent a lot of evenings.

And one in which he could immerse himself in his own reality.

Chapter Four

The room was lovely. Way nicer than the cheaply furnished studio apartment she'd rented closer to the Sierra's Web office. Glen had opened the door and then just left her there, saying he'd bring in her things from his car.

She'd have offered to help him, but he'd seemed uneasy as he'd rushed her from the kitchen through the house. Almost as though he was regretting having her there.

And that's when it hit her that maybe she really had gone off the deep end where the Billingsley case was concerned.

What was she doing? Staying in the home of a man she'd just met? Planning to take up valuable resources at a nationally renowned firm with a full docket of cases to tend to?

At the Sierra's Web offices, everything had seemed like a dream come true. For most of her life, she'd been driven to know what happened to that little boy who'd been stolen from under his mother's nose just a few miles from Lorna's house.

The need had carried her one step at a time to…what? A possible obsession that had her taking a leave from her job without pay and, in the space of a few hours, moving in with a man she'd just met?

Albeit one whose work she'd been following for years. And whose firm was known to protect innocent people from crimes.

The duo of thoughts settled the panic that had been rising inside her.

And a flash memory of the note she'd found on her floor transferred to an evidence bag on a conference table had her a little more willing to settle for a luxury suite rather than having a possible stalker find her and doing lord knew what with her.

She was just taking in the eclectic collection of books on the wall shelf when Glen returned with her two largest bags. Not saying a word as he left them just outside the door and headed back down the hall. Presumably to get the smaller two bags.

She'd jammed in as much as she could. Three months was a long time, and while she'd known she'd have to buy some household items when she got to town, she'd also been very aware of her budget.

Guilt and uneasiness flooded again.

She made great money. Another year and she'd be on the verge of being set for life.

And she was putting off even her own financial security to solve a twenty-three-year-old missing person case that the nation's top professionals had been unable to solve. And over which she had zero jurisdiction.

Was she really that egotistical? Thinking she would be able to do what others had not?

So much so that she'd given hope to a woman whose family needed her to let go and move on.

Selena.

It was one thing for Lorna to sacrifice her own life—putting any potential for relationships, for financial security, on hold—but what was she doing to Selena?

The woman's wedding was only a few months away. She should be dwelling in the happiest, most magical moments of her life. And Lorna was pulling her back.

Or, at the very least, giving her an excuse not to move forward.

Feeding the longing inside a heart that struggled to let go...

The sound of Glen's return—roller bags on the hallway's tiled floor—interrupted her thoughts, and Lorna moved quickly to get her big bags inside the room and out of his way.

Expecting him to drop the bags and disappear until morning—figuring she'd text him at some point to find out what time she had to be ready to head back to Sierra's Web—she was thrown off-balance again as he pushed the smaller bags fully into the room and then stood in the doorway behind them.

Using them like a shield, perhaps—though for whose benefit, hers or his, she wasn't sure—but...not leaving.

Not saying anything, either. Just standing there looking like he might.

Maybe trying to find a way to tell her not to bother to unpack? That he'd be rolling the bags back out because he'd changed his mind about letting her stay?

That idea completely wiped out any worry she'd had about obsession. First things first. She had to have a place to stay that would satisfy Sierra's Web's mandates for allowing her access to their resources.

She couldn't have come so far just to be cut off at the last minute.

"This room is wonderful," she blurted, needing to stop him from telling her it wasn't going to be loaned to her after all. "The diversity of the books alone could keep me occupied every night for a month." Overkill.

She'd be through them in two weeks, max.

But the words had drawn his attention away from wherever it had been as he glanced toward the shelves mounted to the wall perpendicular to the bed. "I'm not even sure what's there," he said, but didn't step past the bag barricade he'd created to find out.

"You don't know the books in your own home?" she asked him, having figured they were all his past reading material that he'd chosen to keep. Wide-eyed with surprise, she glanced at him.

And caught his gaze just as it brushed over her.

Shoving his hands in his pockets, he rocked forward on his feet and said, "Various guests have left them behind. Or Mariah and Kelly did. I don't get back here much."

Her mouth fell open again, but that time she quickly closed it. Taking in what he was telling her. And what he wasn't.

"Your partners Mariah and Kelly?" She asked the question that came first to mind.

He nodded.

Then came the second. "They've both stayed here?"

Had he had a thing with each of them? And they were all still such close friends? As a well of something akin to jealousy hit, she gave herself a mental shake. If he'd been having a thing with them, they wouldn't have been staying in the guest suite.

"They decorated my house," Glen told her, meeting her gaze then, with something akin to a challenge in his.

She smiled then. "Oh," she said. "You really do spend most of your hours in the lab."

"Yep."

And then something else hit. A point that was a whole lot more pertinent to her personal situation than Glen Thomas's possible affairs ever would be. "You mentioned various guests."

He shrugged. "We get out-of-town investigators, new hires who need time to find a place of their own, and those of my partners who don't live in Phoenix and need places to stay when we have in-person meetings. We own an apartment to house them, but when there's overflow…they come here."

Relief flooded her. She felt foolish for her doubts, and happy with a hint of inexplicable excitement too as she gave a big nod and said, "Then you really don't mind that I'm here. You're kind of used to this."

His frown, the easy shrug, as he said, "It's a no-brainer to me," was the clarification that allowed her to open her mind to all the possibilities the next three months could bring.

Case files. All day in the state-of-the-art lab to work on nothing but Simon's case. Spending time with the man she'd looked up to for so many years—even if it was mostly silent. As great as she was at what she did, there was so much more she could learn from him.

"Except one thing…" His words cut off the thoughts dancing through her.

"What's that?"

"I've never had anyone offer to cook."

Right. She'd overstepped. "I'm fine to make do," she rushed to tell him. "I love salads and tuna. I can be in and out in the couple of minutes you envisioned and described. That's what we agreed upon." She nodded again. Letting a bit of the happiness inside her slide out in a small, but very genuine smile.

Until she saw him frown.

What had she done that time?

"I was going to take you up on your offer," he told her. "I like to eat. And I'm not a cook."

It was her turn to frown. She ran a hand through the thick strands of textured hair all over her head. "But your kitchen…" And she stopped. "Kelly and Mariah, too?"

He nodded, but held her gaze.

She smiled.

And, in the matter of the kitchen, the relationship between them became personal.

BRIAN POWERS, ONE of Sierra's Web's top private investigators, had ties to law enforcement in Arkansas. Bonds formed during a missing child case the previous year. In that situation, they'd known the abductor—the imprisoned father of the child—but the man had been torturing his ex-wife by refusing to admit what he'd done with the little girl. Brian had been instrumental in solving the case.

And was on the ground in Little Rock first thing Tuesday morning. He'd made arrangements to secure arrival of the Billingsley evidence box at the Sierra's Web home office by Wednesday. Hud already had the electronic files.

Brian's main focus was on the threatening note that had been lying on Lorna's floor when she got up on Sunday.

Glen filled Lorna in on the details during the ride to work that morning, with occasional glances in the rearview mirror to make brief eye contact with her for confirmation that she appeared to be listening. Better that than travel in a silence that was only going to get more awkward. He'd carpooled to the office with short-term work guests dozens of times over the years. Couldn't remember a single prior instance of the personal discomfort he'd been experiencing since meeting the Little Rock scientist the day before.

He was a loner. An introvert. Not a social guy. His houseguests weren't there to visit him. They were lodging in an extra room. All he had to do was be cordial when paths crossed, like the morning drive. He'd mastered cordiality in the cradle.

So why was he suddenly suffering from an influx of inexplicable emotional upheaval?

As soon as the mental question presented itself to him, the answer followed. A two-point response. First, because the woman in his back seat *had* come specifically to see him. Making him point on a case for the first time in the more than a dozen years since Sierra's Web's inception.

And because she'd tapped into his reason for getting up every morning. Making up for his failure with Sierra. Every day he got up, every case he handled was driven by that failure. But Lorna had seemed to understand that without even meeting him.

She was equally driven.

But didn't yet have the answers that would let her move on to her life's work, as he and his partners had done.

Relaxing as the points hit home with him, Glen felt more like himself as he parked his car and then, after obtaining Jamison's go-ahead nod, exited the vehicle and took Lorna straight to the space he'd set up for her in the lab the day before. Other than when she was accessing equipment too large to move, she was to stay in her area.

And not involve herself in, or access evidence and files pertaining to, any of the other work going on in other work areas.

He stopped at denying her the right to speak with the other forensic experts who would be in the lab that week. Figuring to do so would not only be rude and perhaps border on cruelty, but also a little like telling a puppy that it couldn't roll and play with its newborn womb mates.

Instilling boundaries that went against nature set up both the bound and the bounder for certain failure.

Reminding himself that Dr. Schwann came with impeccable credentials, he left her to get acclimated with her temporary workspace and headed to the corner windowed lab office, where he spent most of his limited desk time. While his office upstairs in the suite had been mostly for show since the new lab opened on the premises, no one had suggested that he give it up.

Nor did he ever intend to offer.

Some things just…were. And he brought in enough money for the firm that it could afford to humor him with some extra square footage.

Besides, if, in the future, he were ever to have another

interview for a possible case selection, he'd need the space upstairs.

And enough was enough. Frustrated with his bizarre change in thought patterns over the previous twenty-four hours, Glen was in full focus mode as he read over the official Billingsley case files Hud had forwarded to him. Taking in what others had discovered, noted, thought, along with theories, suppositions, and unanswered questions. And then, with a second look, just focused on what he thought. What stood out to him, scientifically speaking. Asking himself where evidence could be found. Looking for the obvious as well as the obscure.

There was no way he was going to know the case like Lorna Schwann did. He'd had a couple of hours to familiarize himself with the details. She'd had a couple of decades.

But he felt much more in control of Sierra's Web's involvement going forward as he joined her in her lab space midmorning.

"We need a case plan," he told her, all business from the very first second. "Prioritizing our research and testing." While he was curious as to her perceptions of the lab, he didn't allow himself to dwell there long enough to pursue the thought.

She barely gave him a glance as she reached to the corner of the U-shaped counter space that denoted her personal portion of the lab—an area identical to the spaces occupied by the full-time scientists on staff, all arranged as a perimeter to the equipment they shared. Picking up a lined sheet, she handed it to him.

The list he'd just requested. Glancing over it, he saw nothing denoting the need for a change, recommendation, or an addition, either, and handed it back to her saying, "Get me a copy of that, please." And then, leaving not a single breath for anything other than case work to seep in, continued right on with, "I've gone over the evidence list." She'd mentioned a pen the day before, when he'd asked her what she most wanted to see from that same compilation. "The pen stood out to me, too."

Her gaze landed directly on him for the first time since he'd seen her waiting in the foyer by his front door, already in her lab coat, over a pair of tan pants—her satchel over her shoulder—a few minutes before he'd told her to be there.

He hadn't asked her how she'd slept. If the room was comfortable. Or, more to the point, if there was anything she needed. Extra blankets and towels, even.

Nor had he thanked her for the delicious chicken-and-broccoli casserole she'd left in the refrigerator for him for dinner.

Staring back at her, all those lacks seemed to stack up right in front of him. Thrown between them by her? By him?

Glen blinked against the lapse in his thoughts, and asked, "Why the pen? And what tests?" He had his own theories. Wanted to hear hers.

"The pen because it was found on the grass just behind the bench. And that was the last place Simon was known to be. He'd said he was looking for worms to go fishing."

The toddler had been two. Had had an age-appropriate plastic fishing pole with a one-foot string for line and a big plastic yellow hook—large enough not to be a choking hazard—on the end.

The pole had gone missing, along with the boy. And had never been found.

"And the first test, of course, would be fingerprints. With metal-organic framework crystals, we can coat the pen and lift latent fingerprint residue."

Glen didn't smile, but only because he consciously stopped himself. He'd already reached the same conclusion. If he'd been issuing some kind of capability or trust test, she'd just aced the third question in a row. First, being the list, second, choosing the pen as the most important evidence, and third…

"MOF just solved a case for us last week," he told her. And stopped talking with the details of the long string of robberies of the elderly on the tip of his tongue.

The words might have fallen out in the open regardless, except that Lorna had turned away to the state-of-the-art computer system on the end of her middle counter, with multiple screens mounted on the wall above it. With one click, the screens came on, showing him a series of slides, all on-screen together, depicting the same headshot in various stages of maturity.

"This is what my program does," she said, sounding less like the needy scientist she'd been since he met her and more like an A-list lecturer as she continued with, "I started perfecting the procedure during high school. I took pictures of Simon from birth until two years old—some had been pasted all around town when he went missing, and others I gathered from a birth announcement that had been in the local paper, and from a series of birth-to-two-twin photo shoots that a local photographer had used as publicity for her business. They were my first test case. But I wasn't convinced of the accuracy of my output. Then later, I added in other photos that Selena sent to me. Both of her and of Simon, from birth until two. From there I was able to measure the bones in their faces for each of their first twenty-four months down to minute accuracy. Then I calculated how their bones changed each month, in terms of growth rate and shape, and then compared them to average growth charts, finding that he changed at a slightly slower than average rate. While her growth had been slightly above average. From there, I calculated both of their future looks based on their bones' individual growth patterns and then factoring in their individual growing rates. And ran the program. Selena's had been such a close match even I couldn't believe it."

Glen stared at the screen. Following the science, the things she'd done, but hadn't said, the multiple complicated factoring computations she'd had to have run. "I assume you then ran the program on yourself?"

Leaning forward, she clicked, and the images on the screen changed. Same exact placement, different faces. His gaze tried to linger on each one of them. Beginning to end. His mind sent his focus to the last one.

It could have been taken of the scientist that very morning.

"Of course, if I was out to manipulate Sierra's Web into helping me, and designed this program to look like it works when it really doesn't, I could have just entered pictures of myself in those slots." She said aloud what his mind had already told him.

He shook his head. "To what end?"

For the first time that morning, her striking features softened. He caught a glimpse of the somewhat vulnerable-looking scientist he'd seen the day before.

A woman driven by desperation to set herself free from that which had been holding her captive since she was six years old.

Kelly, their psychiatry expert, could probably give him a rundown of all the ways Lorna had obviously been affected by what had happened when she was just starting school in her small, presumably safe, hometown. Knowing his close college buddy as well as he did, Glen knew Kelly would have a chat with Lorna when she figured she could make it look like no more than a friendly hello. Kelly never had been one to pass up the chance to help someone face past issues in an effort to keep them becoming future ones.

"I'm asking for use of all of Sierra's databases to run this age-progressed photo of Simon and I need you all to believe in it first. That would be the key reason for manipulation. And to that, I want to run photos of you through my program,"

Lorna said, as Glen stood there ruminating about his friend helping her. "I just need you to shoot me over the photos. Preferably with accurate dates, but if those aren't available, at least good estimations of your exact age…" She paused, clicked the screen back to the age progression of Simon Billingsley. "It makes a huge impact when someone can see themselves here," she told him. "You watch me load your photos and stand here with me while the results spit out."

Right. As much as he truly wanted to see the program at work firsthand, personally, with photos he knew for sure hadn't been manipulated in any way, it wasn't going to happen.

"I don't have any," he told her.

She frowned. "While the program works best with at least twenty-four photos over the first two years of life, I can run it with less. The results won't be as clear-cut, but you'll see that they're close enough for everyone to recognize you."

He shook his head. Shrugged. "I don't have any," he repeated. "But I'm sure some of my partners do, and those will do just as well for your purpose here. Convince one of us, you've got us all."

"A birth photo would be in your medical records," Lorna said softly. "And even just a preschool candid shot, or a picture on Santa's lap, would suffice. As long as I know your age at the time of shooting the photo."

Glen's gut tightened. A seminormal occurrence for him. His chest did, too. Which was not. "There is no birth record," he said then, telling her something not even his partners knew. "I was born on a couch in a one-bedroom apartment. And immediately moved out of state because my young mother feared that I'd be taken away from her. No preschool. No Santa photos."

Eventually, there'd been a birth certificate, but the details had been provided to the best of authorities' ability to do so. Not details he chose to share.

He was hot under the collar, literally, for having already said too much.

Lorna blinked. Swallowed hard enough that Glen noticed. And then, still looking him in the eye, she said, "Any of your partners will do. Preferably the one who can provide the photos the soonest." She turned back to her screen.

Without asking a single question.

And Glen, watching her, felt a rush of affection unlike anything he'd known before.

Chapter Five

Used to working in a field where things tended to move slowly—red tape as well as necessary time for test results to come back—Lorna was pleasantly shocked to have a text from Glen that photos were in the drop box assigned to her computer station less than an hour after the man had been standing behind her.

Feeling as though years of weight was being lifted from her shoulders almost overnight, she opened the file. Scrolled. And closed it again. Heading straight for Glen's office.

She understood that trust didn't come free. And that she was coming at them all out of left field. She was the one who'd insisted on having them vet her system with photos they'd provided and a grown person they all knew to verify the almost pinpoint accuracy of the results.

But to use her request—a sign of faith—to test her work ethics?

His office had walls of glass, allowing him to have eyes on the lab at all times. The door was also glass, but her knuckles were spared the hard raps she might have drummed on it, by the fact that the entrance was open.

"I can't use the photos," she said as she was heading through the doorway, not bothering to hide her disappointment. "The date on the newborn photo is only sixteen years ago. Makes this a minor child and that requires parental signature. No way I'm entering those into my system." She'd asked for partner photos. Period.

It was a test. Had to be. If Sierra's Web had wanted to use her program for a case, they'd need only to have asked. With all they were doing for her, that small quid pro quo would have been a given.

As they'd have known.

By the time she was standing directly in front of Glen's desk—staring down at the mathematical equations on the tablet on which he'd been using the stylus currently suspended in midair—she'd taken a breath. Hated the overemotional reaction she'd just exhibited.

"I apologize," she said, trying not to read too much into the way the scientist's mouth was hanging open in shock. "I'm used to being left to work alone. And having my requests respected. I also see things in black-and-white when it comes to protocol and legalities." It hit her then. Her juvenile delinquencies that she'd told him about. Cringing with embarrassment, she said, "Underaged determination aside." And then gave him the full truth. "Actually, *because* of that juvenile record. I learn from my mistakes. Had those misdemeanors followed me, they could have been used to discredit my work on future matters in court. If someone was desperate enough to go that far. When the record was expunged, I vowed to never, ever cross a legal line again."

Judging by the way Glen's gaze wasn't glued on her, she figured she had his full attention. She only wished it was for good cause.

But stood her ground. She still needed photos she could use.

When he seemed to get that she was done talking, he quietly said, "You have parental signature."

She did not. Most assuredly. Kept her mouth shut on the

words and shook her head. Then allowed herself to say, "They must have forgotten the form." But she still didn't feel right about using the photos.

"And a sixteen-year-old girl…why? Why not just one of you? This teenager should have a say in her photos being passed around like this." Frowning, she watched him. Surely Sierra's Web hadn't made it to the best of the best with such lax practices.

Disappointment flooded through her. She'd thought renowned scientist Glen Rivers Thomas was better than that.

Glen stood, pulled a chair from up against the glass sidewall, pushed a switch for the blinds to lower, and motioned for her to have a seat.

As silent as he was, she did so.

When he was back behind his desk, Glen said, "Hud sent you the file himself," as if that explained everything. The softened tone in his voice as he issued the words did far more to get her attention. And convince her that what she needed to know was coming.

Instead of feeling as though she was a mistrusted outsider somehow lacking in credentials and being put to the test, she suddenly felt as though she'd risen to a level above other employees. Made no sense, but there it was. The look in his eyes, the tone of his voice, had her waiting for whatever was to come.

Not so much with anticipation, but with a need to understand what was going on so she could do the job justice.

He picked up his phone. Typed on the screen.

As she waited, trying not to take in anything in the office that could be "other" case related, she kept her gaze on the man she'd wanted to meet for more than a decade. She'd seen photos of him dozens of times. Had watched a video of a lecture he'd given.

Would have figured, with the way she'd built him up in her

mind, the reality would be a bit of a downward spiral—hero coming to life and all. Instead, the creases around his eyes spoke to her of someone serious and dedicated. The way he weighed his words before speaking…a man who took responsibility for what he imparted. The way his eyes seemed to flood with things he wasn't saying. And the body…muscled shoulders and forearms, not the workout-defined kind, but the ones grown by constant activity and probably carrying evidence and heavy equipment…

His phone quacked a duck sound. Lorna jerked back in surprise.

With his gaze attuned to the screen in his hand, he didn't even seem to notice. But set the phone down and looked up at her.

"An official release, from both parents and teenager, will be in your drop box by the time you return to it. And I've been given permission to fill you in," Glen said.

She should thank him for providing what she'd needed and get to work. Her body seemed glued to the seat. He'd asked for and been granted the right to speak with her.

Whatever he had to say meant that much to him.

And she couldn't walk away.

HUD HADN'T CALLED Glen on the random, totally unlike him text he'd sent. Instead, his friend had given Glen exactly what he'd asked for. Without question.

While the fact made Glen nervous, it also gave him a curious sense of strength. Even though drawing strength from others wasn't his thing.

Never had been.

Everything he had to offer the world came strictly from within him.

Mentally noting the oddities to deal with later, he focused

on the woman seated on the other side of his desk. Expecting a wall of professionalism encasing her expressions.

And saw…more than that. Her green eyes almost seemed to glow with life. And yet emanated compassion, too. Something he didn't handle all that well. Coming at him or leaving from him. Pushing his glasses up on his nose, he set forth to bring back the business mode that defined his human interactions.

Except with his partners. And then it was friendship, family, from a distance.

"The photos are of Hudson's daughter," he said, coating himself in practicality. "Hope." So she'd know the girl's signature when she saw it.

"Her name's Hope?" The wide-open eyes, the light in them, were not cloaked for office talk.

Glen swallowed. Gave a slight nod, in acknowledgment of the question, then went on with his soliloquy. A business rundown was all. Not a conversation. Any emotion that accompanied his words was to remain inside him. "He didn't know about her until she went missing a couple of years ago, shortly before her fourteenth birthday." That was the critical part. He spit it out there and ignored the gasp coming from the opposite side of the desk. "The police believed their best shot at finding her was to do a deep dive on her computer. Hope's mother, Amanda, called Hud. She'd been keeping up on him and his career. Knew about Sierra's Web."

When Lorna's mouth fell open, silently, Glen figured he was home free without a lot of back-and-forth rendering of the situation. And forged right ahead, saying, "Amanda had sporadic photos. A lot of them, but with holes in age progression, too. Last night, Hud told both Amanda and Hope about your age progression program. Hope is the one who asked if it would be possible, if there was a way her dad could make a deal with you, to get you to run the program on her. And have it spit out renditions for every month of her life. So that her dad could know them all." He kept to the pertinent facts. "Your request this morning fit so perfectly into the plan, no one questioned getting the photos to you immediately." He'd made it through the potentially emotional portion of the meeting. Was able to bring it right back to the business at hand.

The permissions she'd requested on her way to gaining the database access she so badly wanted.

"So they found her? She's okay? And now her mom and dad are together?"

Glen stared at her silently. She wasn't on her way back to her station.

Nodding, holding his stare with one of her own, Lorna added, "You said that Hudson went home last night and told them both about my program. Home, and they were there." As though he hadn't understood the original question.

Needing to stand, to clear his space, Glen stayed seated right where he was. "Hudson and Amanda are married, yes. They…actually have a little one at home, too." Why on earth he'd added that he did not know.

"They had another baby?" The note of honest happiness in the woman's voice knocked every other thought out of Glen's mind for a second.

Until he caught himself smiling with her. Then, considering that shared expression, flushed with awkwardness. Unsure how to get himself out of the moment.

By wiping the smile off his face. Using his mouth was a way to do so, so Glen said, "Yes." The one word.

No more segues to the grin family.

She still wasn't leaving. Was she actually going to force him to dismiss her? Tell her she was free to go?

"So…why did Hudson abandon Amanda and Hope in the first place?" The question came with a frown, in a thoughtful, as opposed to openly accusatory, tone. As though Lorna was using the situation as a learning experience.

For that reason, Glen said, "He didn't know Amanda was pregnant. They were both living in a children's home. Had turned eighteen. He got a full-ride scholarship in Arkansas and, in spite of their romance, just left. When she found out about the baby, she didn't tell him."

"She didn't want to ruin his chance to make something of himself," Lorna said, nodding—and still frowning.

Glen wasn't so sure she was right. But he had no idea if she was wrong, either. Hud was happy. His family clearly adored him.

Which was all that mattered to Glen.

That and getting her out of his office before he did something else irresponsible.

Like smile at her again.

Just to see her smile back.

LORNA WAS FAR more excited than nervous when she hit Run on the test of the validity of her program using Hope Warner's photos. She knew the program worked.

And to be able to use her own invention to give something back to Sierra's Web in the process of possibly being on the cusp of finding Simon Billingsley was almost more rewarding than she could explain. *If* her access to databases turned up an identity for the photos she'd created from Simon's bone structure and growth patterns. There was always that. The big 'if.'

She stood in her space, waiting for the program's results, unable to wipe the smile off her face. Not that she needed to. With the six-foot-high walls of the individual workstations, she couldn't be seen. She just…didn't generally feel so…hopeful.

Hope giving her hope. She didn't miss the connotation.

Nor, a couple of hours later, did she completely lose that hope when, having been granted full access to all of Sierra's Web's databases, she hadn't found a match for Simon. There were a few more sources to run the current age progression through. And from there, she'd start going backward. In case Simon's likeness had been entered at an earlier age.

After his two-year-old disappearance.

But the light inside her was dimming some. For years, she'd convinced herself if she could just run her likeness of Simon through databases, she'd find him.

Had even pictured herself telling Selena that she'd be able to ask her twin to attend her wedding. And to imagine being able to validate to the woman's family that Selena had been right to continue to hold on to Simon's existence in her heart and mind. To not give up.

While images flew across her screen, and she looked for a match, Lorna wore the headphones she had on sometimes at Stellar, listening to the classical music that helped her focus and going over the official case files that had arrived that morning. Growing her to-do list. And rearranging some priorities, too.

Most of the lab's stations had filled up, but Glen's ship ran tight. From what Lorna had noticed, going to and from Glen's office, the scientists were all as focused as Lorna was. She had no idea how many cases Sierra's Web currently had, but by the concentration she saw around her, she got a better grasp of the fact that many of the jobs they were doing held lives in the balance.

She started to feel like a fraud, temporarily hanging out among them. Until a loud cough behind her had her jumping in reaction and reaching for her headphones at the same time. She turned to see a woman, fortyish or so, in jeans and a long-sleeved T-shirt and tennis shoes, standing behind her. "I'm Augusta, I'm on Hudson's team," the woman said, standing at the outside edge of Lorna's space. "I'm working on a series of cold cases for a sheriff's office in North Dakota. Hud was telling us about your program, and I was wondering if you'd mind running some photos through it for me."

Another bolt of excitement shot through Lorna as she smiled and took the photos, ran the program with them, and sent the results. She felt a little giddy inside at the idea that her work held significance for experts with as much or more experience than she had. A sign to her that, no matter how many failures she had in the next weeks looking for Simon, no matter how many setbacks, doubts, or odd, sometimes not quite welcoming nuances coming at her from her temporary boss, she was where she needed to be.

She'd fought for the chance to finally work Simon's case full-time. To have full access to it. She was in her current circumstance because of a lifetime of hard work. And determination.

It was up to her to make the most of it.

Not to doubt her own legitimacy, her right to be there. Or the drive that had alienated her from so many in her life. If she was obsessed with the Billingsley case, so be it. She was also giving her all to end the obsession.

Not caving beneath the endless weight of it. Or giving up.

She was following her own instincts. Choosing how to live her life, not letting others do it for her. The mental process continued as she waited. And lingered as others packed up for the day and the likenesses of Simon were still running through scheduled databases.

Determining that she'd let it run all night, she stepped out of her area far enough to see if Glen was showing any signs of calling it a night, not wanting to hold him up…and maybe wanting to hear anything he had to say about the Billingsley case. His day.

Or anything else.

He wasn't at his desk. Returning to her space, she glanced toward the screen, toward the flashing images. Except…they weren't flashing.

Heart pounding, she walked slowly toward the screen. Intensely focused. Hardly daring to believe. The image wasn't current. She hadn't found an adult Simon.

But…she had a hit. An image from a missing person case. Dated twenty-one years before. A four-year-old named Billy. Shaking, she stared at the image, at the information on the photo. Hardly daring to take it in, to process scientifically, for fear that she'd somehow prove her program wrong.

Based on the data below the photo on the poster, Billy had been reported missing from Ocean Springs, Mississippi on July 4.

A holiday often spent in parks. Could he have lost his way in another park?

The question shot through her disbelief as she stared, knowing that she was looking at Simon Billingsley.

Tears sprang to her eyes. She had to get to work. Had so much to do. Needed police reports, parents' names. An evidence box containing something with Simon's DNA on it.

And hopefully something that would link the two disappearances.

The two crimes.

No way a little boy just wandered off twice, never to be seen again. It wasn't like he'd been old enough, either time, to hop on a train and take himself somewhere safe.

To provide for himself.

So many questions lingered just out of reach as she initially processed what she was seeing. Answers to be sought.

"Lorna?" She heard Glen's voice before he appeared in the doorway. Heart leaping again at the sound. He had to see what she'd found…

She turned, holding back the urge to grab his arm and

pull him forward, and stilled as she saw him, glasses in one hand, his hand wiping over his face with the other, just as he reached her.

The frown he was wearing was new to her. Not confusion, or discomfort.

Way more than that.

Her stomach flip-flopped, not in a good way. "What's wrong?"

He shook his head, his gaze seeming to ooze concern as he looked at her. And stood there saying nothing.

Beginning to realize that Glen seemed to be silent a lot when he had things to say, she took a step toward him. Reached out a hand and grabbed his arm, just as she'd told herself not to do. Not sure if she was initiating the contact for him or for herself.

He'd come to her. Did that mean his distress had something to do with her?

Or was he just coming to let her know about something holding him up because he was her ride home?

"What's wrong?" she asked again, giving his wrist a squeeze.

To her shock, he slid his upward until his fingers had clasped around hers. "There's been a fire," he said then, holding steady on her gaze. As though holding her up with his look.

She didn't get it. Frowned. "A fire?" And it hit her. "The Billingsley case file has been destroyed?" It was en route. Due to arrive in the morning.

The shake of his head only confused her more. "Your house?" she guessed then, needing to help him find a way to communicate whatever had him choked up. For him more than her, at that point. He was clearly upset. She couldn't help until she knew what she was helping with.

His headshake made her stomach clench that time. She

saw his lips move. Heard words. "Yours." But didn't fully comprehend.

The apartment she'd rented?

"Brian Powers just called."

The agent on the ground in Morrilton?

Yours. His word hit again.

Her mouth fell open.

And all Lorna could think about was the hand she was holding on to like it was her lifeline.

Chapter Six

Glen had Lorna collect her things and took her to the lab's emergency exit, where Jamison was already waiting for them. He hadn't given her time to shut down anything. Just grab and go. He had to get her out of there until they knew more.

Jamison and another local Sierra's Web bodyguard, McKenna Hamilton, flanked them on both sides as they made a beeline to the waiting limousine and ushered them both into the back seat before jumping in front and heading out immediately. Jamison at the wheel.

McKenna was an expert at seeing in a three-hundred-sixty-degree circle and detecting tails. She'd grown up in the area, and split her time between Phoenix and Shelter Valley, a small mountain town forty-five minutes outside the city. Glen wanted to tell Lorna about the hunted millionaire, Joe Hamilton, that McKenna had protected a couple of years before, but sat silently beside her. Needing to be more than he was.

Needing answers even more.

Other than asking if anything survived the fire, she hadn't said a word. No questions. And no balking at orders, either.

The response he'd had to give her was wholly insufficient. He didn't know. Brian had just arrived on scene as the fire trucks pulled up. He'd call when he knew more.

Glen had let go of Lorna's hand when she bent to get in the car ahead of him.

It lay on the seat between them.

He wanted to pick it up again. To hold on. A sensation so out of the realm of his reality that he made certain he didn't do it.

The last thing the gifted scientist needed was to have the man she'd trusted enough to come to him for help wigging out on her.

He could only imagine the horror she must be going through. Imagining the loss of everything she owned.

And while he cared about her pain, sympathized with her loss, his bigger concern at the moment was why. If the fire was due to faulty wiring, something that could have happened, catching her unaware while she lay in her bed asleep at night, then the blaze taking place while she was out of town could be considered a good thing.

But there was the threatening note, first, at her door and then two days later, after she'd left town—possibly showing someone that she was not backing off as advised—a fire? That was too much of a coincidence for Glen to believe.

He'd like to be wrong. Left room for the possibility.

But he'd learned young to leave nothing to faith.

Brian and Hud had agreed that the timing was highly questionable. The investigator vowed not to leave the property until he was certain there was no more evidence to be found.

One way or the other.

Two guards would be patrolling outside Glen's house that night, with Jamison in the guesthouse. McKenna would return with the limo to pick them up in the morning.

Overkill, maybe. Glen's call. On his dollar—not that the firm would blink if it wasn't, but he was insisting. He had more money than he was ever going to need. And Lorna had somehow become a reminder of Sierra in his mind.

He could not allow any chances that he'd make the same mistakes twice.

His issue, his wallet. And no need for anyone else to know that.

Lifting the hand that was itching to hold hers, Glen indicated the limo, them in the back seat, the bodyguards, and said, "This could be overkill." His attempt at offering reassurance.

Lips tight, Lorna nodded.

He respected her silence. Understood it. Should be welcoming it. He would be reacting the same way were he the one who'd just been told his house was on fire.

So why was her lack of communication not sitting well with him?

And why was he focusing on feelings rather than problem-solving?

"I just had an inspection done of both the electric and the plumbing." Lorna's words pulled him back on track. "The house is old, and I didn't have it done when I bought the place."

Was she telling him that she'd known about an issue? And hadn't yet had it fixed? "And?"

"Everything came back as either good or excellent condition. It had been updated when the previous owner purchased it ten years ago."

Not a good piece of information at the moment. He translated it. She was telling him she didn't think his protective measures were overkill.

That she was worried.

Glen covered her hand with his again.

SHAKING INSIDE, LORNA concentrated on the touch of Glen's hand atop hers for the remainder of the meandering drive back to his place. Knowing that the multiple turns meant that McKenna and Jamison were making sure they weren't being followed.

They weren't moving fast enough to be escaping a follower.

Once inside, standing on her own, she started to panic. Her home! All her possessions! She didn't have insurance on either of them. Had opted not to renew until her school loans were paid off. Had figured the risks were minimal, and the financial benefit certain.

Her folks had given her the down payment on the old house in a sweet little neighborhood as a graduation gift. She'd used the savings she'd been building, investing conservatively, since her first job at sixteen—and all through college—to pay the rest. She'd gotten the place at a steal. It needed paint. Some new flooring. The rooms were tiny, and it only had one small bathroom, but she'd fallen in love with it on sight.

She had no insurance…

Had to do something. Couldn't just sit and wait. Anxiety would weaken her. Aware that Glen was watching her, she moved further into the house and toward the kitchen. The last thing she wanted to think about was putting anything in her stomach, but she could cook.

Preparing things she liked made her feel good. And productive, too. Chopping, browning, mixing were therapeutic. Glen had told her she was free to use everything she found in the kitchen with the caveat that she share her final results with him. He'd probably had no idea that she'd be digging into every cupboard in the kitchen, every shelf on both the refrigerator and freezer, pulling out random findings as she went, forming a mental list of dishes she'd make.

And he certainly wouldn't be expecting the cocktail meatballs made with ground beef and onion and grape jelly. The veggie tray. Seasoned homemade croutons with a Parmesanbased warm dipping sauce. And potato wedges. She had all four started within minutes of entering the kitchen.

Comfort food. Every bit of it.

Reaching for a chopping knife, she thought of the set her sister—who was eighteen years older than her—had sent as a housewarming gift. And sliced a bit of a finger, forcing her to throw out the top piece of carrot and waste time with her finger under water.

Meatballs were simmering in jelly and crushed cereal, and a quickly thrown together cocktail sauce—consisting of ketchup, lemon juice, Worcestershire sauce, and spices—was on the stove, bread cubes were in the air fryer, potato wedges in the oven, and she was back to slicing veggies—making heart shapes in the tops of radishes—when Glen appeared in the entryway from the dining room.

A quick glance showed her creased brows behind his glasses, and a grim shape to his mouth, and she returned her attention immediately to the mostly full tray awaiting the bits of red-and-white color beneath her knife.

Even though she knew bad news didn't get better by putting it off, it didn't generally get worse, either.

"You lost most of your garage. Your car." He started in with facts by the time his foot hit the kitchen floor. "But the house is intact. There will likely be some smoke damage. A neighbor was out, saw the smoke coming from the back of the building before the first flame sparked up high, and called the fire department."

"Mr. Waverly takes his dog out every afternoon when he gets home from work." She said the words aloud as they popped into her head. As she might have done at home, where she commonly talked aloud.

And she stopped cutting. Her hands were shaking, and she didn't need any more blood.

"I have car insurance," she blurted then, just standing

there at the counter, knife in hand, looking down at the celery, carrots, and zucchini already on the tray. Wishing Glen had had cucumber instead.

She had car insurance. Whether or not it covered damage by fire, she had no idea. But had time to find out. She didn't need her car right then.

What she needed was to know…

"It was arson, Lorna."

The fact that Glen Thomas was on the same wavelength as her didn't come as a surprise. Nor did his pronouncement.

She'd figured. As had he—hence the elevated protection detail.

She'd made enough veggies to feed them all. Jamison. The two on patrol outside. Her and Glen. McKenna, too, had she stayed.

Aware of the smells emanating from the oven, the sound of the air fryer, the pan of dipping sauce on the back burner, she felt like she needed to be home. In her own house. Alone. Where no one would see.

Except that, from what Glen said, the place would be too filled with smoke for her to stay there.

There'd be fire damage to clean up. She'd lost everything in the garage.

She'd lost the garage.

And it wasn't any of it that was currently overwhelming her.

Putting the knife down, she turned, faced the man she'd spent years wanting to impress. "I apologize for using so many of your groceries. And you don't even have dinner here. Just hors d'oeuvres."

He gave the room a cursory glance. "Brian found mousetraps set all around the perimeter of the house. He noticed the same darkened area on all of them. They'd been sprayed with what the fire marshal suspects is insect repellent. Probably containing picaridin and/or alcohol. We'll know more when the evidence gets to the lab. I'm assuming you don't keep mousetraps out?"

Chin tight, she said, "Actually, I do. But only by the cellar entrance. And I do not spray them with anything. They're the catch and release kind." She named the brand.

Glen's frown increased, and he pulled out his phone. Typed on the screen as he said, "Someone wanting to get away with arson would use the devices you bought, figuring they'd be burned up enough in the fire—assuming all of them had had a chance to light and burn—to destroy the spray."

She leaned back against the counter. "Someone that astute would wear gloves."

He glanced up from his phone, met her gaze briefly, and nodded.

Who was to say that she hadn't sprayed the insect repellent in those traps? Hoping to keep the bugs away from her house as well.

"I had insect repellent in the garage," she told him. Named the brand.

And couldn't look away when his gaze shot to hers.

Their chances of proving who'd set fire to her house had just lessened alarmingly.

GLEN SHOT TEXTS OFF, his mind spinning. He needed to be in the lab. With the traps in hand. They didn't know what they didn't know until he could test for particular insecticides. Prayed there would be some partial fingerprint that didn't belong to Lorna. And had to ask, "What's the insurance payout on your home?"

She nodded. As though she'd been expecting the query. "I let the policy lapse until I pay off the school loans. I'm on a fast track to get that done. I own the home free and clear."

No mortgage to insure. All risk had been on her.

While the news spelled potential disaster for her, it also negated a benefit to her to set fire to her own home.

Pushing his glasses up on his nose, he looked at her. "No one is going to think you did it. Your alibi is golden."

"I could have hired it out." Her tone was professional. Businesslike. He commended her silently. "But why, when I have nothing to gain and everything to lose?"

A conclusion he'd already reached. Just for the case file that would need to rule out any potential suspects. "If what I suspect proves true, we've just learned something about our arsonist," he told her. "He used your traps, your repellent, to point any possibly surviving evidence right at you, which means he's one who assesses all angles. Who plans ahead for possible consequences."

"Who was at my house, in my garage…" she added, her voice dropping off as she paled.

Glen forced himself to stick to the puzzle before him. "According to neighbors, the fire was set when most in the neighborhood were still at work and at school."

"Mr. Waverly doesn't usually get home until five," she said, letting Glen know she was on his train of thought with him.

"The arsonist cased the neighborhood." Glen stated the obvious conclusion aloud. Thinking aloud. "This was done methodically. Not some emotional lashing out."

"If not for Mr. Waverly…or whatever neighbor was home unexpectedly…he'd have succeeded."

He could see the fear in her eyes. The tension in her facial muscles, the set of her shoulders. Lost track of putting the pieces together long enough to say, "Neighbors have turned over what security camera footage they have." Then had to add what she'd soon know. "But there isn't much of it."

"I'm assuming he'd have made himself aware of place-ment, in any case. If he went so far as to break into my garage, to scope out my home, he'd most certainly have known to watch for cameras."

The arsonist was careful. Controlled.

And determined.

Lorna's sigh was loud enough to draw his gaze. He saw the fear flash in her eyes again as she asked, "Why?"

The answer was obvious to him. He'd given it to Hud before Hud had had a chance to tell him that he and Brian had already reached the same conclusion.

"To get you to go home."

She shook her head, her gaze hardening to determination. "But…"

Glen cut her off. "When you came here, your intention was to work the case alone, just to use our resources. Not to pay for our services as well. Correct?"

She held his gaze as she nodded slowly. Her eyes widening. "He wants me to back off the case, just like you said."

It was one time Glen didn't like being right. "At this point, that's the only conclusion any of us are drawing. Brian is still talking to others at Stellar, in the neighborhood, where you shop and bank, to see if anyone saw anything, or knows anything, that might make you a target for something of which you're unaware. But so far, as you said, you lead a quiet life, spending most of your waking hours working."

She blinked, as her brow rose, a flash of surprise before she said, "I didn't know…my entire life is being…" Her words dropped off as she nodded.

"Your parents live in Mississippi, correct?"

She nodded again.

"And you have two much older siblings. Also out of state."

Another affirmative. Along with a deeply indrawn breath.

He was interrogating her. Doing his job. For her sake. No reason for a sudden surge in his oxytocin levels. The hormone that stimulated rises in empathy. Yet, he said, "I'm sorry, I have to ask."

Brows raised again, this time seeming surprised, she said, "It's okay. You're doing so much…and I'm here using up all your groceries, and…"

Glen held up his hand to cut her off. "First, I'm glad you're here." And instantly froze. *Too much.*

Awkward.

Then she smiled, said, "I'm glad I'm here, too."

And for a second there, he forgot what he'd been about to ask next.

Chapter Seven

Lorna had to keep busy, keep a part of her mind occupied with mundane action, or anxiety was going to get her. She'd been fighting that devil since the day Simon Billingsley had gone missing. She hadn't yet been able to rid herself of it. But she'd learned how to control it.

Breaking eye contact with Glen, she moved to the stove, stirred the meatballs. And heard him ask, "Did you tell anyone that you were planning to work on the Billingsley case while you were gone?"

She shook her head.

"Selena knows. Did you tell her you planned to work the case alone?"

She spun to look at him. If they were going to haul Selena Billingsley in for questioning, make a circus out of the young woman's life…the idea was just…ludicrous. "Selena would never try to stop me from working on this case. And besides, what does it matter if I'm working the case alone or not?" She went back to stirring. The dipping sauce that time.

"It might not. We're trying to narrow down suspects. And to assess other aspects of this as well. Does someone know for sure you took a leave to work on the Billingsley case? And if so, how? Do they know you're here? And again, how? Is Sierra's Web at risk?"

She turned so fast at that last question, she dropped the spoon on Glen's spotless tile floor. Eyes wide, she was about to…she didn't know what…when he held up a hand.

Something she was getting used to. Him using a hand to get her to stop talking. It should bother her.

Except that he didn't seem to do it with a sense of taking control. Or cutting her off. More like, out of nervousness.

And a need to stay on task.

The uneasy expression in his eyes, the flash of relief when she fell silent, told her so.

"The firm is currently handling half a dozen cases that put us at equal or greater risk. Every one of us has had our lives threatened, at one time or another. We're trained. And we have precautions in place. And the best way to make sure that no one gets hurt is to be constantly vigilant. Unless you're about to tell me that you're choosing to abandon the Billingsley case to remove yourself from danger, then let's move on."

She nodded. Bent to pick up the spoon. And used the edge of the lab coat she still had on to wipe the floor. Didn't bother to tell him she wasn't quitting. No way she'd give in to threats and fear. The devil won if she did that.

Glen seemed to already know what she was thinking.

Which sent a wave of warmth through her.

Holding on to it, she discovered focus finding its way out of shock. "There's a piece of good news in all of this," she said, finally seeing what he and his team had probably figured from the note she'd been so quick to deny had anything to do with the case. "Someone wants me to stop looking for Simon. Which means there are answers to be found. Someone either knows what happened to him, or is aware that someone else knows."

Lots of *someones* in there.

As he nodded, she had a flash of him in a recorded video she'd seen years ago. More clarity. Her mind working even while her emotions were somewhat scrambled. "I just remembered something." She shared the part he'd want. "Several years ago, while I was working on my doctorate, an instructor asked why I wanted to go into forensic science, and I told her about Simon's case. She suggested I watch a video you'd made on trace evidence chemistry. Said that if anyone could help me figure out what happened to him, you could. She sat and watched the video with me and became my unofficial Simon sounding board while I was in the program. When I graduated, I told her that I hoped to meet you one day…" Her voice trailed off as she felt herself slipping back into personal waters.

A swim he clearly was not the least bit interested in taking. Nor should she be.

Eyes narrowed, he said, "Name?"

"Eva Pettigrew." She couldn't imagine the woman would turn her on to the firm of experts, and then warn her off the case, but if someone had talked to Eva about her, maybe… "Brian can probably still find her in the lab at the university in Little Rock." She named the school and rattled off the address of the lab, too. Watching as Glen typed on his phone.

Shaking again, but more from excitement than fear.

After twenty-three years, "Someone" had finally shown a card in his hand. He existed. Had something he didn't want her to find. Knew she was not going to give up looking for Simon. He feared her. He was out to stop her work.

And Lorna finally had another someone not only supporting her need to find closure for Simon, but who had the resources and willingness to help her make it happen.

The fact that her long-term hero was turning out to be far more than she'd ever imagined he could be, was a small detail better left untouched.

SHE'D WATCHED HIS VIDEO. Had been wanting to meet him for years. Glen heard the rest of what Lorna had said. His mind was on the case.

With a direct attack against her, it couldn't not be.

But as his texts with Hud turned into a couple of phone calls, taken outside on the patio as they discussed an update from Brian and agreed on a plan going forward, Lorna's admission continued to linger.

So much so that, when he hung up, instead of heading straight to his suite—to continue to study, assess, and ask questions that could lead to an avenue that held answers—he headed back out to the kitchen. Justifying the action by the very real fact that Lorna needed the update as well.

He could have called her.

The scents wafting through the house were too much temptation to resist, was what he told himself.

He was also smart enough to acknowledge that the excuse didn't hold weight.

She'd removed her lab coat. Was standing in tan pants that delineated every lovely curve, hips leading to thighs that slimmed with every inch his gaze lowered. "Something smells delicious," he said, when he started to salivate.

Clearly, he needed to eat.

She turned at the sound of his voice and her gaze softened. He liked that it did. And focused on the plate she was filling.

"It's not really dinner food." She repeated a rendition of what she'd said earlier. "But there's enough of it here to fill a household of people so I'm using it as such. You certainly don't have to."

He grabbed a plate from the cupboard. "I've never been a traditional eater," he told her. "Breakfast at dinnertime, big lunch no dinner, forgetting to eat…whatever fits the day. What is all this?"

The veggies and potato wedges, he got. Listened with honest interest as she described the other two recipes. Filled his plate with enough of all four to last him a day or two, and then, without taking time to get through a conscious decision process, moved to the table in the dining room, set his plate down, and pulled out a chair.

It was normal for people to eat at tables. She didn't need to know that the only times in the table's few years of life that it had actually held food and had people seated around it had been the few times he'd had to take his turn hosting Sierra's Web holiday meals. Which he'd had catered.

She'd poured herself some iced tea. Had the glass and her plate in hand, heading toward the kitchen's exit, and he said, "Have a seat," before she had a chance to pass by him on the way to her room.

Breaking one of his own stipulations laid down just the afternoon before.

When she hesitated, he said, "We've got business to discuss."

She sat. He realized he hadn't brought a drink in with him. The wet bar in his suite, complete with a half-sized refrigerator, supplied all the beverages he ever needed at home.

He'd had the kitchen refrigerator restocked the day before, as soon as he'd known that Lorna would be staying with him. Adding to his normal supply of fresh vegetables, milk for cereal, bread, and freezer meals.

Excusing himself, he headed into his suite for his nightly very watered down shot of high-end scotch. He made it tall. With ice.

And didn't explain himself as he sat back down. Just seemed cleaner that way.

It took him a few bites into the odd meal to stop eating long enough to speak. "This is really good," he told her. "I have no idea what you seasoned the meatballs with, or the potatoes, the bread or the dipping sauce, either, but I'm suddenly very glad I spent all the money I did ordering a chef's online spice selection for the complete kitchen."

She pursed her lips. Maybe stopping a smile. He couldn't

tell. "I figured Kelly and Mariah stocked them," she said, her tone sounding like a scientist giving an opinion on a professional matter.

And right, he'd have been better to just leave it alone.

To that end, "I've spoken with Hud a couple of times." Not dinner conversation, but if she was as much like him as he was beginning to expect, she'd be used to eating while she worked on difficult matters. "The interior garage wall, connected to your home, was made out of cinder block, not two-by-fours. It didn't burn. The house itself is secure. Brian's been inside, and because the fire was extinguished before the flames reached the next mousetrap, your living space is surprisingly unscathed. His opinion, a professional cleaning, including air, all vents, windows, and carpeting, and you should be good to go."

She sucked in her lower lip. Nodded. And then took a bite of the meatball on her fork. Showing him nothing of what she was thinking. Feeling.

It was generally the way his relationships went. The way he needed them to go, or he bugged out quick.

Her reticence bothered him. He wanted more.

And if she gave it? What then?

He'd be pushed right back into his cocoon. Had happened the couple of other times he'd attempted to venture out. Being emotionally intimate was just plain foreign to him.

Which was why he'd failed Sierra.

And why he was compelled to sit with Lorna? To know what she was feeling? To be more for her?

Made sense to him, scientifically.

And his meal was almost gone. He took a bite. Swallowed. Looked up to see her watching him. And said, "I need to know where you are with all of this. If you're okay with pressing forward. Not just scientifically, but emotionally." He didn't want her to leave, though he should do. But he couldn't let her stay without making her fully aware of what she appeared to be walking into. "Hud, Brian, and I agree that it's looking more and more like you've opened a hornet's nest." He stopped when her eyes widened, and he saw a twitch in her chin. She put down her fork.

He waited for her to excuse herself to go pack. She studied him for several seconds, then said, "I have no intention of walking this back. I understand if you all have to do so. I have no money to pay for your services. Not now. Though I'm perfectly fine with going on a payment plan, even if it takes me half my life to get it paid off."

He held up a hand. Shook his head. She was on a completely wrong track. He had to give her the rest. "Sierra's Web, as a firm, has taken the case," he told her, his gaze steady and firm on that one. "We made the official arrangements when we took custody of the box of evidence and the case files. I'm sorry if I didn't explain that well enough." He didn't mention that it was the first case he'd ever personally recommended to the firm. Or that he suspected that was the reason they'd taken charge of it so quickly.

She shrugged. Grinned kind of sheepishly and said, "It's also highly possible that I'm far too sensitive where Simon's disappearance is concerned. I tend to expect people to brush me off."

He wouldn't dismiss her. "We expect whoever is threatening you to escalate. We have to assume that he knows you're here. If not from anything you said, then from Brian's presence in town. His request for the case."

She paled again. "You think someone on the police force is behind this? Trying to silence me?"

He hadn't gone there, yet. It was possible Hud or Brian had. His mind focused on the provable evidence part.

He leaned in. Out of his league, and feeling fully in it, too.

"Do you have reason to believe there might be?" he asked. "Something you found? Or suspected?"

She shook her head. But didn't look wholly convinced. "It just kind of always made sense to me, you know? How else did a toddler just disappear on his own, without leaving a trace? The police were called in almost immediately. And never found a hint of evidence that led to anything. That just always seemed odd to me."

He nodded. "Yet from the list of evidence we've seen, it's clear they turned every stone looking for him. Brian says the case file is detailed. Showing a thorough investigation. Every *t* crossed, every *i* dotted. And no questions left unasked. Hud agreed."

She nodded. He couldn't tell if she was disappointed or just not fazed by what he'd said. "You saw the file today, what did you think?" he asked her.

With a startled expression, she said, "I agree with the assessment. But if someone knew something, they'd know how to make sure no evidence turned up, right? As well as they'd know that the investigation had to be all hands on board. The FBI eventually took over the case. If there'd been shoddy police work, it would have come back on Morrilton police. And if someone was aware what was happening, he'd have known that a two-year-old disappearing without a trace would most definitely involve the FBI at some point."

She traced as he did. From detail to detail. Filled with a purpose he hadn't realized had been slowly slipping away, Glen looked her straight in the eye. "We've got the best protection, Lorna, but if we're dealing with someone with police connections, someone who's been able to cover up a missing child for more than two decades, we have to expect him to be the best as well. We might not be able to prevent you from getting hurt."

She shrugged. "You might not be able to protect any of you, either," she said, as though the point was somehow moot.

"We work under that assumption every day. You don't."

"Are you kidding?" She looked at him as though he'd missed something simple and couldn't believe he'd done so. "I've been living with the assumption that I'm in danger every minute of my life since I was six years old."

Glen didn't just understand her words. He knew the feeling she described.

Because he'd been living with a sense of insecurity hanging over him his entire life as well.

And proving facts, finding answers, was his way of taking control of the demons that lurked in the dark recesses of a child's brain.

And the brains of the adults they grew into.

Glen couldn't say what his mind understood.

But he reached out a hand, covered hers and the fork it held, and gave a light squeeze.

Chapter Eight

Lorna was falling in love. She was too much of a realist to ignore the reactions coursing through her. And too much of one to hope, even for a second, that anything could come of it.

Truth was, she'd been half in love with Glen Rivers Thomas since she'd read his first published paper. And while it had only been a day and a half since she'd actually met him, she was in his home, cooking for him, and more importantly, working with him.

Work was his life.

And hers, too.

Made sense to her that, for her, they were a perfect match.

Just as she knew that, as with a lot of things in her life, any feelings she had for him would always be *just* inside her. Her secret. Something she understood that others never would. Something about her that no one would ever know.

But something that could still give her strength. She waited for him to resume eating, and then said, "I found a photo today." She'd been so shocked by the fire, and his reaction to it, the firm's intense attention to it, that she'd almost forgotten the most important thing that had happened that day.

As his hand left the top of hers, she made herself take the bite she'd already forked up to her mouth, get it off the utensil, chew and swallow it.

Then, pulling her phone out of her pants pocket, she tapped, scrolled, held it out to him. "That's a photo of Simon at four, created by my age progression software." Pulling her phone back, she flipped the screen one more time and then held it in front of him. "That's Billy Shaking." She spelled the last name. "He went missing twenty-one years ago from Ocean Springs, Mississippi. He was four. Billy. From Billingsley? A new name the little guy would relate to, feel as his own?"

Glen stood so quickly, his chair back hit the floor behind him. He carried her phone with him, was still looking at the screen as he made a call on his own phone.

His words were curt. No hello or identifying himself. "Billy Shaking. S-h-a-k-i-n-g. Ocean Springs, Mississippi. He was four years old twenty-one years ago. Find everything you can." He hung up just as quickly. Righted his chair. Sat back down, pushing his plate away as he did so.

"I needed to know this a couple of hours ago."

She nodded. Then said, "You had me a bit distracted…"

"Right." Wiping a hand over his face, he looked at her. "I'm not a great boss. Not even a good one."

"That's not what I hear in the lab." Her words fell out softly. Of their own accord more than her conscious choosing.

The surprise on his face was unmistakable. As was the rapidity with which he got rid of it. "I know how I want my lab to run. I know how to get it exactly right. I've never been point on a case before. If you'd like me to turn that portion of this over to Hud, I fully understand. As, I feel certain, would he."

It was almost as though he wanted her to tell him to put his friend and partner in charge. Which was why she almost did so. But something held her back. She had no clear reasoning as she shook her head, but she was absolutely certain it was the right thing to do.

"Simon doesn't need a good boss, Glen," she told him. "He needs answers. As do I. I didn't just come to you on a whim. I'm here after years of following your work, with an ever-growing impression that you could help Simon." She'd already basically told him as much. No point in sugarcoating the obvious.

He didn't nod. He just held her gaze for a long few seconds, and then said, "This is the only photo that popped?"

"I don't know," she told him. "You came in, demanding that I pack up and go immediately. I left the program running."

He stood abruptly again. But left his chair upright. "You want to head back to the lab? Check the results?"

She nodded. Quickly gathering their used plates as she stood. Her insides filling with a curious excitement at the thought of the night ahead.

"Wait." His words made her freeze in place. With a plate in one hand, halfway to topping the one she already had in the other. "We can't," he told her. "McKenna's home already. Jamison would come, but we need him as sharp as possible tomorrow. We can't just go driving in my car out into the night…"

He seemed to be decision-making in spurts. Being the boss. And, filling with tenderness, she almost smiled.

"How about if someone calls them both for an early start in the morning?" she suggested. "We both need some rest, too." Even as the words left her lips, she was fairly certain she was going to struggle to get any sleep that night.

He was looking at her, but didn't speak. And she added, "Simon's been waiting twenty-three years. A few more hours probably isn't going to matter."

His gaze turned piercing as he pushed at the nosepiece on his glasses. "Unless whoever wants you to stop looking for him goes after him, too."

She hadn't thought of that. Truth was, she'd been more than half expecting to find out the little boy had never left Morrilton, that he'd died that day and his body had been disposed of. "If he's alive," she said. And then stared at him, not bothering to try to hide the horror she was feeling. "We have no way of warning him," she said.

Chin tight, he pushed at his glasses. "Which is why we need to be diligent and find out what happened to him as quickly as possible. Hud has members of his team working overnight. And we'll both be better able to 'work our magic,' as my partners always tell me, if we've had some rest. Four in the morning too early for you?"

Two in the morning was too late as far as she was concerned, but Lorna nodded and went in to do the dishes before trying to get some sleep. Her mind was spinning. From fires to twenty-three-year-old dirt in the park. The pen she'd finally have access to the next day. And someone brazen enough to leave a note in her front door slot, telling her to back off.

The same someone who'd returned to set her house on fire?

Wouldn't anyone in the neighborhood have noticed if a stranger had been at her house twice in a couple of days?

It wasn't like she had visitors. Ever.

And...

"Why would a child go missing from his siblings and mother who loved him, and then end up missing again two years later in another state?" Glen's voice sounded from the dining room on the way into the kitchen, and Lorna almost dropped the last of the silverware she'd been putting away.

"There's a dishwasher, you know," he said, in the kitchen then.

She nodded. "Simple tasks help ground my thinking." She answered the second comment first. "Washing dishes, with the warm soapy water, is also soothing."

She saw a curious light in his eyes behind his lenses. As

though highlighted by them. Couldn't let herself get lost there, even silently, with only her knowing.

Not with Simon possibly in danger due to her. Everyone had told her to leave it alone. To trust authorities to do their jobs. Her parents and her siblings, who were almost old enough to be her parents, had all warned that she was getting obsessive, and obsession came to no good.

"I don't know why a child goes missing twice," she said then. "Not as young as he was. And not with the same people. If his mother had lost him twice, then we look at her for negligence, at the very least. If he was prone to wander off, couldn't sense danger, or follow direction, then maybe. But by all accounts, Simon was a precocious little guy. Not only did his family all say so, he said he was going looking for worms to fish with. Complete thought, communicating as such, which is impressive for a two-year-old. His mother said he was talking in sentences while Selena was still pointing and giving her a few words at a time." She was rambling again.

Something that worked in her head. For her. Not her usual way of working with others. She'd just repeated what had been in the report they'd both had access to earlier that day. As though he wouldn't have already read it into his own mental storage.

Glen leaned his back against the counter across from her, an arm across his waist supporting the elbow he cupped with one hand to bring the other to his chin. And she calmed. For no reason other than that he didn't seem to find anything odd about her delivery. "So we have a smart child, who maybe wandered off searching for his worms. Being two, he doesn't realize how far he's gone, or know how to get back. Then what? Someone finds him and takes him to Mississippi? And then he wanders off again?"

Didn't feel right. She shook her head at the same time he

shook his. And she leaned against her counter, hands braced on the granite behind her. "Do you think he remembered being taken? And went missing in Ocean Springs because *that* time he wandered off deliberately? Thinking maybe he could catch a ride home? Little ones don't have the same sense of time, or distance, as we do. Nor can they reason through all the pitfalls before them."

Glen's phone buzzed, drawing her gaze to the front pocket of his pants that the phone was half shoved into. And to the fly there, too.

She didn't linger. To the contrary, she jerked her gaze away as though the sight had burned her corneas. It had burned alright. But nowhere near her face.

Appalled, she stared at the floor. Willing fate to be on her side one time in her life and let him not have noticed her reaction.

"Hud's got the police report from Ocean Springs." Glen's voice, his completely consumed tone, brought her gaze shooting back up at his. He was focused on his phone as though the answer to world famine was there.

Which drew her immediately over to his side. Didn't matter what little foibles she had going on inside her. Most particularly when she saw the words on Glen's screen. Read them right along with him as he scrolled.

Billy Shaking, a four-year-old boy who'd been brought into a hospital emergency room in need of stitches in his hand due to falling on a piece of glass in the park, had disappeared from the treatment cubicle with his mother, introduced as Bea Shaking, as soon as the stitching was complete. The four sutures had been administered by an EMT on duty, and they were told to wait for the doctor to come talk to them.

And for discharge paperwork to be done.

The police report stated that no one had seen proof the woman was the boy's mother. He'd been crying due to injury.

She'd acted like a mother. Had consoled him. No emergency room personnel had noticed anything off about them, until they'd simply vanished.

No one knew where they'd come from, other than a park. The address the woman had given as their residence had turned out to be a library in the next town. And the FBI had been notified.

The case remained open.

There was a bit more. She and Glen read to the end. And then she stared up at him, so close she could see the intensity burning in the gray of his eyes. "Do we think that this woman is the one who stole him?" she asked. Then, without waiting for an answer, continued, "We need to get to the case file. There was a list of people who'd been in the park that day. Who'd been interviewed. What if she was one of them? Had him hidden away until she could leave town unnoticed?"

The fear that shot through her filled her voice as she asked, "How do we prove that?" Before giving him a chance to respond to her previous question.

"We'll figure it out." Glen's tone sounded so certain, Lorna relaxed some. Realized how close she was standing to him, felt the heat emanating off him, and stepped away. "There could be good news here," he said then. "The woman was concerned enough about a clean slice on an otherwise completely healthy boy that she risked exposure to bring him in for treatment. If she did take him from the park in Morrilton that day, it's possible that he was loved and cared for."

Right. Good. She'd missed that nuance. Was on a different tangent. "We need to know if there was any physical evidence left behind," she said. "Did anyone get a tissue the woman used to wipe the boy's tears? Anything she touched?"

"Hud said there was nothing collected at the scene," Glen told her, which was disappointing, but she wasn't dwelling on that.

She nodded. "Makes sense. They'd check her address first. Make sure they were there and okay." The report had said that the hospital initially reported it as a leave without paying event. No reason they'd have pulled a tissue out of the trash. Or saved anything disposable from the event. The room would have been immediately cleaned for the next patient. She had to slow down and let clarity come to her.

She meant to. And in the next second, was looking up at Glen as she said, "I know it was him. Which means that we know for certain he was taken out of Morrilton. We just don't know how, or by whom."

"We're one step closer," he allowed, his gaze locking on hers for long enough that she almost thought he was noticing her as a person, as a woman. But then he blinked, stepped back kind of awkwardly, and she realized he'd just been lost in thought.

And wondered if he'd realized how she'd been looking at him. God, she hoped not. Turning, she headed toward the dining room, through which she'd get to the hallway that eventually led to her suite. "Four a.m.?" she asked, trying for casual. Hoping she at least came off as not shaking like a leaf.

"Yes." His answer was solid. Almost unequivocal. "I'll see you at the front door."

And with the obvious dismissal as an excuse, Lorna strode with purpose all the way to her room. Where she closed the door, and collapsed back against it, her hands clasped together in the middle of her chest.

She was going to find out what happened to Simon Billingsley. She just knew it. He might be deceased, but just the fact that he'd made it to four was wonderful news. Hopeful news.

The fact that someone was trying to silence her was good news, too. Someone was guilty of something pertaining to the little boy's disappearance. She might get hurt in the process of finding Simon's answers. Without them, her life was stagnant.

And the rest…meeting her hero in real life…she'd have to wait until she was home to fully ingest that one. In the meantime, she had to focus on not humiliating herself in front of him while she was there. She needed the memory of her time with him to be a good one.

GLEN WAS IN the kitchen, drinking coffee, half an hour before they were due to leave.

He had a coffee maker in his suite.

Lorna did not.

He'd rested. Knowing she was close, and safe, had helped. He didn't delve into his reasons for thinking that. Just accepted that the job was different than any other. And any out of the ordinary behavior or reaction changes he might experience were to be accepted as a product of his current task.

Made more obvious to him when, before bed, he'd made arrangements for a couple of other forensic experts to take over the rest of his current work. Another first.

And when the Billingsley case was done, so would be the adverse effects of it.

So knowing, he was good to go.

Until she didn't show up in the kitchen for coffee. She'd consumed some the day before. His lack of knowledge of her habits should in no way disappoint him.

And yet it did.

After brief nods of "good morning," the car ride through mostly deserted Phoenix streets in the dark was a silent one. As was their walk through the lab to Lorna's station.

The only portion of that unusual to Glen was that he noticed. And was bothered by the silence. Any other time, he'd have welcomed it.

Lorna's gasp rent him out of the muck into which he'd fallen, even after assuring himself he was good to go. They'd reached her station—her a step before him—and, with dread in his gut, his glance followed hers. Expecting to see an escalated warning, a threat of some kind.

Instead, he stood with her, focused not at all on the woman, but on her computer screen. Filled with various images—piled on top of each other—of potential matches for Simon Billingsley.

Lorna approached slowly, as though hardly daring to believe what she was seeing. "Look at all these." Her voice held wonder. And then she seemed to forget he was even there as she sat down, grabbed her mouse, and started to pull images apart.

There were at least a dozen of them. Rolling a stool in from next door, Glen pulled up next to her. "Print the list of databases," he said, "including social media sites and photo apps. It'll help us narrow down searches for context on these."

Pulling up another screen, she clicked and hit Print. And was already back to her facial recognition screen by the time he'd turned back from her printer with the page in hand.

She'd enlarged a photo, homing in on the background. "That looks like a stream in the background," she said. They were looking at a group of boys, aged ten or so, all wearing baseball caps, sitting on a set of bleachers in front of a dirt field. The highlighted photo was of a boy in the front-row middle. His cap was pushed back on his head, the bill pointing upward. His expression serious, though not instilling a sense of harm or worry.

"I'm not sure it's him," Glen had to tell her.

She nodded. "I know. It's only a three-point marker. But it's not going to hurt to put it in our mix. If we can manage to prove locations of these photos, we can build a map, based on approximate age, and maybe see where Simon's life has led him. We check out every location…even if only one of them is a match…that could be all we need. He might still be

there. Or have been there long enough for someone to recognize him. Remember him."

He'd already been on the same page. And as loath as he
was to leave her anywhere on her own—even in his own secure lab—Glen pushed back from her table. "Send half of
them to me," he said. "I'll dive, you dive, and when we're
through, we meet up to create our map."

She nodded. Was so fully engrossed in her screen, he
would have suspected she hadn't heard him, except that he
saw photos flying into a folder that he knew would be in his
drop box by the time he got to his office.

For once his lack of people skills didn't feel so…awkward.

And he slid fully into work mode with a smile on his face.

Chapter Nine

Hudson Warner sent down a description, with a sketch, of the woman who'd been with Billy Shaking at the Ocean Springs hospital twenty-one years before. There were no women in any of the thirteen photos Lorna and Glen had split between them. She'd taken six, had given him seven, just because he was more familiar with all the resources at their disposal.

And quicker at the work, too. As he should be. He had almost a decade on her, working in the field. Had finished his doctorate at a much earlier age than she had. Something she wanted to hear about, but wouldn't ever ask.

While she was working on gleaning every piece of evidence she could from her six photos, she fed Hud's sketch through her recognition program. With added bone measurements and her more intricate age progression system, the software would clean up the image some. And she'd send it through the same databases that Simon had run through the day and night before.

Members of Hud's team were going through Billy Shaking's file piece by piece, researching everything they could on their end and sending pertinent items down to the lab.

Like the size and location of the scar that would be on the boy's right hand for the rest of his life. It popped on-screen with a message from Hud to her and Glen. Glen responded.

Lorna went back to the first photo on her list—she'd organized them by age, youngest-appearing to oldest—and used a high scale photo enlarger on both right and left hands. Just to be sure.

Only one of the images contained a right hand turned outward toward the camera.

And…she jumped up.

Rushed to Glen's office. "The scar is there," she told him. On a mission, she didn't stop on her way to his desk, or slow down as she joined him behind it. Pushing her hands in on his keyboard, she typed, accessed her screen, and pulled up the image.

Her heart thumped as she viewed his screen.

His hands brushed hers as he typed, and the image appeared on all three of his screens. And with another click, the screens' images split to show the face attached to the hand. "I have him at around eight here," Lorna said. And added, "Based on my software, he was eight. It's a near perfect match."

"Where?"

She shook her head. "I don't know yet. The image popped up from a crowd of kids. Looked like coming out of a school. It was an article about a school day ending for the last time. A new campus had been built. It didn't say where. I was about to look up the location when Hud's image arrived."

"Name of the school?" Glen didn't even take his gaze from the screen long enough to look at her.

"Hamilton Elementary."

He typed. As she'd suspected, there were numerous schools all over the US by that name. He typed again, asking for a Hamilton Elementary school that closed or opened seventeen years before. And got one.

In Panera, Georgia, a small town nearly one hundred miles east of Atlanta. Only three and a half hours from Ocean Springs.

Leaned over to view the smaller print on the screen with Glen as he'd typed, Lorna turned her head with the huge smile she couldn't contain. "We've got him at eight!" she said. And added, "And he was attending school!" She wanted to twirl. To hug someone.

Selena.

Or… Glen. Her eyes locked with his in the midst of that perfect moment. And she was suddenly aware of how close their faces, their bodies, were. How she'd just barged into his personal space.

She'd have been appalled at herself except that he didn't seem to have minded.

He was smiling, too.

HE'D ALMOST KISSED HER. Glen left the lab for some air a minute after Lorna rushed from his office as abruptly as she'd entered it. She'd been hurrying back to her workspace to continue with the work before them. Had said something of the sort.

While he'd remained frozen, both hands clenching the arms of his chair.

He'd known her two days.

She'd "known" him almost a decade. What she'd said the day before, about watching his video…about knowing even then that she wanted to look him up.

Had it been him, with that plan, he'd have watched every video, read every paper. And if she'd done so…which was likely…then that explained why she worked so much like him.

He'd basically trained her to work alongside him.

As he took the stairs up to the firm's main floor, his panic calmed some. To the point of heading right back down. The lab always had security. The detail had doubled.

Still, Glen didn't want to leave Lorna down there alone.

There were many ways to threaten a person, to torment

them mentally. A lot of them accomplished through phone calls and computer screens.

He wanted her to be able to find him, to come to him, the second something hit. It didn't take long for a perp to mentally manipulate. A simple threat to family and she could be turned into someone even she wouldn't recognize.

Just as Sierra's mind had been forever changed by what had happened to her. Leading her on a hopeless chase, somehow believing she could expose an illegal college gambling ring all on her own. She'd taken on powerful people and had lost.

Lorna was as determined to expose what had happened to Simon Billingsley. And Glen was her mentor. She'd come to him for help. Something Sierra hadn't done.

Reentering the lab, he experienced again the sense that his friend was giving him a second chance. The opportunity to change his future by laying the past to rest.

Before he headed back to the critical work awaiting him at his desk, he stopped in to see Lorna. Not even nodding at the other scientists working in the stations he passed.

"I don't know how much you know about cyber criminology," he said, keeping his voice low so no one else heard him. Pulling his stool to her side for the same reason.

"I took classes in it," she said, looking straight at him. "Why?"

"We see a lot of things here that the rest of the world does not," he told her, holding her gaze because the moment was that serious. His message that urgent. In those seconds, nothing else mattered. "Even our own highly trained experts have fallen prey to high-level scams a time or two. If whoever left you that threatening note and then set fire to your office has any idea where you are, or what you're doing, he's likely going to attack you here."

Her gaze narrowed. A change in her eyes came and went. Probably emotion.

"Anything happens on your screen, even a second or two of slowdown, you come find me," he told her. "I'll be here, in the lab, as long as you are. Don't think you're immune. Or be so overly confident in your own mind that you think you aren't susceptible to manipulation. If you recognize anything unusual on-screen, shoot it to Hud immediately and then come find me. Do not respond to anyone or click on anything that appears the least bit suspicious. Not only Simon's answers, but your life, could depend on it. We have top-of-the-line security protocols in place here, but it's not a system problem I'm concerned about." He stopped short of describing in detail the types of manipulation that were concerning him.

She seemed to know, though. She swallowed, deeply, as he'd noticed her do a few other times emotions were high. Gave him a nod. And her continued attention, too, as she said, "You should be concerned about system problems." Her voice sounded weaker than normal. "At least here in the lab, you should be. If someone trying to stop me has any idea that you all are helping me…"

The fear in her eyes was recognizable even to a dolt like him. He covered her hand with his without even thinking about what he was doing. "Don't worry," he told her. "I didn't mean to imply that I saw no threat to us in this situation, just that we work under similar threat every day. We have four of the best hackers in the world on staff, full-time, watching our systems around the clock. If something hits us, they'll know the second it does and will shut us down."

As her gaze calmed, he became aware of the soft warm skin beneath his palm and pulled his hand away. With too much abruptness, he was sure.

So made it worse by standing so fast the stool he'd been seated on rolled a foot behind him. "Do not take my warning lightly or fail to contact me…" he said. And strode from the intimate space.

If the scientist had sensed any of the feelings of attraction he'd been experiencing when around her—if there'd been any chance that she might be encountering some of the same inside herself, for him—he'd likely just quashed the possibility that anything more between them would grow out of the untoward reactions.

And that was a very good thing.

BY MIDMORNING, LORNA had made all the enhancements she could and had turned over researching of the backgrounds of the facial recognition photos from Simon's age progression likenesses to Hudson's team.

She'd just had long enough for a restroom stop and to get a cup of coffee out of the machine in the hallway when Glen messaged her computer screen, telling her that the box of case evidence had arrived from Morrilton.

He was having it delivered to her space.

Not his own.

A sign of his growing trust in her?

She knew better than to take the choice personally—to read too much into things—but did so anyway.

And was eager to get to the evidence. After Glen's warning, she'd much rather run chemical tests on objects than sit at a computer using any kind of software with internet capabilities.

She'd be using the computer. Couldn't do her job without it. Just needed a bit of time to acclimate to Glen's frightening demands as he'd left her earlier. There'd been something very real behind his message to her. She'd bet her life on that one.

And needed to know what that something had been. Had to understand so she could get out of panic mode.

In the meantime, the soon-to-arrive evidence was a much anticipated, welcomed, and long-awaited gift. It was also just the distraction she needed. Something that mattered more than anything that could or could not be coming at her as retribution for not backing down.

Eager to get her hands on the pen, setting up a counter with all the possible materials, tools, supplies, and solutions she could use as she analyzed a twenty-three-year-old—at least—writing implement, she had a flashback to Glen's office earlier that day, the way their faces had been so close together. And then later, again so close, with his hand on hers.

Could the scientist be feeling an attraction to her? But he'd hightailed it away from her, with a curt order, the second he'd seemed to sense their possibly growing closeness. He couldn't have made it any clearer that he had no interest in her as anything other than an employee helping him solve a case.

So why had he covered her hand? Gazed into her eyes so intensely? Was she sending out an overabundance of pheromones? And he recognized the effect they were having on him?

Ellsworth. It was Ellsworth all over again. Paling at the thought, Lorna continued to gather items, inspecting test tubes as she pulled them from packaging. While memories from her ill-fated affair in freshman year washed through her.

The freedom she'd felt, finally being out of Morrilton, where Simon's disappearance had been a shadow lurking every second since it had happened. And being away from her older parents' and siblings' protectiveness, too.

Add to that, she hadn't been the only science nerd. She'd been in a lab full of them. Had felt normal, accepted, understood for the first time in her life.

In her youth and exuberance, she'd thought Ellsworth Connolly had been knocked with the same intensity of romantic feelings for her that she'd had for him. Turned out, he'd only wanted sex.

And after he'd had it a few times, had moved on without

looking back. She'd saved face, of course. Had pretended that she'd only been looking for physical pleasure as well. That she'd never thought they were boyfriend and girlfriend.

She'd also done a deep dive on sexual attraction and the very real existence and effect of pheromones. Had taken a hard look at testosterone as well.

So knew better than to read anything into Glen Rivers Thomas's reaction to her. Clearly, she was a woman who put out an abundance of pheromones when she was attracted to a man.

The thought had her reaching into her satchel for her lavender oil, spreading some on both wrists and her neck. Any exciting message she might be sending to ignite a release of testosterone would be immediately counteracted by the calming scent.

If nothing else, the essential oil's advent into her olfactory receptors was most definitely soothing her.

She was fired up to work, to get Simon's answers and move on—and prepared to stand next to her mentor however many times it happened over the course of the case, feeling nothing but professional admiration.

Worst-case scenario, she'd have to find a way to obtain more oil.

FILLED WITH THE same sense of urgency he'd had when trying to help police find out what had happened to Sierra, Glen signed for the evidence box delivered down to the lab and carried the package immediately to Lorna.

Hands gloved, they worked together, mostly without speaking, carefully removing and cataloging every piece of evidence, until Lorna spied the pen that she'd put first on her list. Glen watched as she picked it up gently, handling it as though it was newly spun glass, as she turned it to inspect every speck on the cylinder's tubing.

"It's got bite marks." Her words were without inflection, as though announcing information to a group, and he respected the professionalism as his own blood started to flow a little faster. Hers had to be churning like a race engine.

After her initial inspection, she handed it to Glen. His focus was all on the teeth marks. "It's not chewed on the end," he said, talking to himself aloud. Something he rarely did. So…talking to her. "Most people chew on the end of the pen."

"It's like someone held it with their mouth." Lorna was close, bending in with him to the bright light attached to one of her tables. She smelled like lavender. A lot of it. His mind noted, but didn't linger. The pen was plastic, ballpoint, re-fillable. Meaning it came apart in the middle.

If it *had* been held in a mouth…he looked up at Lorna.

Her gaze met his and she raised her brow. "What?"

"It's possible that I can get a saliva sample from this," he told her, carefully unscrewing the writing implement. "It's been stored in a climate-controlled dark place. And if there was any trace that seeped in here—" he indicated the en-graved metal ends that screwed together "—we have an even better shot." His mind was spinning over what he knew. "I'll try the Polilight first as it's nondestructive. With the new ad-vances in fiber-optic-based detection, we might get lucky. HRMS—high-resolution mass spectrometry—will be my next choice, but only after we've completed the rest of the testing we need to do." They'd both only handled the pen with two fingers. It was possible he could get a positive result for the presence of saliva without compromising any other po-tential evidence. "The molds for bite marks and metal organic framework crystals we'll need to apply for fingerprints could compromise other existing evidence on the implement, but with the bite marks in the middle, it's fairly safe to assume that whoever bit the pen was holding it by one or the other end of it while putting it between his teeth."

All three tests were long shots.

But it was so often those nearly impossible-to-make connections that solved cold cases. Assuming law enforcement at the time had been competent, everything else had already been checked. Double-and triple-checked.

"Saliva could tell us whether whoever held the pen was a man or a woman. Even if we can't match the sample to a specific person," Lorna said. "That could be key. And might be our best shot."

Which was why he was taking the pen with him. But before he went, there was one other thing he needed to discuss with her.

Pen in one hand, he waved his free one over the table filled with the evidence they'd laid out. From pieces of dirt and what would have been grass, to paint samples from the bench. Trash that had been found in the area, samples of Simon's hair, his toothbrush, pictures of the clothes he'd been wearing that day, as provided by his mother. Crime scene photos. And Glen had to say it. "The level of thoroughness here, along with the number of times this case was revisited over the years, I don't think that Morrilton police had a mole, or that they were in any way involved in Simon's disappearance." A local cop would have had access to evidence. Some should be missing.

Lips pursed, Lorna nodded. "Agreed. Unless there's some key piece that was never here to begin with, was never logged. I don't suspect the entire department. But neither am I ready to rule out the possibility that someone who had access at the time didn't compromise the investigation for some reason. The person would probably be retired now. But could still have fellow officers on the force who would likely have let him know that the case is being looked at again."

Pushing at the nosepiece of his glasses, Glen nodded. Sensing that she was an intellectual match. He was energized just working with her. "I'll have Hud's team look into all members of the force for the past twenty-three years, and Brian can follow up with any in-person interviews," he said from the doorway of her space and then held up the pen. "Be right back."

He made it out of the close space, the proximity that left only air between them, without undue emotional reaction.

But as he headed to the half of his office that housed his own massive private lab, he carried the scent of lavender with him.

Chapter Ten

She'd seen the pen. She'd been yearning to gain access to that cheap little writing tool for years. Ever since she'd first seen the evidence list pertaining to Simon's case. With adrenaline coursing through her, Lorna could hardly believe the difference a few days made in a life.

All those years…all the fear…and she finally had the pen.

It might bring nothing. She knew that. But, so far, it was providing far more than she'd expected. She'd read nothing in any report about teeth marks on the barrel. Had never even considered saliva.

And could hardly believe that she was at Sierra's Web. Working with a nationally renowned forensic scientist. Staying in his home, even. It was all so surreal—it was no wonder she was a bit emotionally off-kilter. Feeling as though finally having full access to Simon's case was twice as exciting as she'd ever imagined it would be.

Feeling as though she was not only respected in her field, but that her work could actually make a major difference in others' lives.

Her entire life she'd been the girl, then the woman, that people patronized. Pitied. Thought of as obsessive. An introvert. Wickedly smart in the laboratory, but outside it, practically invisible. Except as the overprotected youngest member of a family that no one had ever really understood.

She had the pen!

And crime scene photos. A paint sample. Methodically laying them out, arranging them in order of most likely to provide evidence that she could use, she started by clipping the photos to a line hung along the bottom of a section of wall cupboards, studying each one as she did so. Storing the visuals in her mind so they'd be there if something appeared that pertained to any one of them.

They hadn't yet heard anything more on the age progression photos they'd sent upstairs before they left for home the day before. But even without those, she felt confident that they'd uncovered sufficient proof to know that Simon had been alive at eight. That he'd attended school.

Most probably in Georgia.

With gloves on, she picked up the photos of exact likenesses—brand, color, style, and size—of the clothes Simon had been wearing the day he'd disappeared. And started to shake. Descriptions of his outfit had been posted all over Morrilton. She'd looked them all up before. But to see the actual sizes—laid out as an outfit, down to the socks and tennis shoes with the dark scruff on the right toe where he'd dragged it along blacktop—it was like she could almost see the toddler inside them.

She could feel his fear as he'd been lost from his mother, just as she'd been feeling her own panic ever since that day. There'd been no obvious sign of distress in the eight-year-old's likeness. Dare she hope that Simon's case would be one of the few that ended up without tragedy to him, other than having been stolen from his family?

Was she unprofessional to pray that he'd grown up with love in his life?

For some reason, the thought brought to mind the man who'd be returning to her space soon. Glen was such an enigma. His home, while decorated in a lovely, warm fashion, gave no hint of the man himself. Of his life. No personal touches. No mementos lying about or framed photos on tables or walls.

Wait. Staring at a photo of the bench Simon's mother had been sitting on—dealing with a crying Selena with her husband on the phone—the bench behind which Simon had gone to look for worms, she noticed three things.

Marks on the bottom wooden slat of the bench back. They looked like they could be the size of two-year-old fingers holding on to the bench for steadiness while digging in the dirt.

Her gaze traveled immediately downward in the photo and saw the second piece that had caught at her. Disturbed dirt. As though some ants had made a sloppy little hill. Or a little one had been digging.

And third, most importantly, as she raised her gaze again, the marks in the wood's paint, in the midst of those little dirt smudges. Scratches. As though little fingers grasping for balance had slipped, scraping at peeling paint.

Across her space in a second flat, Lorna homed in on the paint sample on her counter. Read the description. A piece of chipped paint found on the ground in front of the bench. Simon had disappeared from the back of the bench. She got why the paint chip hadn't been mentioned in any reports, other than as something a crime scene responder had picked up and bagged.

But, that olive green paint chip proved that the paint on that bench was loose. Falling off. Grabbing the crime scene photo from the clip, along with the small bag containing the paint chip, she rushed down the hall to Glen's office. And through that to the opened door of his lab. Stopping just over the threshold, as she caught sight of herself. Running to him as though he was her friend, her soulmate, not the very temporary boss she'd only actually known, in person, for a few days.

He looked so…professional…so…important…standing in his white coat and black pants, the broad width of his shoulders slightly hunched over the scope he was looking through. His butt, of all things, drew her attention. Firm. Lithe.

The second of impulsivity passed as instantly as it had hit, as Glen turned around. She had evidence in her hand. Pushing the nosepiece on his glasses, he said, "I was just about to head down your way," in a tone that sounded more like a friend, an equal, than a new boss. "We've got some saliva here, a trace. I'm not sure how much information I'll be able to get out of it. May not even be a clean DNA sample…" His words fell off as he looked at the evidence in her gloved hands.

"What did you find?" His tone heightened with expectation.

The fact that he knew she wouldn't be there if she didn't have something potentially significant sent a spark of warmth through Lorna as she advanced further into the room. Or maybe it was excitement from the case that elicited that small thrill. She had the awareness, and it was gone as she held out the photo to him first. "Take a look at the bench back, bottom slat," she said. And waited.

Glen glanced. And then reached for a large magnifying glass, peering at the photo through it. "We're talking about the smudges here, right?" he asked, holding out the photo with the glass directly over the spot she'd seen. Moving in, Lorna's pulse sped up.

"You think they could be fingerprints?" she asked, still not certain, but believing her initial impression.

"Run them through facial recognition. Just those impressions against Simon's fingers as seen in the photos his mother provided." She should have thought of that. Would have if she wasn't so far out of her element. Having been transported to a world that seemed far too good to be true, she looked up at him. "You see anything more there?"

He looked again. And then closer. She held her breath. "Are those scratch marks?"

Smiling inside, doing all she could to contain her outward expression, Lorna shrugged, and said, "If Simon had paint under his nails, or left on his fingers, when he disappeared, we might be able to find traces of it on other items taken from the park and parking lot that day." She held up the small bag containing the paint chip. "Mass spec can give us a complete breakdown. And we've got all those evidence bags containing pieces of trash picked up from the area, including the parking lot. It could tell us from which direction he left the park. Give us an indication if he was driven away in a vehicle or left on foot by the opposite end of the park, onto the sidewalk across the street from the library." She talked about exact distances to each. And said, "I've always thought he was walked out. By way of that sidewalk. There used to be these wooden climbing apparatuses, like little houses and things that kids could play in. The perfect getaway would have been via them. Hiding places as needed. Playtime for Simon. And then rows of trees planted to cut the park off from the street beyond. And into a car. Just that quickly."

Lorna tensed as she realized that she was rambling, once again. Glancing from the paint sample she held to the photo he held, she forced herself to look up at him.

Saw him studying the bench photo again. Then, brow furrowed behind his glasses, he turned his gaze on her. It was piercing. Thoughtful. Assessing.

She felt like a student in freshman science class, worried that she'd failed her final exam. Except that she was confident she knew her stuff. She might be wrong, but her theory held weight.

"Test the paint. Get the compound breakdown. I'll have one of the other scientists start testing the bagged trash." His gaze locked with hers, and Lorna felt tears push at the back of her eyes. A quick blink kept them from showing, but she was never going to forget that moment. The sense of oneness. Something she'd never felt with another human being in her life.

Even the fact that Glen, reaching for his phone, didn't seem to be sharing her feeling of connection didn't diminish the moment.

Intensely, professionally focused or something more personal, she wasn't sure, nor did it matter. He understood the importance of taking every tiny possibility seriously. Not due to obsession. But because that one time he didn't could be the one time it mattered most.

He glanced back at her. "I'm getting with Hud and Brian to see if there's any footage of the street outside the library during the time directly before Simon's disappearance."

Chances of that were slim. But if they kept digging, left no stone unturned, something would turn up.

Lorna was as sure of that as she was that her entire life had been building toward, preparing her for, those few moments, days, or weeks she had with Glen Rivers Thomas.

She'd come into her own, and her future was forever changed.

GLEN DOUBLE-CHECKED HIMSELF as he finally hung up from his partner, and pen in hand, he made his way slowly down to Lorna's space. Bottom line was finding out what had happened to Simon Billingsley. Not any oddness about himself in his dealings with the temporary scientist in his midst. Had to be that way. He was asking others to invest critical time on the matter, and while he was funding the case and had ample resources to do so, wasted expert energy meant some other problem was not being solved.

And solving crimes, giving peace to others, preventing further pain, would always mean more to him than his own personal issues. He wasn't a guy who'd ever have a family at home, or bring ultimate happiness to others. Just wasn't who he was. And while he was perfectly fine with that, it also meant he couldn't let his internal turmoil interfere with getting the job done.

With so much movement in various directions, he was fairly certain any reaction to visiting scientist Dr. Lorna Schwann wouldn't even have room to grow but he checked himself just the same. He needed to ensure success.

And entered Lorna's space, dropping the evidence bag holding the pen on the table, already delivering words in her direction. "Brian had a phone call with Professor Eva Petti-grew a few minutes ago and doesn't believe she said anything to anyone about the Billingsley case recently or in the past, either." Meaning she hadn't revealed what Lorna was up to. And they still had no way of knowing if the person threatening her knew that she'd flown to Phoenix. Or was working with Sierra's Web. He said all that aloud, too.

It wasn't until he saw the look of consternation on her face, noticed the way her hand was running through that tousled hair of hers, that he realized he should have started with case news. She'd been waiting.

The most difficult part of a scientist's job.

The rest, the possible danger she was in, while they be-lieved it to be case-related, was a personal matter.

"There's nothing new on the Billy Shaking angle," he told her. "Unfortunately, street and security cameras weren't a thing yet back then. And the hospital was busy that day."

She nodded. Didn't seem surprised. Or even particularly

disappointed. "We know he was alive at four," she told him. "And that he was in Ocean Springs. It matters."

He agreed. As far as the case went, the Billy Shaking discovery was huge. He just hated to not have more.

For her.

"Same is true for Panera, Georgia, too," he said, adding, "As far as cameras go. Hud's been tied up with formalities and privacy issues there, but just got a judge's order allowing us to have access to Hamilton Elementary student enrollment records. The order is limited. We only get photos that were taken for school use, as those don't come with any perception of privacy, but if our boy was there and had his picture taken with his class, we'll have it soon."

Our boy? As though he and Lorna had birthed the child? Or adopted him? What in the *hell* was he doing?

Giving his all to the case. The answer came silently. On the tail of the internal question.

"He's also put out feelers and has someone on standby in the area to do some canvasing if we determine there's cause. See if anyone who went to elementary school with the boy we believe to be Simon remembers him. Or anything about him. We'd like to have a name first, though. Hopefully the school records will prove fruitful there."

Lorna sat on her stool, hands in her lap, giving him full attention. Her gaze focused. He fully trusted that she was taking in every word.

And would spit them back out as appropriate anyplace they applied as they continued to work to find Simon. The realization gave him a measure of comfort. Knowing that getting the job done successfully meant as much to her as it did to him.

As though he didn't have the whole world completely on his shoulders. Hers were there, too.

Nonsense, when he considered that he'd had his partners

sharing their collective burden since the inception of the firm. But the scientific expertise had all been on him.

And his lab of experts.

The thought did nothing to expel his sudden, new sense of not going it all alone. But he had no time, or desire, to dwell.

He handed her a folder he'd carried down with him. "The reports on the mousetraps recovered from the fire at your home," he told her. Waited while she read what he already knew.

She did so silently, perusing rapidly, and looked up at him. "They were my traps. My prints the only ones discernible— the arsonist wore gloves, obviously."

She glanced down again at the file she held and then, brows raised, back up at him. "Only the ones by the garage had inflammable insecticide in them."

He nodded.

Shaking her head, frowning, she said, "They only meant for the garage to burn? Or thought the whole house would catch, meaning there was little chance the original mouse-traps would survive. They would have wanted to diminish the chance of anyone ever figuring out how the fire started."

Both theories had been discussed. "Hud and the fire marshal think it's the former. A warning to you, but more important, a way to get you home. If the house burned down, there'd be less reason for you to fly back immediately. You'd have had no place to stay."

Her eyes scrunched at the corners as she shook her head. "Maybe, but if a neighbor hadn't alerted the fire department, the place still could have burned."

"Not if whoever set the flame was close enough to call the fire in."

She nodded, her face clearing. And set the file down. A clear indication to him that she was done with the topic.

He wasn't done. Needed her to not be done.

"If, as we believe, this person is after you due to this case, finding out who he is could be the quickest way to solving it," he said. The evidence they were collecting to find Simon was critical.

He couldn't get by the fact that tending to her safety was as much so.

She nodded and looked him straight in the eye as she said, "I learned a long time ago that the only way I can tend to my own safety is to look at the science that can prove facts."

Something changed within Glen as she said the words. He'd heard renditions before. Even partially from her. But standing there in the midst of evidence flooding in, while a threat hung over her head, he had a brand-new sense of the power his lab work, her lab work, scientists' lab work in general, had always had.

More than that, he knew he was right where he was meant to be.

He had her to thank for that.

And would never forget it. Or…he suspected…her, either.

SCIENCE MIGHT NOT tell her what she needed to know. Uneasy, Lorna watched Glen leave her lab, wondering if those mousetraps were hinting to him what they were screaming at her. Someone could be trying to frame her. With the goal of discrediting her as a scientist, and therefore discrediting any work she might be trying to have recognized as valid.

The threatening note…her word against…no one's. They'd been able to prove nothing from it. The envelope had been common, sold in the big-box store in town. She had some in her desk. Paper, ruled, sold everywhere as well. Ink, same. There was no science to prove that she hadn't left the note herself. To draw attention to her own importance. To her work on Simon's case.

Panic could also just be making her paranoid.

But even if the person wasn't out to invalidate her work, science wasn't helping her to find him.

Glen said catching the person after her was possibly the quickest way to solve the case. She saw it differently. Solving the case was the quickest way to finding the person out to get her. They had a hell of a lot more clues to follow with science in Simon's disappearance than the current zero they had with her stalker.

She needed to hear from the tech team regarding the age-progressed photos of Simon. Had she been home, she'd have been on them herself. First.

Then on the evidence currently consuming her lab space. She didn't have to prove that Simon had been at the park that day. Even the potential paint under his little nails, or traces of it on his fingers, if found in trash picked up all over the park—marked with exact location—would only tell them where he'd been in that park after being behind the bench.

Was she being obsessive? Grasping at straws in an unending haystack?

She grew cold as the thought was quickly pushed out by another…was she wasting the valuable resources of one of the nation's top private crime-solving firms?

Could she be in the process of making her professional hero, her mentor, look like a fool?

Tension swarmed through her stomach, her chest felt tight, and Lorna's gaze fell to the pen Glen had returned to her. Legitimate physical evidence. With a possible clue to who might know what happened to Simon Billingsley.

Someone who might have taken him.

The fact came boldly. Stood out clearly in her mind.

Lorna fell down to her stool, light-headed, as fear washed over her. Nausea brought a wave of chills. She always thought of Simon's disappearance as though that was all there was. A disappearance. And her goal—to find him. Dead or alive.

Period.

Because, at six, she hadn't been able to access the bigger truth without hiding in her bedroom closet.

The little boy had been taken.

Which meant, as a child in Morrilton, who played at that same park, so could she be.

And there she was at twenty-nine, still choosing to frame the kidnapping as a boy disappearing, not being taken.

It was time to stop.

To face reality head-on.

To see what Glen saw.

The kidnapper somehow knew that she was getting closer to finding out who he or she was. And so was out to get her, too.

Her worst nightmare, the fear that had shaped her entire life—including years of advanced study, choice of career, inability to trust what she couldn't prove, and being an introvert—had come true.

They were after her, too. Had broken into her garage, used her insect repellent. Had set fire to her home. They'd been on her front porch, just outside her front door, while she'd been in there.

And for all she knew, they were in Phoenix, too. Watching her. Watching Sierra's Web.

Watching Glen.

Thinking of the man, the expressive gray eyes that let her know when to push—when to be silent, when to listen—she got angry. On Glen's behalf. She didn't know his story. Didn't have to know it to see how it had shaped him into a man that she trusted.

She trusted him. No questions asked.

Strength replaced weakness in her muscles, and she stood.

Reached for the pen with a purpose and determination that was deeper than ever before. They thought she'd been obsessed before…they could just watch her going forward.

Fear had been propelling her, her entire life.

Strength was going to see her into her future.

Chapter Eleven

Glen was in his lab, standing in front of his thermocycler, studying results. Determining accuracy based on what he knew a normal report looked like. He'd run the same type of DNA test innumerable times over the course of his career. Had mixed trace of saliva with the proper reagents for single strand duplication. Ran them through the heating and cooling process again and again...

"You haven't eaten all day." The female voice shot through him, not so much with a slice as a rush of warmth, and he took a deep breath. Lorna. The only person who'd ever instilled such a strong reaction in him.

He wasn't pleased that instead of dissipating, the sensations were growing more pronounced.

And while turning around, said, "No one enters my lab without invitation. Text notification. Or knocking. House rule." He recognized the wrapper on the sub in her hand. Realized how hungry he was.

Met her gaze. Shrugged. "It happens," he said, but glanced at the sandwich again.

She handed it to him. Her way of apologizing for the unannounced interruption?

He took it. Met her gaze and said, "Thank you." And then, grasping for the lifeline that would get him back on track, said, "I have the PCR—polymerase chain reaction—results on the saliva." And handed them to her.

In her white lab coat and brown pants that fit her long shapely legs far too well, she handed him a file folder she'd been holding between her arm and rib cage. "I have results, too," she told him.

He reached for them. Caught a whiff of lavender and backed away to one of his main work counters—the one furthest from her—and sat. He took a bite of the sub and then opened the folder.

Then spent the next few minutes reading detailed accounts of spacing between incisors. One, bottom right, was out of alignment. Molars had no distance between them. A canine with more curvature than others. And, based on all of the above, a computer-generated dental arch.

His ham, roast beef, and turkey sandwich was half gone. He turned to look at the woman who hadn't made a sound since he'd sat down.

Standing exactly where he'd left her, she was watching him. Glanced at the report she held and then back at him. Her head arched slightly sideways. Her eyes opened wide.

And he nodded. "We've both concluded, based on our separate evidence from that pen, that it belonged to a woman." Him with a saliva breakdown. Her with the dental mold specifics.

The finding could mean nothing.

And it could be huge.

"Have you run the DNA?" she asked.

He nodded. "Still waiting on results, but based on the sample, I'm not hopeful."

She showed no reaction to the news. "I'm going to run my bite molds against dental records," she said, without any anticipation in her tone.

But her eyes were glowing when she looked at him. "We don't have enough to identify her, but we know we're looking for a woman. Whether she was behind that bench when Simon was, who knows?" She shrugged those feminine, relatively small shoulders that carried so much weight so well and went on. "But if she was even in the park that morning and left before police cordoned off the area and made everyone stay for questioning, it's possible she saw something that was never reported."

"The police sent out multiple public requests, urging anyone who'd been near that part of town that day to contact them," he reminded her. They were scientists who dealt with facts. Not potential visionaries who could see what wasn't right in front of them.

The look in her eyes intensified, and she didn't blink as she stared at him and said, "If you took a kid, would you contact police?"

"Nope." He shook his head. Then nodded. And asked, "Did you eat?"

"It was buy one get one free," she told him, as though sharing their food was commonplace. "I called upstairs and Lindsay told me your favorite and then placed the order for me."

Lindsay, the fifty-seven-year-old woman who'd been running their office since the firm's inception. Along with help from Sarah, the very temporary manager they'd had in the year before to bring their records up to date.

A woman who'd lied to them all—though for good reason.

Glen shrugged away the memory. He'd grown to care about Sarah very much. Just hated that he hadn't seen through her to begin with.

And remembered how Winchester, their financial expert partner, his friend since college, had felt when he'd found out he'd brought a liar into their firm.

The memory gave him pause, as he sat there, completely engrossed in a case he was paying the firm to take on for a woman he'd just met a few days before.

A woman he'd brought into his home.

Almost as though sensing that her presence was creating angst within him, Lorna headed for the door, saying, "I've got to get back. I've got several tests running on things from the evidence box."

She was gone before he had a chance to give her a response.

But left a taunting whiff of lavender scent behind.

LORNA WAS ALONE on her side of the lab by six that evening. Another scientist was working on the far side of the building. She could see a light on over there. But everyone else had gone home. She'd yet to get to know any of them. Had had a couple smile at her, murmur hello, but, overall, there wasn't much mingling going on among Sierra's Web forensic staff.

She appreciated the privacy.

And was getting hungry again. After the excitement of the morning, finally laying hands on the evidence box, testing the pen, getting positive results, she'd spent the next several hours running various tests on bagged evidence. She'd cataloged every single result, but nothing had popped out at her as anything that pointed to puzzle pieces they could use.

Still, the familiarity of the work and the strict guidelines required by protocols were soothing. Brought her back to a self that she was familiar with. Comfortable with. The safe confines of the Sierra's Web lab, along with finally having the time to go through the plethora of evidence from the Billingsley case with no distractions, also contributed to a sense of well-being—a mixture of confidence and security—she'd been missing since she'd left her office at Stellar five days before.

It lasted right up until the lab suddenly went dark. The lights. And all her equipment, too. Grabbing her phone, she turned on the flashlight, and then dialed Glen.

"Stay put," he said, as soon as he picked up. "I'm on my way to you…"

By the time he'd finished the last word, she heard him in the hall as well as through the phone. The call disconnected and he was sliding his phone into the pocket of his lab coat as he entered her space, saying, "Might just be something as simple as a problem with an electrical line." Though, typical of Phoenix in the spring, there was no hint of any storm. What little she'd seen of daylight skies since she'd been there had been clear blue, beneath a sun so bright it lit the world. "The generator should kick on any second."

He stood there, as though waiting for his prophecy to come to be, and when it didn't, pulled out his phone and dialed.

Other than an initial "What's going on?" Glen's side of the conversation was conducted in total silence. She watched his eyes narrow and a frown appear on his forehead.

And felt her stomach drop at the look of concern he shot her way as he hung up.

"Someone from Hud's team noticed what appeared to be an intelligence drone on our surveillance screen late this afternoon," he told her. "It was gone before they could identify it. But an electrical outage on top of that is too much of a coincidence for us to just ignore."

The lifetime of fear she'd just conquered before lunch came rushing back with such strength it took Lorna's breath away. She sat. Forced her mind to focus through the fog. Looked at Glen, because it helped, and said, "So what, we just sit here? What if they're dropping something on the building? Some kind of chemical that could be slowly killing us, even now?" The thought that had seemed completely valid in her head didn't seem as much so said aloud.

She wasn't surprised when Glen, standing a couple of feet away, said, "Then why warn us with an electrical outage?

Why not let us just stay here and work and die in the process?"

She nodded. "And I noticed a couple of gas chromatographs connected to mass spectrometers, on either end of the lab," she said. Letting him know that she was still in possession of a wit or two. The powerful equipment could pick up such small traces of chemical in the air that they'd have been alerted by sirens before they'd been in danger.

That coherent thought led to another. "You think someone tampered with the electric to get people out of the building?"

He shrugged. Cocked his head. Pushed at the nosepiece on his black frames. And finally said, "It's one theory. Maybe the most obvious."

"Or they want to prevent us from finding out something we might be on the verge of discovering." Strength was returning.

"Either way, we're going to wait it out a bit," he told her then. "Hud's the only one still upstairs. The computer lab has around-the-clock experts, and Clive is still down here with us. Security is checking out the entire building, inside and out, while Hud waits to hear back from the electric company."

Fear eased out of her slowly. Almost as though Glen was pulling it out of her and causing it to evaporate with his magical powers.

She searched for something intelligent to say. Something professional, and came out with, "What are we going to have for dinner?"

At which point she grinned. And said, "I was planning to make spaghetti. You have everything I need for the homemade sauce."

"I don't have any spaghetti," he pointed out.

"The boxed macaroni salad mixes come with pasta shells. They give you bursts of sauce flavor as you eat."

Oh, good lord. Bursts of sauce flavor?

With his brow raised, Glen sat down. "Am I making you nervous all of a sudden, because…"

"No." Her blurted response was a little too urgently delivered, but unequivocal. "Exactly the opposite. I'm just trying to focus on plebian things, so I don't start to get claustrophobic down here."

It wasn't until after she'd let that little tidbit out that her brain replayed the *because*. He had been about to tell her something she might have wanted to hear before she'd cut him off.

"I didn't know you struggled with closed-in spaces. You should have said something. We've got a free lab down the way, I can see about combining two of them…"

Lorna shook her head, cutting him off again. "I'm fine here," she told him. Getting finer by the second as they just sat and talked, like regular people, about nonwork stuff. Like they were complete equals. "It's just the unknown source of the threat against me, combined with unexpected drones and unexplained darkness," she said. And then added, "I was still holding out hope that whoever this someone is, they didn't know I was here. Working with Sierra's Web."

"Even if the request for the Billingsley evidence box wasn't somehow leaked, Brian's been in Morrilton for a couple of days," he reminded her. "Flashing his Sierra's Web credentials, asking questions of a lot of people."

Right. She'd known that. Just didn't seem to be very proficient at facing full truths head-on when it came to her own personal safety. Not a fun realization to have.

"I was actually getting ready to head down to see you when the electricity went out," Glen said, his hands propped on his knees, arms straight. Looking as though he had something good to say.

She needed it. "You've got some good news?"

"I have two pieces of information," he said, and then immediately followed that with, "I got a hit on the DNA I extracted from the saliva found on the pen."

Jumping up, Lorna took a step closer to him. Mouth open. "Who is she? Have you found her? Is she being questioned?"

She couldn't believe it. Their long shots really were producing results. Just as she'd always believed they would. Once she was given a chance to pursue them. Science held all the answers.

It took her a second to realize that Glen wasn't even close to jumping up and down. She took a deep breath. Crossed her arms.

And heard him say, "Her name was Michelle Applegate."

Was. Her stomach sank. But they'd been right about the pen biter having been a woman. She waited.

"She was from Searcy." He named the small college town where he'd graduated from college. An hour or so drive from Little Rock. And only another forty-five minutes to Morrilton.

Their proximity had been one of the reasons she'd first been introduced to Glen's work.

"She died wrapping her car around a tree just outside of town. Cause of the crash was excessive speeding and a blood alcohol level half a point over the legal limit." His words hit her with a weight that pushed her back to her stool.

Sitting, she asked, "When?"

"A month after Simon went missing."

"Was kidnapped. Simon was kidnapped." She said the words aloud. Had to hear them. To face them. And then drew the next obvious conclusion. "If she *was* at the park that day and did see something, even if she was involved in the kidnapping—" she stumbled just a notch over the word "—we certainly can't question her about it."

He nodded. "Brian's in Searcy, anyway. Trying to find out if she had family there. The address on record for her is twenty-three years old, so he might not find much."

"And he might," she had to say. "Small towns have a way of remembering. Generations of families do still stay put sometimes."

Hers hadn't. Not after she'd left for college. But then nothing about her youth had been traditional.

"I also wanted to let you know that Hud's tech team has been poring over every twenty-three-year-old record from the area, some from online, some copies that were emailed to them. Based on electric bills, hotel records, credit card receipts, they found a couple of hundred names of people who'd been in the Morrilton vicinity the day Simon disappeared, and who left right afterward."

Disappeared. He was still using the word.

Because, technically, until they found the truth, they didn't know what had happened to the little boy. All they could prove was that he'd *gone missing.* She hadn't been as off base as she'd let herself think.

The thought calmed her some.

"They'll be following up on every one of them," he told her. "As will Brian when he gets back from Searcy either tonight or tomorrow."

The amount of work being done because of a case she'd brought to the firm was overwhelming. And overwhelming her, too. Her refusal to give up, her lifetime of work on every small detail she had, her age progression and facial recognition system, had laid the groundwork. But mostly her belief in the possibility that one two-year-old boy could be found decades later had drawn such effort from so many. That realization brought tears to her eyes.

Glen stood abruptly. Turned to look at the evidence bags she'd yet to get to lined neatly on the counter closest to him. Almost as though he'd seen the moisture she'd blinked from her eyes.

And hadn't wanted to be privy to it.

Taking pity on him, she asked, "Any word from Hud's team regarding the facial recognition photos?"

His back still to her, he nodded. Then said, "Nothing complete yet. We should have a report by morning. If it's done before midnight, they'll shoot it to me at home via our secure server."

At home.

Where he'd be.

And where she'd be, too.

Lorna had no idea where anything that was happening was going to lead. The sudden—so far inexplicable—electrical outage, the threats against her, the almost impossible goal of solving a twenty-three-year-old cold case, the strange emotional tumbles she seemed to be taking, all hung over her. On her. Inside her.

And yet, knowing that she wasn't alone—that Glen was on the tense and potentially life-threatening ride with her—was showing her an inner strength she hadn't known she'd had.

She was just another job to him, but he'd become much more than that to her.

And even though she saw the clear ending to their relationship at case end, she wasn't sorry she'd sought him out. Didn't think she'd ever be.

No matter what came in her future, knowing him had made her life better.

Chapter Twelve

An unidentified drone had crashed into the main electrical wire that fed power to a half-mile radius that included Sierra's Web's office building. It could be several hours before the line was fixed and power was back on. The incident might be a fluke, a coincidence, completely unrelated to Lorna or any of the other cases currently being handled by the firm of experts. Except that the lab remained without backup power. The generator, housed in a fenced area behind the five-story office building, had water in the fuel tank. It hadn't rained in over a month—there was no way that had been a twist of fate. Or an accident, either.

Whether it was a direct attempt to get at Lorna or was targeting Sierra's Web in general was far too soon to guess. Sierra's Web tech experts working from their homes were assisting local officials to try to get an identification on the drone, to determine, if they could, whether it was the same flying object that had been seen hovering over Sierra's Web late in the afternoon.

Any long-running tests in the lab that required power were all on individual battery sources. And with portable power sources, Glen and Lorna had power for their phones. They had flashlights. And a key to the vending machine to open it and grab whatever snacks they wanted for free.

He didn't want any. Neither did Lorna.

"We'll wait it out until dark," he told her, once they were all alone in the lab. Not missing the ironic glance she sent at his missive. They were in the dark, waiting for darkness to fall.

Full security surrounded the building. "Hud's upstairs with a couple of local police officers. When it's dark enough, he'll be escorted out to his SUV, drawing any watchers' attention. At the same time, we'll head out an emergency exit behind the trash compactor. Our car, without lights, and a security team will be waiting for us. We'll be off the lot before Hud and his crew get to his vehicle. Should only be another half hour or so."

"I can't believe this is happening," Lorna said, her gaze concerned, filled with appropriate amounts of worry, but a sense of calm, too. Maybe more so than he was feeling. He had his gun. Knew how to shoot it. And had a black belt in martial arts, too. All the partners did. With refresher courses completed the year before after Dorian, their medical expert, had been taken hostage just blocks from her home. He ran through a mental rundown of what he knew, a checklist of actions to take in any eventuality. Realizing, about halfway through, as he stood at the ready in his office, that perhaps Lorna, who was sitting on the edge of an armchair against the wall, should be made aware of some things before he took action.

"I've got a SIG." He got right to the point. Retrieved the weapon from the top drawer in his desk. Felt better as he checked the chamber, and then shoved the weapon in the waistband of his pants, where it would be hidden from sight by his lab coat.

"I'm fully trained and licensed to use it. I'm certified in self-defense, too," he added.

She was watching him. Not moving. And a full minute later asked, "You ever shoot anyone?"

There was that. He wasn't all that surprised that she'd homed in on the weak point of his preparation. "Never."

"Ever shoot *at* anyone?"

"Nope."

"Ever been in a situation where someone near you *did* shoot at someone?"

"No."

She nodded. And he left it at that.

HE KEPT HIMSELF between her and the only entrance to the room. Lorna noticed. She had to pee, but didn't say so. Figured the urgency was due to nerves. She should be fine once they were in the car on their way home.

If not then, she'd be good for sure when they were safely ensconced in Glen's house. In her current tense moments, his place felt like home to her. A lot more than the burned-out-garage property she owned.

She felt a lot better twenty minutes later, sitting in the back seat of a nondescript beige SUV with Glen as Jamison drove them along a route they hadn't been on before.

Her very temporary boss leaned over to her, and she tilted toward him naturally, to hear him say in a near whisper, "The windows are bulletproof." A piece of information meant to reassure her, but it made her nervous all over again. For their safety, but for another far more practical reason as well.

She chose to focus on the latter. "This has to be costing a fortune," she said softly. "Where's the money coming from?" She'd pay it all back, if it turned out that she'd brought the danger to Phoenix with her. It was just going to take a while.

He shook his head. "Write-off," he said. A company write-off, she translated. And further filled in blanks with her knowledge of how that worked. Sierra's Web was paying their employees, but not taking a cut for themselves. And they'd claim the employee portion as a business expense, or perhaps a charitable donation.

As successful as they were, she imagined they could use the tax break. And knew that she was still going to be sending them money every month for the foreseeable future. At least for the expense that was being incurred on her behalf.

"What do you think are the chances of this all being due to the Billingsley case?" She had her calculation. But trusted his judgment.

"Ninety-five percent."

She'd been at ninety-eight. Didn't bother saying so.

They took another turn. And then another. Traveling roads she'd never been on before. Going west. Glen's property was east. It was one thing to vary the route, but to go in the complete opposite direction?

Jamison and McKenna were both sitting straight, appearing to be watching intently, mirrors and road. They were being paid to do so. Whether the actions were necessary or not.

They didn't appear to be speaking at all.

Someone being paid well to pay attention probably shouldn't be engaging in casual conversation.

She'd ridden with them both a few times, and neither of them had appeared anywhere near as…tense…as they currently did. The constant changing of views. Taking in everything all the time. With very little body movement.

As though they didn't want anyone to know they were watching?

The light in front of them turned red. Jamison didn't slow down. Bracing herself for the sudden stop when the bodyguard realized that he had a red light, Lorna gasped as the man pushed harder on the gas and flew through the signal. And then made a quick turn.

No one said a word, so she didn't. They sat there, four people together in the enclosed space, in utter silence as laws were broken.

Something was very wrong. It didn't take a scientist to figure that one out.

More quick turns. A backtrack, and then a turn south. Glen's home was north.

Tension built within her. To the point of nausea. Light-headedness.

Panic.

That's all it was. She had to refocus. To keep her mind on that which she could affect, not fear that which she couldn't. It was the only way to be ready for whatever challenge presented itself next.

She would be ready. She wasn't going to just disappear...

Glen's hand slid over hers. Just there. Covering her skin with warmth. She needed more. Turning her hand, she put her palm to his, wrapped her fingers through his, held on tight.

And was able to draw a deep, healthy breath when his grip slowly deepened to equal hers.

She might be in imminent danger. With a captor gaining on her. Ready to pounce. But she wasn't two years old. Or helpless.

And she wasn't alone, either.

GLEN REALLY NEEDED to be alone. To face the danger himself. Deal with all the consequences. He'd taken the case. Had he not, Lorna would likely have been in no more danger than she'd been in for the past few years. Without Sierra's Web's resources, she'd been unable to make headway. Had posed no threat.

By bringing Lorna into Sierra's Web's headquarters, he'd also put his firm at greater risk than normal.

Encased in darkness, in the back of the powerful and potentially deadly cocoon, he took the weight of Lorna's smaller frame against him when the car made another sudden sharp turn. And felt himself slide into her with the force of an immediate fast swerve in the opposite direction.

The hand holding hers let go and flew quickly up and over her head to brace his weight against the side of the vehicle. And then…stayed there. Sliding down to lie around her shoulders. Ready to fend off the next move that could crush the air from her lungs.

Her body sank into his, her fist resting on his thigh. He felt as though he was on a roller-coaster ride over the next few minutes. Being whipped side to side, bumping as Jamison took the SUV off road through the desert to come out on a street Glen hadn't even known was there.

The car's Global Positioning System had been turned off. He and Lorna had been instructed to do the same on their phones before they'd left Sierra's Web headquarters. Glen fully understood and commended the choice.

But was growing more concerned about help reaching them in the event that they weren't able to get away from whoever was obviously following them. He'd known Jamison a long time. The man lived on his property. And was as solid as they came when guarding his charges. There was no way he'd be taking them out for some ill-considered joyride.

They slid to Lorna's side of the vehicle again, and he braced her from the side of the interior, and then wrapped his hand more firmly around her shoulder. Just in time for Jamison to hit a bump that sounded like it bottomed out the frame of the vehicle and threw Lorna upward against the seat belt. Her head bumped the rest behind it as she fell back fully into the leather.

He remained silent. Had no words for such a moment. Just held on to her. And as her hand returned to his thigh, flat that time, not in a fist, he covered it with his free one.

They'd opted to form their partnership. They were on the ride together.

And all they could do was hold on.

Lorna almost wept when she recognized the corner leading to Glen's gated community. They were safe.

For the moment.

She had no reason to continue to clutch his thigh.

He had no reason to hold her shoulder. But she noticed that he didn't slide his arm off her shoulders and back over to himself.

Even when they entered the private gate leading to his property.

He held her until the car had pulled into the empty stall in his three-car garage, and the door shut behind him.

At that point, on Jamison's direction, he had to reach into his lab coat pocket for his phone, which necessitated letting go of her. She used the action to pull her hand discreetly back to her own lap. Making certain that no part of her body was touching any part of his.

While McKenna stood guard at the door of Glen's house, Jamison went in to check that the place was secure. Glen, his gaze on the doorway into his laundry room, didn't speak. And in spite of her sudden need to blab, to apologize at the very least, she didn't make a sound.

Not even when they were finally in the house. She stood while Jamison and McKenna gave them a list of instructions. They were to stay away from all windows—couldn't even walk in front of them. And to keep their phones on, location still off, at all times.

Glen had a secure, scrambled internet line at home and so they were permitted to work.

He didn't look her way as they both took in the rules they'd have to live by for the next few hours, at least, until they knew more. McKenna had a make and model of the car that had been following them.

A midsize, black vehicle like a million others. Nothing that stood out.

But she'd seen the driver's face once—when a streetlight had flashed on—and had already called it into the police and Hud.

Hud had said to tell Glen that they should have the guy yet that night. They'd deep dive his phone, his accounts, and stay on him until they knew more.

Glen nodded at that last. Lorna kept glancing at him, wishing he'd look her way, needing to connect with him. To know that he was okay.

That they were okay.

All she got was his look of professional attention on the two bodyguards who'd be supplemented by added security outside the house. The entire place was surrounded and would remain so until they had answers.

"Hud's got a team watching airspace for the night as well," Jamison said as the session seemed to be close to ending. "They'll know if a drone even tries to get close to your neighborhood."

Glen looked at her then. As though she were a total stranger. And said, "We have permission to connect to government satellites."

She nodded. Impressed, actually. And relieved, too.

She didn't see herself sleeping anytime before they knew more. Even if that took more than a day. But she wasn't panicking, either.

Almost two hours had passed since she and Glen had been alone together without bodyguards in their immediate space. She was about to ask Glen what he wanted for dinner, when she heard a car start in the garage.

Eyes open, fear sluicing through her, she looked at him,

standing between the kitchen and dining room, going through mail that had been on the counter. Brought in by security? Or Jamison?

"Did you hear that car?"

Barely lifting his gaze to her, he did spare her a brief glance and then was looking back down at the envelope in his hand as he said, "McKenna's taking the car back to the lab. A couple of forensic experts will be going over it right away, to see if there was any kind of tracking device. It was checked thoroughly before we left. It should have been near to impossible to find us."

"Unless someone saw us pulling out."

"The tail didn't start until we were twenty minutes into the drive and on a route no one knew we'd be on. Including me."

That was news to her. And she'd been with him the entire time since the electricity went off. Obviously, he hadn't shared a lot of the information he'd been given during his one-sided conversations. It had seemed as though he'd kept her in the loop all along. He'd relayed information every step of the way.

But he'd withheld some, too.

She made a mental note of the fact. Focusing on doing that, rather than on the spear of hurt feelings that shot through her.

Clearly, he didn't trust her as completely as she trusted him. She had mentally entrusted her life's work, and her safety, to his keeping.

"You want that spaghetti?" she asked.

He nodded. Threw the unopened envelopes in the trash. She caught a glimpse of one. Clearly some kind of gold credit card offer. He still wasn't looking at her.

Because she'd touched his leg? Or because he'd kept his arm around her? Was it her he was upset with? Or himself?

Lorna turned her back on the situation and opted to start dinner. Cooking soothed her. And her homemade spaghetti sauce took a while to simmer, with her adding spices to taste throughout.

"You want a beer?" Glen asked, pulling a bottle out for himself.

She wasn't much of a beer drinker. Or one who consumed alcohol except on special occasions, but her nod contained some gusto as she accepted the opened bottle he handed her and he reached in for another for himself.

Expecting him to be out of the room before he'd even swallowed his first gulp, she turned to reach for the pan she wanted. And heard a stool at the counter bar scrape against the floor. Glancing over, she saw Glen sitting there, scrolling on his phone.

Connected to the secure Wi-Fi, she was sure.

And set to work, much more pleased to have him there, than to be in any part of the house alone.

Just until she got her mojo back.

And maybe had a chance to find a dose of the inner strength that he seemed to bring to the fore within her.

Chapter Thirteen

Glen wasn't reading much of what was flashing on his phone. He'd opened a news source and randomly scrolled, while his mind cataloged the events of the past few hours. Starting from the time the electricity went out.

He needed to get to work and couldn't do that without a concise plan of action, formed from scientific examination of what he knew—which would lead to what he had yet to find out.

And from there to a list of priorities.

He also had to get his awareness of Lorna as a woman, not a scientist, out of his mind. And, even more importantly, out of his body.

It was like the woman had donned some kind of cheap pheromone perfume right before the lights had gone out.

He'd been turned on innumerable times in his life. Never even close to what he'd been experiencing that day. With that woman.

Who was licking tomato juice off her finger as she walked to the sink. And then rinsed the digit he'd just had a fantasy about suckling on.

Drying her cleaned hand, she moved past him toward the dining room. "Where are you going?" His question came out far sharper than intended.

"To get my computer." She'd stated her intention, but remained at a standstill, as though waiting for his approval before continuing.

And he stood. Didn't want her out of his sight for any length of time. Or in any part of the house with windows that accessed the front of the house. Just a gut instinct—or fear based on Jamison's warning to stay away from windows.

Not based on proof of an immediate threat directly outside his home.

Which left him no way to explain. "I'll get it for you," he said, and because he was closer to the mark, was able to cut her off before she had a chance to stop him.

She'd dropped her satchel in a living room chair while they'd been debriefed by their bodyguards. He picked up the satchel, but went further, too, all the way back to the suite she was using, to grab the laptop she'd mentioned having set up in there, as well.

Information gleaned the day she'd moved in when he'd grilled her about her protocols. Both of her devices had ample space to store everything she needed, with duplicate files. And only transferred information back and forth between the two of them through manual plug-in, one to the other.

She was careful. Smart. Didn't use any cloud storage. As he'd already assured Hud.

She was the only person he'd ever met who was as careful as he was to protect the sanctity of every single test, or pool of research, that he did.

The thought brought a sense of understanding.

Feeling himself slipping off some invisible precipice, Glen quickly gathered up the plugged-in machine and adapter, and with the satchel on his shoulder, headed back to the breakfast bar that separated a portion of the kitchen from the dining room.

Lorna was back at the stove, browning hamburger on the

burner next to the one where she'd been filling a big pan with canned tomatoes, tomato sauce, and various other things he'd ordered up for delivery while reading recipes he thought he'd like to try.

And then had never gotten around to trying.

And, standing there, her laptop on the counter, it occurred to him to ask, "Did you check the dates on those cans?"

"Yep." She threw him a grin. One that couldn't have been at all sexy, but had seemed to his wayward gaze to be. "I learned that lesson last night."

He grinned too, then. While taking in his positioning of her laptop. And then her satchel.

Looking everywhere but the field of vision in which he'd catch any glimpse of her.

LORNA DIDN'T HAVE a lot of experience with men. She'd dated. Had planned the night she lost her virginity in college. Not having had sex had become like a stigma to her. Everyone had done it. Talked about it. Scientifically, sex had implications that she didn't quite believe. So she'd made arrangements with a guy she liked and trusted for a onetime thing. It hadn't been great for either one of them. She'd enjoyed a night or two of preplanned sex with a guy she'd gone out with during grad school. She'd just never found anything that drew her to seek out male companionship over her work. Anytime she'd had free had been spent in the lab with the Billingsley case.

Or at home, relaxing. Cleaning. Cooking. In a peace that had been…peaceful.

Standing there in Glen's kitchen, she took off her lab coat, leaving her in the close-fitting light beige short-sleeved knit shirt she'd put on with brown pants that morning—a lifetime ago—and stole a glance at Glen as she threw the coat over the back of a bar stool.

Needing some kind of sign from him, an acknowledgment of the connection they'd shared during the harrowing drive home. Even if just to talk about how frightening the trip had been.

He was back on his stool, his thumb moving along his phone's face.

Then, almost as though the strength of her need had reached him, he looked up and caught her gaze, and stood again. Turning away abruptly, he took a couple of steps, and, without slowing, or turning back, said, "Going for my computer."

Leaving her with a strong impression that his path had been an escape route. Not that she was any good at discerning such things.

Or would have any idea how to interpret his strange behavior.

At the moment, with them locked in, danger lurking, and everything hanging in a state of not knowing, she wasn't sure she wanted to decipher his current state.

Her sauce was simmering. The meat was covered, on warm, and waiting to go join the nicely spiced tomato-based liquid. Her computer called out to her.

And while Glen did, too—call to her—silently, inside her—she opted to give her attention to that which she trusted. That in which she was fully confident of her abilities to discern, process, and accomplish. Settling herself on a stool two down from Glen's former perch, she noticed that the beer bottle he'd left behind was still three-quarters of the way full and took a third sip from her own.

She was running through the mental to-do list she'd just made, already knowing the two things at the top of her list. First, she had to try to clean up the one partial fingerprint she'd managed to lift, with the use of metal-organic framework crystals, from the end of the pen. She had a couple of powerful programs, along with learned techniques, to aid in the process. She needed it to be as clean as it could be to run it against Michelle Applegate's print—if there was one.

And to run a check for the woman's dental records as well. Lorna's bite mark mold was extensive enough to get a match on that one.

In her mind, the tests were imperative. That pen had stood out to her the first time she'd read about it in the list of evidence taken from the scene. Maybe because it was the only halfway valid piece. The only thing that indicated a visitor to the park, not the park itself.

It was possible that Michelle hadn't been the only one to handle the pen.

Focused fully on the case, she was fine and had a decent plan.

Until Glen had been gone for more than five minutes.

And, looking at his still-full beer bottle, she wondered why he hadn't returned.

He could be in the restroom, she told herself.

Or working where he could be alone. That thought carried far more weight. And left her feeling heavier, too.

Why offer a beer, and take one for himself, just to leave her alone with both bottles?

Was he that eager for homemade spaghetti?

And she'd been thinking he didn't want to leave her alone until they had some answers about the day's adverse events. Hoping so, at any rate.

He'd insisted they remain together at Sierra's Web once things had gone haywire. She had just kind of thought the protocol would remain in place once they were home as well.

It wasn't like he was the one who suggested she work in the kitchen. She was the one who'd said she was going for her computer. She'd also been busy preparing a meal for them while he'd just been sitting there.

His offer had been polite. Simply that. Nothing more.

"I talked to Hud." Glen's sudden return startled her so much she jumped in her chair. She hadn't heard him coming. But then, he was only just then coming around the corner through the dining room. Had started to talk to her before he'd arrived.

Something he seemed to have a habit of doing.

Some might find it irritating. She thought it was kind of endearing.

Or maybe just preferred to think about his habit for a second longer, to prolong having to deal with whatever he had to say.

The serious tone in his voice had warned that the news wouldn't be good, even before she'd seen the stiff expression on his face.

He had his laptop under one arm. Just stood there holding it as he said, "The drone spotted earlier hovering over Sierra's Web had no visible registration numbers, and I doubt it would have been registered with the national database, in any case."

She nodded. Followed his information clearly. Agreed with his assessment. Tension escalated within her.

"However, the signals it put out made it possible for Hud's team to identify it as the same make and model of the drone that damaged the electrical cable."

Heart beating harder, she stared at him. "It was the same drone."

He shrugged, gave a brief headshake. "We can't say that for sure. Only that it was the same make and model. One that Hud's team can't find on the market."

"You're telling me it was a homemade drone?"

Another shrug and then, "All we know is that the signals it puts out don't match any known to be commercially for sale."

"So, what, it's a government thing? Like some kind of classified mission?" Even just saying the words was surreal.

She couldn't wrap her mind around what they could mean. Or come up with possible implications.

Glen's headshake was a comfort that time. He continued to hold her gaze as he said, "Not one that anyone knows about. We've got contacts with the FBI, who put out feelers."

Of course they did. Have the contacts.

It was why she'd come to Glen, to Sierra's Web. They could take her case without red tape or specific guidelines to be met. And they were more connected than any single source she'd ever heard of.

And, picking up her beer, taking a long sip, she frowned. Still holding her bottle, needing more from the liquid courage than it was providing, she asked, "So what's your theory?" Because she sure as hell didn't have one.

"At this point, just that Sierra's Web was likely the target."

He was still meeting her gaze, so she didn't look away. Didn't want to lose a second of the connection he offered.

"Which we kind of already assumed," she managed to get out.

"There was no forensic evidence on the generator. Other than a piece of earth that had been mussed."

"To cover up a footprint," she blurted out. Her mind finally gaining strength on her overactive emotions.

"That's the logical conclusion."

"How was the fence surrounding it breached?"

"Nothing showed up on the surveillance cameras. And there was no obvious explanation. The team had night work lights out there, brushed for fingerprints over every inch of the fence. The lock was intact."

"When was the last time the generator was used?" The question popped out. And Lorna took another sip of beer.

Glen picked up his as well, took a sip, before saying, "I'm not immediately aware of the date, but it's checked every month. Last check was seventeen days ago. Nothing shows on camera since then. Police are following up with the company we hire to service our alternate power sources."

Something struck her then. "Including the instruments in the lab running on their own power?"

He nodded.

And she was afraid she was getting where he'd been going all along. She'd noticed the equipment in her lab had capabilities to run on its own high-powered battery source. She just hadn't had cause to use it.

"So someone outside of Sierra's Web could know I was there." Where it went from there, she hadn't yet figured out.

"Someone knew that I had a vacant space in the lab outfitted and operational on Monday."

Sticking with the facts. She appreciated his approach. But the conclusion was fairly obvious.

"You think someone who doesn't want me to succeed with the Billingsley case was able to find out who serviced the backup power sources at Sierra's Web, and was able to find out there that a new lab was being used?"

He sipped. And shrugged.

"Then why the drone surveillance?"

"I've already added two new labs in the past six months," he told her, still standing by the stool he'd vacated earlier. "A new lab in and of itself isn't verification of who's occupying it."

She frowned then. Set her bottle down. Went to stir sauce that didn't need her attention yet. "The drone was meant to fly until I came out," she said as she stirred. Speaking as though she was discussing whether or not to have bread with dinner. "But since it was discovered, they went to plan B."

"That's the current theory."

Well, at least she was capable of finding the same conclusion the experts at Sierra's Web had reached. She dismissed the thought as having no merit.

Hated that she'd even had it. Such mental processes spoke of a lack of confidence. Something she hadn't started to exhibit until she'd flown to Phoenix.

She'd rather live with the anxiety than start to doubt herself.

The thought pulled her up straight. Propelled her back to her computer.

And as Glen sat down in the stool one over from her, using the same power source as her to plug in his laptop, she engaged herself fully in the search for answers.

Allowing herself to be glad that he was at work beside her.

As much as Glen yearned to be sitting someplace safe with Lorna, his arm around her, her hand on his leg, he knew he had to shake the memory. To leave it behind.

Just as he had to step off the Billingsley case. His personal commitment to Lorna's dedication to the case—his own need to find out what had happened to the little boy to bring his twin peace—didn't carry enough weight to keep him on it. Sierra's Web had taken a direct hit. It was all hands on deck until they knew who and why.

He was aware of the scientist, though. Knew every time she stood to fiddle with her sauce. Was aware that she washed out the frying pan she'd used to brown the hamburger.

Heard her chopping before the smell of onions bothered the corners of his eyes. And wondered if they were bothering her, too.

But he didn't look up. Or allow himself to wander from his own investigations and various conclusions. From the messaging he was doing with Hud.

He didn't even allow himself a glance when she announced that dinner was ready. But he responded when she asked, "You want it in the dining room again?"

So much. Yes, he did. "No." His response came out more

abruptly than intended. He couldn't apologize for that. Couldn't look up, get that personal, get distracted. But he saw her shadow elongated on the kitchen tile. She was holding two plates. "I'll take it right here."

The plate, with fork and napkin, appeared. It smelled so good his mouth watered. "Thank you," was all he said.

But didn't move, didn't even breathe, until she sat down beside him. Rather than choosing to eat alone at the table behind him.

He was halfway through the meal—still with visual focus on his computer screen—had finished his bottle of beer, when she got up again. Her hand entered his field of vision. His bottle disappeared. He heard the two crash together in the trash and then the refrigerator open.

Another bottle appeared where his empty had been. And she asked, "What are you working on?"

She'd walked behind him. Would have seen his screen.

And he looked over at her. "I'm going through all the cases I've worked on, specifically the ones on which the work my lab did had a significant effect. Most recent first, but going out two years. Paying attention to factors such as wealth or connections of perpetrator, loss of that wealth or jail time as a result of that case."

She was back on her stool, lifting her opened bottle to her lips. Not at all an appropriate time for him to notice the roundness of her breasts against the shirt holding them so seductively.

And so not a normal Glen mindset. He was channeling a much younger Hud at the moment.

"You're making sure that today's threat doesn't have some other source." Lorna's words, the concerned frown his gaze finally made it up far enough to see, brought him back from a precipice that he had to avoid revisiting at all costs.

He nodded. Noticed what he perceived to be a warmth in

the green eyes staring back at him. And returned himself to his screen. His gaze, at least.

The one-of-a-kind scientist beside him battled with the words he was looking at for control of his thoughts.

Chapter Fourteen

Lorna took a long sip of her second beer. She wasn't much of a drinker, but didn't feel any adverse effects. He'd had a light brand in his refrigerator. Less alcohol.

But maybe able to provide some calming effect on the emotions roiling through her. She'd managed to clean up the partial fingerprint some. Had already searched the database for Michelle Applegate's prints. Was waiting on that result and checking—with Sierra's Web access over Glen's secure server—the National Crime Information Center to see if she got a hit on the bite mark mold she'd taken off the pen.

While waiting was and always had been a normal and expected part of her job—a part she'd often welcomed as it gave her mind a minute to rest and think of pretty things, or food—she was finding her current waits excruciating.

Partly because she was working on the Billingsley case and awaiting valid and pertinent information, not just chasing a long shot.

Partly because of the very real threat of danger hanging over their heads.

And also because of the man beside her.

In the car earlier, when she'd put her hand on Glen's thigh, she'd felt a couple of seconds of intense emotion. Not even a little bit like fear.

She'd wanted to raise her hand further. To touch him intimately.

The instinct had been so strong, she'd felt warmth between her legs. For the first time ever. She'd read about such physical reactions to the sexual act. Understood the science of it.

Had always been a bit skeptical about the truth behind the results.

"Hud just sent an update from Tony, the tech expert still working on the Billingsley facial recognition photos based on your age progression system." Glen's words, or rather his voice, busting into her sexual thoughts where he was so thoroughly present, sent another burst of warmth to her lower regions.

One that was instantly quashed as his words registered. "And?" she asked, staring at him.

He didn't look back at her. Acted as though he was reading from his screen, but didn't sound like he was reading as he said, "The boy in the elementary school in Georgia— he was eight, in third grade. Name was Billy. Not Shaking, though. Billy Simmons."

Her heart leaped. "Billy Simmons. Simon Billingsley! It has to be him!" Tears sprang to her eyes. It was really happening! Finally happening!

Her fingers itched to grab her phone and call Selena. She didn't, of course. Knew better than to reach out to anyone in her life while the potential threat hung over her.

And focused on Glen, instead. "So what did he find? Does Tony know where Billy is?"

When Glen finally looked over at her, a bit of the joy leaked from her system. His expression was...all scientist. And not one who'd just solved a case. "Similar to Billy Shaking, he just disappeared. At least as far as records go. He was in school for the second half of that year. No record of him returning after the summer break. And no requests for his records to have been forwarded to another school. Nor were there incoming records when he was enrolled. A woman had come in, claiming to be his mother. She'd had a birth certificate for him and a driver's license for herself under the name Anita B. Simmons. Gave an apartment address for them. Said she'd homeschooled him. And, unfortunately, that's all we know."

Okay. They weren't there yet. But they were definitely on their way. "I see a pattern here," she said, eyes wide-open as she spoke to Glen, while his focus appeared to still be on her. Not his screen. "A single woman. Trying to tend to a young boy's needs…" She stopped when she got to the end of the part she liked.

"One who was obviously on the run." Glen provided the rest. He continued to look at her, holding her gaze captive.

"We're a step closer," she told him. Smiled.

Saw his gaze deepen. And her nipples hardened.

The beer wasn't working as a calming agent.

She felt the warmth below again, too. Needed her lavender. And immediately excused herself to the restroom.

MICHELLE APPLEGATE HAD no known family. She'd grown up in foster care. And while there was no evidence pointing to her *not* having been in Morrilton the day that Simon went missing, there was also nothing that pointed to her being there then.

Her pen was found close to the time of the little boy's disappearance. "It stormed two nights before Simon vanished," Glen said as Lorna washed up dinner dishes. She'd had that perfume on when she'd returned from the bathroom.

He'd been a case of *want*s and *can't have*s ever since.

Was doing his best to focus on the one thing that had always consumed him to the exclusion of all else. Was unsettled to find that working two acute cases at once wasn't even enough to keep his mind from wandering in Lorna's direction.

And the perfume?

There was only one logical explanation for her to have donned it. She was a scientist. She'd know that the olfactory system responded sexually to certain scents.

She wanted to turn him on.

It was that thought that was maintaining forefront position in his head, no matter what he tried to do to displace it. He wasn't alone in his bizarre reaction to the scientist.

Made sense, really, since she was so much like him in other ways.

She wanted him as much as he was suddenly wanting her. Human beings were wired to feel attraction.

The realization didn't open any doors or put possibilities on the table, but it did oddly relax him some. Soothed him to know that he wasn't alone in the bizarre change in hormonal reactions that week.

There wasn't anything wrong with him.

And they had a couple of cases to solve. The current danger hounding her and Sierra's Web. And the Billingsley case. Feeling more like himself than he had since the electricity had gone out, Glen looked over at Lorna and said, "While we can't prove that Michelle Applegate was in the park during the time of Simon's disappearance, we *can* prove that her pen was dropped there within a twenty-four-hour period beforehand. First and most obvious, a pen lying in the dirt during a storm would have shown trace of mud…"

Lorna jumped in to say, "…There was no sign of any PFAS—per-and polyfluoroalkyl substances—on the implement. I specifically tested."

PFAS, the "forever" chemicals, were in all rain on earth.

Her hands wet, the dish wand she was holding suspended over a plate, she locked gazes with him. Seemed to tell him that she needed something from him. More than just his lab or his help to solve her case. More than protection from the unknown danger following her.

And he was in turmoil again. Troubled.

He could decipher pages of chemical coding. Find trace elements of minute evidence on a piece of grass. But he could not figure out how to interact with the scientist staying in his house.

LORNA DIDN'T FINISH her second beer. Nor did she let it sit in front of her, tempting her. She poured it down the sink. And, dishes done, put her mind on that which she could control. The work awaiting her on her computer.

She had no ability to create the outcome, but she could make darn sure there was one. As many of them as it took to find Simon Billingsley. The boy had been alive at four in Mississippi. At eight in Georgia. There had to be more.

If anyone could produce evidence from underneath Simon's fingernails shortly after he disappeared, then she'd have a paint sample chemical breakdown to compare it to.

Glen continued to scroll and type. Messaging with his partners. Researching cases. They didn't speak. She didn't need to do so.

Just having him there, working beside her, kept her focused on her own work.

Kept thoughts of the demons out in the dark at bay.

As the night grew later, and fatigue started to set in, she flipped from enhancing and studying more photos she'd shot that day of evidence taken from the park to the databases running, saw that the system was still searching, and felt a stab of panic in her stomach.

Took a whiff of her wrist. Inhaled the muted scent of lavender. And, with her stomach relaxing, looked back at her screen to see results…just sitting there.

Finally.

"The bite mark is a match to Michelle Applegate," she blurted aloud. And then, hearing Glen's fingers flying on his keyboard, glanced over. Sorry to have interrupted him. Her information wasn't newsworthy. Just confirmation of what they'd already known.

She opened the screen she'd been working on, a series of photos of items taken from the far end of the park, the area across from the church, enhancing and enlarging every inch of every photo, one portion at a time, to search for any sign of bench paint, of a two-year-old-size footprint. Focused. And yet, still noticed that Glen had stopped typing.

"You were hacked, Lorna."

His soft words, issued with more warmth than he used in the lab, drew her gaze slowly to his face. Filled with shock, she stared at him, trying to glean the ramification of what he was telling her.

Her work at Stellar? Her age progression system.

"You paid for the subs today with a personal credit card."

She nodded. "Lindsay needed it to phone in the order."

"Your card was hacked."

Oh. So… "There were a bunch of bogus charges on it?" she asked. Filling with relief. Money wasn't life. And most fraudulent charges could be reversed. Most particularly if caught early.

Which they just had been.

Glen had glanced back at his screen. Was staring at it silently. She figured adding up the amounts, to give her a figure in one fell swoop.

"Your card was hacked on Saturday," he said. And then glanced at her again, his gaze steady. Serious. And seemed to be full of strength, too.

Saturday. The day before she'd left town?

"There's been no fraudulent use of the card, Lorna. Someone has been tracking your usage."

And it hit her. She shivered. Got hot. And then cold again. "Whoever left the note…telling me to back off…" She paused, staring at Glen. "I didn't use that card until lunch today…"

Her words dropped again. Feeling sick, mouth slightly open, she just stared at him. The drone. The electricity outage. Water in the generator's fuel tank. All because of her.

He held her gaze. She read no accusation coming from his gray eyes. And her mind became clearer. "The fire. He didn't know where I was. Just wanted me to come home. One of the theories…"

Glen shrugged. But gave one single nod, as well.

Her chest tightened. "Who?" she asked. Bracing herself for the next question. Was he in custody?

Glen's headshake seemed as though he'd read her mind. Was answering the unspoken question, not the one currently hanging spoken, in the air between them.

"Hud's team is working on that. Whoever he is, he's got impressive tech experience. The hacking. The drone. And the anonymous hiring of a local employee…"

"The what?" She cut him off.

"The generator. An employee at our backup power supply source is in custody. He admits to adding water to the gasoline supply in the generator. Apparently, he's stolen some of the fuel to resell on the dark web and knew just where and how to access the fencing without being caught on camera. More cameras will be installed on the Sierra's Web office building back lot before morning."

Stomach tight, feeling sick and anxious, and wishing she hadn't had beer or dinner, she sat sideways on her stool, facing Glen, but holding her own hands on her own lap.

"The guy was contacted via email. Was offered ten thousand dollars to disable the generator in a way that wouldn't be noticeably detectable."

She swallowed. "Hud's team is trying to break the encryption on the email source, but, so far, is being pulled into a high-speed tech chase."

And she got it. "Whoever doesn't want me finding out what happened to Simon has a lot of money. Enough to buy top-tier information technology experts, an arsonist, this battery guy, and probably whoever was chasing us tonight as well?"

His nod was one slow movement. Up and down. No shrug.

"With that kind of wealth, he could also have law enforcement on the payroll."

Glen didn't break eye contact as he said, "That possibility is on the table, though there's been no evidence that anyone in the Morrilton police is holding out on us. Or putting up roadblocks to prevent us from accessing any and all records."

She wanted to believe. "That you know of." The words came out of her mouth, shining a light on her trust issues. "How would we know if they're hiding something from us if we don't know it exists?"

He did shrug at that. And then raised his brow, his gaze as serious as she'd ever seen it as he said, "The question is… do you want to continue with the Billingsley case or go into protective custody in another state until we catch this guy?"

As she opened her mouth even before he'd delivered the last word, he held up his hand and gave a sharp shake of his head. "Before you make any kind of choice or commitment, you need to know that Sierra's Web won't be bullied. We've taken on the case, made commitments to local and state law enforcement agencies, as well as the FBI, as part of having done so. We'll get the job done."

She heard what he was saying. She was no longer needed. And for a second, was tempted to tuck tail and run. That second, the six-year-old girl inside her came forth, afraid to play in the park, or even sit on a swing for fear that someone could grab her off it from behind and run with her before anyone had a chance to see.

But with one blink, that girl was gone. Replaced by the woman she'd become. "I won't be bullied, either," she said. "This is my case. I have to see it to the end."

She'd promised that little six-year-old, and Selena and Simon, too. She had to have the strength to take back what the kidnapper had taken from all three of them. And so many others.

Something seemed to change in his eyes. A light of some kind. A glint. And his lips softened, too, as he nodded.

And then, without another word, she turned back to her computer.

Choosing to believe that she'd somehow pleased him with her response, Lorna ran a hand through her short, thick, chaotic hair, and joined him in getting back to work.

NO ONE COULD protect her better than Sierra's Web could. The partners, all their experts, weren't superhuman, but together, as a whole, they were the closest thing to it.

Glen told himself that was the reason that he was so pleased that Lorna had chosen to stay and see her case through to the end. It was certainly one of them. The most important one.

And yet, as he stole a glance over at her while awaiting a response from Hud on the list of cases Glen had sent to him, Glen couldn't deny that he was also glad to have a little more time with the intriguing scientist.

He found himself finding a bit of pleasure even in hard and scary times with her, just because she was there. More so than he'd ever enjoyed being in the company of anyone else.

And that scent...

"Oh!" Her exclamation sent a shock wave of guilt through

him. One that quickly dissipated when he realized she was fully engrossed in whatever was on her computer screen, not catching him in the act of watching her.

Or reading his thoughts.

He leaned over, trying to get a glimpse of her screen. "What's up?"

Shaking her head, frowning, she didn't take her gaze from her screen. "I just found Michelle Applegate's fingerprint in the Searcy police database. Nothing came up in any of the national databases, so, on a hunch, I tried the local one. She'd been picked up for theft a couple of times as a juvenile."

"So we have our three-prong confirmation that she owned the pen and was likely the only one handling it before it was left in the park that day." He welcomed the conversation. Was relieved to be back working on the case.

Not thinking about the woman with whom he'd partnered to bring it to its close.

"No." She shook her head after speaking. "The fingerprint doesn't match. Not even a little bit."

With that last sentence, she turned to look at him.

And Glen's pulse ticked up.

Chapter Fifteen

Someone else had touched Michelle Applegate's pen. Probably after she had, since it was the only viable print on the writing implement.

What a day.

Lorna had spent more than two decades thinking about the Billingsley case. One of those decades, she'd been actively seeking answers in the boy's disappearance.

And in one day she had more evidence than those ten years had brought her.

Add to that the fact that the anxiety she'd been afraid of facing had been brought to life as well. The danger she'd feared had materialized.

Someone wanted to stop her from living her life's course. Whether they wished her dead or just stopped, she couldn't say, but it seemed obvious, with the lengths the guy was going to, the number of accomplices he'd already paid, that her death wouldn't be any spilled milk he'd cry over.

If it even was a *he* who was after her. Maybe Michelle had had a boyfriend. Who'd taken a two-year-old boy to sell him?

And the woman who bought him wanted to be a good mother to him but had ended up with a life that she had to live on the run.

Maybe she'd put in for adoption. Had thought the two-year-old had been obtained legally and had been in need of a mother.

Could Simon have just wandered off and ended up in the back seat of someone's car? She shook her head at the thought.

Energy thrummed through her. She'd been through more in twelve hours than she'd experienced in her entire life.

Parts of her, muscle and bones, mostly, were tired.

And she dreaded the thought of heading to the back of the house alone. To lie in the dark. Imagined herself lying there, exhausted, with a spinning mind that wouldn't let her sleep.

"You ever see the original *CSI*?"

Glen's words drew her gaze to him. He looked…she didn't know what. Different. Less boss and more just…person.

"Every episode," she told him. "That's how I got a lot of my ideas for investigative avenues when I was a kid."

He smiled. A real, complete facial expression that took her breath away. He was so incredibly…handsome…when he relaxed. More like a movie star than the so-serious expert forensic scientist that he was. And with those black-framed glasses, he made a perfect Clark Kent. Superman's alter ego.

She was more tired than she'd realized, entertaining such fantastical thoughts.

"Feel like watching one now?"

She saw Glen's lips move. Heard his words. Wasn't sure she'd translated them correctly in her brain. "You want to sit here and watch a television rerun?"

He shook his head and, having taken his question literally, embarrassment washed over her. Until he said, "I was thinking maybe in the den."

She didn't know there was a den.

"It's between my suite and the laundry room," he told her. "Along the garage wall of the house. Downside to the space is that there are no windows, but for right now, that sounds good to me."

A room without windows sounded wonderful to her, too. As did not being alone just yet. She smiled, and said, "Lead the way."

Figuring the man for a mind reader—if she could believe in such things.

More likely, they were similar enough in composition that he understood some of the things she wasn't saying.

And even more believable...he'd smelled her lavender and knew that she was having to resort to essential oils to help herself calm down.

Whatever the reason, Lorna shut down her computer as he did and, also following his example, carried it with her to a room that wouldn't be so alarming in the dark.

No windows. And Glen.

As perfect as her life ever got.

"I HAVE TO stay online," Glen said even before he'd reached the small room that he almost never occupied. There was a plug on one end of the dark brown, wall-to-wall, soft suede sectional sofa Kelly and Mariah had picked out for the space. He aimed for the corner seat, plugging in and placing his laptop on the big flat arm of the two-seat biggest piece. Hud and the team were sending constant updates, and he couldn't afford to miss one.

Not with their lives on the line.

"Are there two plugs?" Lorna asked, moving from the far end of the sectional over toward him. "I can't find one over here."

"It's covered by the corner piece." He pointed to the sectional's middle and held out his hand for her plug.

It was awkward that their electronic needs required them to share the two-seat section, but made the one ottoman less of a hassle as they could share it rather than have to decide who got it. He'd offer it to her. She'd say she didn't need it. They'd go back and forth, and regardless of who ended up using the thing, neither of them would feel great about it.

A bit dismayed when he realized how far his thought processes had tumbled, Glen grabbed the remote control out of the console mounted into the other end of the sectional and clicked to turn on the large-screen television mounted on the wall across from him. It and the sectional were the only two pieces of furniture in the room.

Lorna had already settled in her seat, having run her computer cord behind the cushion at her back, and Glen was careful to position himself as far from her as the space left to him would allow. Putting a good foot between them. He needed a minimum of four.

They'd been at it almost twenty hours, with a harrowing ride thrown in. He wasn't ready for sleep. Didn't intend to leave her alone until they'd apprehended the driver of the vehicle that had barreled straight at them with such speed at one point, the force of the crash would have smashed them into a wall. Hence Jamison's rough turns and cross-country maneuvers.

If not for the bodyguard, they'd have all likely been dead.

Something Glen had only found out about himself half an hour before. And had to relay to Lorna before she left the safety of the den. His sense of duty made the choice mandatory. His need to shield her from more trauma was putting up a good fight in the meantime.

They were fully protected. Unless a bomb fell on them.

Glen gave a mental shake of his head at the thought and focused on bringing up the first episode of the original *CSI* series he'd downloaded to stream. Because he'd never used the television, doing so required signing in, but he got there.

Sat back and allowed himself a brief glance in Lorna's direction, having felt her gaze on his back the entire time he'd been one-letter typing by using the remote to scroll across the screen.

She was engrossed in her computer screen.

Not him.

With a mixture of relief and a bit of disappointment, too, Glen pulled his own computer onto his lap.

LORNA LOST TRACK of the crime being solved on the television screen. Aware of Glen next to her—wondering if any of the work he was doing had anything to do with her or the Billingsley case—she mostly just wanted to lay her head on his shoulder and take a nap. Just for a minute or two.

To escape the tension that had become her life.

Professional, fear-based, emotional, and sexual, too. She'd arrived in Phoenix, and her entire life had seemed to expand with overwhelming rapidity.

As she continued to work on evidence photos, she tuned in for a couple of lab scenes on the screen, too. The methodology was outdated, but she took note of the human thought processes that led the "scientists" to successful conclusions.

Mostly she noted that, even on television, forensic science required patience and putting in long hours with little gain, until that one piece of information clicked. And solved the whole case.

That's what she was looking for.

The one miniscule piece that was going to open the floodgates. Or, even just by itself, prove what had happened to Simon Billingsley.

And hopefully lead them to the man the boy had become.

They'd made great strides in the few days she'd been in Phoenix. Enough to propel her for the rest of her life, if that's what it took, to bring the case to a close.

But they still were no closer to knowing what had happened to that two-year-old child twenty-three years ago in the park. Nor did they know where Simon currently resided. Or even if he was still alive.

The television silenced and she looked up to see the paused screen.

"Hud's team is following a lead." Glen's words, coming from right beside her, sent a trigger of hope to her heart.

Looking over, she met the familiar sight of him focusing on his screen and waited.

"They've made it through more than a hundred of the people who, based on various things such as electric bills, hotel and apartment rentals, credit card receipts and shop records, were all in Morrilton the day Simon disappeared and left within a day or two afterward. Some left and returned. Others were just passing through…"

His words dropped off. His hands stilled on the keyboard, and then suddenly, Glen turned to look at her. His gaze was almost apologetic and most definitely concerned as he said, "Tonight, in the car…when the ride got…scary…the car that was following us…actually, first tried to broadside us into a wall."

She swallowed as her mind immediately switched gears, leaving the day twenty-three years ago to jump into the most recent past. But instead of homing in on the idea of possibly being smashed like a pancake, she looked Glen in the eye, her expression steady, and said, "That's why we're in here."

He nodded and did not look away.

Her lips pursed. She understood that he'd previously withheld the information it had been her right to know. But felt a rush of warmth, too, at his inability to keep his secret. Glen Rivers Thomas was a stand-up guy. Just as she'd gleaned from the hours of watching videos of his lectures and speaking engagements.

She could trust him. Wanted to thank him for telling her.

Was too filled with an overflow of affection for the man to find words appropriate to the situation. Ended up with, "You said Hud's team was following up on a lead…pertaining to the day Simon disappeared…"

His expression cleared, returned to the professional look she was accustomed to, allowing her to also feel more like herself as he said, "There's a woman, Annabelle Gravestone, who paid cash for a room at the motel out by the highway. One night only."

Lorna's adrenaline surged. "The night before Simon disappeared?" She wouldn't hang around afterward, not unless she wanted to get caught.

Glen nodded.

"And?"

He shrugged. Shook his head. "That's it. Which is what makes this too coincidental to ignore. There's no record of her in town. No credit card receipts. Not even at the gas station. The motel didn't require a car registration, nor did it have surveillance cameras back then. Brian visited the place this evening. Saw the logbook for himself."

"Dilly has always kept meticulous records," Lorna said, with a bit of warmth. "She's in her seventies now, but I remember her from Halloween. She'd always host a haunted maze, with the walls made out of hay. I don't remember what she charged, but it was always crowded, and I heard kids at school talk about it."

He glanced at his computer and then back at her. "You didn't ever go?"

She rolled her eyes. Shook her head. "Even if my four over-protective 'parents' would let me, I was too scared to do it. You know how easy it would be for someone to snatch a kid out in the dark like that?"

And yet, it had never happened. There'd been protocols in place, she'd learned as she got older. And still had had no desire to attend. Not anything she wished to dwell on as she sat locked in for her own protection. With real danger at her back.

"This Anabelle Gravestone…where is she now?" Hudson's team would have run a background check first thing.

Glen shook his head as he said, "They haven't been able to find any record of her. Ever. Anywhere."

"She checked in with a fake name. Annabelle Gravestone is an alias."

"And all we have to go on is a name in this Dilly's record book. She didn't remember the woman at all."

Another dead end, and yet, "We're one step closer," she told Glen. Because her instincts were telling her they were.

As were others, since they'd brought the woman to their attention.

Glen glanced at her again, and as she spoke, his look lingered. "We've got four-year-old Billy Shaking with a woman who disappeared…"

"Then eight-year-old Billy Simmons, with a woman who disappeared," he added with a single nod of his head.

"And now Annabelle…" She stopped, mouth hanging open as a thought occurred to her.

"What?" Glen's tone sounded anticipatory. And she almost smiled at him. Before she caught herself.

"Say we've got just one woman. Who stole Simon to begin with. Moved him around for obvious reasons. She not only had no proof that he was hers, no birth certificate, but there were missing child reports within a four-state radius. By the time he's four, they're in Mississippi. At eight, Georgia…" She was babbling. He was nodding. Humoring her? Or being patient, waiting for her to get to the point?

She did one last mental self-check before suggesting, "We need to be looking at the names we have for the mystery women," she said. "Simon has been given names with significance. Names that are derived from who he is legally. If this is one woman, following a pattern, she'd possibly do the same for herself. Even if she just did it for little Simon…to call him names that he could relate to and remember to answer to, she'd need to do the same for herself for the same reason. Would be really suspicious if a little guy didn't know his own mother's name."

It was a long shot. A really, really long one.

But if she didn't go in search of miracles, she might never find one.

GLEN SENT A message to Hud immediately. Asking for one of his algorithm experts to design code that would transpose letters and be able to search databases for content based on those letters. He gave a brief outline of the theory driving the request, giving Lorna credit as he did so.

Hit Send. Glanced over to see Lorna focused back on her screen next to him. And, as exhausted as he was, felt more alive than he had since Sierra died. Maybe his friend really was up "there" somewhere, helping him get a second chance.

Forgiving him for the fact that she hadn't had one.

Negating the thought even as he had it—there was no scientific proof to back it up—he saw Hud's almost immediate response and clicked to see if his friend agreed that Lorna's idea held weight.

Or was going to question Glen's having given it enough merit to make the request in the first place.

He saw the words at the top first. On it.

And then dived immediately into the longer paragraph below it. Expecting to read a rundown of exactly how the new piece of the puzzle was going to work.

But saw something else entirely. He read the words twice. Mentally cataloged the details, and then said, "We have another likely photo match for Simon." He kept his gaze on his screen. Didn't dare to take a risk of falling into the emotion he knew would be shining from Lorna's gaze.

Even when she remained silent, he didn't look. Just kept right on with, "In Baldwin, Michigan. A little fishing town forty-five minutes from Lake Michigan's eastern shore."

She hadn't needed to know the global positioning aspect. He delivered it anyway. Giving himself a few seconds to slow down his suddenly overactive metabolism. Lorna's age progression program was working beyond what he'd even imagined it could. They were getting closer and closer to solving her case.

And in the space of just a few very long days, that job had become personal to him.

As had she.

Chapter Sixteen

Lorna waited for Glen to continue. The way he was study-ing his computer, she figured he was still reading the new message for himself. Didn't mind the second or two to take a deep breath. To prepare just in case the news was not good.

To that end, she kept her gaze on the man who'd proven himself to be kind. Fair. And honest. The man she was never going to forget.

One who'd drawn her up out of her science enough to notice him in a very healthy, adult way. Not that being at-tracted to Glen was necessarily healthy for her. But finding out that she was capable of experiencing such feelings—fleet-ing though they probably were, scientifically speaking—was a very welcome surprise.

Keeping her hands positioned on the keyboard on her lap, she watched her unknowing mentor push at the nosepiece on his glasses. "The boy's name is Will Simonson."

Her heart thudded as everything else inside her froze. Billy Shaking. The little guy had probably been shaking when he was kidnapped. Billy Simmons. He'd remembered he'd been called Simon. Will Simonson. Different versions of the same name. It couldn't be a coincidence.

Glen closed his laptop. Set it on the double-wide, flat arm of the sectional next to him, and fear filled her. Simon was dead.

They'd succeeded. They'd found him and…

Gray eyes filled with something she hadn't seen in them before turned on her. Cutting off her thoughts. And most of her breath, too. "The photo that popped up from your program had been taken as part of a marketing plan from a firm out of Detroit," Glen said, sounding different to her, too.

She couldn't read him. And tensed.

"He'd won an academic scholarship to the University of Michigan. But after the photo was published, he disappeared. A record search turned up no Will Simonson prior to his arrival at Baldwin public schools. The records present upon his admission to the high school there were falsified. His only parent information was a mother, and there've been no hits on that identity since."

The chemicals bursting through her, endorphins, serotonin, dopamine, oxytocin, and probably pheromones, too, held Lorna upright as relief weakened her to the point of falling into a huddle of gratitude.

Staring at Glen, not even trying to hide the sheen of tears in her eyes, she said, "High school. How old was he?"

"Sixteen."

She blinked. "He won an academic scholarship to a top school at sixteen?"

"Which he had to forfeit, yes."

There was that. But… "If he's that sharp, he'd have found another way to get an education," she said. Then, with hands shaking, lifted her fingers to briefly touch the back of them to Glen's cheek. "Sixteen, Glen! That's only nine years ago! Because you took a chance on me, we have our boy at sixteen!"

His gaze warmed, softened, and then seemed to gleam.

She watched as he started to lean slowly toward her.

Reached up to touch his face again.

And then he kissed her.

She tasted like summer.

Smelled like a flower garden.

Glen couldn't pull away. Couldn't stop his mouth from remaining on hers. Not while her lips were moving so tentatively against his.

And her hands on either side of his face were holding him to her.

He opened his mouth. She did the same, and he accepted the invitation, slipping his tongue inside to meet hers.

Her hand left his cheek and dropped. His eyes flew open, figuring she was ready to push him away, and, instead, saw her computer slide off her lap and tilt upright between the cushion and the furniture's frame.

Hard and needing her, he deepened the kiss. It would have to end. He knew that. No way he could take off his clothes with his very temporary hire.

But, God, he wanted to. Like he'd never wanted to before.

With a fire that seemed to consume him, even as his brain reminded him that he had limits.

She moaned. Licked his lips, and then met his tongue again. He suckled lightly. Almost lifted his hips up in his need to find friction against his penis but focused on her lips instead. On showing her in the way he could how desirable he found her.

It was just a kiss. Nothing more.

Until the hand that moved her computer moved again. He waited for the touch of those soft fingers against his day's growth of beard.

Pushed his face lightly into the hand that still held him, while he took another soft pull on her tongue.

And nearly came off the couch when the hand meant for his face cupped his penis instead. Like a woman who knew exactly how to get what she wanted out of a man. The pressure was light, but she'd managed to encompass almost all of him. And let the tips of her fingers trail lower, to his most delicate area.

He moved. He couldn't help it. Spreading his legs, he made access easier for her. Just for the second her exploration could last. Moved his body so that her hand slid all the way to his tip, and all the way down to cup him between the legs, too.

He was letting her do as she wanted with him. And would find the strength to resist taking what he most needed.

When her other hand left his face and lowered between them, Glen braced for the will to be strong enough to endure all ten of her fingers down there without losing control.

He kissed her harder. Let his tongue sink deeper.

It was only a kiss. He was only going to kiss her.

Her second hand didn't make it to his penis. She stopped at his hand. Lifted it, and he moved his fingers, trying to wrap around hers as she'd nonverbally asked him to do in the car.

She let go of his palm before he got the chance to complete his task. Placing his hand very firmly against one very full round breast. With an unmistakably hard point at the center apex.

Then pushed herself against him. Rubbing against his palm.

God help him.

He didn't have it in him to reject her. But didn't cup her as every instinct he had was screaming at him to do.

Until she went for his second hand. Brought it up against her second breast, and then, without breaking contact with his lips, slowly lowered herself down on the cushion.

"I'm your boss." The words were torn out of him. Right against her lips.

"No, you're the only man who's ever made me want this," she replied. Quite clearly. So clearly, he opened his eyes. And found himself staring straight into hers.

"You want me," she challenged.

"Of course I do," he nearly growled back. "I'm human."

She nodded. "And now, so am I. Feeling fully and completely human. Is that okay with you?"

Hell yes, it was okay. It was better than okay. It was…unbelievable. Throwing off his glasses, he answered the question with another kiss.

One that was hungry and deep and leading to more.

When the woman was willing, and the man was willing, and there was no payroll involved, and it felt so incredibly good, why did they have to stop?

As his pants were unzipped, and his hands slid under her top to unfasten her bra, he forgot the question.

Forgot everything but the moments they were sharing. The touching. The eventual entering. The movement. In and out. Up and down. Again and again.

Until she cried out. Her body pulsed around him. And he exploded. Into several bursts. And eventually fell down to his shoulder against the couch, slid his arm beneath her, and felt her head settle against his chest.

He wasn't sure what had just happened. How it had happened.

Or what happened next.

But he knew one thing for certain.

It was no longer just a kiss.

LORNA HAD NEVER been so embarrassed. Or so incredibly satiated, either. Which was further cause for embarrassment.

Coming on to him like some overzealous fan was bad enough, but had he sensed her virginal response to being turned on? Everything had hit her so fast, been so shockingly powerful, that she hadn't calculated at all.

If not for Glen's going for his wallet as she'd pulled his pants down, she wouldn't even have remembered to use protection.

She'd known girls in college who'd been so thoughtlessly randy. Had figured their tales to be highly embellished out of a need to justify such foolish behavior.

She'd just been so…she didn't know what. Trying her best to get into the clothes that were tangled and partially inside out, she thrust her foot into a pant leg and met with resistance. Shoved harder and said, "I apologize for…" then stopped.

Where did she start?

"I'm the one who owes the apology." Glen's pants, she noticed from one covert glance from the side of her eye, were already in place, fastened and buckled. "You're a guest in my home. You're under my employ. I've never behaved in such an abominable fashion in my life."

He'd behaved badly? Her foot met air. Finally, she had one leg in her pants. Waited until the other was through, button was in buttonhole, and zipper all the way up, before saying, "I came on to you, Glen." Was proud of how practical she sounded.

How more like her scientific self she was beginning to feel again.

Whatever unstoppable force had come over her was dissipating with a speed she welcomed. Refastening the bra that had never come off, she reached for her shirt. His was already on, buttoned. He was also already into one sock and one shoe.

He was a sock, shoe, sock, shoe man.

She was sock, sock. Shoe, shoe. Had read that meant either that she was very organized and couldn't fathom one foot fully ready to walk on stones while the other wasn't even partially ready. Or that she was compassionate—didn't want to leave one foot completely bare while the other was fully clothed.

Glen's way was more efficient. Only had to lift each foot once.

He was fully dressed. Glasses and all. She had her shirt on but was still barefoot.

When had they bared their feet?

While her bra strap had still hung over one arm?

Humiliating heat washed through her again. Had her feelings for him been so obvious he'd taken pity on her? Would they still be able to work together?

What in the hell had she done?

For the first time in her life, she was actually making progress in finding out what had happened to Simon, and she blew it.

For *sex*?

She was fully dressed. Had nothing else to do with herself, except stand there. Sit. Or grab her computer and walk out.

To a dark house. With windows that led to a world where danger lurked because someone wanted her gone.

An unknown entity who had already tried to kill her. Her mentor. And innocent security employees, too.

"You initiated physical contact, yes," Glen said out of the blue, drawing her gaze to him. She stood frozen to the tile floor and watched as he reclaimed his seat and looked straight back at her.

Something he'd avoided enough for her to know that he was taking their situation head-on. Which calmed her some. Not enough to sit down next to him, though.

She trusted him. Wasn't sure just how much she could trust herself at the moment.

He didn't appear to be about to hold her actions against her.

At least not in terms of ending their association.

Vacating the case.

Didn't mean it wasn't about to happen. It wasn't like she could rely on her own judgment at the moment.

A delicious chill passed through her. Followed by a cold one. Her body thrummed from his touch. And down below…she could feel the aftermath. But it didn't fit the current situation.

Didn't fit her life's goal.

And there she stood. With no words coming to her that she deemed worth speaking. Watching the man who'd acknowledged her guilt in the debacle she'd made, and said nothing else.

He'd glanced at his computer. Seemed to study the screen some. But hadn't touched it.

The look in his eyes, when he turned them toward her, reminded her of the man she'd met the first day in his office. Her stomach clenched and her heart sank as she saw him open his mouth to speak.

"Fear stimulates adrenal glands," he said. "Intense fear, intensely so. Adrenal glands also are affected by great joy, such as finding out that a toddler you've spent your life seeking made it to age sixteen."

She could hardly breathe. Couldn't look away. Her brain was in full receiving mode. And was processing, too. "Dopamine is a neurotransmitter that makes us feel good."

Chin jutting, he held her gaze and nodded as she said, "It comes from the endocrine system.

"Through the thalamus, which is traditionally thought to be the source through which sexual messages come to our bodies," she added.

Eyes narrowing, he continued to watch her as he said, "Our adrenaline was raised to critically high levels during the drive home and further stimulated by the news that we're likely dealing with an unknown power with money who's hired any number of others to cause harm to us."

She nodded, took a step closer. "And then the good news, along with our shared situation and forced solitary confinement…"

"…created a surge of sexual desire that forced action."

"Just like one would dart after a toddler running into the street," she said. Finding semblances of herself in the science. The logic.

She was educated. Aware. In control. She wasn't immune to natural human responses.

"Had either one of us had a surge of cortisol…" He let the word drop with raised eyebrows and a tilt of his head.

The hormone stimulated by fear or stress would have stopped them.

Which meant…they'd both been willing participants.

She nodded slowly. Then summarized where the conversation had led them. "So we have nothing to worry about," she said. "We know why it happened. It meant nothing more than a normal human reaction to an overabundance of stimuli."

As though satisfied that they had no problem between them, Glen picked up his computer, slid it to his lap, and said, "We emptied ourselves of what could have become debilitating hormones in a healthy way."

Grabbing her own laptop out of the slot into which she vaguely remembered shoving it, Lorna sat down.

He spoke scientific truth. Which set her free.

Mostly.

As she struggled to focus, she told the recalcitrant, hormone-overload-induced parts of her that were trying to argue the point to shut up.

Chapter Seventeen

Glen stared at his screen. Tried to get his mind back in gear. Saw three more names that had come in from Hud before the midnight deadline they'd decided would be when the two of them knocked off for the night and got a bit of rest.

Three names in addition to Annabelle Gravestone. People that Hud's team had marked as possible kidnappers, based on the initial activity pull. All names that the overnight tech team would be researching over the next few hours.

Glen cared. Didn't dare allow himself any emotional surge as more evidence crept under their microscope.

And knew that, like Hud, he and Lorna had to take a break. Their physical encounter was in-his-face proof of what happened when one was pushed beyond healthy limits.

He'd regret what happened. There was no doubt in his mind about that. Once he was rested. Sleep deprivation led to hormonal imbalance.

Until then, he was living on thin ice. And, so knowing, had to be responsible to that fact.

"It's midnight," he announced, closing his laptop with no next step in mind.

Lorna nodded. Closed her laptop as well. Looked over at him and said, "You mind if I sit here for a while and watch some television? I'm not going to sleep if I go lie down right now in the dark in a room with windows."

Looking over at her, he was hit all over again with how, in some ways, they were so alike. He wasn't sure he was going to sleep at all. Had been on his way down a road where he grabbed a pillow and blanket and camped out in the hall outside her suite.

As though his being out there could make some kind of difference to her welfare if a hired hit man managed to make it past Sierra's Web security and break in her window.

He'd hear the break-in.

Could alert others.

"You mind if I sit awhile as well?" he asked her.

Something flashed in her eyes. Relief maybe? He knew he felt some when she nodded and turned and faced the screen as he picked up the remote. Rather than locking gazes with him.

Which was what had gotten them into trouble earlier.

They watched another crime scene episode. Didn't speak at all. And then it was over. "You want to try to get some rest?" Glen asked, feeling less het up, but no closer to finding relief in unconsciousness.

She turned to look at him. "You mind if I sit here for a while longer?" A repeat of her earlier request to stay. As if the question was all she had between being okay and lying in fear. "I'll keep the television down low. Or just play a game on my phone," she added.

"You mind if I hang out, too?" he asked right back, just as he had before. Able to look at her without feeling the threat of self-betrayal.

She gave him a tired grin. "It feels safer, huh?" she asked.

He nodded. Turned on the next episode. And woke up three hours later with his feet up on the ottoman, his head back against the corner of the cushion, and Lorna's head on his shoulder.

He didn't move. Didn't want to disturb the quiet moment. Or her.

Didn't even know she was awake until she said, "Tell me about Sierra." Her voice was a near whisper, almost sacred sounding.

Glen didn't even consider not doing as she asked. In that moment of quiet with danger seeming to lurk all around them, confessing his failings where his friend was concerned seemed…right. Just.

He told her how their friend had been made to partner with a jerk in one of her classes. How Sierra had bested the guy, and he'd ended up forcing sex on her.

And then he stopped talking. Just sat there, horror creeping up over him.

He'd been working under the impression that he was somehow making past mistakes up to Sierra through his association with Lorna, and then he'd gone and taken a male/female working relationship and turned it into…

A finger touched his lips. Soft. Gentle. "If anything, I forced you." The voice came softly, too. But filled with confidence. "And when you were on the brink of pulling back, I called you back with a stark truth. Practically begging you not to stop the sensations I was experiencing for the first time in real life."

He turned his head to look at her then. "It was all the things you said, Glen. A surge of adrenaline-induced hormones that had to find release with nowhere else to go. Coupled with proximity and the fact that we get along well. Please leave it at that. Don't make my first orgasmic experience into something we both have to regret."

The tension reigniting in Glen dissipated. With a blink and a slight grin, he nodded. And though he was discussing the worst time in his life, and living through the most personally dangerous, he felt better within himself than he had in…maybe ever.

"TELL ME WHY you blame yourself for Sierra's death." Lorna held her breath as she said the words aloud. She'd been waiting for Glen to tell her more.

Was she only intuiting that he held himself responsible in some way for his friend's death? From the time or two he'd mentioned the woman after which his firm was named, but more from the times he hadn't?

Figuring Glen had been in love with the woman.

And that he blamed himself for failing to protect her.

It wasn't any of her business.

So why did she feel as though it was? Feel driven to help him if she could. He'd done so much for her. Over the space of years. Didn't matter that most of it had been without his knowledge or direct contribution. He'd done more for her in the past three days than anyone else had been able to do in a lifetime.

If she could give even a little bit back…

"Sierra changed after the semester of that ill-fated partnership." Glen's words broke into her thoughts. Head back against the couch, he was staring outward. "I knew she and Win had a secret thing going on… I'd seen them once when I'd gone to his dorm room…but I never said anything. I didn't want to make things awkward, you know, for the group of us. I figured if they had problems, they'd work them out."

He stopped. She waited. Leaning her own head on the cushion behind her. The predawn early morning quiet permeated the room. Leaving the rest of the house vacant-feeling.

"I loaned her my car." Glen's voice was barely discernible, and yet rang loudly in her ears. Lifting her head, she looked over at him. Watched as with lids wide-open, he stared toward the upper wall in front of them and said, "Which wasn't all that odd. I was the only one with wheels at the time and everyone borrowed them. But Sierra least of all. Until, suddenly she was borrowing my car all the time."

He broke off. Didn't move except to blink. "I knew it was odd." He turned his head toward her then, catching and holding her gaze as he said, "But I didn't ask her about it." A sheen came over his eyes. He shook his head. Looked back to the ceiling and said, "If I'd only asked…"

He seemed to be done. Everything inside Lorna screamed at her that he couldn't stop there. Not because she needed to hear the rest, which she did, but for him. "What happened?" She barely got the words out through the emotion tightening her throat.

She'd looked up the case years before, when she'd been verifying the validity of scientist Glen Rivers Thomas. Most particularly because her first introduction to his work had been issued as coming from Dr. Glen Rivers. And a subsequent year, it had Dr. Glen Rivers Thomas.

She hadn't been sure it was the same man.

Her research had shown her more than she'd ever expected to find. Not about the man's name. But about his firm. His partners. Their friend who'd died when they'd all been in college together.

Sierra had died. There'd been few details beyond that. Searcy police had been involved in another case at the same time a missing Sierra had turned up dead. The vagueness of details had led Lorna to suspect suicide had been the cause of death.

And… Searcy. Same place Michelle Applegate had died. Years before Glen's friend Sierra. No wonder Glen seemed to be reliving his past.

Seeing the man's furrowed brow, Lorna pushed where otherwise she might not have done. "What happened?" she asked again.

Could Michelle Applegate have been involved in Simon's disappearance? Had she been Annabelle Gravestone? And then hadn't been able to live with herself?

About to raise the question to Glen, her thoughts about Simon's case completely escaped her as he said, "She'd been hell-bent on getting justice for what had happened to her, without admitting to anyone—including Win—that it had happened." His words seemed to flow, as though they'd given up the fight for silence, as he continued. "She discovered that the guy had a gambling problem. That he was involved in some large-scale illegal sports betting venture, with a serious bookie at the helm. She intended to expose him, them, but ended up getting herself killed, instead."

The look on his face, the tone in which he'd delivered those last words, had her heart speaking before her brain could think. "It wasn't your fault, Glen. You couldn't help that she didn't tell you what was going on."

Turning his head, he looked over at her, and said, "I loaned her the car that was the only means by which she could have found out what he was doing, could have followed him as much as she did. Or known where he met his bookie."

"Sounds to me like she was determined enough to have rented a car," Lorna said quietly. Because the practicality behind her words seemed so obvious.

And maybe they were to one who was on the outside. Hearing the story for the first time. Glen blinked again. Cocked his head against the couch as he continued to hold her gaze. "I was the one who helped the police find her," he said, sounding neither pleased nor displeased with that piece of information. "I'd found a note in my car, just had some scribbled numbers on it that I'd been trying to decipher, like maybe they were some kind of code. The detective who was looking for her recognized the numbers. They led police to the bookie. To Sierra's attacker. And to her body."

The truth stabbed Lorna. Sierra hadn't committed suicide. She'd been murdered. For trying to expose evil. Which was what the Sierra's Web partners, and she, too, had been trying to do for their entire adult lives.

Sitting back, closer to Glen, she put a hand up behind his shoulders, lightly riffling her fingers through his short strands of hair for a second as she laid her head on his shoulder.

And fell back to sleep.

GLEN WOKE TO the sight of the clock on the television screen. Five-thirty. Which in Arizona in April meant that the sun was coming up.

They'd made it through the night.

And had to get back to the lab. Lorna's head lifted from his shoulder as soon as he took a deep breath, leaving him with a cold spot where there'd been warmth. She reached for her computer as he stood and pulled his lab coat back on.

Dreading the awkwardness that he was certain the moment was about to bring, he dived right in with a plan. "I'll walk down with you to your suite," he said, words falling out of him as though he'd had them preset. "We'll keep low in the living room, below the windowsills. The hall is good. Then you crawl into your suite only long enough to get whatever you need to get ready for the day." He gathered his computer as he spoke. Moved to the door of the room. "There's a bathroom in the hall," he told her. "No windows." The bath in her suite had a garden tub with a beveled window on the wall above it.

Lorna didn't speak, but was one step behind him as he walked toward the living area. "My bath is windowless, so I'll use that one. I'll keep the door open to my suite, so you can get to me if you need to. And keep my phone right outside the shower, too."

Ducking low then, he crossed the living area as quickly as he could, stood as he reached the hallway to her suite, and pulled the gun out of the pocket of his lab coat. Handing it out to her. "You take this."

She almost ran into him as he stopped. Had been following him that closely. But she backed up as she shook her head. "I'm one of those who'd be more in danger of losing the thing and having it used against me," she told him, then stepped past him.

Managing to do so without touching him at all.

Glen waited while she retrieved her belongings, listening intently, but not watching. And when he heard the click of the hall bathroom door closing behind her, he hurried to his side of the house and a quick cold shower.

Shaving could wait until their stalker was caught.

LORNA AND GLEN made it to Sierra's Web without any drama at all. Afraid to hope they'd turned a corner, knowing they hadn't until the attempted murderers—and whoever had paid them—had been caught, she headed straight down to the lab when Glen went up to meet with his partners. McKenna was to be her escort for the day. Jamison would be keeping Glen safe.

Electricity was back on for the entire area that had been blacked out. Backup generators were in place and in working order.

The technician who'd admitted to tampering with the fuel source had been charged and was sitting in a jail cell. The payment he'd received had been sent through an untraceable Bitcoin source to then be exchanged into American dollars and passed on to an offshore account that sent electronic payment to the man in Phoenix.

A much too elaborate system just to hire a low-level employee to sabotage a fuel source. The mechanism was in place to finance schemes on a considerably larger scale.

And Lorna was in love with the man sponsoring her presence at the high-end firm that was keeping her alive.

She'd seen it coming. Hadn't done anything to try to stop it. Might not have been possible, but she hadn't even tried.

Truth was, she wasn't sorry. She was going to hurt when she left. Would long for him throughout the years ahead. But she'd do so with a smile, too. He'd shown her proof that physical ecstasy really existed. She'd experienced exquisitely perfect moments in his arms.

Beyond that, she'd never been under any impression or held out any hope that they'd actually become a couple someday. Her mind was too realistic for those kinds of childish dreams. They hadn't made promises that would be broken. So her heart wouldn't break either.

He'd given her a wonderful memory.

She was finally in the know, sexually speaking. Would be forever grateful.

And would never forget.

The mental discourse, which turned into a self-imposed order of action without debate, allowed Lorna to focus fully on the workday in front of her. With most of the available Sierra's Web experts pulled from work on Simon's case to finding the source of the attacks against her, Glen, and Sierra's Web, she had to give full effort to the reason behind it all. Finding out what happened to Simon Billingsley.

At Winchester Holmes's insistence—Win being Sierra's Web's financial expert partner—she'd put holds on her credit cards, leaving only one debit card active. And at the financier's bidding, had left only a minimal balance in the account for any incidental spending she might need to do. He then had her purchase a plane ticket departing that night to Panera, Georgia—Simon's location at eight. And had her pay the higher price to make the ticket refundable.

An investigator would be meeting the flight she didn't actually board. Looking for anyone else who might be attempting to follow her when she landed.

Hudson was hoping that when the hacker accessed her account a second time, his team would get him. They'd set up spyware that should give them access to even an encrypted account.

Her instincts were telling her to focus on Annabelle Gravestone and any possible links to Michelle Applegate. She could use her age progression software to run an age regression on the photos that were printed of Michelle in the Searcy newspaper after the accident. And one from her high school yearbook, too. They'd been in her inbox from Brian that morning.

For inspiration she printed out photos Selena had provided her years ago of her mother. Pregnant. And, at the hospital right after Selena and Simon had been born, too. Sharon Billingsley had passed away from anaphylactic shock, after reaching her hand into a barrel that contained a bees' nest, when Selena was in high school. Which was when Selena had started contacting Lorna.

Glen showed up at the entrance to her space after his meeting upstairs, and her heart lurched. He was unshaven. Because of the situation she'd put him in.

Seeing the dark stubble on his chin, her thoughts went immediately to the feel of it between her breasts. Her thalamus shot into gear, and she stiffened, trying to keep up appearances while she dealt with the unexpected interference. She'd made her resolve.

Her night with the scientist had been a one-off. Period.

"Who's this?" Glen asked as McKenna—who'd been spending a lot of time communicating on her phone and watching surveillance cameras from there, too—vacated the space.

He was pointing to Sharon, not Michelle, his expression as he studied the photo and then glanced at her serious and focused. And so would she be.

"It's Sharon Billingsley," she told him, and herself as well. Reminding herself what mattered. And it sure as hell wasn't her own physiological pleasure. "I had these posted in my lab at Stellar," she said next, and then added, "I'm going to find out what happened to Sharon's little boy."

He nodded. Looked at the computer screen that was currently flashing a series of lines and blurs as her program ran. "I'm running age regression on Michelle Applegate from the photos Brian sent over." And before he could ask, she said, "I don't know what I'm hoping to find. I'll know it if I see it. Maybe I'll find a photo of her in middle school with a friend. We could age progress the friend and run it by Dilly, just in case she remembers it." She flushed even as she made the suggestion. "Or see if we get hits on the age progression of the friend in Searcy. I'm already running the photo Brian sent in all the databases we have—new sources who went online, that kind of thing." She nodded toward a second screen with blurred images speeding across it.

His nod was instant, as though he approved of the choice. "I'd like to see them, too, once they're complete."

He wasn't looking at her. Nor had he said why he'd stopped in to see her. Lorna's heart lurched again. Drawing focus from the work she was there to do. She couldn't be bothered about whether or not Glen was upset with her.

Regretting what had happened between them.

Or wondering if he'd want one more go at it, since she'd likely be at his place again that night. Unless he was ready to tell her he was kicking her out? She wouldn't blame him. It would be for the best, actually, considering what a ninny she was being right then.

"No hit on the plane ticket yet," he said, leaning in toward the photos of Sharon that she'd posted on the cork wall above her evidence table. "Thanks for doing that, by the way. Win said you followed his instructions exactly, and immediately."

Was he praising her? Or pleased? As a flood of warmth hit her stomach, she shot down an immediate emotional barrier. Physiology aside...just...no.

"Why wouldn't I?" she asked, when she should have remained silent. He'd expressed appreciation. Why was she making more of it than it was?

Her question had been rhetorical. Could have been why he didn't respond. She had no explanation for her own ridiculous distraction where he was concerned. They'd had sex. It was done.

And a wave of intense emotion shot through her a third time when Glen spun around to face her. "We might have a lead on the offshore account," he told her. Met her gaze, looked away, and brought his eyes back to hers again. And, as an entirely unrelated-to-sex-and-love excitement shot through her, he held up his hand.

"We've got no names, no identities yet, but Hud's team was able to find activity involving the account as far back as twenty years."

"Twenty years!" Her voice rose—not in decibel, but in pitch.

His gaze remained steady. Serious. "Doesn't mean it's related to Simon," he told her. "I don't want to get your hopes up. Just means that whoever is trying to prevent you from finding out what happened to Simon has been laundering money for a couple of decades. Might be that Simon's disappearance interrupted something else that was going on at the time. Drug or arms trade. Or even just local theft from company assets. Hud's looking into all possibilities."

She nodded. Understood what he was telling her. They had a plethora of possible connections—clues—and still not a single answer to explain how Simon Billingsley had disappeared without a trace twenty-three years before.

He was still looking at her. She stood still. Silent. On edge.

Giving him time. Needing to know what was going on in that brilliant mind of his.

She waited in vain.

After a breathless number of seconds, he turned and walked out.

Chapter Eighteen

Had Glen not been so embroiled in the two clearly related cases, he'd have buried himself in his lab, in data, and stayed there until he was over whatever ailment had beset him. He didn't get sick. And he most certainly didn't need hours to recover mental and physical equilibrium after a sexual encounter.

Encounters with the opposite sex had always been out of sight, out of mind with him. Which was why he didn't date much. That, and the fact that he wasn't out of his lab long enough to have many women express interest in him.

So was that the problem? Lorna having expressed such a large dose of interest? And in his own home, to boot?

Had to be. The logic inherent in the answer settled him. His seemingly emotional reactions to her, as an individual, were merely the result of an oversaturated hypothalamus.

Anything else, like the idea that he could be falling for her, as in man to woman, hooking up, partners…was fantasy. He'd attended several of his partners' weddings over the last few years. Fully accepted that they believed they were in love. Wanted them to continue to believe.

Even though he knew better. Love had no scientific basis. Not in the sense of one person loving another over all else for as long as they lived. Science told him that feelings of affection came and went, just like sexual arousal and anger.

He was not falling for his very temporary and alluring housemate. He was merely oversaturated by her physical interest in him.

He tried the idea on a second time. Backed up with scientific proof. Found it valid. Got through a morning's worth of emails, reading reports from other scientists in his lab who were all working on their own assigned cases, giving feedback. At the top of his game. Productive as always.

Until a non-work-related, personal question popped into his head.

Are you going to do it again? Immediately backed up with, *While she's at your house.* And then, *Since you're both consenting adults.*

Throwing up a hand at the inexcusable interruption, he shook his head. Then wondered if the headshake was an instinctive negative response to the question asked, or a rejection of it outright for having trespassed on his workday.

Was in the process of rejecting the analysis of the rejection when the subject of his conundrum walked in the door. In the navy pants and white-and-navy polka-dot sleeveless button up she'd come out of his hallway bathroom wearing that morning, she strode right in without knocking.

Then froze. Her lab coat flew behind her as she rushed back out.

Standing, ready to go after her, alarm shooting through him, he stopped when a text sounded. Thinking the sound indicated an incoming missive from Hud, possibly related to Lorna's distress, he opened and read as he headed to the outer room of the lab, past his office.

Sorry for the intrusion. May I come in?

The message was from Lorna.

Who was standing in the doorway watching him read her text.

Punching in a *Y,* he hit Send and turned to head back to his lab. Giving his body a second to calm down from the immediate physical reaction he'd just experienced, seeing her standing there—her flyaway short dark strands reminding him of how his fingers had felt running through them the night before.

By the time he'd reached his stool, his hard-on was still there—covered by his lab coat. And he'd answered his earlier question, too. Yes. If she was still at his house that night. And was willing. He'd have sex with her again.

Sexual desire waned with time and repetition, and he needed to get the woman out of his system.

"I think I found something, Glen!" She'd barreled in behind him, full of emotion. Responding immediately to her tone, he turned, looked at the sheets of paper she was holding.

The prints of Sharon Billingsley. Taking them as she handed them to him, he studied the likenesses, four of them in total. Glanced up to see her looking at him expectantly. Her green eyes alive with a light that was wholly captivating.

To the scientist in him.

"I measured the stomach on those pregnancy photos," she told him. "One was from when Sharon was pregnant with her older daughter, Beth, Selena's sister, who has tried to get Selena in counseling to get over Simon and get on with her life…"

She stopped. Took a deep breath. And then said, "The other is supposedly of Sharon pregnant with Simon and Selena."

Pushing at the nosepiece on his glasses, Glen raised a brow as he glanced at Lorna. "Supposedly?"

"I measured the belly," she said then, her gaze darting from the photo to his face and back to the photo again—leaving him feeling as though he'd been touched. But her words hit, too, and he pulled the photos closer. Then set them on his main worktable, pulling the high-powered lamp over from its wall mount to center it directly above the images.

Lorna appeared beside him, her arm up against his as she leaned in. "They're exactly the same size," she told him. "I had them up on-screen. Those photos are of the same pregnancy. And if you do a life-size enlargement, there's no way that that belly contained two full-grown babies."

Frowning, he turned to her. "What are you saying?"

She shrugged one shoulder, shaking her head, but she met his gaze head-on. Professional to professional. "I have no idea. Except that for some reason, Sharon Billingsley gave her daughter a pregnancy photo of her and Simon that wasn't actually of her pregnancy with her and Simon." She slid another photo onto his table, directly under the light. "This was taken right before Selena and Simon were born," she said.

The image depicted a very pregnant belly covered with a hospital gown. "In this previous photo, with Beth—" she pointed to the first of the two full photos of a very pregnant Sharon Billingsley "—the baby has clearly dropped. She's carrying her down low. Same with this one." She pointed to the second photo of fully dressed pregnant Sharon. "But look here, with the twins right before birth, she's so filled with child that the bump is like a table coming out of her rib cage. I never paid much attention before. And she's upright in those two and lying down in this one. But when I enlarged them and measured…no way two pregnancies are going to measure the same, even in the same woman. And most definitely not when one is a single birth and the other is multiple."

She was right. And onto something. Whether it had a significance to the case or not, he couldn't say, but the cause of his distraction had just brought his attention fully back to the case. "I'll call Dorian," he told her, naming his medical expert partner, newly married Dr. Dorian Michaels. "She can put in a request for medical records."

Lorna glanced at him, so close that he could see the darker green ring around the iris in eyes clearly filled with concern. "Since Sharon is dead, and this case has taken a dangerous turn, could she do so without having to get permission from the family?"

He nodded immediately. And stepped back just as fast. "It could take a few hours longer. We'll need to get a warrant. But I agree, that's the way to go."

And the other thing...sex again...assuming she came on to him, that was the way to go, too.

Lorna had to keep her distance from the man. They were getting closer to Simon. Her brain hummed with an energy she'd never known before. On any forensic science problem she'd ever had. Or ideas regarding Simon's disappearance, either. No way could she let her immature little bout of sexual awakening hamper Simon's right to be found. Dead or alive, the little boy deserved to be known for who he'd been. The life he'd been born into.

Glen hadn't yet kicked her out of his home. Maybe he couldn't, due to the protection detail they shared. Not without revealing to his partners what they'd done.

It was up to her, as his guest, to make certain that he was not put in any further situation that could be awkward for him. Or risk one arising out of future unprofessional actions. They'd lit a fire. Put it out. Had escaped suffering any burns from the choice. And needed to walk away from it. A repeat performance would offer no guarantees of escaping unscathed.

McKenna brought lunch in. The woman was kind. And professional. She didn't chitchat. Or even hint that she'd sensed something going on between Lorna and Glen. Lorna took that as a huge win. And didn't ask if Glen had had lunch.

The man didn't seem to make nutrition a priority, and with the long hours they were keeping, along with an unexpected expenditure of energy the night before, he had to eat. The thought nagged at her to the point that she finally texted him, just to shut herself up.

Did you have lunch?

And heard back almost immediately. Y.

Just that. Even after she sent a thumbs-up, nothing else came through. But it turned out to be more than enough to get her thoughts out of the personal mud and back into the work she'd spent so much of her life trying to accomplish.

She got a hit on age-regressed photos of Michelle on some social media posts, and a couple of local Searcy news publications that had been digitized. Most of them with friends. From there she pulled out individual photos of others in the images, and started them through facial recognition databases, and then, specifying Morrilton only, into social and news sources as well.

Some of the original Michelle posts, and the couple of new mentions, contained names to go with the people pictured. And while she waited, she did searches on those names, looking for any that were in the system with fingerprints she could use as a comparison to the partial print she'd managed to lift from the pen she'd received in the evidence box the previous morning.

The work was slow, potentially tedious, but Lorna was in her element. Doing what she loved to do.

For a cause that meant more to her than any other.

Her computer had just shot another photo up to the small

icons delineating finds when Glen's voice came from behind her. "Turn everything off."

She jumped. Banged her knee on the counter she'd had her stool pushed up to. And without turning around, immediately shut down. Then, heart pounding, spun around.

He was gone.

OUT IN THE HALL, Glen finished his conversation with Hud, then turned to get back to Lorna, only to bump into her as she came toward him.

Reaching out, he steadied her, his hands—one still holding his phone—on her arms. Saw the fear in her gaze and pulled her into his office, shutting the door behind them before walking her back to the privacy of his lab.

Taking a seat on the stool he'd only vacated a few minutes before, he said, "It's okay," and motioned for her to take a seat. "Hud's team has been fending off attempts to breach our protocols all day, at the same time as studying what the hacker might be looking for, as well as any identifying information that could lead us to him."

She nodded. Chin tight and eyes still intent with concern, she didn't break eye contact with him. Nor did she speak.

"He's only trying to access your work," Glen said then. "Which makes no sense since so many of us are working on this case now."

With a brief headshake, she said, "Makes total sense to me. He knows that I'm the spearhead. It could be assumed that the case is mine and everything is being reported to me."

She was right. To someone unfamiliar with Sierra's Web's inner workings, he could see merit in the theory. But didn't like what came with it.

"This fits particularly well if we're dealing with someone who's personally aware of you. Of your lifelong mission to find Simon. To the exclusion of most everything else."

She nodded. Chewed her lower lip, but didn't crumble.

"Let's see what happens next." He said what Hud had just expressed to him. "With your system off, let's see what he does. Where he goes. If he disappears."

She ran a hand through the distraction her hair had become to him. And wide-eyed, asked, "Are you sure this place is safe? Secure? He could have a bomb here or something."

Glen wanted to take her hand so badly that he shoved his underneath his thigh instead. Sat on it. "We have sensors that detect explosives and have had protection personnel all over the building and the block surrounding it since before we arrived this morning. Airspace is being monitored as well. In addition to all our normal safety protocols. This is not the firm to mess with."

He thought he detected a hint of a grin forming on her lips, but didn't allow himself to linger long enough to verify his opinion. Instead, he picked up a folder from his worktop— one he'd just put together, intending to take to her when Hud's call had come in—and handed it to Lorna without a word.

And watched as she slowly opened it, started reading, and then read faster. When she had the gist of what he'd handed her, she stared over at him. "I don't get it," she said, but from her frown he knew she wasn't talking about the information she'd just ingested. "This says that Sharon Billingsley only gave birth one time. To Beth."

Holding her gaze, almost as though they were passing far more silently than verbally, he nodded.

"So who gave birth to Simon and Selena?" She asked the question that had been passing between them. And then said, "Unless Sharon did. At home. With a midwife. And then, what? Just never saw her gynecologist again? Except—" she held up the folder "—it says here that she had regular visits. Including six months before she died."

He nodded.

And she stood up. "I have to call Selena. We need her DNA." She glanced at the folder again. "We have Sharon's. She gave it when Simon went missing." She paused then. "Why would she do that? If she knew she hadn't given birth to him?"

She'd caught up to Glen, as he'd known she would. He shrugged, and said, "Makes you wonder what in the hell is going on here, doesn't it?"

With an intense look at him, she said, "I need to speak with Selena."

"Already being arranged," he told her, then glanced pointedly at the phone she'd pulled out and added, "Not with that."

Her questioning look turned to one of understanding, and he said, "Brian is going to reach out to her on a burner phone. When we're certain her call isn't being traced, he'll be patched through to a scrambled internet connection here." He nodded to his computer screen.

Glen believed that Simon's sister was more likely to take the call, accept the news, and cooperate with Lorna than a private detective she'd never met. Most particularly with her family trying to catch her acting far enough out of normal boundaries to enact an intervention on her behalf. Which was why he'd insisted on the protocol.

"Wait," Lorna told him. "Selena and I only communicate through phones we both purchased just for that purpose." She ripped a corner of the folder he'd given her. Grabbed a pen and wrote. "That's her number. Hopefully she'll pick up from Brian's unidentified number. Or, per our predetermined agreement between the two of us, call the number back later if she isn't alone when his call comes through. I'm guessing, since she knows I'm off somewhere working on the case, that she will."

As she spoke, Glen gleaned some new insight into the woman he'd had sex with, slept with, the night before. Simon's case had been personal to her since the day the boy disappeared, due to the fear it had instilled within her that was with her still, though maybe in different formation. But her bond with Selena was deeper than he'd first assumed. Than she'd led him to believe.

He made his call to Hud, relayed the slight change in plan in terms of Brian's call to Selena, and then glanced at Lorna as he hung up. Needing to reach deeper, for no reason pertinent to the case. "You and Selena have more in common than Simon's unexplained disappearance," he said, holding her gaze with a steady one of his own. The separate phones for their conversations were glaring. "Your parents, your family, your older siblings—they're like Selena's older sister, her fiancé, whatever family she has. You share the fact that everyone around you thinks you're obsessed with something that you know has answers waiting to be found. You're hiding your work from your family as much as Selena is hiding from hers. For the same reason."

With a head tilt, she said, "Selena is certain that Simon is waiting to be found."

"And you?"

"I never let myself think that far. What I know is that the answers are there. And I need to find them. No one else is even looking. And if Selena is right, and her twin is still alive, how is he ever going to find his true self, or have a chance at a whole life, if I don't find him?"

He nodded. Then very quietly said, "And how are you ever going to be able to let go of the fear if you don't have the strength to meet it head-on and make the bad guys pay for what they did?"

Her eyes took on a sheen of tears.

And Glen had to fight not to take the woman into his arms and hold on tight.

Chapter Nineteen

Lorna's conversation with Selena didn't end up happening until she and Glen were back at his place that evening. Simon's twin hadn't picked up the call. And Glen and Lorna's transport plans had changed as well. They'd been picked up just after four—far earlier than Glen ever left the office— from the helicopter pad on the roof of the building and flown to an undisclosed location where they'd disembarked to find McKenna and Jamison waiting in another SUV—navy this time—with windows made of bulletproof glass. The drive to Glen's had taken less than half an hour.

Glen had gone for a beer for each of them when they entered his place, and they'd both moved to the small den, as though they'd had a conversation about doing so. "We can have frozen dinners when we get hungry," Glen had offered as he'd handed her the beer. At which time she'd reminded him they had leftover spaghetti. The way she'd been feeling, worrying sick about Selena and how to reach her without endangering the younger woman, or putting herself or Sierra's Web at further risk, had been a good appetite suppressant.

Sitting in the small space with Glen again had done the rest. How was she going to get through the entire evening with their scent from the night before seeming to linger in the room?

She'd been saved from answering herself by Selena's call back, which was patched through to Glen's computer via the Sierra's Web encrypted network.

Selena had been in joyful tears when Lorna had started in by telling her about having found evidence of Simon at four, eight, and sixteen. She'd described the photos. And her twin's accelerated learning capabilities.

Taking a deep breath, she glanced at Glen and then dived into the rest. "Have you heard much about the day you and Simon were born?" She asked the woman something they'd never discussed in detail before.

Which was only then striking her as odd. Lorna had heard the story of her own birth so many times, from four different perspectives, that she figured she could write a book about it and be fairly accurate.

And yet, all the times she and Selena had discussed the past...

"Not much." Selena's response cut off Lorna's thoughts. "Just that we came really fast. An hour after Mom got to the hospital. She was in labor with Beth for almost twenty hours. Dad didn't even have time to get to the hospital before we arrived," the woman added.

And with another glance at Glen, who raised his eyebrows as though asking if she still wanted to be the one to speak to Selena about the DNA request, Lorna stared at the computer screen showing a conversation with only boxes bearing numbers for callers. "We got your mother's medical records today, Selena," she said, and took a deep breath. Then said, "There's no record of her having given birth to you and Simon."

"Well...that's crazy! The records are missing!" she said immediately following the first proclamation. And then, "Whoever took Simon took them!"

The idea was far-fetched, but not impossible. Lorna continued to stare at the screen. And decided to let Selena's assertion stand. "We need your DNA, sweetie," she said then, her voice soft as it often was during her emotional exchanges with the younger woman. "Just to confirm that you're her biological child."

"This is ridiculous!" Selena said again. "I can't…wow. You're really asking this of me? You're the one person who's always known, just as I have, that…"

"I'm still that person," Lorna cut in. "And you know me. You know I have to prove everything I believe…"

She glanced at Glen as she said the words, looking for his understanding of her personal quirk, only to see him regarding her as though she was a specimen on his table. Needing tests before he could ascertain what he was dealing with.

"You've already got Mom's DNA," Selena said. "She gave a sample when Simon disappeared. She told me so. And you've got Simon's, too, obviously." The FBI had collected that the day the little boy disappeared from the park.

She nodded to the computer screen. Swallowed through a tight throat. "And I'm waiting to run them until I have yours," she said, not bothering to add that she'd been unable to run the test with her system still down, and hackers still trying to access it. They'd been about to use Glen's lab when they'd been informed that they were leaving early.

"Fine." Selena's tone wasn't just angry. The younger woman was hurt. "I just can't believe this. After all this time. I sure as hell never thought mine and Simon's biological connection would be in question. And to imply that Mom wasn't our mom! As though you think she somehow had something to do with Simon's disappearance!"

Blinking, her throat dry and tight, Lorna clung tight to the beer bottle in her hand and said, "I'm not implying anything. To the contrary, I'm planning to prove what we've both known all along." She crossed her fingers as she said the words.

Saw them that way, lying on her lap, and immediately un-

crossed them. Whatever was happening to her, the unchar-
acteristic segues from the science that sustained her, she'd
get through it.

Just as soon as Simon's case was solved.

When she heard a sniff come over the line, she bucked up,
found her own strength, and said, "Selena? It's going to be
okay. We're making incredible progress. I have pictures to
show you of your twin brother at sixteen…" She let her voice
trail off on the miraculous note. Sitting there with Glen, with
a whole team supporting her, while Selena still sat alone, with
everyone thinking she was emotionally at risk for believing
her brother was still alive. For thinking she'd see him again
someday. Hoping that her own faith would bolster Selena,
she held on.

And heard, "But what if the DNA proves that we aren't related?" The words were mostly just whisper, interrupted by
tears. "I don't know who I am without Simon out there. I've
had this sense of him my whole life, and if I find out that it
was all just in my head…"

"Don't." Lorna's tone was firm. And maybe louder than
necessary. "Simon needs you to be holding on to that connection, Selena," she continued, drawing from research she'd
done on twins shortly after Selena had first contacted her,
telling her that she could feel that her brother was alive. "It
could help lead him back to us."

She didn't look at Glen as she spoke. She couldn't show
him under a microscope what she believed. But after her
years talking to Selena, she couldn't discount the woman's
certainty that she knew her twin was alive, either.

"Selena?" she asked, as the line fell silent.

"Yeah?"

"A private investigator—his name is Brian Powers—is on
the line. He works for Sierra's Web and will make arrangements with you to get the sample of your DNA, okay?"

"Yes." The word was wobbly. But fully understandable through Selena's tears.

"Continue to believe your brother is out there waiting for you to find him."

"Why? Maybe everyone is right. Maybe I am just obsessed."

The words cut into Lorna. "You are not obsessed. Just hold tight, and either I or Brian will be in touch tomorrow, okay?"

"Yes."

The connection with Brian's phone cut off then, before Lorna could give more words of hope she wasn't certain she felt.

Not where Selena and Simon were concerned. Or their mother, either.

Selena had lived with Simon during the first two years of their lives. The collection of photos she'd seen proved that. The woman could just be feeling that connection—to a boy her age who'd shared her life with her. Needing to feel him in the horrible aftermath of his disappearance. And, as a result, when her family later fell apart.

Her father needing to move on. Her mother unable to let go. The big sister who spent more time at her dad's house than with Selena and her mother. Clinging to Simon had been her constant. Had gotten her through college and into a healthy, loving relationship.

And with one phone call, Lorna had just stripped it all away.

Glen's hand appeared in her peripheral vision, then dropped, as though he didn't know what to do with it. "It's not your fault." His words were soft, but issued with certainty.

And while she appreciated his kindness…for the first time since she'd met him, she didn't believe him.

Glen felt Lorna's sense of failure deeply. Personally. Or… maybe he was feeding off hers and feeling his own.

"I purposely gave Sierra her space," he said softly, leaning back against the couch, his beer bottle held with both hands on the cushion between spread knees. "I knew that she was on some kind of mission—though I'd hoped it was to plan a secret wedding to Win or something—but I didn't check in with her. Just gave her my car, thinking that was all it took to be a friend. If I'd asked a single question—or told any of the others that she was using my car a lot—if I'd had her back at all, she might still be alive today."

He wasn't speaking for himself. But for her. Because she *had* asked the question. Hundreds of them. Hundreds of times. And they were making incredible progress. Far more than he'd expected when he'd taken her case on just four days before.

"From what I've read and what you said, she likely would have lied to you, Glen. Had you asked why she needed the car so much. She was on a mission of her own. Something she was driven to do. And you...you brought her justice."

He heard the logic in her words. Wanted to believe them. But the conversation wasn't about him. Or Sierra. Exactly the opposite. Turning his head, he looked over to see her staring blankly straight ahead. "You did what I didn't, Lorna. You ask the questions. Even when it's hard." Like the need to explain to Selena why they needed her DNA. "You've had Simon's back for decades, and Selena's, too, for several years."

Driven by an unwavering personal need to find answers, she was like him. But she was so much more than he'd ever been, too. The woman oozed compassion, and Glen had spent his entire life fighting not to let himself get caught up in anything he couldn't control. Emotional closeness being first on the list. Where he pulled back, she pushed forward. Sierra and Simon were proof of that. She talked when she was uncomfortable. He became mute. Her hair was wild and unruly. His was carefully maintained.

"I've been driven by my own need to find the answers,"

she said softly. "And now I'm asking myself why I continued to push so hard. I took a leave of absence from a lucrative job. Not only have I put my own life in danger, but now yours and others', too, as well as creating havoc at Sierra's Web. And for what? To find answers that aren't going to change the past, but could bring pain and suffering into the future? Selena has a good life. Is about to get married. Yes, she wants answers, but if I hadn't been there, giving her an excuse to continue to hang on to hope that Simon's kidnapping could be solved, she'd have eventually moved on. Moved away from what really has become an obsession. For both of us."

She lifted the beer bottle to her mouth. Took a couple of swallows, like it was water not an alcoholic beverage. Glen wanted to reach out a hand. To slow her down. But held back. Guzzling one bottle of beer, if she came to that, wasn't going to hurt her. He wouldn't offer a second.

Or he would, and let her make her own choice. Because that's who he was. What he did.

"Instead, I encouraged her to believe that the past could be resolved, only to hurt her in the end. I've always known that we might not find Simon alive. I just never thought about how that would make her feel. I was out to find her answers because I somehow thought they would set us both free. But free from what? Hoping?"

Glen heard the truth in her words. Respected them. She'd never said she was going to find Simon. Only that she had to find out what happened to him. "I'm guessing you never told Selena that you'd find her brother alive," he said, watching her watch the wall. He was fighting for something that wasn't even his, but that felt vitally important to him, anyway. "You didn't give her false hope.

"Having a passion for something, and more importantly, having the strength and determination to follow through on something you think others failed to do—that needs to be done—makes you an admirable human being, Lorna. Someone to be praised, encouraged." He stopped talking. Heard himself getting into a place that went deeper than his mind. And was far more personal than their brief association would withstand.

Her head turned. He could feel her look at him. He had to fix what he'd done. Get them back on track. "We have to turn over a lot of stones to find the one under which the key is hiding," he started, feeling inane, but gaining strength, too. Turning to look at her, he said, "Justice needs to be served, Lorna. It's why we have laws, law enforcement, courts. It's why we do what we do."

She nodded. Peeled at the label on the top of the beer bottle that was still three-quarters of the way full. Wasn't arguing, but, based on the scraps of paper becoming a carefully laid pile in her lap, his words weren't helping, either.

"Selena and her family members need to know, even if they don't like the answers," he said then. "People learn to live with the not knowing, but it's always there. An entity that lingers. And shapes future feelings and choices. It's an unrest inside that is a constant reminder of loss of control. Of inability to help yourself." The words came up out of him. And once started, they didn't stop. "Closure, while painful in the moment, will allow Selena to put the past to rest."

He heard his own words. Knew them to be absolute truth. And held her gaze steadily as he let her glean that from him.

He also heard buzzing inside him. Realization knocking at him from the inside out.

And for a second there, wished he'd never met the woman who'd managed to turn his entire world upside down in just four days.

LORNA DIDN'T FEEL GREAT. The dark turn the evening had taken lurked within and around her. But Glen's words made sense out of her emotional chaos. Enough so that she knew she had to stay and find the answers she'd flown to Phoenix seeking.

Selena could very well be heartbroken. Most assuredly if she found out that not only was Simon not her twin brother, but her mother wasn't her biological mother, either.

Didn't mean she hadn't been a great mother. Or hadn't loved Selena to distraction. Which was what she'd tell the woman the next time they spoke.

What she should have said on the line earlier.

She wasn't herself. Meeting Glen in person, working beside someone who shared her path, her attraction to him, the sex, leaving it all behind as soon as they found out what happened to Simon…so not the quiet, peaceful life she'd made for herself.

But worth it. She needed to move past finding Simon's answers.

And Selena…the answers could very well be life-changing. Painful. But she'd be set free, too. Able to live and love to the fullest, giving her all to her husband, her future family, without holding back.

Glen had been right about that.

And so many other things.

He'd also just revealed something that—while she kept telling herself to let it go—she had to ask him about. Rising enough to put down her beer bottle on the built-in console in the next section of the couch, she turned toward him as she sat back. They should eat. She needed to get out to the kitchen long enough to reheat the pasta she'd made.

The thoughts were there. Practical. Correct. Provable, even.

And she didn't move. Other than the muscles it took to say, "The way you spoke about living with the not knowing…that wasn't just book learning." She was staring right at him. Saw the slight move in his jaw. As though he was biting down.

Or bracing himself.

She had no right to push. She was there solely on his grace.

And he'd just praised her for seeking answers that hadn't been found.

"What didn't you know?" she asked softly. And when he didn't answer, "Or don't you know still?"

He could tell her to shut the hell up. Or get up and leave her sitting in the small room alone. He could expel her from his home and Sierra's Web, too.

He took a sip of his beer. And then another. She recognized the need for a second or two of liquid comfort.

They both knew that alcohol was not going to help any of the situations they were facing.

The fact that they were back there, in the room where they'd had incredible sex. A small room with no windows and minimal furnishings. A room that had called them back.

Because it was windowless. But so were the separate bathrooms where they'd showered that morning. She couldn't speak to his, but hers was large enough to fit a small table and chair. Had sufficient electrical outlets and the ability to take care of one's vital functions, too.

She continued to pin him with her stare. Because he continued to sit. He had something to say. And when he was ready, she'd be there waiting.

Another two minutes passed. Lorna wasn't all that hungry. Had no place else to be.

"My parents got pregnant with me in high school." His voice, when he started speaking, sounded like something she'd heard on his video lectures. And as she'd been then, she was glued to every word. Understanding that they were in a sacred moment. "Mom's home life wasn't good. My father's family was extremely conservative. They feared my paternal grandparents would force them to give me up for adoption." He stopped.

She didn't move. Wanted to put a hand on his arm. Or slide her fingers through his. But kept them firmly clasped together. Silent seconds ticked by.

"According to her, they ran off to get married, but couldn't get a license without parental signature. And couldn't afford one, either. My father got a job, they managed to get a one-room apartment, and by the time I was born, they were seventeen and could go on public assistance for health care."

He was stating facts as he knew them, with no discernible emotion attached. Focusing on practicalities. Lorna focused between the words. Looking for what he might not be able to say. Hadn't found anything. So she gave up and just listened.

"My father died on the job—he was working construction and fell off a three-story scaffolding—when I was a year old. My mother did her best, but never quite handled losing him. She'd never go back to the homelife she came from. And was afraid that my father's parents would take me from her, and I grew up in and out of foster care. She couldn't build a life for us, but she wouldn't give me up for adoption, either. She disappeared when I was in high school. Just left without a forwarding address."

Lorna's heart cried out. She so badly needed to reach out to him. To give him soft warmth. Instead, she blinked back the tears that might make him uncomfortable. He was talking to a colleague. Not a lover.

"A few years ago, I got a call. She was dying. Wanted to see me."

And he didn't go. The thought hit her hard. Stole her breath from her lungs. There was no science that could give him answers.

She shouldn't have pushed.

"When I got to the hospital…"

Lorna couldn't hold back the tears as he paused, staring at his beer bottle. He'd gone. Thank God, he'd gone.

"She told me that Rivers, the name we'd always gone by, was her last name. That my father's last name was Thomas. And that's when she told me about everything else, too. Their high school pregnancy. All of it."

Glen Rivers Thomas. He'd answered a question she'd had—why the addition of Thomas to his name. He'd found his answers. Her eyes flooded anew. She blinked. Tried to hold back the tears.

"She told me his parents' names. And where they'd lived when I was conceived."

Wow. He really did know what it meant to find the answers. Her tongue buzzed with questions. She smiled, wishing he'd turn to look at her. That she felt free to give him the big hug she suddenly needed to bestow. There really were happy endings.

Except that... Glen was frowning. "They weren't happy to see you?" she asked hesitantly. Then more words poured out. "Didn't believe that you were their grandchild?" He'd have had DNA take care of that one quickly enough. And it occurred to her... "They were already gone?"

His gaze, when he looked at her, seemed to prepare her for something...shameful? "I've never looked them up," he told her.

And with a tightening of facial muscles, she stared.

"Then maybe that's what we do to pass the time tonight," she said. "What's the worst that can happen? You find out you lost your chance? Or that they're creeps? At least you'll have your answers." Picking up her computer, she brought up Sierra's Web's secure server and looked over at him.

"What are their names?"

She understood why he knew what it meant to not have the answers. And more, had heard the intensity in his voice earlier when he'd insisted that any answers she gave Selena would be a blessing in the long run, as they'd set her free.

Selena wasn't the only one who needed closure. The only one living in an emotional cage.

And Lorna couldn't give up without removing the bars.

She had a mind that sought answers at all costs.

And she was going to provide them.

For the boy who'd been stolen when she was six years old. For his twin sister.

And for the man Lorna loved, too.

Chapter Twenty

"Carla N. and Steven G. Thomas." Glen gave her the names. As much as his instincts were telling him he was going to regret the move—that as soon as Lorna was gone, he'd come back to his senses—in the moment, he felt a curious sense of relief. "My mother's name was Tricia Rivers. My father's was Steven Glen Thomas."

It wasn't like anything he'd said would have any permanent effect. Lorna was a temporary workmate. Not one of his partners.

All of whom would most definitely have found Glen's grandparents, even if they hadn't told him about doing so, if he'd told any of them that he knew their names.

He'd explained the legal addition to his own name—filed for him by Savannah, their law expert partner—as a choice to honor his dead father. One of his mother's last requests. Which it had been.

He'd just held back the part about there being grandparents.

And possibly other family.

The idea of finding them, meeting them, made him want to lock himself up in his lab and stay there. He wasn't a family guy. Didn't feel like he wanted to be.

And yet...he heard his own words again. Issued for Selena,

but hitting him in a way that had kind of shocked him. *People learn to live with the not knowing, but it's always there. An entity that lingers. And shapes future feelings and choices. It's an unrest inside that is a constant reminder of loss of control.*

Which made maintaining control a number one priority. Meaning the parameters of his life had to be kept minute enough that he was in constant control. As in…a lab that he rarely left? Because it was the only place he felt completely comfortable.

And, God help him, safe?

Until a woman barged into his world, fitting into it enough that he gave her entrance into that lab, and then showed him a glimpse of himself completely out of control.

As he'd been the night before in Lorna's arms.

And wanted to be again.

Was that it then? He was upending his life, going down a rabbit hole of emotional conflict—possibly involving a family of strangers—to justify another night of sex?

Glen slumped against the couch, pulled back inside, too. But he didn't tell her to stop.

"Surprisingly, there are quite a few Carla and Steve Thomases coming up," Lorna said, her tone studious, her expression a bit of a frown as she focused on her screen. Typing, then reading, typing, then reading. "Do you know what state your parents were living in during high school?"

"She said Texas. I'm not sure she was telling the truth." But the Thomas thing…there'd been no doubt about that one. His mother had looked him right in the eye, in spite of the tears flooding hers, and begged him to honor his father by bearing his name.

"Texas marriage records are online," she said as she typed. "I'm assuming at this point that your father's conservative parents were married."

He'd assumed the same. Sipped his beer. Thought about

the hours it was going to take to get Selena's DNA to the lab. The searches being done on Annabelle Gravestone, Michelle Applegate, and age progression photos of Simon Billingsley, too. The record searches being done in Michigan.

The paint chip Lorna had found in the evidence box and tested, so they'd have a basis for identification if anything else showed up with that paint. Twenty-three years later.

The tiny fingerprint scratches she'd seen in the paint on the back of the bench. In between all her other tests, she was meticulously checking every piece of evidence picked up in the park the day Simon disappeared. Looking over every single one of them for signs of his little fingers. Of paint. A tearstain. Saliva trace.

Just as he'd be doing if he was working the case full-time.

Someone that thorough, she was going to find his grandparents. If not that night, then sometime soon.

Another sense of relief hit him along with instant rejection of any idea of him being part of a family. But the knowing, having the answers, allowed him to let go.

"Selena needs the answers you're finding for her," he said aloud. Ruminating, which was odd for him, but what the hell, everything about the minutes he was living was out of the realm of anything he'd have ever imagined. "How can she let go until she knows what she's letting go of?"

Bad grammar. Accurate thought.

He couldn't let go until he knew what to let go of. Were they alive? Dead? What kind of lives had they lived? Were there others? Kids, grandkids? How old were they? Still married? He'd opened his mind to one question—dead or alive—the only one he'd knowingly contemplated, and a slew of others followed.

Didn't faze him much. One answer or a dozen. He'd take them in.

So he could do the one thing he always did, except for Sierra's Web and, peripherally, his partners.

He'd let them go.

LORNA WAS ON a mission.

She could leave when the Simon Billingsley case was officially closed, without a broken heart, if she knew that her being with Glen had allowed her to complete an act of love for him.

He'd given her the way. Something he could easily have done himself, probably quicker than her, anytime over the past several years, and hadn't.

She didn't know why he'd chosen her as his conduit.

But she was not going to let him down.

She carried her computer with her out to the kitchen, where she and Glen crouched together and stayed low as they prepared a tray of food and beverages. A plate of the various fruits he had left. Oranges, apples, which she sliced. Grapes. He grabbed a package of sliced Havarti cheese. She took the grape jelly she liked to eat with it. They had crackers. Some ham slices she'd found in the freezer and thawed and cut up. Some chips and salsa. And a couple of the packaged chocolate cupcakes she'd found in a cupboard.

He wasn't saying much. Asking whether she liked something or not. Hadn't asked what she'd found, if anything. She didn't say. Nor did she look at her computer while she was out there. She was storing up the memory of her very first picnic with a man.

Made sweeter by the fact that they were alone together in his home, and she was in love with him.

No one would ever know that last part. So it didn't matter that the world would scoff at a scientist believing herself in love after only knowing a man for four days.

Sometimes all it took was four days to live a lifetime.

Or get over one.

And, if truth were known, she'd been half in love with Glen for years. Had learned so much from him. Was as good a scientist as she was because of him.

Then, meeting him—his honesty, the compassionate way in which he'd seen her need, the danger she was in, and had opened his home to her, a complete stranger, had all made the falling a no-brainer.

Even the fact that he'd let two of his partners furnish his home for him. The way he kept trying to cook even when he didn't like a lot of the dishes that resulted.

His ability to admit that he wasn't good at something. Or many things.

His willingness to do the hard work—even when it meant exposing his own emotional battles.

And the way her body responded to him…that was what had finally catapulted the scientist inside her. Her own chemical reactions had proven to her that Glen was unlike any other man she'd ever been with.

And like the scientists they were, once back in the den, they'd both been engrossed in their computers over the hour that they'd nibbled off the tray on the ottoman in front of them.

Until Glen broke the silence they'd been sharing. "Hud's off for the rest of the night. Brian has already shipped Selena's DNA, overnight express. It'll be at the lab in the morning. His overnight team will have a complete report for us by morning on Michelle Applegate and any woman they can identify from the various photos turned up in social media and in Searcy news. They're using your program to run further age regression on those photos as well. The coding team is working on the hacker. It's tedious work, following twenty years of twisted trails, but they have been able to verify, through coding fingerprints, that the person trying to hack into your work at Sierra's Web is tied to that offshore account. Whether just being paid from there, perhaps laundering money through it, or having set it up to begin with, they don't yet know."

It was maybe the most words she'd ever heard him say all at once. Was glad for the update. And wasn't quite ready to give him her own report. "Give me five more minutes," she told him.

It was late. They'd need to rest. She was hoping on separate portions of the sectional. Or, at least, her on one portion of it if he chose to do as Jamison had suggested and pull the mattress off his bed and sleep on the floor.

When he picked up the tray and left the room, she felt his absence like a physical pang. It was already starting. The separation that would be coming in the days ahead. When the danger was gone. And Simon's answers had been found.

Forcing herself to concentrate on the very important task at hand, she completed the slideshow report she'd spent the past hour creating. And was ready and waiting, watching the doorway for him, as he returned.

He'd taken off his lab coat. Had his gun in hand. And her heart started to thud. "You saw someone?" she asked. And then, before he could respond, added, "Heard something?"

He looked...just far too good as he shook his head, the short hair a bit rumpled and far too sexy with the two-day growth of dark stubble on his chin. Without the lab coat, his shoulders and the breadth of his chest were more clearly delineated. And those thighs...the muscle between them...

She cut off the instant spate of distraction she'd sent herself on at the sight of the gun, and saw him slide the gun between the cushion and couch end just below the wide arm where his laptop sat as he said, "No. Jamison gave the all clear. The crew outside is in place and on patrol."

So didn't that mean...and the gun there...that he *was* planning to stay in there with her?

Didn't matter. Not at the moment. "You want to watch one episode of *CSI*?" he asked, picking up the remote from the console on the other side of her before crossing back over to take his seat.

"Can we talk for just a minute?" she asked instead, feeling her chest tighten some around her. Needing to be whatever it was he would need over the next minutes.

His lips pursed, his chin jutted, and he shrugged. But the television stayed off.

Moving over just enough for them to share view of her computer screen, she pushed for the first slide to appear. "Carla and Steven Thomas were married fifty-three years ago in Dallas, Texas. She's seventy-three, he's seventy-five."

The words were in large print on her screen as well.

"This is Carla," she said then, and tapped to switch to the next slide. She'd found several photos, had pulled them all in, but the largest one, in the center, was within the past year.

Glen didn't make a sound. Didn't move.

After a few seconds, she said, "This is Steven," and clicked again. The largest photo wasn't a current photo, though there were two of those on-screen as well, one size smaller. The old black and white front and center was of a much younger Steven. Around Glen's age. And the resemblance…she didn't know if he could see it, but it had caught her instantly.

"They had three children," she said, and clicked another time. Two of the photos were of women in their sixties. One was of a much younger man. His photo from a high school yearbook.

The women's names and addresses, along with marital status and husbands' names were written beneath their photos. "June and Meredith both still in live in Dallas. As do their parents," she told him.

And then, before going any further, said, "Steven is a retired minister. Carla is a homemaker and from what I could find, was a preacher's wife in every sense of the word. Meredith is a lawyer, still practicing in a firm that specializes in family law. June is a sixth-grade teacher, and has been at the same school for thirty years."

She flipped one more time. "Meredith had two kids. Mike and Ashley. Both are married. Ashley has four-year-old Jason. June had one child, a daughter. Kylie. She's twenty-nine and still single." Pictures of all three kids—his biological cousins—were on-screen.

She'd found a family photo, with every member present, including spouses, on social media, celebrating Carla and Steven's fiftieth anniversary, but hadn't included it, or a number of other pieces of information she'd stumbled upon, in the slideshow.

He had the answers he'd most critically need. Including cell phone numbers. From there it was up to him what he sought to learn. Or not.

Tears filled her eyes as she stared at her screen. An entire family.

And he'd been excluded. Had grown up with no one to call his own except a woman who could neither provide regularly for him, nor find it in her heart to give him up.

Lorna's heart cried out for him. Not so much in pity, though there was sadness and regret there for him—but more in need to wrap her arms around him and let him feel how incredibly special he was.

How much he was wanted.

And how very much he was loved.

But it wasn't her place. He had his partners. They were his family.

She'd served her purpose.

And might spend more time than she thought grieving when she had to tell him goodbye.

HE HAD HIS ANSWERS. Just like that. There they were. He could let go. Sitting in his little den that he'd been in maybe twice since he'd moved in, Glen couldn't escape the sense of surreality encompassing him.

He'd had the most incredible sexual encounter of his life in that space less than twenty-four hours ago. His life was in danger, and he wasn't running away from the source. He was continuing to do the job he'd been born to do. Even if it meant dying in the process.

He'd told a woman he'd known four days something he'd never told anyone. Had opened a personal door he'd believed forever closed.

And he had a family. Grandparents. Aunts. Cousins. A minister. A lawyer. A schoolteacher. A preacher's wife who was at home to raise her kids.

Had they even looked for his dad when he and Glen's mom ran off?

Did they know their son had had a son? Or that he'd died soon after?

Or were they, like Selena Billingsley, living every day with a gaping hole filled with questions and no answers? In need of a company like Sierra's Web to dig deep enough, hard enough, to find out what had happened to their son?

Thinking of the situation from the outside in—sitting there with the answers before the possibility of questions had even become apparent to him—Glen realized that he wasn't going to get his closure, his freedom, until he finished the job Lorna had started.

"We have no way of knowing if they're aware of what happened to their son," he said aloud. Working the case. Fully realizing there might not be one. The Thomases could have their answers. They might have known all along that their son was dead. That Glen was out in the world. They might have chosen to turn their backs on a situation that wouldn't fit their pretty family picture.

"They have a family headstone at the cemetery attached to the church Steven retired from." Lorna clicked. Pulled up a photo of the building, the cemetery, and the angled, but still legible headstone bearing the last name of Thomas. "I found it through an obituary from when Steven's mother died fifteen years ago."

Steven's mother. Glen's great-grandmother. Who'd still been alive for over half of his life. The pang went deeper that time. And he shrugged it off. The work he was doing wasn't about him. It was about providing answers so others could let go.

With his head back on track, he saw what Lorna had obviously seen. What she clearly thought he should see. His father's name was there. With a birth date. But no death date.

"Like Selena, they deserve answers," he said, his tone calm. He understood. It's what his firm did. Provide answers to those who needed them.

Lorna didn't respond. He didn't look at her. She'd clicked the screen back to Steven's images. He reached and scrolled back one to Carla. Saw a client in need. "It should probably be done in person," he said then. Focused on getting the job right.

"Probably." Lorna's tone, like his, was professional.

He glanced at her—saw a warmth in her gaze he didn't need. Nodded and picked up the remote, turning on the television. "I'll tend to that after the Billingsley case is resolved," he said, wanting the matter dropped.

Maybe he was procrastinating. The choice also seemed right.

As did putting an arm around Lorna, like in the car the other night, inviting the weight of her head at the apex of his chest. Human contact to get through the difficult moments they were living.

And when, halfway through the show, he felt the weight of her deepen against him, heard her steady even breathing denoting sleep, he tipped his head back just to rest his eyes for a bit, too.

Chapter Twenty-One

Lorna woke just before dawn. The windowless room gave her no clue to the hour, but the clock on the television screen let her know that it was time to get up.

She just didn't want to move. Lying on the couch, with Glen's arm hooked around her waist, she didn't want to wake him. Vaguely remembering when he'd wordlessly laid them down together, she didn't think she'd stirred the rest of the night.

But the second she felt his arm stiffen slightly against her, she sprang quickly into action. Sitting up, she ran a hand through her hair. Stood, allowing him room to rise at his leisure, and set about unplugging her laptop and gathering it against her.

He did the same, but where she'd have darted wordlessly out the door, he paused, looked at her, and said, "Same drill as yesterday morning?"

Sweet relief warmed her. She nodded. And much later that morning, was still thinking about the way his eyes had lingered on her as they'd left the room.

Glen Rivers Thomas was not an easy man to get close to. She'd seen him with the experts who worked for him, and there was always an invisible step back. Then that morning, as they'd had an in-person conference with Savannah,

Dorian, Winchester, and Hudson down in Glen's office—with Kelly and Mariah on video call—she'd watched him with his partners. Had witnessed a trust she'd never before seen in a workplace. And a very clear affection, too. But still—it was as though he wore a hands-off sign when it came to anything more than work or superficial conversation. A message they all seemed to respect.

None of them mentioned Glen's newfound family. Maybe they'd talked as friends earlier, without her present—they were, after all, in a business meeting—but she didn't think so. The news was huge, a life-changer, and Glen was acting as though the day was the same as any other.

Compartmentalizing. She understood. And reminded herself that it was none of her business. Hoping that at some point her heart would catch up with her brain.

She'd assumed the meeting had been called for a report on the Billingsley case. With so many different angles being looked at, involving various teams, and Sierra's Web having been targeted as well, it made sense to her that the group would convene.

Instead, the conversation had been arranged for an entirely different purpose. As Lorna stood in her lab awaiting DNA results on Selena, Simon, and Sharon Billingsley and using the time to get through more of the twenty-three-year-old evidence that had been sent from Morrilton, the previous hour's turn of events replayed silently in her mind. Over and over again. If she'd had a hand free, she might have pinched herself just to get the reality check over with and accept that she'd made a deal with Sierra's Web that would end her financial shortcomings.

We'd like to recommend, first and foremost, that you copyright your age variation program. Savannah had been the main speaker. Actually, other than head nods, smiles, and a definitive *please* from Hudson, she'd been the only speaker.

The firm wanted to pay for exclusive rights to use her program, giving them the ability to share with law enforcement as appropriate, but also the ability to protect against its misuse. With cybercrimes and generative artificial intelligence becoming more prominent, they wanted to do all they could to ensure that her tool wasn't used for harm.

She hadn't dared glance at Glen. Her fingers had been shaking as, left alone with the lawyer after the brief meeting, she'd gone through the online process to file for registration of copyright, and then had signed the contract she'd been presented.

Her entire life she'd let herself be made to feel like an obsessive crackpot. And in the space of a few days, her work had become distinguished enough to be of exclusive value to a nationally renowned firm. One she'd been a fan of since her first year of college.

Because of Simon Billingsley.

And Glen's willingness to help a determined but desperate scientist get on with her work.

Hud's team hadn't yet come in with a morning report.

She'd made it through a little more than half of the plastic evidence bags containing every little piece of anything the crime scene investigators had picked up from the Morrilton park twenty-three years before. Was determined to get through them. Leaving no stone unturned. And reached into the pile they'd become on the end of her table. Taking what her fingers fished out.

A piece of foil. Half of a condom wrapper was her first thought, and, with evidence gloves covering her hands, pulled the two-inch, clearly torn, paper-thin substance out to dust it for prints. If nothing else, they could hope to trace someone who'd seen someone lingering in the park the night before, or early in the morning the day that Simon disappeared. Someone possibly planning a kidnapping? A couple having sex, not wanting to get caught, would likely be attentive to who could be in the immediate vicinity.

The material, while foil on one side, was paper on the other. With what looked like a torn orange shape. Part of a product emblem of some kind? She'd check out the source, but fingerprinting came first. Placing the scrap of trash on the glass beneath her mounted, lighted magnifying glass, she picked up her magnetic brush. And froze.

There, in the corner of the ripped packaging, was clearly a speck of color. Olive green. Heart thudding, she lowered the magnifying glass, enlarging the image. Still there. She wasn't imagining the dot of something.

Could just be paint from the printing on the wrapper. Her instincts wouldn't let her settle for that. Determining that she had to test that speck first, rather than risk losing it to fingerprint dust, she meticulously removed the small sample and, adding the proper chemicals, put her mass spectrometer to work. And then, presented herself back at the source for fingerprinting.

Her nerves were climbing within her, tensing around the butterflies also seeming to take flight within her abdomen, when she saw the print formation take place. She'd run it through every database known to Sierra's Web, but had to rule someone out first.

Michelle Applegate. The biter of the pen.

Her brain was just processing the information on her computer screen, not yet even fully comprehending what was in front of her, when the spectrometer signaled an end to the process she'd been running. Turning to that, she stared.

Glanced back at her screen.

And, hands shaking, picked up her phone and called Glen.

"COME DOWN NOW." The voice was Lorna's, but not a tone he'd ever heard before. With dread in his gut, he dropped his phone in his pocket, grabbed his gun out of his drawer, and sped toward her lab.

No way she'd talk to him, her temporary boss, or even a friend, like that unless there was an emergency. It didn't occur to him, until he rounded the corner of her space and saw her sitting there alone and completely well, that perhaps he should have alerted security before rushing into danger.

On her stool in front of her main worktable, her eyes were wide, turned toward him, as he barged in like the place was on fire. Not an impossibility, considering the other assaults that had happened on their properties that week. "You okay?" he asked, taking his first full breath since he'd answered his phone.

She nodded, but still looked…oddly ready to cry…as she watched him approach. She glanced at her computer screen, so he did, too. And then she motioned toward spectrometer results. And pointed at a small piece of ripped trash beneath her microscope. An evidence bag that identified where it had been collected.

"It's part of a wrapper to one of those little bags of character-shaped cheese crackers," she said. "It must have been given to him, to distract him, keep him quiet. He ripped it open, a piece stuck to his little fingers, and he brushed it off. Probably with the side of his leg." She was rambling. But the picture she built formed solid, like a video replay in his mind.

"Simon was out by the road, across from the library, just like you thought." She'd got a match from the paint sample collected under the bench.

"And Michelle Applegate was with him." He put into words the news that was almost too sacred to speak aloud. They'd found her holy grail. At least part of it.

Lorna nodded. "At least, she gave him the crackers. Her print is clear on this end of the paper. He likely took the bag from her, holding it just above where she had."

They didn't have Simon's fingerprints. But they had his DNA. Which could verify that what the evidence was telling them was true. Either way, Michelle had been at the bench where Simon had been taken, and the bench paint, which had been scraped—conceivably by Simon's little fingers—had been on a small bit of trash picked up at the edge of the road across the park from the bench.

"I knew that pen was important," she said then. Looking up at him with a sheen of tears in her eyes.

And in that second, he knew, without question, that she was vitally important, too.

EVEN WHILE LORNA struggled to accept that she was actually getting the answers she'd been seeking all her life—as that darkest of all dark days in the park that she'd imagined un-countable times in her mind was coming to life with facts—a pall hung over her.

She was getting her answers, just as Glen had received his the night before, but what about Selena? Was Simon's disap-pearance the shadow in her life? Or was it something larger? More sinister? A child gone. Another left with a woman who probably hadn't given birth to her?

Or Simon?

If Sharon Billingsley wasn't Simon or Selena's mother, then who was?

Glen was still in her lab, talking to Hud on the phone, when her thermocycler signaled PCR results. Her hands were shak-ing as she approached. For the first time since she'd started her search for Simon's answers, she didn't want to see results. Didn't want to know.

The scientist in her drove her forward anyway.

And the woman in front of her wept. A flood of tears burst forth, rolling quietly down her face. She wiped them away as she reached in her satchel for the phone purchased for Selena calls only and dialed Brian's burner phone.

"Selena and Simon are a match for full siblings, and Sharon is most definitely their mother." She left the message as professionally as possible and hung up, still shaking with the news.

The truth didn't explain why Sharon had provided Selena with pregnancy and birthing photos that didn't match, nor did those wrong photos matter. The woman had lost her two-year-old son. And later, because of it, her marriage. She couldn't be blamed for photograph mismanagement. Misplacement. Possible destruction due to the pain remembering caused. Or to possible blocks in her memory, as she looked back at happier times.

Cell phone images hadn't been a thing back then. Or even a possibility. Phones with cameras hadn't been available in the US until a couple of years after Simon was born. She'd checked just that morning.

And didn't want to turn around. Glen's voice was no longer deep in conversation on the other side of her lab. She felt his heat directly behind her. Needed to turn around, to hold him and be held. Instead, she said, "You heard?"

"I see." His tone alerted her to more going on. As though he was calculating the information in front of him in light of something else. Weighing possibilities.

Backing up a step, running her butt into the table behind her, she turned. Looked up at him. "What?"

"Hud found his hacker," he told her, without a hint of a smile.

Bracing herself, mind racing to figure out how that could possibly be bad news, trying to think of anyone she'd be shocked to find as the culprit, she slowly asked, "Who?"

"Devon Billingsley."

Instead of her butt just touching the table built into the

wall behind her, Lorna leaned her entire weight against it. "Selena and Simon's father? That's impossible! He died a few years ago. I went to his funeral, Glen. I stood in the back, didn't tell anyone who I was, but I was there. It was open casket. I saw him."

And Selena and Beth, too. Sisters who'd been at odds a lot of times, but who'd held on to each other, through the service. And afterward.

It took her a second to realize that Glen was nodding. "The code traced back to him," he clarified. "And Hud's team were finally able to hack enough encryptions and trace enough stop points to find the account that the first deposits into the offshore account originated from. Cryptocurrency wasn't a thing then, so it was a bit easier for them to follow back."

He stopped, as though giving her time. There'd never be enough to help her, so she said, "And?"

"It came from a private account Devon Billingsley opened not quite a year before Simon and Selena were born."

She shook her head. Confused. "What, he was opening an offshore college fund account for his future children?"

Glen's headshake warned her she wasn't going to like what was coming. "There were regular withdrawals from the account. Starting from two months after the account was opened, and ending when Simon was in high school. All by the same person."

She had to ask again. "Who?"

"Annabelle Gravestone."

Her mouth fell open. "The woman at the motel. The one Dilly didn't remember."

He nodded.

Staring at him, she tried to draw from his intelligence, his experience. "She didn't remember her because she'd never seen her before," she guessed. In a small town, if Annabelle had been around much, Dilly would likely have run across her.

He shrugged.

And she couldn't take a dead end. "Did they trace that account? Do we know who this Annabelle Gravestone is?"

She'd known his headshake was coming before it happened. The news he'd had to impart hadn't been good. She just didn't know how bad it was. If more was coming. And as hard as the moments were, she was grateful that Glen was giving her breaths along the way to accept what she was hearing.

"Other than that one hotel registry and the bank account, a woman by that name doesn't seem to exist. As you already know, Hud's team completed all the standard searches when we found the hotel registry. There are no birth records, marriage licenses, or death records by that name. A check on the surname didn't bring up anything, either. They did a deeper search last night and still came up empty."

He sounded sorry.

Which made her feel less alone. More determined.

As she focused, the facts gelled inside her. Her DNA results for Sharon, Simon, and Selena. The discrepancy in photographs. The bank account. "Surrogacy." She blurted the word. Stared at Glen. "Devon was paying a woman to have a baby for him and Sharon. Back then it wasn't as much an accepted thing like it is now. Surrogacy implantation generally involves multiple embryos with the hope that one takes. Multiple births are sometimes a result."

It fit every detail. And then some. Adrenaline flowing, she stared at Glen. And then stilled. "You said the payments to Annabelle Gravestone continued until Simon would have been in high school."

He nodded. She frowned. "Doesn't make sense that a father is paying money to an account before his son and daughter are born, for their birth, but then continues to pay for..."

She broke off. "What if the agreement wasn't just for the birth? What if the Billingsleys agreed to pay the woman for a certain number of years? Or...until her death?" For the unknown—at that point fictitious—woman's sake she hoped it wasn't the latter.

Glen's gaze had been intent the entire time she was blathering. As she finally fell silent, he said, "There's merit in the surrogacy theory," he told her. "Most particularly based on the pregnancy photos with Sharon, and the timing of the start of the payments. Even say we go with the idea of an agreement that provided extended payments for whatever length of time...that doesn't explain who's using the offshore account now to pay people to sabotage you, Sierra's Web, and this investigation."

The obvious answer was, "Someone doesn't want us to find out what we're finding out." A lot of little things that led to big possibilities without any proof to tie them together.

Looking at Glen, seeing him, the man who'd trusted her with a very personal situation the night before, another thought struck her. "What if Simon's surrogate was on a payment plan, but did take him? What if Simon found out at some point? Knows that he has a twin sister. But loves the woman he'd grown up to believe was his mother. Wanted to protect her. Maybe she told him about the offshore account. And maybe now it's him that's trying to shut us down? To protect her. And himself. Maybe he doesn't want to be found."

Glen had known for a few years, at least, that he could have family who might want to meet him. He hadn't even bothered to do an internet search.

Nor had he shown much reaction when she'd "introduced him" to them the night before.

He'd grown up as he had. Meeting what might have been wasn't going to rewrite history. But it could be the birth of a plethora of regret. So much that even the possibility of close family in his future hadn't been enough to prompt action.

Recognizing the similarities in her newest theory regarding Simon and Glen's life, Lorna's entire perspective downshifted. What if she'd spent her entire life trying to fix something that wasn't considered broken by the life that had been stolen? And Selena—what would it do to the girl to know that her entire life had been spent missing her twin brother, thinking that she was feeling him, when the reality might turn out to be that he'd had the chance to reach out and had chosen not to know her?

"I'm guessing there's been no other activity on that account since those regular payments stopped, until this past week," she said. Because he'd have mentioned it, if there had been.

Glen's nod was long and slow. "You're correct."

Lorna's entire system deflated. As though air had been let out of her skin. She felt like an old prune. One who'd once had potential to be of good taste to someone who liked prunes, but who'd been so busy trying to find someone who didn't need answers, to bring justice for someone who didn't want justice, that her greatest possibilities had dried up. She'd been so single-mindedly focused on finding out what happened to Simon Billingsley that better options for her talents, her focus, had passed her by.

Not that it was all about her. Just…the idea of telling Selena…if indeed the theory panned out…

She shut the rest of the thought out to say, "We don't know that that's the case," she told Glen. "That Simon doesn't want to be found and is hiring people to stop us. We've got to follow this through, every clue, every idea, every possibility, until we find Simon Billingsley, or whatever he might be calling himself right now. Until we hear the truth from him, we don't have our answers."

When Glen nodded his agreement, she didn't feel great, but she was able to draw in a deep breath.

She didn't have to tell Selena anything…yet.

And had bought herself some time to prepare for the immense heartache that she was beginning to see in her own future as well.

On many levels.

Chapter Twenty-Two

Glen couldn't stop thinking about his family. Biological relatives, he amended the thought. Over and over as he kept seeing, in his mind's eye, that headstone on Lorna's screen—a son listed with no death date.

And his own youth, one move after another, in a home, back with his mother, in another home—his growing up was more of a cluster than any kind of childhood should have been.

Family was such a nice word. Conjuring a system by which one felt accepted, cared about. Secure. Where one was always wanted. Welcomed. Celebrated.

In reality, family was sometimes a guise behind which painful secrets hid.

While Lorna returned to checking more evidence, Glen put himself on Devon Billingsley. Hud's team had sent a report on him, and Glen studied it, looking for anything he could use to find scientific proof to fill in the what-ifs and maybes to give them some kind of real proof about what had happened twenty-three years ago. To lead them to why someone didn't want them to know about the past. So they could find out who was threatening Lorna Schwann's life.

He didn't kid himself that the danger had passed. Though there'd been no new attempts on her life in the past twenty-four hours, that was only because Sierra's Web had the means to protect the firm and, within its fold, protect her, too.

Experience had also taught him, and his partners, that the longer danger lurked, the more desperate perpetrators became. Time was of the essence.

And one small detail could be the break in the case. That's where he, and the science he lived his life by, came in. Devon Billingsley might have just been a husband and father who was trying to hide the fact that his wife wasn't carrying their children. Sharon could have gone away for a few months and come back with the children.

Or there could have been something more underhanded going on. The money could be completely unrelated to Simon. Or Michelle Applegate. Lorna had just found evidence that tied Michelle and Simon together, but there was nothing that looped in Devon or Annabelle. Not to Simon's disappearance, nor to the money.

They knew from the original police report that Devon had been on the phone with his wife, who was consoling a hurt child—Selena—when Simon had disappeared from right behind her.

And there… Glen's gaze glued to one line in the pages of information Hud had sent up that morning. A twenty-three-year-old fingerprint that had been held within private company records unearthed by Hud's team. A firm Devon had done business with that required fingerprinting. Hud had called the company himself to get the prints sent over. He had Devon's fingerprints.

Bringing up all the evidence that he and Lorna had collected, Glen started a series of tests. To pull DNA from the fingerprint, to separate strands of the DNA for comparison, and to compare to the other prints they'd collected during the case—for starters. Lorna had managed to find several unidentified prints in the mass of evidence she'd been going through.

His mind was still calculating all of the tests he could run, determining order of priority, after the DNA, which he already had running, when he got a hit.

On the first piece of evidence he'd tested—but only to rule it out. Not because he thought for one second that...

He cut the thought off as he picked up his phone. Dialed Lorna. And when she picked up, said, "Devon Billingsley is a perfect match for the half print you got off that pen."

And then he called Hud. He and Lorna were the science people. The rest of his partners would put the pieces together. But he was certain, as was Hud, that he and Lorna had found critical missing links. His match to half a fingerprint might not stand up in court, but in the realm of clues to lead investigators to the connections that would allow them to find the final answers, it was conclusive.

They were nearing the end of the case.

Good or bad, it would soon be over.

But, for once, Glen didn't feel like celebrating.

LORNA WAS IN her lab, processing evidence, when McKenna barged in. "Let's go, now!" she said, grabbing Lorna's arm and pulling her toward the hall. Afraid she was about to die, Lorna stayed with the bodyguard, allowed her to rush her along with an arm behind her back. Was about to run by the doorway to Glen's downstairs suite when McKenna pushed her toward the door. "Get to the lab. Stay there."

The woman's words propelled her forward even as the bodyguard rushed away, leaving Lorna alone. Until Glen appeared in the door between his office and lab. She ran toward him, and when he grabbed her in his arms, she held on. Shaking. Ready to cry.

But didn't stay long. She had to be strong. To be part of the solution, not a victim. Pulling away, she dropped to a stool.

"Members of Hud's team have been monitoring the offshore account, while others are working to get to its current source. Two new payments just hit. One here in Phoenix. And one in Michigan."

Michigan! She concentrated on the one that didn't involve the city where she currently sat. "That's the last known location we have for Simon. Nine years ago."

He nodded. Watched her solemnly, and she connected the dots. Phoenix—where she'd already been targeted after arriving in town to find out what happened to Simon Billingsley. And Michigan—where Simon was last known to have lived.

"Our investigation put Simon in danger," she said.

Pulling a stool over close to her, Glen sat and said, "Based on what we know, that's one theory. Hud's team is adamant that we haven't been hacked. No one knows what kind of searches we've been doing. We didn't lead whoever this is to Simon." But she might have. She'd done searching, too. He paused, pushed the nosepiece of his glasses, and the movement brought his lab coat forward. Giving her a clear sight of the gun in his pocket.

She looked from it to him, and he said, "Local law enforcement are following up on the payment that was sent to an account here in Phoenix."

Yeah, there it was. The part she'd been trying to avoid thinking about. "That's why we're in here." Her lips pursed as she said the words.

Glen cocked his head, took a breath, and said, "Everyone else has been asked to leave the building. No one else is being allowed in." He held her gaze for a second and then added, "Out of an abundance of caution."

Feeling weak and helpless as she sat there, Lorna was

all about caution. She'd thrown it to the wind by coming to Phoenix. To Sierra's Web. To Glen.

And seemed to have opened a Pandora's box filled with more fear and pain than she could have imagined.

GLEN AND LORNA had been locked up for half an hour—mostly talking over everything they knew, had read, or proven about the case, and watching the machines currently running the tests Glen had started, hoping for a miracle—when Hud called down. Glen put his partner on speakerphone.

"Using Lorna's suggestion to run anagrams of Simon Billingsley's name, with emphasis given to words starting with *B* and *S*, we got several hits and, with help from investigators on the ground, narrowed them down to a twenty-five-year-old male in Grand Rapids," he said. "Bill Simeon. Agents got to him an hour before he was due to leave work."

"Was it Simon?" Lorna blurted the words, her mouth hanging open. Eyes wide, she'd grown pale, and Glen felt uncharacteristically invested in the answer as well. More so than he had in a long time.

With all the cases he'd worked over the years, too many to count, he'd grown somewhat complacent.

"We're still waiting on fingerprint results, but he's in custody, safe, and was certain that we had the wrong guy until we asked about a scholarship he'd forfeited nine years ago."

Lorna jumped up, hands to her face. "Oh, my god! We've got him? We found Simon?" She was walking a small circle in front of the phone.

"Still waiting on the fingerprints," Hud repeated, and Glen understood. They had no definitive proof that the high-school-aged photo Lorna's program had matched to the two-year-old who'd gone missing was their boy.

"Oh, my god," Lorna said again, still walking back and

forth by the phone. "Did he say why he kept changing his name? Or…or…who the woman was he was with is? Does he have a scar on his hand?"

"He does." Hud's voice came over the line. "And as to the rest, he insists he grew up with his mother. He's seen photos of her pregnant with him and holding him in the delivery room…"

"A baby photo could be anyone," Lorna interjected. Then put her hand over her mouth.

"He explained periodic name changes and their moving around a lot when he was growing up by the fact that his mom had an abusive boyfriend who kept finding them."

"And the money?" Glen asked, his eyes on Lorna. "Did he know about the money his mother was getting?"

"His mother!" Lorna called out over Glen's question. "What's her name?"

"Anne Simmons. We're running a check on that now."

Lorna, stopping in front of the phone Glen still held, said, "Selena. Does she know?" Urgency filled her tone.

"Not yet. Nor does he know about her. Or even that he was kidnapped. Not until we get the prints back, confirming his identity. But there's something else you two need to know."

Glen recognized the grave tone in Hud's voice and, bracing himself, he stood, instinctively putting himself between Lorna and the door.

"Police found a bomb planted in Bill Simeon's car."

Glen's gut tightened, and he put his hand in his pocket, slid his fingers around the butt of his gun. Fearing it wasn't going to be enough. A paid-for hit, bought by money from the same offshore account that had paid a known assailant against them earlier in the week. The hit man had just planted a bomb.

"You two need to stay put," Hud finished. "Don't leave that lab for any reason. I'll get back with you as soon as I can."

The call clicked off and Lorna stood there staring at Glen. She was shivering. Shaking her head. Her eyes wide. "We found him," she said, her throat sounding tight with tears.

And Glen did what he had to do. He reached out for her, took her in his arms, held her close. His body blocking hers from the doorway. Lorna had sacrificed so much because she wouldn't give up on one two-year-old kidnapped child and his twin sister. Her lifetime dedication to what she believed in, her drive, her strength, her mind, her compassion were suddenly like chemical reads coming from his mass spectrometer, delineating clear proof that she was priceless.

No way was he going to let *anyone* get past him to hurt her. He'd die first.

LORNA'S HEAD WAS SPINNING. It was over. Decades of work and within hours, it was done.

She couldn't sit down. Couldn't slow down. Had only made it through the short drive from Sierra's Web to Glen's house because he'd been holding her hand between both of his, keeping her in her skin, the entire time it took for Jamison to drive them there.

And now that she was in the house, she had no idea why she'd thought she could agree to Glen's suggestion that she just stay the night at his place rather than checking in to a hotel before her flight out in the morning. His reasoning—she had to come back to collect her things, anyway, the bed had already been slept in so one more night wasn't going to make a difference, and it would save her the cost of the hotel—had seemed logical an hour before.

While they'd been waiting for law enforcement to track down the man who'd agreed sometime overnight to cause her bodily harm in exchange for money, she and Glen had talked about his newfound family. She'd pushed the issue. Driven by an extreme overload of emotion—that compounded as fingerprint proof came in to verify that Bill Simeon, Will Simonson, Billy Simmons, and Billy Shaking were all Simon Billingsley—Lorna had convinced herself that the sterility of Glen's lab gave them a scientific bubble in which to speak.

Her heart wouldn't let her completely hide behind that curtain, however. Her departure from Glen's life had been growing more imminent each time the phone had rung, and she'd known she might not get another chance to help his heart find a measure of peace. And, if the fates were being kind, a bit of happiness, too.

He hadn't shared her perspective. Had barely entered the conversation before he was back out of it. But she'd appealed to his fairness to at least arrange for law enforcement to pay the elder Thomases a visit and give them the details of their son's death. Nothing else. Just when and how he'd died.

Holding back that closure was unkind. They deserved to have a completed entry on that headstone, not a gaping unknown that allowed hope to prevent them from fully grieving.

She'd heard him on the phone with Hud, arranging to have a call made to Carla and Steven Thomas, informing them that their son had died. Giving Hud brief details of the time and cause of death. If Hud had asked questions, Glen hadn't answered them. Glen had had a call back that it was done during the drive home. But hadn't seemed to stay on the line long enough to get any of the details.

The drive home. His. Not hers.

It was done. The case was done. Everyone who'd broken laws, who was still alive, was in custody. She was safe. Free to go.

Had a flight out in the morning.

She still couldn't wrap her mind around it all. Focused on that which she could take in.

"You coming?" Glen's voice pulled her from hanging out between the door and the living room to the kitchen. He'd invited her, as they'd arrived at his place, to have a glass of wine with him.

A salute to the work they'd done together. To the brother and sister twins who'd already been reunited by phone, and who'd be meeting in person later that night. Simon hadn't wanted to wait another day to fly to Arkansas once he'd heard Selena's voice on the phone.

And the rest of that story drove her into the kitchen for Glen's proffered glass of wine. At least it was the reason she was allowing herself to think. More than the wine, she needed conversation. With him. The only person who'd understand.

More like, the only person in her life who'd be able to fully participate in the conversation. Telling herself she only needed a debriefing, she clinked the glass he held up to hers, took a sip, and slid onto the far end bar stool she'd occupied two nights before.

Made no sense how two decades seemed like weeks, and two nights seemed like decades.

When Glen took the stool he'd occupied before as well, leaving an empty one in between them, she relaxed some. He was making it easier to pretend that they were just co-workers spending one last evening together. Not lovers parting forever.

He'd pulled out more of the cheese and crackers they'd consumed the other night—still in their packages. They lay there on the counter, all wrapped up, waiting.

She didn't think she'd get one swallow down. The liquid had been hard enough.

"I still can't believe a man would give up his own son. That he'd actually help someone steal a two-year-old from his mother. And then continue to live a lie, letting the poor mother grieve, for the rest of their lives," she said, rattling off what was sticking out most in her mind from all of the shocking details that had been showered on them, a little at a time, during their hours in Glen's lab.

Glen huffed, and said, "I'm just glad that all of our evidence, piled on one piece at a time by the FBI interrogators as they threatened Selena's uncle with the kidnapping charges in addition to attempted murder for hire and arson charges, did the trick." Hud had told them that as more and more evidence had been laid out before Dale Billingsley—naming him as the suspect—the man had sung like a canary. And subsequently, had produced all the missing evidence to finally reveal the truth of what had happened in the Morrilton park twenty-three years before.

With Hud's team so far into the series of chains that led to the offshore account, and with them watching the account 24-7, they'd been able to trace the two most recent originating payments to Devon Billingsley's younger brother, Dale. An arrested would-be assassin picked up in Phoenix later in the afternoon had identified the man as well. Unlike the bomber in Michigan, the Phoenix gun for hire had refused to do the work without a face-to-face with the boss. He'd flown to Little Rock the day before to meet with Dale.

She shook her head and had to ask, "Do you really think Devon fell that far in love with the surrogate that was carrying his children as Dale testified?"

Glen, looking at his wine, shrugged. Then reached out to the crackers. Taking a couple and opening the cheese, he ripped the corner off a slice to make a little sandwich between the crackers. A sure sign he wasn't going to answer.

Any other time, she'd have let the question drop.

She was too close to a precipice herself to do so. "Seriously, Glen. Even if we just accept that he fell in love with her during the months she was carrying his children. If she was as sweet and alone as Dale said..."

"And as beautiful," Glen put in somewhat derisively.

"Anyway, I get that part. And then, with her hemorrhaging during the birth and ending up unable to ever have children of her own… I even understand how he could get pulled into that mess…but to give away his own son?"

Dale had said that Devon had been working twelve or more hours a day, seven days a week, getting his investment firm off the ground. That he hadn't wanted any more children, but because Sharon had wanted them so badly and had suffered such debilitating postpartum depression after her own first pregnancy with Beth—which had resulted in her being unable to have more children—he'd finally agreed. She'd promised to do all the work, all the feedings, take on all the care of the new baby herself.

Only to find out that they were having twins. Sharon had been thrilled. But hadn't been able to keep up with all the feedings, changings, every two hours all night long. And Devon had been seeing Anne Gravestone, Annabelle Gravestone, aka Anne Simmons—the surrogate—in the spare time he hadn't had. He'd been meeting her for lunch. In a hotel close to his office. Throughout the pregnancy and for the two years after the babies were born, too.

She'd begged him, again and again, to let her take one of the babies she'd birthed. The shocking part was, he'd eventually given in to her. He'd been helping her out financially all along and simply continued to do so—with the caveat that she never contact him again.

"The part that's hardest for me is the uncle," Glen said then, breaking into her thoughts. "How does a man get so twisted up in his dead brother's financial success that he's willing to commit murder, even of his own biological nephew, in order to keep the wealth for himself?"

Lorna sipped from her wine. Thought about family. About Selena, who'd adored her uncle Dale, having to face the fact that he'd known about her brother's whereabouts all along.

And her father…being the cause of it all… Lorna hoped that she hadn't done more harm than good in finding Simon.

According to both twins, who'd called her separately while she'd still been in Glen's office, she was a miracle worker and they owed her everything for life. She took the memory as she had the first round, with a shrug. And washed both away with another sip of wine.

Thought about the brothers who'd pulled off a horrible deed and lived with it for decades, without giving anyone any hint of what they'd done. Devon had confessed to Dale shortly after the kidnapping about what he'd done. And bought his younger brother's silence with an offer to be his vice-president in the company that was finally starting to show enough profit that he'd been able to buy up a couple of small businesses. With plans to get to larger ones.

Dale had taken a big hit when Devon passed away and Dale got a look at his older brother's will. It had read that all his assets were to be split between Beth, Selena, and his closest biological male relative. With Simon gone, that meant Dale. But when Selena had mentioned that there was a gifted forensic scientist taking a leave of absence to find her brother, Dale's world had spun out of control.

"How does a father give away his own son—albeit to someone who desperately loved him and offering enough support to know they'd be okay—and then watch his remaining loved ones grieve all those years? And for what? Amazing business success?"

"He and Sharon split the very next year," Glen reminded her. She hadn't been thinking of Sharon. And hoped again that Selena would be okay. And that Beth would be more supportive now that she knew that Selena had been right all along to not give up on Simon. By all accounts Beth had adored the little guy.

Glen took another couple of crackers, put some cheese

between them, and handed the snack to her. When she took it, he said, "At least he signed over guardianship of Simon to Anne. Not that it would have held up in court, but it gave her some security, having his signed written wishes. Though weird that she didn't seem to have kept her copy. At least not that Simon found after her death."

"I'm guessing that once he reached a certain age, she destroyed the paper. She wouldn't want to risk Simon finding it."

Dale had kept Devon's copy, though. And another agreement with Michelle Applegate to pick up Simon in the park and deliver him to Anne outside of town. Michelle and Anne had been in the same foster home together years before in Searcy and Anne had watched out for Michelle. And Michelle had been amply rewarded for her hour of crime.

If you didn't consider that she'd died a month later.

And the rest, Devon on the phone with his wife while she tended to an injured Selena, giving Michelle the perfect chance to persuade Simon to follow her quietly by tempting him with his favorite treat—well, other than the treat part, that had just been a cruel twist of fate. Depending on who was judging.

Lorna wasn't so sure that Michelle's dropping of the pen that had been used to sign agreements was a twist of anything but design, though.

That pen had called out to her from the very first time she'd heard of its existence. And in the end, it had led them to her, and to Devon, too. Lorna liked to think that Michelle had offered her own confession the day that the crime had first been committed. Maybe hoping that Simon would be returned home before his life was irrevocably changed.

The thought settled her spinning mind, her jittering nerves, into a new sense of determination. She'd been able to reunite one family. Bringing aching hearts with empty holes together.

And sitting right next to her—and filling her heart as well—was a member of another family that held empty places.

Taking a deep breath, knowing that she was charging into a new kind of danger, she looked over at Glen and said, "Is it time yet?"

The offshoot question got him to look at her. "Time for what? *CSI?*"

Her gaze became more pointed. She raised her brows and said, "Time to let some grieving parents know that out of the ashes, comes love."

Just like with Simon and Selena.

Glen emptied his glass of wine. Set it on the counter. Walked out of the room.

And left her sitting there.

SHE WASN'T ALL WRONG. Glen peed. He washed his hands. Ran a hand over his day's worth of stubble as he looked in the mirror. He saw a lot there. Potential. Intelligence. Ability. Steadfastness. He didn't see…love.

What he saw was a man inexplicably desperate to get back out to the kitchen. To convince his fellow scientist that there was no rush to contact the Thomases. They'd lived thirty-five years without him. Didn't even know he existed, according to the report that came back from the police who met with them. The Thomases had specifically asked if there'd been any children. The police had told them the truth. They had no idea.

His partners didn't know for sure, either. Nor were they asking. Glen knew they suspected. They were all extremely bright people. And the only family he had.

But Lorna, a woman he'd known less than a week, not only knew his life story, but was influencing his choices regarding it?

It wasn't right.

He glared hard at the mirror.

So why did it feel right?

Feel.

He hated the word.

Hated even more that he'd spent time that morning studying the science of emotion. He knew the physicality, of course. But forensics didn't call on the use of any of it. Nor had his life.

Looking at the gray eyes staring back at him, expecting the familiarity with which he greeted himself every morning to shave, he saw something else entirely.

A demand.

For honesty.

Followed by a question. How could you be honest about something you hadn't figured out yet? Something that could be fleeting?

The dead stare back at him contained…nothing. So Glen left the mirror behind and went back out to his houseguest for one more night.

It was the polite thing to do.

And…the only thing he wanted to do.

She was standing at the counter, peeling potatoes. "I thought I'd make some chicken noodle soup, my style," she said. "You can freeze it in single-portion bags and have it there when you want it."

She'd poured him a second glass of wine. Her glass was full as well. And he almost grinned. Soup was a stopgap. She wasn't done with him and the Thomas thing yet.

He was catching on to her and her current activity, making him soup, translated to him as "This isn't over."

The oddest part was the relief that flooded him at the thought. He took a step toward her. And then another. Driven from someplace within him that had never driven before.

Didn't have license from him to do so, either.

"What I want is to know if you'd be willing to stick around an extra day or two," he said. Heard the words. Weighed them. Liked them.

And knew they weren't what he needed to be saying.

She'd spun around, half-peeled potato in one hand, the peeler in the other, mouth hanging open. He'd made her speechless.

Kind of liked that he could. Then shook his head and said, "I was thinking that maybe I shouldn't show up on the Thomases' doorstep alone. All the unsaid things…the emotion…a third party there would probably make it easier for them."

He knew it made the whole concept more palatable to him.

But when he'd heard the joy in Simon's voice earlier, and the thankful tears in Selena's…when he'd heard her talk about how she'd never given up, how she'd been waiting twenty-three years…he'd known that there was more on his plate that needed doing. His biological grandparents had been waiting for nearly thirty-six years.

"May I make a suggestion?" Lorna asked, going back to her peeling.

"Why are you suddenly asking permission to do so?" he shot back. Tense. Not at all sure how to get his world to quit changing by the second.

She turned again, hands still filled. "Then I won't ask. I'll just say, I think you should call first. Just showing up on their doorstep, a complete stranger knocking on the door, is going to have them in a questioning, perhaps somewhat untrusting, mode. Or, at the very least, polite mode. The shock of your message will hit them hard. And maybe that's not how they'd want their first time seeing their grandson to go."

Call them first. He nodded. Needed it done before he thought himself out of it.

With a sense of unreality, Glen pulled out his phone. And

dialed the number he'd programmed in that morning, when he'd been alone in his lab and had opened his email to find a copy of the slideshow Lorna had presented him with the night before. He'd spent precious time needed elsewhere to go through it. More than once.

When he heard the phone ringing, he pushed to put the call on speaker and dropped his cell to the counter. By the third ring, Lorna was standing beside him. Hands empty. Until one of hers threaded fingers through one of his.

"Hello?" The voice was female. Upbeat sounding.

His grandmother? Glen had nothing.

"Is this Mrs. Carla Thomas?" Lorna asked, sounding upbeat as well.

"Yes, who's this?"

"I'm calling for a friend," Lorna said. "Is Reverend Thomas there as well?"

"Yes, we're having dinner. What can we do for you, dear?" Glen bowed his head. Stared at the grooved granite at the edge of his counter.

Lorna squeezed his fingers. "Can you put me on speakerphone?"

"Of course. Who did you say this is?"

"Who is this?" a male voice stated then. Not unkindly, but sounding determined to get an answer.

"My name is Dr. Lorna Schwann. I'm a forensic scientist."

"Oh, God, Steve. It's about Stevie…" The woman's voice crumpled.

"It is about your son," Lorna said then. And, giving Glen's fingers another squeeze, said, "Sort of." When she paused, and silence hung on the line, Glen looked up at her.

As soon as she caught his eye, she nodded and said, "It's actually about my friend, another forensic scientist, whose name is Glen Thomas," she said.

Glen saw the tears filling her eyes as he heard a double

gasp on the other end of the line. "I'm sorry to interrupt your dinner, sir, ma'am." Words came out of him. He hadn't planned them. "I know you heard some hard news this afternoon, and I just wanted to let you know the rest of it. I didn't really know your son. I was only a year old when he died. But I grew up hearing about how wonderful he was. And I've lived my life to honor him. I just wanted you to know."

He moved his free hand to push his screen to end the call, and Lorna grabbed it.

"You're our grandson?!" Carla's squeal held disbelief, but more delight than Glen had ever heard in his life. He'd call it pure joy if he had such a thing to compare it to. "We have a grandson! Stevie's son!" The woman's voice was clearly shaken.

"Son, is this true?" The male voice sounded a little less emphatic as well.

"I'm Steven Glen Thomas's son." Glen gave them the facts. It was what he had. And who he was, too. The guy with the facts.

"I can't…" Carla's words broke off in tears.

"Son… Glen…please…can we come to you? Can we meet you?" Steve's voice held more emotion than Glen had ever expected to hear. More than he'd ever heard from himself.

They had the right. "Yes," he told them.

And heard Lorna say, "As soon as you'd like."

Yes, that was good. Get it done. And if it was soon, he had a better chance of convincing her to stick around until it happened.

He sure as hell had enough work to keep her busy. Would pay her for her time.

His thoughts went along the path he could handle as he heard Lorna and the Thomases making plans. Lorna told them where Glen lived. They were going to call the airlines. And call back with the time they'd be landing the next day.

He heard the call end, too. With many thanks. And his own quickly uttered "See you tomorrow," tacked on at the end. The call clicked off from their end.

See you tomorrow? Had he lost his mind?

But when Lorna dropped his hands and went back to peeling potatoes for soup to be stored in one-serving packages, Glen seemed to have more sense about him than he'd ever had.

Or none at all.

And if that was the case, he hoped he'd lost it for good as he said, "So, are you willing to stick around an extra day or two?"

She didn't answer.

But he was too determined to do his normal walk away. She'd taught him that. Her twenty-three-year-long determination had brought a family back together. "Or longer," he added. "I've got plenty of work to keep you busy. And Sierra's Web pays well."

Her back stiffened. Not a good thing. She'd get a cramp. He reached out with both hands, gripping her lightly as his thumbs worked out the tension. He'd done the same for his mother after a long night of her carrying trays in the restaurant where she worked.

And until that moment, had forgotten doing so.

"I don't want you to go," he told Lorna. Something he'd told his mother many times, too. She'd left him behind, in whatever home he'd been assigned to, every single time.

"I'm no good at relationships. Ask any of my partners. They'll tell you. Even as a friend, I pretty much suck."

Leaving her soup materials on the counter, she turned, her gaze serious, intent, as she stared up at him. "I think I'm in love with you, Glen. Can you handle that?"

Love. "Noradrenaline floods the brain, heart rate increases, and other brain areas are deactivated."

She didn't frown. Or turn away. Inexplicably to him, she smiled. "Yep. But it's way more than that, my man, and I think, someplace inside, you know that, or you wouldn't be standing here asking me to stay."

He didn't have a ready answer to that. Most notably, the immediate rejection he'd have uttered as recently as the week before. Or a turn away with a stony silence that precluded further conversation.

It just made no sense, him a man of science, thirty-five, and never in a long-term relationship, falling for a woman in less than a week.

"You trust science," she said softly, her hands on his waist. Bringing to his attention that his were still on her shoulders.

He kept his eyes locked on hers. He knew he was good there. "I do," he said.

"And you trust me."

"Implicitly."

"You'll learn to trust love, too, Glen."

Not you'll learn to love. But learn to trust. The distinction might not matter to anyone else. For him, it was everything.

He could feel love. He could give love. He'd been doing so for years. From a distance. He loved every single one of his partners. And their kids.

He just didn't trust it to last. Theirs for him, not the other way around.

"I trust you," he said to Lorna. He trusted her not to leave if she said she was staying.

Tears sprang to her eyes then. She lifted up to kiss him, but he wasn't done with business yet. "Will you be staying here?" he asked. "In this house. With me?"

"Are you asking me to?"

He checked himself on the question, found the answer waiting, grinned, and said, "Yes, I am."

She kissed him then. Hard. Hungrily. With tongue and

lips fully involved. As they stumbled their way to his bedroom. To make love, not just have sex. On a bed, not a couch.

Twice.

Eyes opened, eyes closed. Speaking. And silently. Urgently, and more tenderly, too.

And later, when, dressed in pairs of his gym shorts and T-shirts, they returned to the kitchen for her to actually make the soup she'd started, Glen thought about marriage in his and Lorna's future together. About a lifetime. Maybe even a family someday.

And trusted that, like his grandparents, they were all on their way.

* * * * *

COMING SOON!

We really hope you enjoyed reading this book.
If you're looking for more romance
be sure to head to the shops when
new books are available on

Thursday 20th November

To see which titles are coming soon, please visit
millsandboon.co.uk/nextmonth

MILLS & BOON

LET'S TALK
Romance

For exclusive extracts, competitions and special offers, find us online:

�f MillsandBoon

𝕏 @MillsandBoon

📷 @MillsandBoonUK

♪ @MillsandBoonUK

Get in touch on 01413 063 232